Innocent Blood

INNOCENT BLOOD

P. D. James

BOOK CLUB ASSOCIATES

London

First published in 1980
by Book Club Associates
by arrangement with Faber and Faber Ltd
Set by Latimer Trend & Company Ltd Plymouth
Printed in Great Britain by
Whitstable Litho Ltd, Whitstable

British Library Cataloguing in Publication Data

James, Phyllis Dorothy
Innocent blood.
I. Title
823′.9′1F   PR6060.A4671/

ISBN 0–571–11566–7

Contents

Book One

PROOF OF IDENTITY

1

The social worker was older than she had expected; perhaps the nameless official who arranged these matters thought that greying hair and menopausal plumpness might induce confidence in the adopted adults who came for their compulsory counselling. After all, they must be in need of reassurance of some kind, these displaced persons whose umbilical cord was a court order, or why had they troubled to travel this bureaucratic road to identity? The social worker smiled her encouraging professional smile. She said, holding out her hand:

"My name is Naomi Henderson and you're Miss Philippa Rose Palfrey. I'm afraid I have to begin by asking you for some proof of identity."

Philippa nearly replied: "Philippa Rose Palfrey is what I'm called. I'm here to find out who I am," but checked herself in time, sensing that such an affectation would be an unpropitious beginning to the interview. They both knew why she was here. And she wanted the session to be a success; wanted it to go her way without being precisely clear what way that was. She unclipped the fastening of her leather shoulder bag and handed over in silence her passport and the newly acquired driving licence.

The attempt at reassuring informality extended to the furnishing of the room. There was an official-looking desk, but Miss Henderson had moved from behind it as soon as Philippa was announced, and had motioned her to one of the two vinyl-covered armchairs on each side of a low table. There were even flowers on the table, a small blue bowl lettered "a present from Polperro". It held a mixed bunch of roses. These weren't the scentless, thornless buds of the florist's window. These were garden roses, recognized from the garden at Caldecote Terrace: Peace, Superstar, Albertine, the blossoms overblown, already peeling with only one or two tightly furled buds, darkening at the lips and destined never to open. Philippa wondered if the social worker had brought them in from her own garden. Perhaps she was retired, living in the country, and had been recruited part-time for this particular job. She could picture her clumping round her rose bed in the brogues and service-able tweeds she was wearing now, snipping away at roses which were due for culling, might just last out the London day. Someone had watered the flowers over-enthusiastically. A milky bead lay like a pearl between two yellow petals and there was a splash on the table top. But the imitation mahogany wouldn't be stained; it wasn't really wood. The roses gave forth a damp sweetness; but they weren't really fresh. In these easy chairs no visitor had ever sat at ease. The smile which invited her confidence and trust across the table was bestowed by courtesy of section twenty-six of the Children Act 1975.

She had taken trouble with her appearance, but then she always did, presenting herself to the world with self-conscious art, daily remaking herself in her own image. The aim this morning had been to suggest that no trouble had in fact been taken, that this interview had induced no special anxiety, warranted no exceptional care. Her strong corn-coloured hair, bleached by the summer so that no two strands were exactly the same gold, was drawn back from a high forehead and knotted in a single heavy plait. The wide mouth with its strong, curved upper lip and sensuous droop at each corner was devoid of lipstick, but she had applied her eyeshadow with care, emphasizing her most remarkable feature, the luminous, slightly protuberant green eyes. Her honey-coloured skin glistened with sweat. She had lingered too long in the Embankment Gardens, unwilling to arrive early, and in the end had had to hurry. She wore sandals and a pale green open-necked cotton shirt above her corduroy trousers. In contrast to this casual informality, the careful ambiguity about money or social class, were the possessions which she wore like talismen: the slim gold watch, the three heavy Victorian rings, topaz, cornelian, peridot, the leather Italian bag slung from her left shoulder. The contrast was deliberate. The advantage of remembering virtually nothing before her eighth birthday, the knowledge that she was illegitimate, meant that there was no phalanx of the living dead, no pious ancestor worship, no conditioned reflexes of thought to inhibit the creativity with which she presented herself to the world. What she aimed to achieve was singularity, an impression of intelligence, a look that could be spectacular, even eccentric, but never ordinary.

Her file, clean and new, lay open before Miss Henderson. Across the table Philippa could recognize some of the contents: the orange and brown Government information sheet, a copy of which she had obtained from a Citizens Advice Bureau in north London where there had been no risk that she would be known or recognized; her letter to the Registrar General written five weeks ago, the day after her eighteenth birthday, in which she had requested the application form which was the first document to identity; a copy of the form itself. The letter was tagged on top of the file, stark white against the buff of bureaucracy. Miss Henderson fingered it. Something about it, the address, the quality of the heavy linen-based paper apparent even in a copy, evoked, Philippa thought, a transitory

12

unease. Perhaps it was a recognition that her adoptive father was Maurice Palfrey. Given Maurice's indefatigable self-advertisement, the stream of sociological publications which flowed from his department, it would be odd if a senior social worker hadn't heard of him. She wondered whether Miss Henderson had read his *Theory and Technique in Counselling: A Guide for Practitioners*, and if so, how much she had been helped in bolstering her clients' self-esteem—and what a significant word "client" was in social-work jargon—by Maurice's lucid exploration of the difference between developmental counselling and Gestalt therapy.

Miss Henderson said:

"Perhaps I ought to begin by telling you how far I'm able to help you. Some of this you probably already know, but I find it useful to get it straight. The Children Act 1975 made important changes in the law relating to access to birth records. It provides that adopted adults—that is people who are at least eighteen years old—may if they wish apply to the Registrar General for information which will lead them to the original record of their birth. When you were adopted you were given a new birth certificate, and the information which links your present name, Philippa Rose Palfrey, with your original birth certificate is kept by the Registrar General in confidential records. It is this linking information which the law now requires the Registrar General to give you if you want it. The 1975 Act also provides that anyone adopted before the twelfth of November 1975, that is before the Act was passed, must attend an interview with a counsellor before they can be given the information. The reason for this is that Parliament was concerned about making the new arrangements retrospective, since over the years many natural parents gave up their children for adoption and adopters took on the children on the understanding that their natural parentage would remain unknown. So you have come here today so that we can consider together the possible effect of any enquiries you may make about your natural parents, both on yourself and on other people, and so that the information you are now seeking, and to which you have, of course, a legal right, is provided in a helpful and appropriate manner. At the end of our talk, and if you still want it, I shall be able to give you your original name; the name of your natural mother; possibly—but not certainly—the name of your natural father and the name of the court where your adoption order was made. I shall also be able to give you an application form which you can use to apply to the Registrar General for a copy of your original birth certificate."

She had said it all before. It came out a little too pat. Philippa said:

"And there's a standard charge of two pounds fifty pence for the birth certificate. It seems cheap at the price. I know all that. It's in the orange and brown pamphlet."

"As long as it's quite clear. I wonder if you'd like to tell me when you first decided to ask for your birth record. I see that you applied as soon as you were eighteen. Was this a sudden decision or had you been thinking about it for some time?"

"I decided when the 1975 Act was going through Parliament. I was fifteen then and taking my O-levels. I don't think I gave it a great deal of thought at the time. I just made up my mind that I'd apply as soon as I was legally able to."

"Have you spoken to your adoptive parents about it?"

"No. We're not exactly a communicative family."

Miss Henderson let that pass for the moment.

"And what exactly did you have in mind? Do you want just to know who your natural parents are, or are you hoping to trace them?"

"I'm hoping to find out who I am. I don't see the point of stopping at two names on a birth certificate. There may not even be two names. I know I'm illegitimate. The search may all come to nothing. I know that my mother is dead so I can't trace her, and I may never find my father. But at least if I can find out who my mother was I may get a lead to him. He may be dead too, but I don't think so. Somehow I'm certain that my father is alive."

Normally she liked her fantasies at least tenuously rooted in reality. Only this one was different, out of time, wildly improbable and yet impossible to relinquish, like an ancient religion whose archaic ceremonies, comfortingly familiar and absurd, somehow witness to an essential truth. She couldn't remember why she had originally set her scene in the nineteenth century, or why, learning so soon that this was a nonsense since she had been born in 1960, she had never updated the persistent self-indulgent imaginings. Her mother, a slim figure dressed as a Victorian parlour-maid, an upswept glory of golden hair under the goffered cap with its two broderie Anglaise streamers, ghost-like against the tall hedge which surrounded the rose garden. Her father in full evening dress striding like a god across the terrace, down the broad walk, under the spray of the fountains. The sloping lawn, drenched by the mellow light of the last sun, glittering with peacocks. The two shadows merging into one shadow, the dark head bending to the gold.

"My darling, my darling. I can't let you go. Marry me."

"I can't. You know I can't."

It had become a habit to conjure up her favourite scenes in the minutes before she fell asleep. Sleep came in a drift of rose leaves. In the earliest dreams her father had been in uniform, scarlet and

14

gold, his chest beribboned, sword clanking at his side. As she grew older she had edited out these embarrassing embellishments. The soldier, the fearless rider to hounds, had become the aristocrat scholar. But the essential picture remained.

There was a globule of water creeping down the petal of the yellow rose. She watched it, fascinated, willing it not to fall. She had distanced her thoughts from what Miss Henderson had been saying. Now she made an effort to attend. The social worker was asking about her adoptive parents:

"And your mother, what does she do?"

"My adoptive mother cooks."

"You mean she works as a cook?" The social worker modified this as if conscious that it could imply some derogation, and added: "She cooks professionally?"

"She cooks for her husband and her guests and me. And she's a juvenile court magistrate but I think she only took that on to please my adoptive father. He believes that a woman should have a job outside the home, provided, of course, that it doesn't interfere with his comfort. But cooking is her enthusiasm. She's good enough at it to cook professionally, although I don't think she was ever properly taught except at evening classes. She was my father's secretary before they married. I mean that cooking is her hobby, her interest."

"Well, that's nice for your father and you."

Presumably that hint of encouraging patronage was by now too unconsciously part of her to be easily disciplined. Philippa gazed at the woman stonily, noted it, took strength from it.

"Yes, we're both greedy, my adoptive father and I. We can both eat voraciously without putting on weight."

That, she supposed, implied something of an appetite for life, not indiscriminate since they were both appreciative of good food; perhaps a reinforcement of their belief that one could indulge without having to pay for indulgence. Greed, unlike sex, involved no commitment except to one's self, no violence except to one's own body. She had always taken comfort from her discernment about food and drink. That, at least, could hardly have been caught from his example. Even Maurice, convinced environment-alist that he was, would hardly claim that a nose for claret could be so easily acquired. Learning to enjoy wine, discovering that she had a palate, had been one more reassuring affirmation of inherited taste. She recalled her seventeenth birthday; the three bottles on the table before them, the labels shrouded. She couldn't recall that Hilda had been with them. Surely she must have been present for a family birthday dinner, but in memory she and Maurice celebrated alone. He had said:

15

"Now tell me which you prefer. Forget the purple prose of the colour supplements, I want to know what you think in your own words."

She had tasted them again, holding the wine in her mouth, sipping water between each sampling since she supposed that this was the proper thing to do, watching his bright challenging eyes.

"This one."

"Why?"

"I don't know. I just like it best."

But he would expect a more considered judgement than that. She added:

"Perhaps because with this one I can't distinguish taste from smell and from the feel of it in the mouth. They aren't separate sensations, it's a trinity of pleasure."

She had chosen the right one. There always was a right answer and a wrong answer. This had been one more test successfully passed, one more notch on the scale of approval. He couldn't entirely reject her, couldn't send her back; she knew that. An adoption order couldn't be revoked. That made it the more important that she should justify his choice of her, that she should give value for money. Hilda, who worked for hours in the kitchen preparing their meals, ate and drank little. She would sit, anxious eyes fixed on them as they shovelled in their food. She gave and they took. It was almost too psychologically neat. Miss Henderson asked:

"Do you resent them for adopting you?"

"No, I'm grateful. I was lucky. I don't think I'd have done well with a poor family."

"Not even if they loved you?"

"I don't see why they should. I'm not particularly lovable."

She hadn't done well with a poor family, of that at least she could be certain. She hadn't done well with any of her foster parents. Some smells: her own excreta, the rotting waste outside a restaurant, a young child bundled into soiled clothes on its mother's lap pressed against her by the lurch of a bus, these could evoke a momentary panic that had nothing to do with disgust. Memory was like a searchlight sweeping over the lost hinterland of the self, illuminating scenes with total clarity, the colours gaudy as a child's comic, edges of objects hard as blocks, scenes which could lie for months unremembered in that black wasteland, not rooted, as were other childish memories, in time and place, not rooted in love.

"Do you love them, your adoptive parents?"

She considered. Love. One of the most used words in the language, the most debased. Héloïse and Abelard. Rochester and Jane Eyre. Emma and Mr Knightley. Anna and Count Vronsky. Even within

16

the narrow connotation of heterosexual love it meant exactly what you wanted it to mean.

"No. And I don't think they love me. But we suit each other on the whole. That's more convenient, I imagine, than living with people that you love but don't suit."

"I can see that it could be. How much were you told about the circumstances of your adoption? About your natural parents?"

"As much, I think, as my adoptive mother could tell me. Maurice never talks about it. My adoptive father's a university lecturer, a sociologist. Maurice Palfrey, the sociologist who can write English. His first wife and their son died in a car crash when the boy was three. She was driving. He married my adoptive mother nine months afterwards. They discovered that she couldn't have children so they found me. I was being fostered at the time so they took over the care of me and after six months applied to the county court and got an adoption order. It was a private arrangement, the kind of thing your new Act would make illegal. I can't think why. It seems to me a perfectly sensible way of going about it. I've certainly nothing to complain of."

"It worked very well for thousands of children and their adopters, but it had its dangers. We wouldn't want to go back to the days when unwanted babies lay in rows of cots in nurseries so that adoptive parents could just go and pick out the one they fancied."

"I don't see why not. That seems to me the only sensible way, as long as the children are too young to know what's happening. That's how you'd pick a puppy or a kitten. I imagine that you need to take to a baby, to feel that this is a child that you want to rear, could grow to love. If I needed to adopt, and I never would, the last thing I'd want would be a child selected for me by a social worker. If we didn't take to each other I wouldn't be able to hand it back without the social services department striking me off the books as being one of those neurotic self-indulgent women who want a child for their own satisfaction. And what other possible reason could there be for wanting an adopted child?"

"Perhaps to give that child a better chance."

"Don't you mean, to have the personal satisfaction of giving that child a better chance? It amounts to the same thing."

She wouldn't bother to refute that heresy, of course. Social-work theory didn't err. After all, its practitioners were the new priesthood, the ministry of unbelievers. She merely smiled and persevered:

"Did they tell you anything about your background?"

"Only that I'm illegitimate. My adoptive father's first wife came from the aristocracy, an earl's daughter, and was brought up in a Palladian mansion in Wiltshire. I believe that my mother was one of the maids there, who got herself pregnant. She died soon after I was born and no one knew who my father was. Obviously he wasn't a fellow servant; she couldn't have kept that particular secret from the servants' hall. I think he must have been a visitor to the house. There are only two things I can remember clearly about my life before I was eight; one is the rose garden at Pennington, the other is the library. I think that my father, my real father, was there with me. It's possible that one of the upper servants at Pennington put my adoptive father in touch with me after his first wife died. He never speaks about it. I only learned as much as that from my adoptive mother. I suppose Maurice thought that I'd do because I was a girl. He wouldn't want a boy to bear his name unless he were really his son. It would be terribly important to him to know that a son was really his own."

"That's understandable, isn't it?"

"Of course. That's why I'm here. It's important for me to know that my parents really were my own."

"Well, let's say that you think it important."

Her eyes dropped to the file. There was a rustle of papers.

"So you were adopted on the seventh of January 1969. You must have been eight. That's quite old."

"I suppose they thought it was better than taking a very young baby and having broken nights. And my adoptive father could see that I was all right, physically all right, that I wasn't stupid. There wasn't the same risk as with a young baby. I know that there are stringent medical examinations, but one can never be quite sure, not about intelligence anyway. He couldn't have borne to find himself saddled with a stupid child."

"Is that what he told you?"

"No, it's what I've thought out for myself."

One fact she could be sure of; that she came from Pennington. There was a childhood memory more clear even than that of the rose garden: the Wren library. She knew that she had once stood there under that exuberant seventeenth-century stuccoed ceiling with its garlands and cherubs, had stared down that vast room at the Grinling Gibbons carvings richly spilling from the shelves, at the Roubiliac busts set above the bookcases, Homer, Dante, Shakespeare, Milton. In memory she saw herself standing at the great chart table reading from a book. The book had been almost too heavy to hold. She could still recall the ache in her wrists and the fear that she might drop it. And she was certain that her real father had been with her; that she had been reading aloud to him. She was so sure that she belonged at Pennington that sometimes she was tempted to believe that the Earl had been her father. But the fantasy was unacceptable and she rejected it, faithful to the original vision of the visiting aristocrat. The Earl must have known if he had fathered a child on one of his servants, and surely, surely he wouldn't have rejected her totally, left her unsought and unrecognized for eighteen years. She had never been back to the house, and now that the Arabs had bought it and it had become a Moslem fortress she never would. But when she was twelve she had searched in Westminster reference library for a book on Pennington and had read a description of the library. There had been a picture too. The confirmation had jolted her heart. It was all there, the plaster ceiling, the Grinling Gibbons carvings, the busts. But her memory had come first. The child standing beside the chart table holding the book in her aching hands must have existed.

She scarcely heard the rest of the counselling. If it had to be done, she supposed that Miss Henderson was making a good enough job of it. But it was no more than a statutory nuisance, the way in which uneasy legislators had salved their consciences. None of the arguments so conscientiously put forward could shake her resolve to track down her father. And how could their meeting, however delayed, be unwelcome to him? She wouldn't be coming empty-handed. She had her Cambridge scholarship to lay at his feet.

She said, wrenching her mind back to the present:

"I can't see the point of this compulsory counselling. Are you supposed to dissuade me from tracing my father? Either our legislators think I have a right to know, or they don't. To give me the right and at the same time officially try to discourage me from exercising it seems muddled thinking even for Parliament. Or do they just have a bad conscience about retrospective legislation?"

"Parliament wants adopted people to think carefully about the implications of what they're doing, what it could mean for themselves, for their adoptive parents, for their natural parents."

"I have thought. My mother is dead, so it can't hurt her. I don't propose to embarrass my father. I want to know who he is, or was if he's dead. That's all. If he's still alive, I should like to meet him, but I'm not thinking of bursting in on a family party and announcing that I'm his bastard. And I don't see how any of this concerns my adoptive parents."

"Wouldn't it be wise, and kinder, to discuss it first with your adoptive parents?"

"What is there to discuss? The law gives me a right. I'm exercising it."

Thinking back on the counselling session that evening at home, Philippa couldn't remember the precise moment when the information she sought had been handed to her. She supposed that the

19

social worker must have said something: "Here, then, are the facts you are seeking" was surely too pretentious and theatrical for Miss Henderson's detached professionalism. But some words must have been said, or had she merely taken the General Register Office paper from the file and passed it over in silence?

But here it was at last in her hands. She stared at it in disbelief, her first thought that there had been some bureaucratic muddle. There were two names, not one, on the form. Her natural parents were shown as Mary Ducton and Martin John Ducton. She muttered the words to herself. The names meant nothing to her, stirred no memory, evoked no sense of completeness, of forgotten knowledge resurrected at a word to be recognized and acknowledged. And then she saw what must have happened. She said, hardly realizing that she spoke aloud:

"I suppose they married my mother off when they found out that she was pregnant. Probably to a fellow servant. They must have been making that kind of tactful arrangement for generations at Pennington. But I hadn't realized that I was placed for adoption before my mother died. She must have known that she hadn't long to live and wanted to be sure that I would be all right. And, of course, if she were married before I was born the husband would be registered as my father. Nominally I suppose I'm legitimate. It's helpful that she did have a husband. Martin Ducton must have been told that she was pregnant before he agreed to the marriage. She may even have told him before she died who my real father was. Obviously the next step is to trace Martin Ducton."

She picked up her shoulder bag and held out her hand to say goodbye. She only half heard Miss Henderson's closing words, the offer of any future help she could give, reiterated advice that Philippa discuss her plans with her adoptive parents, the gently urged suggestion that if she were able to trace her father it should be done through an intermediary. But some words did penetrate her consciousness:

"We all need our fantasies in order to live. Sometimes relinquishing them can be extraordinarily painful, not a rebirth into something exciting and new, but a kind of death."

They shook hands, and Philippa, looking into her face for the first time with any real interest, seeing her for the first time as a woman, detected there a fleeting look which, had she not known better, she might have mistaken for pity.

2

She posted her application and cheque to the Registrar General that evening, 4 July 1978, enclosing, as she had done previously, a stamped addressed envelope. Neither Maurice nor Hilda was curious about her private correspondence but she didn't want to risk an officially labelled reply falling through the letter-box. She spent the next few days in a state of controlled excitement which, for most of the time, drove her out of the house, afraid that Hilda might wonder at her restlessness. Pacing round the lake in St James's Park, hands deep in her jacket pockets, she calculated when the birth certificate might arrive. Government departments were notoriously slow, but surely this was a simple enough matter. They had only to check their records. And they wouldn't be coping with a rush of applications. The Act had been passed in 1975.

In exactly one week, on Tuesday 11 July, she saw the familiar envelope on the mat. She took it at once to her own room, calling out to Maurice from the stairs that there was no post for him. She carried it over to the window as if her eyes were growing weaker and she needed more light. The birth certificate, new, crisp, so much more imposing than the shortened form which had served her, as an adopted person, for so long, seemed at first reading to have nothing to do with her. It recorded the birth of a female, Rose Ducton, on 22 May 1960 at 41 Bancroft Gardens, Seven Kings, Essex. The father was shown as Martin John Ducton, clerk; the mother as Mary Ducton, housewife.

So they had left Pennington before she was born. That, perhaps, wasn't surprising. What was unexpected was that they should have moved so far from Wiltshire. Perhaps they had wanted to cut themselves off entirely from the old life, from the gossip, from memories. Perhaps someone had found him a job in Essex, or he might have been returning to his home county. She wondered what he was like, this spurious accommodating father, whether he had been kind to her mother. She hoped that she could like or at least respect him. He might still live at 41 Bancroft Gardens, perhaps with a second wife and a child of his own. Eighteen years wasn't such a long time. She used the telephone extension in her room to ring Liverpool Street Station. Seven Kings was on the eastern suburban line and in the rush hour there were trains every ten minutes. She left without waiting for breakfast. If there were time, she would get coffee at the station.

The 9.25 train from Liverpool Street was almost empty. It was still early enough for Philippa to be travelling against the commuter tide. She sat in her corner seat, her eyes moving from side to side as the train racketed through the urban sprawl of the eastern suburbs; rows of drab houses with blackened bricks and patched roofs from which sprang a tangle of television aerials, frail crooked fetishes against the evil eye; layered high-rise flats smudged in a distant drizzle of rain; a yard piled high with the glitter of smashed cars in symbolic proximity to the regimented crosses of a suburban grave-yard; a paint factory, a cluster of gasometers; pyramids of grit and coal piled beside the track; wastelands rank with weeds; a sloping green bank rising to suburban gardens with their washing lines and tool-sheds and children's swings among the roses and hollyhocks. The eastern suburbs, so euphoniously but inappropriately named, Maryland, Forest Gate, Manor Park, were alien territory to her, as unvisited and remote from the preoccupations of the last ten years as were the outer suburbs of Glasgow and New York. None of her school friends lived east of Bethnal Green, although a number, unvisited, were reputed to have houses in the few unspoilt Georgian squares off the Whitechapel Road, self-conscious enclaves of culture and radical chic among the tower blocks and the industrial wasteland. Yet the grimy, unplanned urban clutter through which the train rocked and clattered struck some dormant memory, was familiar even in its strangeness, unique despite its bleak uniformity. Surely it wasn't because she had been this way before. Perhaps it was just that the scenery flashing by was so predictably dreary, so typical of the grey purlieus of any large city, that forgotten descrip-tions, old pictures and newsprint, snatches of film jumbled in her imagination to produce this sense of recognition. Perhaps everyone had been here before. This drab no man's land was part of everyone's mental topography.

There were no taxis at Seven Kings Station. She asked the ticket collector the way to Bancroft Gardens. He directed her down the High Street, left down Church Lane, then first on the right. The High Street ran between the railway and the shopping arcade of small businesses with flats above, a launderette, a newsagent, a greengrocer and a supermarket with shoppers already queuing at the check-outs.

There was one scene so vividly recalled, validated by smell and sound and remembered pain which it was impossible to believe she had imagined. A women wheeling a baby in a pram down just such a street. Herself, little more than a toddler, half stumbling beside the pram, clutching at the handle. The square paving stones speckled with light, unrolling beneath the whirling pram wheels, faster and faster. Her warm grip slipping on the moist metal and the desperate fear that she would lose hold, would be left behind, trampled and kicked under the wheels of the bright red buses. Then a shouted curse. The slap stinging her cheek. A jerk which nearly tore her arm from its socket, and the woman's hand fastening her grip once more on the pram handle. She had called the woman auntie. Auntie May. How extraordinary that she should remember the name now. And the child in the pram had worn a red woolly cap. Its face had been smeared with mucus and chocolate. She remembered that she had hated the child. It must have been winter. The street had been a glare of light and there had been a necklace of coloured bulbs swinging above the greengrocer's stall. The woman had stopped to buy fish. She remembered the slab, bright with red-eyed herrings shedding their glistening scales, the strong oleaginous smell of kippers. It could have been this street, only there was no fishmonger here now. She looked down at the paving stones, mottled with rain. Were these the ones over which she had stumbled so desperately? Or was this street, like the terrain each side of the railway, only one more scene from an imagined past?

Turning from the High Street into Church Lane was stepping from drab commercial suburbia into leafy privacy and cosy domesticity. The narrow street, its verge planted with plane trees, curved gently. Perhaps centuries earlier it had indeed been a lane leading to an ancient village church, a building long since demolished or destroyed by bombing in the Second War. All she could see now was a distant stunted spire which looked as if it had been fabricated from slabs of synthetic stone, and topped by a weather-vane instead of a cross because of some understandable confusion about the building's function.

And here at last was Bancroft Gardens. Stretching out of sight on either side of the road were identical semi-detached houses, each with a path running down the side. They might, she thought, be architecturally undistinguished, but at least they were on a human scale. The gates and railings had been removed and the front gardens were bounded with low brick walls. The front bay windows were square and turreted, a long vista of ramparted respectability. But the uniformity of the architecture was broken by the individuality of the residents. Every front garden was different, a riot of massed summer flowers, squares of lawn meticulously cut and shaped, stone slabs set about with urns bearing geraniums and ivy.

When Philippa reached number 41 she stopped, amazed. The house stood out from its neighbours by a garish celebration of eccentric taste. The grey London bricks had been painted a shiny red outlined with white pointing. It looked like a house built with immense toy bricks. The crenellations of the bay were alternately red and blue. The window was curtained with net looped across and caught up with satin bows. The original front door had been replaced by one with an opaque glass panel and was painted bright yellow. In the front patch of garden an artificial pond of glass was surrounded by synthetic rocks, on which three gnomes with expressions of grinning imbecility were perched with fishing rods.

As soon as she had pressed the doorbell—it let out a musical jingle—Philippa sensed that the house was empty. The owners were probably at work. She tried once more, but there was no reply. Resisting the temptation to peer through the letter-box, she decided to try next door. At least they would know whether Ducton still lived at 41 or where he had gone. The house had no bell and the thud of the knocker sounded unnaturally loud and peremptory. There was no reply. She waited a full minute and was lifting her hand again when she heard the shuffle of feet. The door was opened on a chain, and she glimpsed an elderly woman in apron and hairnet who gave her the unwelcoming suspicious stare of someone to whom no morning visitor at the front door bodes other than ill. Philippa said:

"I'm sorry to disturb you, but I wonder if you can help me. I'm looking for a Mr Martin Ducton who lived next door eighteen years ago. There isn't anyone at home there and I thought you might be able to help."

The woman said nothing, but stood transfixed, one brown claw-like hand still on the door-chain, the only visible eye staring blankly at Philippa's face. Then there were more steps, firmer and heavier but still muffled. A male voice said:

"Who is it, Ma? What's up?"

"It's a girl, she's asking for Martin Ducton."

The woman's voice was a whisper, sibilant with wonder and a kind of outrage. A chubby male hand released the chain, and the woman stood there, dwarfed by her son. He was wearing slacks topped with a singlet. On his feet were red carpet slippers. Perhaps, thought Philippa, he was a bus driver or conductor relaxing on his rest day. It hadn't been a good time to call. She said apologetically:

"I'm sorry to trouble you, but I'm trying to trace a Mr Martin Ducton. He used to live next door. I wondered whether you might know what happened to him."

"Ducton? He's dead, isn't he? Been dead best part of nine years. Died in Wandsworth Prison."

"In prison?"

"Where else would he be, fucking murderer? He raped that kid, and then he and his missus strangled her. What's he to do with you then? You a reporter or something?"

"Nothing. Nothing. It must be the wrong Ducton. Perhaps I've mistaken the name."

"Someone been having you on more likely. Ducton he was. Martin Ducton. And she was Mary Ducton. Still is."

"She's alive then?"

"As far as I know. Coming out soon, I shouldn't wonder. Must've done near ten years by now. Not that she'll be coming back next door. Four families have had that place since the Ductons. It always goes cheap, that house. Young couple bought it six months ago. It's not everyone fancies a place where a kid's been done in. Upstairs in the front room it was."

He nodded his head towards number 41, but his eyes never met Philippa's face. The woman said suddenly:

"They should've been hung."

Philippa, astonished, heard herself reply:

"Hanged. The word is hanged. They should have been hanged."

"That's right," said the man.

He turned to his mother.

"Buried the kid in Epping Forest, didn't they? Isn't that what they did with her, Ma? Buried her in Epping Forest. Twelve years old she was. You remember, Ma?"

Perhaps the woman was deaf. His last words were an impatient shout. She didn't answer. Still staring at Philippa, she said:

"Her name was Julie Scase. I remember now. They killed Julie Scase. But they never got as far as the forest. Caught with the kid's body in the car boot they was. Julie Scase."

Philippa made herself ask through lips so stiff that she could hardly form the words:

"Did they have any children? Did you know them?"

"No. We weren't here then. We moved here from Romford after they were inside. There was talk of a kid, a girl, weren't it, who was adopted. Best thing for the poor little bugger."

Philippa said:

"Then it's not the same Ducton. This Ducton had no children. I've been given the wrong address. I'm sorry to have troubled you."

She walked away from them down the road. Her legs felt swollen and heavy, weighted bolsters which had no connection with the rest of her body, yet which carried her forward. She looked down at the paving stones, using them as a guide like a drunkard under test. She guessed that the woman and her son were still watching her, and when she had gone about twenty yards she made herself turn round and gaze back at them stolidly. Immediately they disappeared.

25

Alone now in the empty road, no longer under surveillance, she found that she couldn't go on. She stretched her hands towards the brick wall bordering the nearest garden, found it and sat. She felt faint and a little sick, her heart constricted like a hot pulsating ball. But she mustn't faint here, not in this street. Somehow she must get back to the station. She let her head drop between her knees and felt the blood pound back into her forehead. The faintness passed but the nausea was worse. She sat up again, shutting her eyes against the reeling houses, taking deep gulps of the flower-scented air. Then she opened her eyes and made herself concentrate on the things she could touch and feel. She ran her fingers over the roughness of the wall. Once it had been topped with iron railings. She could feel the coarse grain of the cement-filled holes where they had pierced the brickwork. Perhaps the railings had been taken away in the war to be melted down for armaments. She gazed fixedly at the paving stone under her feet. It was pricked with light, set with infinitesimal specks, bright as diamonds. Pollen from the gardens had blown over it and there was a single flattened rose petal like a drop of blood. How extraordinary that a paving stone should be so varied, should reveal under the intensity of her gaze such gleaming wonders. These things at least were real, and she was real—more vulnerable, less durable than bricks and stones but still present, visible, an identity. If people passed, surely they would be able to see her.

A youngish woman came out of the house two doors down and walked towards her, pushing a pram with an older child trotting beside it and holding on to the handle. The woman glanced at Philippa, but the child dragged his steps, then turned and gazed back at her with a wide, incurious gaze. He had let go of the pram handle and she found herself struggling to her feet, holding out her arms towards him in warning or entreaty. Then the mother stopped and called to him and the child ran up to her and grasped the pram again.

She watched them until they turned the corner into the High Street. It was time to go. She couldn't sit here all day fastened to the wall as if it were a refuge, the one solid reality in a shifting world. Some words of Bunyan came into her mind and she found herself speaking them aloud:

" 'Some also have wished that the next way to their father's house were here, and that they might be troubled no more with either hills or mountains to go over, but the way is the way, and there is an end.' "

She didn't know why the words comforted her. She wasn't particularly fond of Bunyan and she couldn't see why the passage should speak to her confused mind in which disappointment,

26

anguish and fear struggled for mastery. But as she walked back to the station she spoke the passage over and over again as if the words were in their own way as immutable and solid as the pavement on which she trod. "The way is the way, and there is an end."

3

When he was working, and that was most of the year, Maurice Palfrey used his room at college. The sociology department had swelled since his appointment as senior lecturer, borne on the sixties' tide of optimism and secular faith, and had overflown into an agreeable late eighteenth-century house owned by the college in a Bloomsbury square. He shared the house with the Department of Oriental Studies, colleagues notable for their unobtrusiveness and for the number of their visitors. A succession of small, dark, spectacled men and saried women slid daily through the front door and disappeared into an uncanny silence. He seemed always to be encountering them on the narrow stairs; there were steppings back, bowings, slant-eyed smiles; but only an occasional footfall creaked the upper floor. He felt the house to be infected with secret, mice-like busyness.

His room had once been part of the elegant first-floor drawing-room, its three tall windows and wrought-iron balcony overlooking the square gardens, but it had been divided to provide a room for his secretary. The grace of the proportions had been destroyed and the delicately carved overmantel, the George Morland oil which had always hung in the business-room at Pennington and which he had placed above it, the two Regency chairs looked pretentious and spurious. He felt the need to explain to visitors that he hadn't furnished his room with reproductions. And the conversion hadn't been a success. His secretary had to pass through his room to get to hers and the clatter of the typewriter through the thin partition was so irritating a metallic *obbligato* to his meetings that he had to tell Molly to stop working when he had visitors. It was difficult to concentrate during meetings when he was aware that she was sitting next door glowering across her machine in sullen, ostentatious idleness. Elegance and beauty had been sacrificed for a utility which wasn't even efficient. Helena, on her first visit to the room, had

27

merely said: "I don't like conversions" and hadn't visited again. Hilda, who hadn't appeared to notice or care about the room's proportions, had left the department after their marriage and had never come back.

The habit of working away from home had begun after his marriage to Helena when she had bought 68 Caldecote Terrace. Walking hand in hand through the empty echoing rooms like exploring children, folding back the shutters so that the sun came through in great shafts and lay in pools on the unpolished boards, the pattern of their future together had been laid down. She had made it plain that there would be no intrusion of his work into their domestic life. When he had suggested that he would need a study she had pointed out that the house was too small, the whole of the top floor was needed for the nursery and the nanny. She was prepared, apparently, to wash and cook with the aid of daily help, but not to look after her child. She had enumerated their necessities: the drawing-room, dining-room, their two bedrooms and the spare bedroom. There had been no study at Pennington; the suggestion seemed to her eccentric. And there could hardly be a library. She had been brought up with the Wren library at Pennington, and to her any other private library was merely a room in which people kept books.

Now, when he had long ago worked through his grief—and how accurately some of his colleagues had described that interestingly painful psychological process—when he could distance himself even from humiliation and pain, he was intrigued by the moral eccentricity which could, apparently without compunction, father on him another man's child, yet which was outraged by the thought of abortion. He recalled their words when she had told him about the child. He had asked:

"What do you want to do about it, have an abortion?"

"Of course not. Don't be so bourgeois, darling."

"Abortion can be thought of as distasteful, undesirable, dangerous or even morally wrong if you think in those terms. I don't see what's bourgeois about it."

"It's all those things. Why on earth should you suppose I want an abortion?"

"You might feel that the baby would be a nuisance."

"My old nanny is a nuisance, so is my father. I don't kill them off."

"Then what do you want to do?"

"Marry you, of course. You are free, aren't you? You haven't a wife secreted away somewhere?"

"No, I haven't a wife. But my darling love, you can't want to marry me."

28

"I never know what I want. I'm only really sure of what I don't want. But I think we'd better marry."

It had been the commonest, the most obvious of cheats, and he the most gullible of victims. But he had been in love for the first and only time, a state which he now realized didn't conduce to clear thinking. Poets were right to call love a madness. His love had certainly been a kind of insanity in the sense that his thought processes, his perception of external reality, even his physical life, appetite, digestion, sleep, all had been disturbed. Small wonder that he hadn't calculated with what flattering speed she had singled him out during that short holiday at Perugia, how short the time between that first appraising look across the dining-room table to getting him into her bed.

It was true that she only knew what she didn't want. Her needs had seemed to him reassuringly modest, her unwants had all the force of strong desire. He was surprised that they had found the house in Caldecote Terrace so quickly. All districts of London were apparently impossible for her. Hampstead was too trendy, Mayfair too expensive, Bayswater vulgar, Belgravia too smart. And they had been restricted in choice by her refusal to contemplate a mortgage. It was useless for him to point out the advantages of tax relief. A nineteenth-century earl had once mortgaged Pennington, to the embarrassment of his encumbered heirs. A mortgage was bourgeois. In the end they had found Caldecote Terrace in Pimlico and here she had given him, however casual the gift, the four happiest years of his life. Her death, Orlando's death, had taught him all he knew about suffering. He was glad now that no premature knowledge had despoiled those first few months of grief. It hadn't been until two years after his marriage to Hilda, seeking medical advice on their childlessness, that he had learnt the truth; that he could never father a child. That period of mourning for a woman who hadn't existed, for a son who wasn't his son, now seemed to him a debt discharged, not without honour, a secular grace.

He had grieved more for Orlando than for Helena. Helena's death had been the loss of a joy to which he had never felt entitled, which had never seemed quite real, which he had hoped, rather than expected, would last. Some part of his mind had accepted her loss as inevitable; death could not part them more completely than could life. But for Orlando he had mourned with an elemental violence of grief, a wordless scream of anguish. The death of a beautiful, intelligent and happy child had always seemed to him an outrage, and this child had been his son. His grief had seemed to embrace a cosmic fellowship of suffering. He had indulged no inordinate hopes for Orlando, foisted on his child no high ambition, had asked

29

only that he should continue to exist in his beauty, his loving-kindness, his peculiarly uncoordinated grace.

And it was because Orlando had died that he had married Hilda. He knew that their friends found the marriage an enigma. It was easily explained. Hilda was the only one among his friends, his colleagues, who had wept for Orlando. The day after his return from the funeral at Pennington—the depositing of Helena and Orlando in the family vault had symbolized for him the final separation, they lay now with their own kind—Hilda had come into his office with the morning post. He could remember how she had looked, the white schoolgirl's blouse, the skirt which she had pressed that morning—he could see the impress of the iron across the front pleat. She stood there at the door looking at him. All she said was: "That little boy. That little boy." He had watched while her face stiffened and then disintegrated with grief. Two tears oozed from her eyes and ran unchecked over her cheeks.

She had only known Orlando briefly on the few occasions when his nurse had brought him into the office. But she had wept for him. His colleagues had written and spoken their condolences, averting their eyes from a grief they could not assuage. Death was in poor taste. They had treated him with sympathetic wariness, as if he were suffering from a slightly embarrassing disease. She only had paid Orlando the tribute of a spontaneous tear.

And that had been the beginning. It had led to the first invitation to dinner, to their theatre dates, to the curious courtship which had merely reinforced their misconceptions about each other. He had persuaded himself that she was teachable, that she had a goodness and simplicity which could meet his complicated needs, that behind the bland gentle face was a mind which only needed the stimulus of his loving concern to break into some kind of flowering—what, he was never precisely sure. And she had been so different from Helena. It had been flattering to give instead of to take, to be the one who was loved instead of the one who loved. And so, with what to some of his colleagues had seemed indecent haste, they had come to that registry office wedding. Poor girl, she had hoped for a white wedding in church. That quiet exchange of contracts could hardly have seemed to her or her parents like a proper marriage. She had got through it in an agony of embarrassment, afraid perhaps that the registrar had thought that she was pregnant.

He was suddenly aware of his restlessness. He walked across to the tall window and looked out over the dishevelled square. Although the slight rain had now stopped, the plane trees were bedraggled and scraps of sodden litter lay unmoving on the spongy grass. This slow dripping away of the summer matched his mood. He had always

30

disliked the hiatus between academic years when the detritus of the last term had scarcely been cleared away, yet the next was already casting its shadow. He couldn't remember when the conscientious performance of duty had replaced enthusiasm, or when conscientiousness had finally given way to boredom. What worried him now was that he approached each academic term with an emotion more disturbing than boredom, something between irritation and apprehension. He knew that he no longer saw his students as individuals, no longer had any wish to know or communicate except on the level of tutor to student, and even here there was no trust between them. There seemed to have been a reversal of roles, he the student, they the instructors. They sat in the ubiquitous uniform of the young, jeans and sweaters, huge clumpy plimsolls, open-necked shirts topped with denim jackets, and gazed at him with the fixity of inquisitors waiting for any deviation from orthodoxy. He told himself that they were no different from his former students, graceless, not very intelligent, uneducated if education implied the ability to write their own language with elegance and precision, to think clearly, to discriminate or enjoy. They were filled with the barely suppressed anger of those who have grabbed for themselves sufficient privilege to know just how little privilege they would ever achieve. They didn't want to be taught, having already decided what they preferred to believe.

He had become increasingly petty, irritated by details, by the diminishing, for example, of their forenames, Bill, Bert, Mike, Geoff, Steve. He wanted to enquire peevishly if a commitment to Marxism was incompatible with a disyllabic forename. And their vocabulary provoked him. In his last series of seminars on the juvenile law they had talked always of "kids". The mixture of condescension and sycophancy in the word repelled him. He himself had used the words "children" and "young people" punctiliously and had sensed that it had annoyed them. He had found himself talking to them like a schoolmaster to the lower third:

"I've corrected some of the grammar and spelling. This may seem bourgeois pedantry, but if you plan to organize revolution you'll have to convince the intelligent and educated as well as the gullible and ignorant. It might be worthwhile trying to develop a prose style which isn't a mixture of sociological jargon and the standard expected from the C stream of a comprehensive school. And 'obscene' means 'lewd', 'indecent', 'filthy'—it can't properly be used to describe Government policy in not implementing the recommendations of the Finer Report on one-parent families, reprehensible as that decision may be."

Mike Beale, chief instigator of student power, had received back his last essay muttering under his breath. It had sounded like "fucking bastard" and might indeed have been "fucking bastard" except that Beale was incapable of an invective which didn't include the word "fascist". Beale had just completed his second year. With luck he would graduate next autumn, departing to take a social-work qualification and find himself a job with a local authority, no doubt to teach juvenile delinquents that the occasional minor act of robbery with violence was a natural response of the underprivileged to capitalist tyranny and to promote political awareness among those council house tenants looking for an excuse not to pay their rents. But he would be replaced by others. The academic machine would grind on, and what was so extraordinary was that essentially he and Beale were on the same side. He had been too publicly committed and for too long to renege now. Socialism and sociology. He felt like an old campaigner who no longer believes in his cause but finds it enough that there is a battle and he knows his own side.

He stuffed into his briefcase the few letters he had found waiting for him in his cubby-hole that morning. One was from a Socialist Member of Parliament enlisting his help with the General Election which he took for granted would come in early October. Would Maurice talk on one of the television party political broadcasts? He supposed he would accept. The box sanctified, conferred identity. The more familiar the face, the more to be trusted. The other was yet another appeal to him to apply for the chair in social work at a northern university. He could understand the concern among his colleagues about the chair. There had been a number of recent appointments outside the field of social work. But what the protesters couldn't see was that what mattered was the quality of the academic work and of the research, not the discipline of the applicant. With the present competition for chairs sociology needed to demonstrate its academic respectability, not pursue a spurious professionalism. He was becoming increasingly irritated by the sensitivity of colleagues, unsure of themselves, feeling morbidly undervalued, complaining that they were expected to remedy all the ills of society. He only wished that he could cure his own.

He put away the last few papers and locked his desk drawer. He remembered that tonight the Cleghorns were coming to dinner. Cleghorn was one of the trustees of a fund set up to investigate the causes and treatment of juvenile delinquency, and Maurice had a post-graduate student who was looking for a research job for the next couple of years. The advantage of giving regular dinner parties was that when one was angling for a favour an invitation to dine didn't look too blatant a ploy. Closing the door, he wondered without much curiosity where Philippa had been going that morning

32

so early, and whether she would remember the Cleghorns and get home in time to do the dining-room flowers.

4

When she finally got back to Liverpool Street, Philippa spent the rest of the day walking in the City. It was just after six when she returned to Caldecote Terrace. The rain had nearly stopped and was now so fine that it fell against her warm face as a drifting mist needled with cold. But the pavement stones were as tacky as if it had fallen heavily all day, and a few shallow puddles had collected in the gutter into which occasional dollops dropped with heavy portentousness from a sky as thick and grey as curdled milk. Number 68 looked just as it did when she returned from school on any dull summer evening. This homecoming was outwardly no different from any other. As always the basement kitchen was brightly lit and the rest of the house was in darkness except for a light shining from the hall through the elegant fanlight of the front door.

The kitchen was on the lower ground floor at the front of the house. The dining-room, which was at the back, had french doors to the garden. The whole of the raised ground floor was taken up by the drawing-room; this, too, had access to the garden by a flight of delicately carved and moulded wrought-iron steps. On summer evenings they would carry their coffee down to the patio to the chairs under the fig tree. The walled garden, only thirty feet long, enclosed the scent of roses and white stocks. The patio was set about with white-painted wooden tubs of geraniums glowing blood red in the peculiarly intense light before the setting of the sun, then bleached as the patio lamps were turned on.

The light was always on in the north-facing kitchen, yet Hilda never drew the curtains. Perhaps she had never realized that, to the upper world, she moved on a lighted stage. She was there now, already starting on the dinner. Philippa crouched down, clutching the railings, and peered through at her. Hilda cooked with a peculiar intensity, moving like a high priestess among the impedimenta of her craft, consulting her recipe book with the keen unblinking scrutiny of an artist examining his model, then briefly laying her hand on each ingredient like a preparatory blessing. She cleaned and tidied the rest of the house obsessively, but as if nothing it contained had anything to do with her; only here in the organized muddle of her kitchen was she at home. This was her habitat. Here she lived doubly caged behind the protecting iron bars on the windows and the spiked railings above, seeing the world pass as a succession of desultory or hurrying feet. Her pale lank hair which normally fell forward over her face was strained back from her eyes with two plastic combs. In the white apron which she invariably wore she looked very young and defenceless, like a schoolgirl preoccupied with a practical examination, or a newly engaged maid coping with her first dinner party. And it wasn't because she worked in the kitchen that she looked like a servant. All but the wealthiest of the mothers of the girls at school did most of their own cooking. Cookery had become a fashionable craft, almost a cult. Perhaps it was the white apron, the worried eyes which seemed always to expect, almost to invite a rebuke, which made her look like a woman precariously earning her keep.

Philippa had forgotten that the Cleghorns and Gabriel Lomas were coming to dinner. She saw that the meal was to begin with artichokes. Six of them, solidly ornamental, were ranged on the central table ready for the pot. The kitchen, under the glare of the twin fluorescent lights, was as familiar as a picture on a nursery wall. The one wicker chair with its shabby patchwork cushion. It had never been necessary to buy a second since neither Maurice nor Philippa made it a habit to sit in the kitchen chatting with Hilda while she cooked. The shelf of paperback recipe books with their greasy crumpled covers, the calendar hanging beside the wall-mounted telephone with its garish blue picture of Brixham Harbour, the portable television set, black-and-white since the one colour set was in the drawing-room. Philippa couldn't remember ever seeing Hilda sitting alone in the drawing-room. Why should she? It wasn't her drawing-room. Everything in it had been chosen by Maurice or by his first wife.

Philippa had never heard Maurice speak of Helena, but it never occurred to her that this was because he continued to grieve for her or because he was sensitive to Hilda's feelings. She had long ago decided that he was a man who kept his emotions in compartments. That way there could be no messy spillage from one life to another. From time to time she had felt a vague curiosity about Helena Palfrey, glamorized and dignified as she was for ever by an early and dramatic death. Only once had she seen a picture of Maurice's first wife. It had been at a bring-and-buy sale held at school in aid of Oxfam. One of the parents had donated a bundle of glossy society magazines. They had sold well, she remembered. People were happy to give a penny or two for the brief pleasures of nostalgia and recollection. They had flicked through them giggling.

"Look, here's Molly and John at Henley. My dear, did we really wear skirts that length?"

Browsing through a bundle displayed for sale, she had seen with a shock of surprise and recognition, Maurice's face. It was a younger Maurice, strange yet utterly familiar, wearing the startled half-fatuous smile of a man suddenly caught by the camera who hasn't had time to decide what expression to assume. It had been taken at a wedding. The caption said: "Mr Maurice Palfrey and Lady Helena Palfrey chatting to Sir George and Lady Scott-Harries". And there they were, not chatting to anyone, but staring into the lens, champagne glasses in their hands, as if toasting this second of their joint lives ephemerally recorded in microdots. Lady Helena Palfrey, smiling, stood taller than her husband in her wide-brimmed hat and ridiculously short skirt. Dark hair framed a face which looked no longer young; bony, almost ravaged, heavy-browed. Philippa had torn out the cutting and had kept it, secreted in one of her books, for almost a year. From time to time she had taken it over to the light of her bedroom window to peer at it obsessively, willing it to disclose some clue to the woman's character, to their love, if love there had been, to their joint life together. Eventually, frustrated, she had torn it up and flushed it down the lavatory.

And now, with an equal intensity, she peered through the railings at Maurice's living wife. She was bent over the central table, carefully rolling out fillets of veal. It looked as if the dinner guests were to have veal in wine and mushroom sauce. They would praise the meal, of course; the guests invariably did. Philippa remembered having read that it was the last war which had finally killed the English reticence about the quality of a meal. Now most of the women, and sometimes the men, praised, enquired, exchanged recipes. But with Hilda the praise became effusive, strained, almost embarrassingly insincere. It was as if they needed to reassure or propitiate her, to give her worth in her own eyes. For the whole of her marriage her husband's guests had treated her as if cooking were her only interest, the only topic she could talk about. And now perhaps it was.

There were footsteps coming down the street. Philippa scrambled to her feet, wincing at the pain in her cramped legs. She felt suddenly faint and had to grasp at the spikes of the railings for support. She remembered for the first time that she had walked for nearly seven hours through the streets of London, round the parks, in and out of the City churches, along the Embankment, without stopping to eat. Painfully, she made her way up the steps to the front door.

She turned her key in the lock and passed through the inner porch with its twin panels of Burne-Jones stained glass, an allegory of spring and summer, into the pearl-grey quietness of the hall. She smelled the usual faint smell of lavender and fresh paint, so faint that it was almost illusory, a conditioned response to the familiar objects of home. The delicate banister rail in polished pale mahogany supported by elegant balustrades unwound from its scroll and curved upwards drawing the eye to the stained glass of the landing window. The two panes were a continuation of the ones in the porch; a garlanded woman with a cornucopia spilling the fruits of autumn, bearded winter with his faggots and stave. To an earlier taste their self-conscious aestheticism and period charm would have been despised; now Maurice, who didn't particularly like them, wouldn't have dreamed of having them removed, probably knowing to a pound the value they added to his property. But the rest of the hall was his taste, his or that of his first wife; the low shelf with his collection of Staffordshire historical groups, bold against the shiny white wood; a pale elongated Nelson dying black-booted in Hardy's arms; Wellington, Field Marshal's baton on his hip, mounted on his charger Copenhagen; Victoria and Albert with their blond idealized children grouped before the Grand Exhibition; a lighthouse rising from a turbulent sea of unchipped waves, with Grace Darling straining on her oars. Above them, in incongruous proximity but looking somehow right since both combined strength with delicacy, were Maurice's three nineteenth-century Japanese prints in their curved rosewood frames; Nobukazu, Kikugawa, Tokohumi. Like the Staffordshire, which as a child she had been allowed to dust, they were part of her childhood, ferocious warriors with their curved swords, pale moons behind delicate blossomed boughs, the soft pinks and greens of the slant-eyed women in their kimonos. Had she really only known them for ten years? Where then had been those other hallways, forgotten except in nightmares, with their dark dados, the lank greasy macintoshes hanging inside the door, the smell of cabbage and fish, the claustrophobic horror of the black cupboard under the stairs?

Without taking off her coat she went down to the kitchen. Hilda came out of the pantry, a box of eggs in her hand. Without looking at Philippa she said:

"I'm glad you're back. We've got the Cleghorns for dinner. Can you do the table and the flowers, darling?"

Philippa didn't answer. She felt very calm, light-headed with tiredness, her anger spent. She was glad that she had no need to discipline her voice, that she was in complete control. She closed the kitchen door and leaned her back against it as if barring Hilda's escape. She waited until Hilda, getting no answer, looked up at her. Then she said:

"Why didn't you tell me that my mother was a murderess?"

But she needed to discipline herself after all. Hilda looked so ridiculous, stuck there speechless, mouth gaping, eyes wide with fright, the personification of stage horror, that she had to make a conscious effort to stop herself breaking into nervous laughter. She watched while the box of eggs dropped from Hilda's parting hands as if she had willed them to fall. One bounced free and cracked open, spilling an unbroken dome of yellow, shivering in its glutinous pad of white. Instinctively Philippa stepped towards it. Hilda cried out sharply:

"Don't step in it! Don't step in it!"

Moaning, she seized a cloth and dabbed at the yolk. There was a splurge of yellow over the black and white tiles. Still kneeling, she muttered:

"The Cleghorns, they're coming to dinner. I haven't done the table yet. I knew you'd find out! I told him. I always said so. Who told you? Where have you been all day?"

"I applied for a copy of my birth certificate under the Children Act. Then I went to 41 Bancroft Gardens. There was no one in, but a neighbour told me. Then I spent the day walking in the City. After that I came home, I mean I came back here."

Hilda was still scrubbing at the tiles, smearing the yellow mucus. She said wildly:

"I don't want to talk about it, not now! I've got to get on with dinner. The Cleghorns are coming. It's important to your father."

"The Cleghorns? How can it be? If they want something from him they'll hardly complain if the food isn't up to expectations. And if he wants something from them, then he's wasting his time if their decision can be swayed by whether the veal is the best they've eaten since they found that intriguing little inn in the Dordogne."

She explained patiently:

"Look, they don't matter. I matter. Why didn't you tell me?"

"How could we? A thing like that. They killed that girl. Raped and murdered her. She was only twelve! What good would it have done, your knowing? It wasn't your fault. It was nothing to do with you. I don't want to think about it. It was horrible, horrible! There are things you can't tell a child, ever. It would have been too cruel."

"More cruel than letting me find out?"

Hilda turned on her with a sudden flash of defensive spirit.

"Yes, cruel and wrong! You don't mind so much now. At least you're grown up. You have your own life, your own personality. It can't destroy you now. You wouldn't be talking like this if you really cared. You're excited and angry, and I suppose you're shocked, but you aren't really hurt. It isn't real to you. You stand outside life and look at it as if you aren't really part of it. You watch people as if they're acting on some kind of stage. That's how you were looking down at me just now. You thought I didn't know you were there, but I did. You don't really care what your mother did to that child. It doesn't touch you. Nothing does."

Philippa stared at Hilda, disconcerted by this unexpected percipience. She cried:

"But I want it to touch me! I want to feel it!"

She thought:

"It's because I don't really believe it yet. All my past is fabrication. This is just a new story, a different angle, to be explored and experienced. Then I shall return to the reality I fabricated for myself, to that unknown father striding across the lawn at Pennington. It is these newcomers, not he, who are the usurpers."

Hilda was rinsing out the floor-cloth under the tap, muttering above the splash of the water.

"When you came in just now—you knew what you were going to say. I expect you practised it in the train. But you aren't really unhappy. You're not as unhappy as you would have been if you hadn't got your Cambridge scholarship. You're like your father, neither of you can bear to fail."

"You mean I'm like Maurice. I don't know whether I'm like my father. That's one of the things I mean to find out."

"It was Parliament, that Act they passed. They had no right. It was breaking faith with adopters. When we took you on we thought that you'd never be able to find out who your parents were."

"Took you on." Was that how Hilda had always seen her, as an obligation, a responsibility, a burden? Probably Hilda had never really wanted her. Why should she? A baby adopted from birth, pitiful, dependent, responsive, might have done something for Hilda's frustrated maternal feelings. But what satisfaction could she have expected from a difficult and resentful eight-year-old whose parents had suddenly been taken from her, had disappeared without explanation? No, it had been Maurice's doing. Maurice had demanded his experimental material. But the idea of adoption must have been Hilda's. She must have been the one who had originally agitated for a child. Maurice wouldn't have cared one way or the other. But if there had to be an adopted child to satisfy Hilda's thwarted maternal instinct, then he would at least ensure that they chose one with intelligence but from the worst possible background. If he couldn't have a child of his own, at least he could rear one for the glory of sociological theory. It was surprising that he hadn't selected a second female, carefully matched for age and intelligence, to monitor their joint progress. After all, every experiment needed a control. How he and Hilda must have enjoyed their secret! Was this what had kept their odd marriage intact, the titillating confederacy of deceit?

She said:

"I could have applied to a court for permission to see my birth certificate once I came of age. That's always been the law, even if people didn't realize it."

"But you wouldn't have done that, and if you had, at least we'd have been warned. Then we could have told the court and the judge wouldn't have given you permission. But even if he had, it would still have been better than learning it when you were a child."

"And all those stories? My mother being a servant at Pennington and dying soon after I was born. Did you concoct them together?"

"No, that was me. He just wanted to tell you that we didn't know who your parents were. But I had to tell you something when you asked. The story just grew."

"And that bit about the letter my mother wrote, the letter to be handed to me when I'm twenty-one?"

Hilda gazed up at her, puzzled.

"I never told you that. What letter? I didn't say anything about a letter."

So that part must have been her own fabrication. Together she and Hilda, in unconscious collaboration, had created and embellished their joint fantasy, a small detail there, a touch of local colour, snatches of imagined conversation, small descriptions. Sometimes Hilda had been forced by Philippa's obsessional questions into embarrassed evasions, but Philippa had always put these down to Hilda's embarrassment at any mention of Pennington and Maurice's first wife. But she had done it very cleverly, you had to give her that. The story had hung together without obvious inconsistencies. Philippa's mother had been a parlour-maid at Pennington. She had given birth to an illegitimate child and had died shortly afterwards. The baby had been fostered by people in the village, now dead, and then by foster parents in London. Maurice had heard about her on one of his return visits to Pennington after his first wife's death, and had suggested to Hilda that they should foster the child. The fostering had been successful and had led six months later to adoption. There was no one now to disprove any of it. The present Earl had sold Pennington nine years previously and had taken refuge from taxation and the exigencies of his ex-wives in the south of France. Very few of the original servants lived in Pennington village and none still worked in the house. It had subsequently been sold to an

Arab and was now closed to the public. It would have been difficult to disprove the story and Philippa had never had any inclination to try. It had, she realized now, conformed too neatly with her own private imaginings. She had believed it because she had wanted it to be true. And even now, one small part of her mind obstinately refused to relinquish it.

She said bitterly:

"You'd be a good liar in the witness box. I wouldn't have credited you with that much imagination. I knew that it embarrassed you to talk about my mother but I thought that was because she came from Pennington. It must have amused you, fooling me for all these years. I hope it was some compensation for having me foisted on you."

Hilda cried:

"It wasn't like that! I wanted you! We both wanted you! When I found out I couldn't give Maurice a child. . ."

"You make a baby sound like an orgasm. And if that's all he married you for—and I can't think why else—it's a pity he didn't send you to a gynaecologist for a certificate of fertility before you went off together to the registry office."

They heard the quiet thud of the front door closing. Hilda said:

"It's your father! Maurice is home!"

She spoke wildly, terrified, like a woman awaiting a drunken husband. Then she dashed to the bottom of the stairs and called:

"Maurice! Maurice! Come here!"

The footsteps hesitated, then came deliberately down the stairs. He stood in the kitchen doorway watching them. Hilda cried:

"She knows! She found out about that clause in the Children Act. I told you she would. She's got her birth certificate. She's been to Bancroft Gardens."

He said to Philippa:

"How much do you know?"

"How much is there? That I'm the child of a rapist and a murderess."

She was glad that he didn't love her, that neither of them loved her, that there was no risk that he would come across to her in spontaneous pity and smother all the shock and misery in his arms. He said calmly:

"I'm sorry, Philippa. I suppose this moment was inevitable, but I wish it didn't have to happen."

"You should have told me."

He placed his briefcase on the table, calmly moving the artichokes to make room.

"Even if I agree, and I don't, there hasn't been a moment since the adoption when it seemed the right time to tell. What time

40

precisely would you have chosen? When you were adjusting to living here, when you were eleven and taking the examination into the South London Collegiate, when you were coping with adolescence, working for O-levels, A-levels, the Cambridge scholarship? Ten years pass very quickly, particularly when punctuated with the crises of childhood. With some news, the later the better."

"Where is she now?"

"Your mother? At Melcombe Grange in the pre-release unit. It's an open prison near York. She's due out I believe in about a month's time."

"You knew that!"

"I've had an interest in her release date, naturally. But that's all. She's not my responsibility. There's nothing I can do about it."

"But I can. I can write to her and ask her to come to me. I've saved the money for my European trip. I can take a flat in London and look after her, at least for the two months before I go up to Cambridge."

The idea, spontaneous, surprising even to her own ears, seemed to have come from outside herself, an impulse not subject to her will. And yet she knew even as she spoke the words that this was what she must do, what she had intended to do from that first moment of learning that her mother was alive. She didn't think about her motives; this wasn't the moment for that egotistical indulgence. But her heart told her that they were corrupt, that this histrionic gesture was born, not out of compassion for that unknown mother, but out of her anger against Maurice, her misery, her own complicated half-acknowledged needs.

He had turned away from her and she couldn't see his face. But his voice was suddenly hard. He said:

"The idea is stupid and dangerous, dangerous for both of you. You owe her nothing, not even the conventional obligations of a child to a parent. All that was expunged with the adoption order. And there's nothing that she has that you need, nothing that she can give you."

"I wasn't thinking of obligations. And there is something I need that she can give me. Information. Knowledge. A past. She can help me to find out who I am. Don't you understand? She's my mother! I can't wipe that out any more than I can wipe out what she did. I can't suddenly learn that she's alive and not want to meet her, get to know her. What do you expect me to do? Go on as if today had never happened? Concoct a new fantasy to live by? Everything you and Hilda have given me is pretence. This is real."

Hilda gave a small ridiculous sound between a snort and a sob.

41

Maurice turned and slowly lifted his briefcase from the table. Suddenly he looked and sounded very tired. He said:

"We'll talk about it after dinner. It's a nuisance that the Cleghorns are coming, but we can't put them off at less than an hour's notice. As I said, there's never a convenient moment for this kind of news."

5

She dressed with care. The guests were only to be the Cleghorns and Gabriel Lomas to even up the numbers, but it wasn't for them that she put on her favourite evening skirt of fine pleated wool and the high-necked green-blue tunic; she was dressing for herself. The skirt and top fulfilled what she most demanded of clothes, that they should be dramatic but easy to put on and sensuously agreeable to wear. She took care with her hair, brushing it until her scalp smarted, then winding it in a high top-knot, curling two thin strands with a wetted finger to lie against each cheek. Afterwards she stood and surveyed herself in the full-length glass. This is how I see myself. How do I look to others?

It surprised her that she was so calm; that the long, bony, honey-coloured face, with its high cheekbones, was so clear in its outlines, the eyes so unclouded. She had half expected the image to fudge and quiver like a reflection seen in a distorting mirror. She stretched out her hands, and fingers splayed to meet fingers encountering the cold glass.

She began to pace slowly round the room, looking at it with the appraising eyes of an inquisitive stranger. It stretched the whole length of the house on the top storey where two attics had been converted into one large, low-ceilinged room. Maurice had furnished it for her to her taste when she was twelve. Unlike the rest of the house it was modern, functional, sparsely furnished, giving an impression of airiness, of being suspended in space. It was very light with windows at each end. The southern window gave a view of the small walled garden and York stone patio, of plane trees, of the multitudinous and varied roofs of Pimlico. The furniture was modern, the bed and fitted wall units in pale wood. At this desk she had worked for O- and A-levels and for her Cambridge entrance. On this bed she and Gabriel had groped and twined in that first unsuccessful attempt at making love. The phrase struck her as ridiculous. Whatever they had been making together, it hadn't been love. He had said, gently at first, and then with controlled irritation:

"Stop thinking about yourself. Stop worrying about what you're feeling. Let yourself go."

But that she had never been able to do. How could you let go of something which you had never felt was yours to relinquish? To let go implied the utter confidence of undisputed possession, the assurance that nothing of oneself could be violated by that transitory, terrifying loss of control.

It surprised her that this initial sexual fiasco hadn't resulted in an estrangement. Like her, he couldn't tolerate failure. And afterwards, unsatisfied and frustrated, she hadn't even managed the expedience of pretence or the grace of generosity. It had been a bad time to recall the warning of his sister; Sarah's voice, cool, amused, a little spiteful:

"My brother seems to look on the upper sixth as his private harem. He's AC/DC by the way. Not that it matters. But it's as well to know these little details before you try to plug in your kettle."

Pulling on her dressing-gown, she had said:

"Why did you bother? Was it to prove that you can make it with a woman?"

And he had replied:

"What were you trying to prove? That you can make it at all?"

But he had, if anything, been more attentive, more apparently devoted since that disastrous evening, and she suspected that he knew perfectly well why she played her part in their charade. He was high on her list of objects of use and beauty which she planned to take with her to Cambridge. Having the rich and amusing Honourable Gabriel Lomas in tow would do her absolutely no harm with her contemporaries at King's.

Settling down at this desk to write a history essay on the first Saturday morning after the room had been completed, she had learned an early lesson, that undeserved good fortune was resented. Mrs Cooper, Hilda's cleaning woman, had been brought up by Hilda to admire the room. Hilda involved her in any new domestic arrangements, apparently in a desperate attempt to pretend that they liked each other. But Mrs Cooper, unpropitiated, persisted in calling her "madam" and held aloof as if to demonstrate that ten shillings an hour and a free lunch could buy obsequiousness, but it couldn't buy affection. She had stared round the room before giving her customary unenthusiastic verdict. "It's very nice, madam, I'm sure." But she had lingered a few seconds when Hilda left, then coming quickly up to Philippa had pushed her face close to her cheek. The words had come in a hiss of sour breath.

"Bastard. I hope you're grateful. It isn't right. All this for a bastard when decent kids have to make do four in a room. You ought to be in a Home."

Then her voice had again become respectful:

"Coming, madam."

Philippa could recall still the shock and anger. But she had learned control. There were no tantrums now. Words, she had discovered, were more effective than screams, more hurtful than kicks and blows. She had said coolly:

"You shouldn't breed four children if you can't afford them. And I expect they'll go on living four to a room if they're as ugly and stupid as you."

After that Mrs Cooper had handed in her notice, but without giving a reason, and Hilda, as Philippa knew, had been left with an added weight of inadequacy and failure.

She walked across to the bookshelves and ran her hand along the spines of the books. Here was the orthodox library of an upper-middle-class student. With these volumes you could pass an A-level in English literature whatever the year or the syllabus; with luck and a good memory you could even achieve a Cambridge entrance. It wasn't easy to deduce the girl's personal taste, except perhaps that she preferred Turgenev to Tolstoy, Proust to Flaubert, Henry James to Dickens. But here were no battered childhood favourites passed from generation to generation. True the accepted upper-middle-class children's classics were present; the *Just So Stories*, *The Wind in the Willows*, Carroll, and Ransome and Nesbit. They looked read, but they looked, also, as if they had been bought new for this privileged child.

Here on these packed shelves was enough knowledge, wisdom, imagination to sustain her for life. For what life? There wasn't a word which she herself had written, yet it was in this accumulation of other men's thoughts and experiences that she had looked for an affirmation of identity. She thought:

"Even putting on the clothes of my choice was only putting on myself. Naked in the bathroom just now, who was I? I can be described, measured, weighed, my physical processes recorded, given a name, real or unreal, for the convenient documentation of a life. But who am I? Whoever I am, nothing of me comes from Maurice and Hilda. How could it? They've done nothing but provide the props for this charade, the clothes, the artefacts. Even this soliloquy is contrived. Some part of me, that part of me which one day will make me a writer, is watching another me choosing

44

the words to think, deciding what emotions are appropriate to feel."

She opened the immense fitted wardrobe and rattled the hangers along the rail. The swaying skirts and dresses emitted a faint scent which she recognized as familiar. It must be her own. This girl liked expensive clothes. She bought little but she bought with care. She wore only wool and cotton; obviously she disliked synthetics. She smiled at the facile irony.

She moved over to the noticeboard of charcoal-coloured cork fitted to the wall above the desk unit. It was patterned with post-cards, obviously bought on holidays or at art galleries, a school timetable, notices cut from newspapers of forthcoming art exhibi-tions, *aides-mémoire*, two invitations to parties. She examined the postcards. Hans Holbein's delicate portrait of Cicely Heron; Augustus John's etching of W. B. Yeats; a Renoir nude from the Musée du Jeu de Paume; a Farington aquatint of London Bridge in 1799; a George Brecht. How could one deduce this unknown girl's taste in art from such capricious pickings? They told one nothing except which galleries she had visited.

In this room, she had concocted for herself over ten years a whole mythology of identity. It was slipping away from her now, that dead discredited world. She told herself, nothing has changed; I am the same person as I was yesterday. But who was I yesterday? The room reminded her of a designer's room in a furniture store, its carefully chosen objects disposed around to give the illusion of an absent owner, but one who had no reality except in the designer's mind.

She recalled Hilda's face bending over her to tuck her in at night.

"Where am I when I'm asleep?"

"You're still here, in bed."

"But how do you know?"

"Because I can see you, silly. I can touch you."

Only, of course, she very seldom did touch. The three of them lived distanced. That hadn't been Hilda's fault. When Philippa was tucked in at night she had lain rigid, rejecting the final, and in the end merely dutiful, kiss, hating that moist encounter of the flesh more than the rough tickle of the blanket which Hilda always drew from under the sheet and tucked against her face.

"But you know you are here because you can see and touch me. When I'm asleep I can't see or touch anyone."

"No one can when they're asleep. But you're still here in your bed."

"If I went into hospital and had an anaesthetic, where would I be then. Not my body, where would *I* be?"

"Best ask Daddy."

"When I am dead where will I be?"

"With Jesus in heaven."

But Hilda had spoken that heresy against Maurice's atheism without conviction.

She was drawn again to the bookcase. Here, surely, if anywhere, an answer was to be found. And here, ranked together, were the first editions of Maurice's books, all inscribed in his hand with the name he had bestowed on her. It was surprising in view of this industry that no university had offered him a chair. Perhaps others prominent in his discipline detected in him a dilettantism, a less than wholehearted commitment to his subject. Or was it simpler than that? Perhaps the rebarbative arrogance of some of his public criticisms irritated or repelled them, as she suspected it might do his pupils. But here they were, the most recent fruits of his intellectual preoccupations, elegantly written for a sociologist, impeccable in scholarship and style, or so the critics said, the books which partly explained Maurice. Now, of course, she saw that they explained her too. *Nature and Nurture: Genetic and Environmental Interactions in Language Development. Tackling Disadvantage: Social Class, Language and Intelligence. Genes and Environment: Environmental Influences on the Concept of Object Permanence. Schooled to Fail: Class Poverty and Education in Great Britain.* Had he planned one day to add another? *Adoption: A Case Study in the Interaction of Heredity and Environment.*

Last of all she comforted herself with a long look at her most prized possession, the Henry Walton oil painting of the Reverend Joseph Skinner and family which she had chosen as Maurice's gift for her eighteenth birthday. It was an extraordinarily attractive and competent painting with none of the slightly sentimental charm of some of his later works. Here was all the elegance, the order, the confidence and the formal good manners of her favourite period in English history. The Reverend Skinner and his three sons were mounted, his wife and two daughters were seated in a barouche. Behind them was their solid decent house, before them their carriage drive, their shadowed lawn set with oaks. They could have had no crises of identity. The long Skinner faces, the high-arched Skinner noses proclaimed their lineage. And yet they spoke to her, telling her only that they had lived and suffered, endured and died. And so in her time would she.

6

Harry Cleghorn who, at forty-five and already balding, still managed to retain his reputation as an up-and-coming politician, looked to Philippa so like a successful Tory back-bencher that she supposed his political career to have been inevitable. He was strongly muscled with a smooth, high-coloured skin, hair so black that it looked dyed, and a moist, rather petulant, mouth whose lips, red at the outlines as if lipsticked, revealed when he spoke an under-bleb of soft pale pink. As far as Philippa could see, he and Maurice had nothing in common except their appearance together as members of the same television chat show and their status as television personalities. But what else did they need to have in common? Differences of background, temperament, interests or political philosophy all faded in the unifying glare which the television studio lights shed on the company of the elect.

Nora Cleghorn faced her across the table, her over-made-up face softened by the candlelight. She must have been attractive when she was twenty to those who liked fair doll-like prettiness, but hers was a beauty which faded early, depending as it did on a pert perfection of skin and colouring, and not on bone structure. She was a silly woman, excessively proud of her husband, but few people disliked her, perhaps because there was something endearingly naive about a belief that membership of the House of Commons represented the summit of human aspiration. She was, as usual, over-dressed for an informal dinner party, gleamingly metallic in a sequined, sleeveless top over a velvet skirt. As their shoulders brushed in the doorway she smelled to Philippa of hot moist coins which had been steeped in scent.

If Nora Cleghorn were over-dressed, so was Gabriel Lomas, since he was the only man wearing a dinner jacket. But with Gabriel one knew that sartorial eccentricity was deliberate. Maurice apparently liked him despite—or could it be because of—his affectation of an extreme right-wing Toryism. Perhaps it made a change from the majority of his students. For his part, Gabriel sometimes seemed to Philippa to be excessively interested in Maurice. It was from Gabriel that she had learnt most of what she knew about Helena Palfrey. Since she had almost total recall of any conversation which really interested her, she could perfectly remember one snatch of conversation.

"Your father is like all rich Socialists, there's a Tory inside which he's struggling to keep down."

47

She had replied:

"I don't think Maurice qualifies as a rich Socialist. You shouldn't be misled by our life-style. He inherited this house and most of the furniture and pictures from his first wife. Maurice's background is perfectly respectable from the comrades' point of view. Dad was a post-office supervisor, leading light in the union. Maurice hasn't rebelled, merely conformed."

"He married an earl's daughter. I don't call that conforming. Admittedly an eccentric earl who is somewhat of an embarrassment to his class, but there's nothing suspect about his lineage, no Victorian creation there. Admittedly, too, knowing Lady Helena, people wondered why marriage, until she produced a baby seven months later, the only seven-month prem to weigh in at eight and a half pounds."

"Gabriel, how on earth do you get to know these things?"

"An addiction to petty gossip acquired during childhood, long summer afternoons in Kensington Gardens listening to Nanny and her cronies. Sarah, grossly over-dressed, sitting up in the huge, shabby family pram, me trotting by the side. God, the suffocating boredom of those perambulations round the Round Pond! Be grateful, privileged little bastard that you are, that you were spared them."

Now as they started on their artichokes, Gabriel was indulging in a minor Maurice tease, pretending to believe that a recent Labour Party political broadcast by a group of Young Socialists had been put out by the Tory Party.

"Naughty of them, although I don't think it will make them any converts. And if they wanted to scare us I think they rather overdid it. Surely even the young comrades don't actually mouth such a risible combination of spurious philosophy, class hatred and discredited economic theory. And where on earth did they find those singularly unattractive actors? Positively scrofulous most of them. I don't think there's been any research to examine the correlation between acne and left-wing opinions. It might be rather an interesting project for one of your post-graduate students, sir?"

Nora Cleghorn said wonderingly:

"But I thought it was supposed to be a Labour broadcast."

Her husband laughed:

"You'd certainly be well-advised, Maurice, to keep the young comrades under wraps until after the election."

The political discussion was under way as was inevitable. Conversation between Maurice and Harry Cleghorn, thought Philippa, was seldom memorable being usually either a reiteration of their previous television encounter, or a rehearsal for their next. She

48

detached her mind from arguments which she had heard so often before and glanced across the table at Hilda.

Ever since early adolescence, Philippa's reaction to her adoptive mother had been an urge to alter her, to upgrade her, to make her over as she might a dull but still serviceable winter coat. In imagination she applied make-up, as if by the judicious application of colour the face could be given definition, rescued from its pallid inconsequence. She had a half-shameful vision of confronting Maurice with a wife transformed, presented with her compliments for his approval, a procuress of his pleasure. Even now she hardly ever looked at her adoptive mother without mentally changing her hairstyle, her clothes. About a year ago, when Hilda had needed a new evening dress, she had tentatively suggested to Philippa that they should shop for it together. Perhaps the invitation had conjured up for her an idealized relationship of mother and daughter, a feminine excursion, half frivolous, conspiratorial. It hadn't been a success. Hilda hated all shops other than those which sold food, was embarrassed by the presence of smarter customers, confused by too abundant a choice, over-deferential to the assistants, shy about undressing. The last store to which Philippa in desperation had taken her had had a large communal dressing-room. What inhibitions of the flesh, she wondered, had caused Hilda to shrink desperately into one corner, trying with ridiculous prudery to undress under cover of her coat while all around her girls and women stripped unselfconsciously to their bras and pants. Philippa had foraged out, desperately hunting among the rails. Nothing looked right on Hilda. Nothing could, since she wore it without confidence, without pleasure, a mute uncomplaining victim offering herself to be adorned for some sacrificial dinner party. In the end they had bought the black woollen skirt she was wearing now, topped by an over-fussy and ill-cut Crimplene blouse. It was the last time they had gone out together, the only time that she had tried to be a daughter. She told herself that she was glad that she need never try again.

Harry Cleghorn's slightly hectoring voice—all his utterances had the resonant boom of the hustings—broke into her comforting disparagement of Hilda, Hilda whose only skills were cooking and deceit.

"Your party claims to understand the so-called working class, but most of you haven't a clue about what they're feeling. Take an old woman living south of the river and holed up on the top of one of your tower blocks. If she can't go out to shop or collect her pension because she's afraid of being mugged, she isn't free in any real sense of that word. Freedom to move about safely in your own capital city is a damned sight more fundamental than the abstractions that the civil liberties lobby prates about."

"If you could explain how longer prison sentences and tougher detention centre regimes would make it safer."

Nora Cleghorn licked sauce vinaigrette from her fingers.

"I do think that they ought to hang murderers."

She spoke in a brightly conversational voice as though, thought Philippa, she were referring to a neighbour's unaccountable omission to hang curtains. There was a moment of complete silence as if she had dropped something precious. In her mind Philippa heard the tinkle of smashing glass. Then Maurice said evenly:

"They? You mean we ought. As it's not a duty I personally would care to perform, I can hardly expect someone else to do it on my behalf."

"Oh, Harry would do it, wouldn't you darling?"

"There are one or two I can think of I wouldn't exactly flinch at launching into eternity."

And this led them, as Philippa knew it would, to a discussion of the century's most notorious child murderess, the name which came up whenever people discussed capital punishment, the touchstone by which liberals tested their response to the death penalty. Philippa wondered if her own mother had served for a longer than normal time because her early release might have stimulated agitation on behalf of that other, more notorious child-killer. She glanced across at Hilda, but Hilda's face, half hidden by the two swathes of hair, was bent low over her plate. Artichokes were a convenient starter to an embarrassing meal. They required careful attention. Cleghorn said:

"Having decided that it is wrong to hang murderers, we are now waking up to the fact that they don't conveniently die in prison or just fade away. We're also waking up to the fact that someone has to look after them and that if we don't pay society's custodians properly for a disagreeable job we won't find anyone willing to do it. But obviously, sooner or later, the woman will have to be paroled. I suggest that it might be later."

Nora Cleghorn said:

"But isn't she supposed to have got terribly religious? I think I read somewhere that she wants to go into a convent or nurse lepers or something."

Gabriel laughed.

"Poor lepers! They seem always to be selected as the sacrificial victims of someone's contrition. You'd think they had enough troubles already."

Cleghorn's moist lips fastened on the succulent heart of his artichoke, like a child's on a dummy. A trickle of sauce ran down the side of his mouth. His voice was half muffled in his linen napkin.

"I don't mind who she nurses as long as she keeps away from their children."

His wife said:

"But if she has really reformed, she wouldn't be agitating to get out of prison, would she?"

Cleghorn spoke impatiently. Philippa had noticed before that he was indulgent to his wife's inanities, but became irritated when she spoke sense.

"Of course she wouldn't. That's the last thing she'd be worried about. After all, if she's hankering to do good, a prison is as suitable a place as any. All this talk about contrition is nonsense. She and her lover tortured a child to death. If she ever comes to an understanding of what she's done, I don't see how she could bear to go on living, let alone start planning for a life outside."

Gabriel said:

"So we must hope for her own sake that she is unrepentant. But why all this public interest in the state of her soul? I suppose that society has a right to punish her to deter others, and to demand what assurances are possible that she's no longer dangerous before letting her out. What we haven't the right to demand is repentance. That's a matter between her and her god."

Philippa said:

"Of course. It's as arrogant as me, a Gentile, proclaiming that I've forgiven the Nazis for the holocaust. The statement has no meaning."

Maurice said drily:

"As little meaning as the statement that repentance is between her and her god."

Cleghorn laughed:

"Now Maurice, leave the theological argument for your encounter with the Bishop. What are they paying you for the new series, by the way?"

The conversation turned to contracts and the foibles of television producers. There was no more talk of murder. The meal dragged on through the veal, the lemon soufflé, and finally to the leisurely coffee and brandy in the garden. It seemed to Philippa that she had never lived through a longer day. She had woken that morning as a bastard; how short but how endless the hours which had legitimized her into horror and disgrace. It was like experiencing birth and death simultaneously, each separately painful yet both part of the same inexorable process. Now she sat, drained, under the patio lamps and willed the Cleghorns to go.

She was beyond tiredness. Her mind was preternaturally clear yet it fastened on unimportant details which it invested with an egregious significance: Nora Cleghorn's bra-strap slipping down a sequined shoulder, her husband's heavy signet ring biting into his little finger, the peach tree gleaming silver under the patio lamp; surely if she stretched out her arm and shook the trunk its leaves would tinkle down in a shower of glistening pellets.

By half-past eleven the talk had become disjointed, perfunctory. Maurice and Cleghorn had completed their academic business and Gabriel, with his half-ironic formality, had taken his leave. But still the Cleghorns lingered in what seemed an obstinate endurance, long after a damp chill had crept across the garden and the purple sky was stained with the arteries of the dying day. It was nearly midnight before they reminded each other that they had a home, said their protracted goodbyes, and made their way through the garden gate to the mews garage and their Jaguar. Philippa was free at last to go to her room.

7

The letter was more difficult to write than even the most challenging of her weekly school essays. It was astonishing that a short passage of English prose should take so long to compose, that even the most ordinary words should carry such a charge of innuendo, condescension or crass insensitivity. The problems began with the superscription. "Dear Mother" seemed a startling, almost presumptuous beginning; "Dear Mrs Ducton" was offensively, almost aggressively formal; "Dear Mary Ducton" was too obviously a trendy compromise, a confession of defeat. In the end she decided on "Dear Mother". That, after all, was the relationship between them, the primal, unalterable, biological tie. To admit the fact needn't imply that it was any more than that.

The first sentence was comparatively easy. She wrote: "I hope that it won't distress you to receive this letter, but I exercised my right under the Children Act 1975 to apply to the Registrar General for a copy of my birth certificate. Afterwards I went to Bancroft Gardens and learned from a neighbour who you were."

There was no need to say any more. In that last sentence infamy

52

was plucked from the past, briefly held, then dropped. The words were bloodstained. She went on:

"I should very much like to meet you unless you would much rather not; I could come to Melcombe Grange on any visitors' day if you would let me know when it would be convenient."

She deleted the second "much" and hesitated over the last five words, but decided on reflection to leave them in. The sentence didn't satisfy her, but at least it was short and the meaning clear. The next part was more difficult. The words "released", "paroled", "licensed" or "set free" were pejorative but it was extraordinarily difficult to avoid them. Quickly she scribbled an alternative draft:

"I don't want to force myself on you, but if you haven't anywhere to go . . . anywhere to stay . . . if you haven't finally decided on your plans after you leave Melcombe Grange, would you care to come to me."

But the last seven words sounded as grudging and patronizing as an invitation to an unwelcome guest. She tried again:

"I shall be taking up my Cambridge scholarship in October and hope to find a flat in London for the next couple of months. If you haven't finally decided on your plans after you leave Melcombe Grange and would care to share the flat, that would be agreeable for me, but please don't feel that you have to say yes."

It occurred to her that her mother might worry about her share of the rent. Presumably she wouldn't leave prison with very much money. She ought to make it plain that no payment was involved. She began to write that the offer was without obligation, but that bleak commercial note was too reminiscent of a sales catalogue. And there would, after all, be obligations. The demands she would be making of her mother couldn't be satisfied with money. In the end she decided the details could await their meeting. She ended the draft:

"It will only be a small flat—a room for each of us and a kitchen and bathroom—but I hope to find one which will be reasonably central and convenient."

Convenient for what, she wondered. Covent Garden Opera House, the West End shops, the theatres and restaurants? What sort of life was she implying? What was she visualizing for this stranger who would walk into freedom, if licence from a life sentence was ever freedom, carrying the weight of a dead child? She copied out the draft neatly and signed the letter Philippa Palfrey. She read it through carefully. It was, she thought, disingenuous. She wondered whether her mother would see through the careful words to the truth. There was no real choice for her. She was, in effect, being once again hunted down. The meeting between them was inevitable;

if not now, it would come later. There was nothing her mother could do to prevent it.

Perhaps it would have been more honest and, since style depended on honesty, more satisfying to have written the brutal truth.

"If you have nowhere satisfactory to go when you're released from prison, would you care to share a flat with me in London until I go up to Cambridge in October? It can't be longer than that; I'm not intending to alter my life for you. I need to know who I am. If you need a room for two months it would seem a fair exchange. Let me know if you'd like me to come up to Melcombe Grange to talk about it."

She heard two sets of footsteps mounting the stairs. Then there was a knock. That must be Hilda. Maurice—taught perhaps by Helena—would never have knocked. They stood there, side by side, like a deputation, dressing-gowned; Hilda in her flowered quilted nylon, Maurice in his fine scarlet wool, looking diminished and vulnerable, bringing with them a childhood bathtime smell of soap and powder. He said:

"We have to talk, Philippa."

"I'm too tired. It's after midnight. And what is there to say?"

"At least do nothing until you've seen her, spoken to her."

"I've already written. I'll post it tomorrow, today I mean. The offer means nothing if it isn't made before we meet. I can't look her over first as if she were goods on approval."

"You propose then to commit yourself, for weeks, for months, perhaps even for life, to a woman you don't know, who has done nothing for you, who will be nothing but an embarrassment to you, whom you probably won't even like. The fact that she happens to be a murderess is irrelevant. It's quixotic, Philippa. Worse, it's self-indulgent stupidity."

"I didn't say anything about commitment."

"Of course it's a commitment. You're not engaging a junior clerk. If she doesn't give satisfaction you can hardly throw her out. What else is it but a commitment?"

"A sensible arrangement to help her over these first two months outside. All I propose to do is to make the offer. She may not even want to see me. If she does it won't necessarily mean that she'll want to share a flat. She's probably made other arrangements. But if she hasn't found anywhere to go, then I'm free for the next few months. At least she'll have a choice."

"It's not a question of her finding somewhere to go. If she hasn't a family willing to take her back, then the probation service will have found somewhere for her. She won't be homeless. They don't

54

parole lifers unless the aftercare arrangements are approved by the Home Office as satisfactory."

Hilda said nervously:

"Aren't there hostels, places like that? I've heard they're quite nice. She'll probably go to a hostel just until she's sorted herself out, found herself a job."

She spoke, thought Philippa, as if her mother were a convalescent being discharged prematurely from hospital. Maurice said:

"Or she'll join up with some woman she's met inside. I don't suppose she's spent all those years entirely alone."

"You mean a lover? A lesbian?"

He said irritably:

"It's not unknown. You know nothing about her. She let you go out of her life, no doubt because she thought it for the best. Now do the same for her. Hasn't it occurred to you that you may be the last person on earth that she wants to see again?"

"Then all she has to do is say so. I shall write first. I'm not proposing to arrive at the prison unannounced. And if she gave me up it's because she had no choice."

Hilda's voice was a thin wail of protest.

"But you can't just leave! What are people going to think? What can we say to your friends, to Gabriel Lomas?"

"It's nothing to do with Gabriel. Tell them I'm abroad until October. That's what I was going to do anyway."

"But they're bound to see you in London. They'll see you with her!"

"What if they do? She won't be branded on her forehead with the divine stigma. I'll think of something to tell your friends if that's all you're worried about. And it's only for a couple of months. People do leave home occasionally."

Maurice came into the room and walked over to the Henry Walton. Studying the picture, his back to her, he said:

"How much have you read about the murder?"

"I haven't read anything. I know that she killed a child called Julie Scase after my father raped her."

"You haven't consulted the newspaper reports of the crime?"

"No, I haven't the time to grub about in the archives, and I don't want to."

"Then I suggest that, before you do anything foolish, make any decision, you get hold of the newspaper cuttings and the trial report and learn the facts."

"I know the facts. They were told to me this morning with brutal explicitness. I'm not going to spy on my mother before I meet her. If I want any more facts, she can give them to me. And now, please, I'm very tired. I'd like to go to bed."

8

Two days later, on Friday 14 July, Norman Scase celebrated simultaneously his fifty-seventh birthday and the last day of his career as a local government accounts clerk. He had told his colleagues that he had been left a modest legacy by an uncle, sufficient to enable him to freeze his pension for three years and to take a premature retirement. The lie worried him; he was unpractised in lying. But something had to be said to explain how a middle-grade unqualified clerk who, to their knowledge, had worn the same suit to work for the last five years could afford the indulgence of an early retirement. He could hardly tell them the truth, that the murderess of his child was due to be released from prison in August and that there were arrangements which he had to make, matters to which he must now devote the whole of his time.

Celebration was not a word he would have used either for the birthday or for his last day at the office. He would have been grateful to have been allowed to slip quietly away as he had at the end of every working day for the last eight years; but there were rituals in the treasurer's department from which not even the least sociable and most private member of the staff was exempt. It was the custom for members of staff who were leaving, getting married, being promoted or retiring to mark the occasion with an invitation either to tea or to sherry, depending on their status and habits and the degree of importance which they attached to the impending change. The invitation was typed by courtesy of the typing pool for those too lowly to have a personal secretary, and circulated by the junior clerical assistant with the miscellaneous departmental notes, circulars and periodicals which went the rounds. On its first appearance Miss Millicent Yelland, the senior personal secretary, would start collecting for a present, tripping conspiratorially from room to room with an envelope to receive donations and a greeting card on which contributors would sign their names under variously worded messages of farewell or good wishes. The choice of card was invariably left to Miss Yelland. At fifty-four she had sublimated her maternal instincts by taking upon herself the role of mother of the division, and had for the past fifteen years promoted, without noticeable success, the fiction that they were all one happy family.

She always took a great deal of trouble, browsing along the racks in the Army and Navy Stores and in the Westminster Abbey Bookshop, and even venturing occasionally as far as Oxford Circus.

For more senior staff she usually chose a dog. Dogs were always acceptable, evoking in her mind a mixture of vaguely-felt emotions and aspirations, loyalty and devotion, rough tweeded masculinity, mysterious upper-class activities on grouse moors and among the heather, a restrained good taste. Since a country cottage, with its suggestion of shared connubial bliss, was unsuitable for a widower, and it was impossible to associate Mr Scase with anything as frivolous as bambis or black cats, she decided on a moorland scene featuring a shaggy dog of indeterminate breed with a pheasant in its mouth.

When she examined the card again in her office she had a qualm of doubt. The pheasant, at least she supposed it was a pheasant, looked so very dead, pathetic really, with its drooping neck and glazed eye. It was hardly what you would call a cheerful card. She hoped that Mr Scase didn't disapprove of blood sports. And when one came to examine it, the expression on the dog's face was really most unpleasant, almost gloating. Well, it would have to do now. She had spent thirty-three pence from the collection of ten pounds— a disappointing sum, but then poor Mr Scase had never particularly put himself out to be popular—and it would be an idiotic waste to buy another card. It was a pity that he was so difficult to choose for. On the death of his wife, eight months ago, about which he had been as reticent as he was about any of his private concerns, she had sent a mourning card on behalf of the division, a silver cross wreathed with violets and forget-me-nots. Afterwards she had wondered whether her choice then had been suitable. He had worked in the division for nearly nine years yet they knew virtually nothing about him except that, like herself, he commuted to Liverpool Street from one of the eastern suburbs. They seldom met on the station and sometimes she wondered if he deliberately avoided her.

Some years previously, emboldened by two glasses of cheap sherry at the office Christmas party, she had asked him whether he had children, and he had replied "No." After a few seconds he had added, "We did have a daughter, but she died young." Then he had flushed and turned aside as if regretting that brief confidence. She had been made to feel tactless and inquisitive. She had murmured something about being sorry and had moved away, replenishing the outstretched glasses and responding to the office banter. But afterwards she had told herself that to no one else had he spoken about his child, that the confidence, even if involuntary, had been to her alone. She never mentioned it either to him or in the office, but cherished it as a small secret which somehow affirmed her worth in his eyes. And the knowledge of his private tragedy lent him an interest, almost a distinction, which intrigued her. After the death of his wife she found herself indulging a private fantasy. They were both lonely. And he was thoughtful, conscientious. The junior staff didn't appreciate him, just because he insisted on punctuality and a proper standard of work. It took an older woman, a mature woman, to appreciate his qualities. Perhaps here was someone who would be a friend and later, who knew, more than a friend. It wasn't too late for her to make a man happy. She would have someone other than Mother to cook for and care for. But she knew she would have to make the first move.

Inspiration came to her from the advice column of her woman's magazine, where one of the readers wrote that she was interested in a boy in her office, but he had never been more than polite and friendly. There had been no invitation, no date. The answer had been explicit. "Buy two theatre tickets for something you think he'll like. Then tell him that you've been given the tickets unexpectedly and ask whether he'd care to see the show with you." It hadn't been an easy ploy for Miss Yelland to put into effect. There had been the difficulty of persuading a neighbour to sit with her mother, the problem of deciding what tickets to buy. In the end, feeling that music was the safest bet, she had queued for two expensive seats for a Brahms concert at the Royal Festival Hall for a Friday night. On the Monday she spoke to him. The few stiff words had been over-rehearsed and her invitation sounded ungracious as well as insincere. He hadn't answered her at first, keeping his eyes on his ledger, and she began to wonder whether he had heard. Then he had got clumsily to his feet, looked briefly into her eyes and murmured:

"It's very kind of you, Miss Yelland, but I never go out in the evenings."

She had read in his eyes not merely embarrassment, but a kind of panic. Afterwards, scarlet with humiliation since the rejection had been so absolute, she had sought solitude in the ladies' cloakroom. Tearing up the two tickets she flushed them down the lavatory. It was, she knew, a stupidly extravagant gesture. The concert was a popular one; the booking office could almost certainly have disposed of the tickets. But the gesture was some small comfort to her pride. She had never approached him again, and it seemed to her imagination that he became even more reserved, withdrew more completely beneath his carapace of quiet efficiency. And now he was leaving. For nearly nine years he had circumvented her loving-kindness. Now he was escaping for good.

The formal goodbye was arranged for twelve-thirty, and by one o'clock Mr Willcox, the chief accountant in the division, who undertook these ceremonies for staff whose status didn't warrant the personal appearance of the treasurer, was in full flood:

"And if any of you were to ask me, as his senior officer, what I regard as the salient feature of Norman Scase's work in this division, I shouldn't need to hesitate for a single second before giving you my judgement."

He then hesitated for a nicely-judged half-minute, giving the assembled division time to assume expressions of brightly anticipatory interest as if this fascinating question had indeed been on their lips, while the deputy senior accountant cast lugubrious eyes at the ceiling, the junior personal secretary giggled and Miss Yelland smiled encouragingly at Scase across the throng. The smile wasn't returned. He stood there, holding the canteen glass in his hand, half filled with sweet South African sherry, and stared slightly over their heads. He had taken the usual trouble with his appearance, neither more nor less. The formal blue suit was a little shabby now, the sleeves polished by the friction of desk top and ledger. The shirt collar was crumpled but very clean, and the nondescript tie precisely knotted. Standing there, a little apart, like a man under judgement, he reminded Miss Yelland of someone; a picture, a photograph, a newsreel, not someone known to her. Then she remembered. It was one of the accused in the dock at Nuremberg. The mental image, impious, offensive, shocked her; she flushed and gazed fixedly into her sherry as if detected in a solecism. But the memory remained. She fixed her eyes again resolutely on Mr Willcox.

"It would be expressed in a single word," he pronounced, and proceeded to use a thesaurus. "Conscientiousness, attention to detail, methodicalness"—he slipped a little over this and Miss Yelland wondered whether there was such a word—"complete reliability. Whatever he has put his hand to, that task has been carried through to the end with accuracy, neatness and with complete reliability."

His deputy, lowering his eyes, swallowed his sherry in one gulp, since it was not a taste voluntarily to let linger on the tongue, and thought that if there were a more bloody boring, damning valediction, then he had yet to hear it. He was intrigued by Scase's early retirement. The legacy, of which he had heard rumours, must have been quite a sum if he could afford to go three years early—unless, of course, he had found himself another job and was keeping quiet about it. But that seemed unlikely. Who, these days, would want to take a fifty-seven-year-old chap without qualifications?

And so the self-satisfied rhetoric boomed on. Sly innuendoes about what Scase would do with his retirement; congratulations only half jocular, he couldn't prevent the note of envy from creeping in that he could afford to freeze his pension and retire three years before he was due to go; the final conventional wish that he would enjoy a long, prosperous and happy retirement and that the division's little gift would be used to provide some small luxury which would remind him of their affection and respect. The cheque was handed over, there was a brief outbreak of self-conscious clapping in which Mr Willcox joined with a curiously soundless and rhythmic clasping and releasing of his palms like a half-hearted cheerleader at a revivalist meeting, and all their eyes swivelled and rested on Scase. He blinked at the envelope which had been pressed into his hand, but he didn't open it. One might suppose that he didn't know the convention, that he was supposed to pretend he couldn't find the flap, raise a gratified eyebrow at the size of the cheque, exclaim over the design on the card, and study the inscribed names. But he clutched it in his delicate hands as a child might do, uncertain if it were really his. He said:

"Thank you very much. I shall miss the division in many ways after nearly nine years."

"Nine years hard," someone called out, and laughed.

He didn't smile.

"After nearly nine years," he repeated. "I shall buy a pair of binoculars with your kind gift, and they will remind me of old friends and colleagues in local government. Thank you."

Then he smiled. He had a singularly sweet smile, but it was so transitory that those who saw it were left wondering whether there had indeed been that extraordinary transformation. He put down his unfinished drink, shook hands with one or two closest to him, and left them.

Back in the small room which he shared with two other clerks, he had already packed his few belongings in a plastic carrier bag; his cup and saucer carefully wrapped in yesterday's *Daily Telegraph*; a ready reckoner and dictionary; his toilet bag. He gave a last look round. Nothing remained to be done. Making his way to the lift he wondered what they would have said, how they would have looked, if he had spoken quite simply what was in his mind.

"I have to retire early because there is something I must do in the next few months, a task which will take a great deal of time and planning. I have to find and kill the murderess of my child."

Would the ring of nervously smiling faces have frozen into stark disbelief, the mouths set in their conventional smirks have broken into embarrassed laughter? Or would they have stood in a surrealist charade, still smiling, still nodding, toasting him in their cheap sherry, as if the dreadful words were as meaningless as Mr Willcox's pompous platitudes? The thought that he might actually hear himself speaking the truth had come to him during the last seconds of Mr Willcox's peroration. He hadn't, of course, been seriously tempted to such folly; but it surprised and slightly offended him that so iconoclastic and so melodramatic a conceit should have entered his mind. He was not given to the grand gesture, either in thought or action. Killing Mary Ducton was a duty which he neither wanted to escape, nor could escape even had he wanted to. Certainly he planned to commit a successful murder, in the sense that he intended to avoid detection. It was justice, not martyrdom, that he sought. But never until this afternoon had it occurred to him to wonder what his colleagues would think of him as a prospective killer, and he felt obscurely denigrated, his serious purpose cheapened into melodrama, that the thought should have occurred to him now.

9

He took his usual way home over Westminster Bridge, across Parliament Square, down Great George Street and into St James's Park. The quicker way to Liverpool Street Station and the eastern suburban line was by Waterloo and the City line, but he preferred to walk each evening over the river and take the underground from St James's Park. Since Mavis's death he had been in no hurry to get home. There was no hurry now.

St James's Park was crowded, but he managed to find room on a bench beside the lake. Carefully he lowered the holdall with his few belongings and placed it on the path beneath his feet. Staring at the lake through the boughs of a willow, he realized that he had sat in this identical spot eight months previously, in his lunch hour on the day after his wife's death. It had been an unusually cold Friday in November. He could remember a smudged sun high above the lake like a great white moon, and the willow fronds slowly shedding their pale lances on to the water. In these burgeoning rose beds there had been a few tight red buds, blighted by the cold, their stems choked with dead leaves. The lake had been bronzed and wrinkled with, at its centre, a great salver of beaten silver. An old man, surely too old to be employed by the council, had shuffled along the path past him, spearing the sparse litter. The park then had held an air of sad decrepitude, the handrail of the blue bridge worn by tourists' hands, the fountain silent, the tea house closed for the winter. Now the air was loud with the staccato chatter of tourists, the shrieks and laughter of children. Then, he remembered, there had been one solitary child with his mother. The gulls had risen squawking before his harsh, cracked laughter, and he had stretched out his arms, willing their plump bodies to fall into his palms. Under the far trees patches of early snow had lain between the clumps of grass like the discarded litter of the dead summer.

Remembering that day he could almost feel again the November cold. He shut his eyes against the sunlit greenness of the park, the sheen on the lake; blotted out the calling voices of the children and the distant beat of the band, and willed his mind back to the hospital ward in which Mavis had died.

It had been an inconvenient day and time to die, the Thursday of the major operation list, and at four in the afternoon when the trolleys were coming back from the theatre. These things, he had sensed, were better managed at night when the patients were settled or asleep, when there was time for the nursing staff to turn aside from the battle and minister to those who had already lost it. The staff nurse in charge, harassed, had explained that normally they would have moved his wife into a side ward, but the four side wards were occupied. Perhaps tomorrow. There was the unspoken commitment that if she could die more conveniently then she could die with more comfort. He had sat by her bed behind the drawn curtains. Their pattern was forever fixed in his mind, small pink rosebuds on a green background, cosy, domestic, a prettification of death. They were not completely drawn, and he could glimpse and hear the business of the ward, trolleys being wheeled beside the waiting beds with impersonal efficiency, the long-gowned nurses steadying the swinging drip-bottles, voices and passing feet. From time to time a ward orderly put her head round the curtains and asked brightly: "Tea?"

He took the cup and saucer, thick white china with two lumps of sugar already dissolving in the spill of brown liquid.

Both her arms lay outside the coverlet. He held her left hand, wondering what dreams, if any, peopled the uplands of her valley of the shadow. Surely they couldn't be as tormenting as the nightmares which, in the weeks following Julie's death, had made dreadful her nights so that he would wake to her shrill screams, to the hot sweet smell of sweat and fear. The world she was inhabiting now was surely gentler, or why would she lie so still? The passing expressions of her face, which he watched with detached interest, were the transitory hints of emotions which she could no longer feel: a peevish frown, a sly unconvincing smile which reminded him disconcertingly of Julie as a baby when she had wind, a petulant frown, the illusion of thought. From time to time her eyes flickered and her lips moved. He bent his head to listen.

"Better use a knife. It's more certain. You won't forget?"

"No, I won't forget."

"You've got the letter?"

"Yes, I've got the letter."

"Show me."

He took it from his wallet. Her eyes focused on it with difficulty. She stretched her right hand trembling towards it and touched it as a believer might touch a relic. She tried to fix her eyes on it. Her jaw dropped and began to quiver as if the effort of concentrating on that oblong of creased white paper had released the final disintegration of muscle and flesh. He took her dry hand in his, and pressed it against the envelope. He said:

"I won't forget."

He remembered when she had written the letter. It had been just one year before, when the cancer had first been diagnosed. They had been sitting together, distanced, on the sofa watching a television programme about the birds of Antarctica. After he switched off she had said:

"If I don't get better you'll have to do it alone. That might not be so easy. You'll need an excuse for finding out where she is. And after she's dead, if they suspect you, you'll have to explain why you traced her. I'll write a letter, a letter of forgiveness. Then you can say that you promised me on my deathbed to deliver it into her hand."

She must have been planning that, thinking it out all the time they were watching the programme together. He could still remember the sudden jolt of disappointment and fear. Somehow he had believed that her death might release him, that he wouldn't be expected to carry the burden alone. But there was to be no escape. She had written the letter at once, sitting at the kitchen table, and had placed it in an unsealed envelope remembering that he might need to show it to someone, someone in authority, someone who might let him know where the murderess was. He hadn't read it at the time, and he hadn't read it since. He had carried it with him in his wallet. Until this moment, so short a time before her death, she had never mentioned it again.

She sank into unconsciousness. He sat on stiffly beside her, letting the dry hand rest beneath his. A lizard hand, inert, repellent, the loose skin sliding beneath his touch. He told himself that it had cooked for him, worked for him, cleaned his house, washed his clothes. He tried to picture these things, tried to stimulate pity. It meant nothing. He felt pity but it was a diffuse impersonal hopelessness at the inevitability of loss. The ward seemed loud with

63

ineffective activity, meaningless suffering. He knew that if he wept it would be for all of them there, sick and healthy alike, but most of all for himself. He had to make an effort of will not to draw his hand away. He was helped by the thought that the staff nurse might draw back the curtains and would expect to find him sitting thus linked, dispensing the final consolations of the flesh. Love had died. The woman had throttled it to death when she throttled the life out of their child. Perhaps it hadn't been very strong to die so easily and thus vicariously, but it had seemed strong. They had loved, as surely every human being did, each to the limit of his capacity. But they had failed each other at the end. Perhaps she had been the most culpable because the stronger. But somehow he should have been able to help her back to a kind of living. Now there was one way left in which he wouldn't fail her. Their joint purpose must now be his alone. Perhaps the death for the woman would be both an expiation and, for him, a release into some kind of life, a justification of the long, lost years.

She had nourished grief and revenge like a monstrous foetus, ever growing but never delivered. Even her general practitioner, wearily drawing his prescription pad towards him and writing yet another letter for a psychiatric outpatient appointment, made it plain that he thought she had grieved long enough. Grief, after all, was an indulgence, having no merit, no social value, rationed out like coins to the deserving poor, a commodity the strong and self-reliant were too proud to need. Perhaps, he thought, the Victorian habit of formal mourning had its uses. At least it defined the accepted limits of public indulgence. A year in black for a widow, he remembered his grandmother had told him, then six months in grey, then in mauve. Those expensive conventions were not, of course, for her but she had observed them with approval in the large town houses in which she had served as a parlour-maid. How long in black, he wondered, for a raped and murdered child. Not long perhaps. In his grandmother's time there would have been a replacement within a year.

How easily humanity subscribed to the universal commercial imperative: business as usual. You have your life to live, they had told Mavis, and she had gazed at them with huge uncomprehending eyes since, so obviously, she no longer had her life to live. You must think of your husband, her doctor had commanded, and indeed she had thought of him. Lying stiffly, speechlessly, side by side in the double bed of that back suburban bedroom, he had stared into the darkness and seen her thoughts, self-reproachful, like a darker cloud against the blackness of the ceiling, or a contagion spreading from her brain to his. Never once had she turned to him. She had occasionally stretched out a hand, but when he had taken it had withdrawn it as if the flesh which had impregnated her had become repulsive. Once, shy and with a sense of betrayal, he had made himself speak to their doctor. The answer, glib and professional, had done nothing to help. "She associates physical love with grief, with loss. You must be patient." Well, he had been patient, patient unto death.

She was trying to speak again. He bent down and caught her breath, sour-sweet with intimations of decay, and had to resist the temptation to put his handkerchief to his mouth to shield him from contamination. He held his breath and tried not to swallow. But in the end he had to take her death into himself. It took her several minutes to get out the words, but when they came between the gibbering lips her voice was surprisingly clear, gruff and deep as it had never been in life.

"Strong," she said. "Strong."

He didn't know what she meant by that word. Was it a final exhortation to him to stay strong in resolution? Or did she mean that the murderess was strong, too strong for him to overcome her if he came unweaponed to the kill. Standing there in the dock of the Old Bailey she hadn't struck him as particularly tall or robust; but perhaps that court, so unexpectedly small, so anonymous, panelled in plain oak, diminished all human beings, guilty and innocent alike. Even the judge, scarlet sashed under the royal coat of arms, had shrunk to a bewigged marionette. But the years in prison wouldn't have made her less strong. They looked after you in prison. You weren't over-worked or under-fed. When you were sick they gave you the best medical care. They saw that you got your exercise. When he and Mavis had talked together about the killing, they had planned to throttle the woman since that was how Julie had died. But Mavis was right. He was on his own now. He had better use a weapon.

He hadn't wanted her to die like this, in bitterness and hate. This too the murderess had taken from them with so much else. Love, the solace of responsive flesh; companionship, laughter, ambition, hope. And of course Julie. Sometimes to his surprise he almost forgot Julie. And Mavis had lost her God. Like all other believers she had made Him in her own image, a Methodist God, benign, suburban in his tastes, appreciative of cheerful singing and mildly academic sermons, not demanding more than she could give. The Sunday morning chapel had been more a comfortable routine than an imperative to worship. Mavis had been brought up a Methodist and she was not a woman to reject early orthodoxies. But she had never forgiven God for letting Julie die. Sometimes Scase thought

E
65

that she had never forgiven him. Love had died chiefly because of guilt; their joint guilt; her blame of him, his blame of himself. She would return to it again and again.

"We shouldn't have let her join the Guides. She only agreed because she knew you were keen, that it would please you."

"I didn't want her to be lonely. I remember what it was like when I was a child."

"You should have called for her every Thursday. It wouldn't have happened if you'd called for her."

"But you know she wouldn't let me. She told us that Sally Meakin always walked home with her across the recreation ground."

But Sally Meakin hadn't. No one had, and Julie had been too ashamed to ask for him to call for her. She had been like him as a child; unattractive, solitary, introspective, coping as best she could with the irrational terrors and uncertainties of childhood. He had guessed why she hadn't taken the short-cut home across the recreation ground. It must have seemed limitless in its dark emptiness, the swings tied up for the night but creaking in the wind, the great upward sweep of the slide gaunt against the sky, the dark recesses of the shelter, smelling of urine, where in the daytime the mothers sat with their prams. So she had walked alone the long way round, down unfamiliar streets, made less frightening because they were so like her own, bordered with cosy, comfortable semi-detached houses with their lighted windows, comforting symbols of security and home. And it was there in one of those dull streets that she had met her murderer. It must have been because the rapist and his house were both so ordinary that he had been able to entice her in. They had warned her punctiliously against speaking to strange men, accepting sweets, going away with them, and they had always thought that her timidity would protect her. But nothing had protected her, neither their warnings nor their love. His guilt was less now. Time didn't heal, but it anaesthetized. The human mind could only feel so much. He had read somewhere that even the tortured reached a point beyond which there was no more pain, only the thud of unregarded blows, a limbo beyond suffering that was almost pleasurable. He remembered the first cup of tea he had drunk after Julie's death. He couldn't have forced himself to swallow food, but suddenly he had been intensely thirsty, and the taste of the strong, sweet tea had been marvellously good. No tea before or since had tasted like that. She had only been dead a matter of hours and already the voracious, the treacherous body was able to experience pleasure.

Now, sitting in the sun with his few belongings on the ground between his feet, he accepted again the burden laid upon him.

He would seek out his child's murderess and kill her. He would try to do it without danger to himself since the prospect of prison terrified him, but he would still do it whatever the cost. The strength of this conviction puzzled him. The will for the deed was absolute, yet the justification eluded his questing mind. Surely it wasn't just the need for revenge. That had long ago ceased to motivate him. His grief for Julie, at first almost as lacerating as Mavis's, had long ago faded into a dull acceptance of loss. He could hardly now recall her face. Mavis had destroyed all their photographs of her after the murder. But there were pictures which he kept in his mind, recalling them almost as a duty, an *aide-mémoire* of grief. Taking his daughter into his arms for the first time, the infinitely small cocooned body, the gummed eyelids, the secretive meaningless smile. Julie toddling towards the sea at Southend, clinging tightly to his finger. Julie in her Guide uniform setting the table for dinner with anxious care, qualifying for her hostess badge. Nothing he did to Mary Ducton at whatever cost could bring her back.

Was it the need to keep faith with Mavis? But how could you keep faith with the dead, who by the very act of dying had put themselves for ever beyond the reach of treachery or betrayal? Whatever he did it couldn't touch Mavis, couldn't harm or disappoint her. She wouldn't return a querulous ghost to reproach him with his weakness. No, he wasn't doing it for Mavis. He was doing it for himself. Was it, perhaps, that after nearly fifty-seven years of living he needed to prove himself, nonentity that he was, capable of courage and action, of an act so terrible and irrevocable that, whatever happened to him afterwards, he could never again doubt his identity as a man? He supposed that it might be so, although none of it seemed relevant to him. But surely it was ridiculous, this sense that the act was inescapable, pre-ordained. And yet he knew that it was so.

The sun had gone in. A chill wind moved across the lake, shaking the willows. He felt under the bench for his holdall and made his way slowly to St James's Station and home.

On Thursday 20 July, three days after she had received her mother's reply, Philippa took a day return ticket to York and travelled up on the nine o'clock train from King's Cross. The brief information sheet which had been enclosed with her prison visiting order stated that the bus to Melcombe Grange left the York bus station at two o'clock promptly. She was in a state of restless excitement which drove her to action and movement. It would be easier to pass the waiting hours exploring York than to linger in London for a later train.

At the station bookstall at York she bought a guide book, then checked the time of the return train. Then she walked indefatigably down the narrow paved streets of the walled city, Fossgate, Shambles, Petergate, between the timber-framed houses and the elegant Georgian façades, down secret alleyways and in and out of spice-smelling shops, through the eighteenth-century Assembly Rooms, the medieval Merchant Adventurers Hall, hung with the splendid banners of the Guilds, the portraits of their benefactors, through the remains of the Roman baths and into ancient churches. She walked in a medieval dream in which the varied delights of the city, colour and light, form and sound, imposed themselves on a consciousness which was simultaneously heightened yet detached. And so at last she passed under the statue of St Peter, through the west door and into the cool immensity of the Minster. Here she sat and rested, looking up where the great east window stained the quiet air. She had bought a cheese and tomato roll for her lunch, and found herself suddenly hungry, but was reluctant to offend the susceptibilities of other visitors by eating it there. Instead she fixed her gaze where God the Father sat in majesty among His creation, glorified in the splendour of medieval stained glass. Before him was an open book. *Ego sum alpha et omega.* How simple life must be for those who could both lose and find identity in that magnificent assurance. But for herself that way was closed. Hers was a bleaker and more presumptious creed; but it was not without its comfort and she had no other. Now with myself I will begin and end.

She arrived early at the bus station and was glad that she hadn't lingered over her lunch since the bus, a double decker, rapidly filled. She wondered how many of the passengers were visitors to the prison, how often the same people travelled month after month the same route. The destination board made no mention of the prison but stated simply that the bus went to Moxton via Melcombe. Some passengers seemed to know each other and called out a greeting or edged their way down the aisle to sit together. Most of them carried baskets or humped bulging tote bags on to the rack. About half the passengers were men and they too were laden. But it wasn't a gloomy company nor, she thought, oppressed by any sense of stigma. Each might be carrying a private load of anxiety, but this afternoon, travelling through the bright air, each bore it more lightly. The sun burned through the windows, scorching the plastic seats. The bus smelled of hot leather, bodies, newly baked cakes and the strong grass-scented summer breeze. Almost merrily it bore its chattering load through sparse villages, down green shadowed lanes where the laden boughs of the horse chestnuts scraped against the roof, then with a grind of gears, upwards to a high narrow road which ran between dry stone walls. On either side stretched the close-cropped fields, white with sheep.

Only three passengers on the lower deck seemed immune to the general air of cheerful well-being, a middle-aged grey-haired man, dressed with careful formality, who had taken his seat beside Philippa just before the bus moved off and who spent the journey gazing out of the opposite window and restlessly turning a plain gold ring on his third finger, and two middle-aged women who had settled themselves behind her and who talked for most of the journey, one of them in a querulous whine.

"It's want, want, want with her, every bloody month. It's all very well, I said, but I can't do it. I'm keeping your bloody kids on social security, bread 20p a loaf and I can't do it. It's wool this month, if you please. Twenty balls! She's knitting herself one of those jerkin things. George won't visit any more. He won't put up with it, not George."

Her companion said:

"They got wool in Paggett's sale."

"That's no bloody good. It has to be that new French wool. Eighty pence an ounce, if you please. And what about the kids? If she wants to knit, Darren could do with a pullover. I've got no bloody time for knitting, I told her, stuck in the house, three kids under eight. Pity they don't let her out to look after them herself. I'm the one who's in prison, I told her. I'm the one who's been bloody well sentenced."

And through it all the grey-haired man sat staring through the window, pulling on his ring.

From time to time she slipped her hand through the flap of her shoulder bag and touched the envelope containing her mother's letter. It had arrived on Monday 17 July and had been posted two

69

days previously. It was as short and businesslike as Philippa's own and she knew it by heart.

"Thank you for your letter. Your offer is kind, but I think you ought to see me before you decide. I shall understand if you want to change your mind. I think you would be wise to change it. I have applied for a monthly visiting order for you and if you care to come I am of course always here." It was signed simply Mary Ducton.

The note of sardonic humour in the last line intrigued her. But then, perhaps it had been meant to intrigue. She wondered if it was a self-protective device, a way of lowering in advance the emotional temperature of this first meeting.

Twenty minutes later the bus slowed to turn left down a narrower road into a valley. The signpost said "Melcombe 2 miles". They drove through a village of stone houses, past the Melcombe Arms and a general store and post office, over a humped bridge spanning a shallow fast-running stream, then alongside an eight-foot stone wall. The wall was old but in an excellent state of repair, and it seemed to stretch for miles. Then suddenly it ended and the bus shook to a stop outside two immense wrought-iron gates. They stood wide open. On the wall the notice painted black and white was stark. "H.M. Prison. Melcombe Grange."

It was, she thought, a not entirely unsuitable house for use as a prison for all its stolid domestic origins. It was a sixteenth-century brick-built mansion with wide projecting wings at whose junction with the centre block two heavy castellated towers rose like watch-towers. The rows of tall mullioned windows, coruscated by the sun, were secretive, transomed with stone bars. The doorway was formidable, its heavily ornate porch symbolic of strength and security rather than of the grace of hospitality. It was easy to see that the estate had been institutionalized. The sweep to the main door had been widened to provide a marked parking space for half a dozen cars, and to the right of the house she could see a row of prefabricated huts, craft rooms perhaps or extra dormitories. On the lawn to the left of the main path three women wearing bibbed overalls were tinkering, not very energetically, with a recalcitrant lawn-mower. They turned to stare at the stream of approaching visitors without apparent enthusiasm.

The openness, the absence of custodians, the beauty of the house stretching before her in its ageless calm disconcerted and confused her. The bus had gone on its way bearing the last few remaining passengers to the next village. She had forgotten to ask the time of the return journey, and she experienced a moment of irrational panic that, without this information, there could be no return journey, that she was condemned to be stranded here in this prison which was so alarmingly un-prisonlike. The visitors, sure of themselves, knowing what awaited them for good or ill, were streaming down the wide gravel path towards the house. Their shoulders dragged with the weight of their bags. Even the grey-haired man was carrying a bundle of books bound with a strap. Only she was coming empty-handed. She walked slowly after them, heart thumping. One of them, a black girl of about her own age, her hair minutely plaited and decorated with green and yellow beads, glanced back then waited for her. She said:

"You're new, aren't you? Saw you on the bus. Who d'you want?"

"I'm visiting Mrs Ducton. Mrs Mary Ducton."

"Mary? She's in the stable block with my mate. I'm going there. I'll show you."

"Oughtn't I to report to someone?"

"You report to the warden's office over at the stables. Got your V.O. have you?"

Seeing Philippa's look of momentary incomprehension, she said: "Your V.O. Visiting Order."

"Yes, I've got that."

Her companion led the way round the side of the house to a set of converted stables, across a cobbled yard and through an open door to a small office. There was a woman prison officer there in uniform. The black girl handed over her visiting order and dumped her bag on the small table. The woman officer rummaged through the contents with brief expertise. She said in a pleasant Scottish accent:

"My word but you're smart today, Ettie. It beats me how you have the patience to thread in all those beads."

Ettie grinned and shook her neatly decorative head. The beads danced and jangled, red, yellow and blue. The prison officer turned to Philippa. Philippa held out her pass.

"Oh yes, you're Miss Palfrey. This is your first time, isn't it? The Governor thought you'd like some extra privacy so I've put a notice on the sitting-room door. You'll be all right there for an hour at least. You show Miss Palfrey the sitting-room, will you Ettie, there's a good lass, I can't leave the desk just for a moment."

The room was a little way down the corridor on the right. A cardboard notice with the word "engaged" was hung on the door. Ettie didn't open it, but gave the door a gentle kick and said:

"Here you are. See you on the bus maybe." Then she was gone.

Philippa opened the door slowly. The room was empty. She shut the door and leaned against it for a moment, glad of the comforting strength of wood against her back. Like Miss Henderson's office, this room had a spurious comfort. It was a place of transit but without the ostentatious vulgarity of an airport departure lounge;

71

unpretentious, stuffy, over-crowded with furniture which looked as if it had been rejected from a dozen different homes. Nothing it contained was memorable. It was designed to be used and then mercifully forgotten. No transient would look back on this room with regret or be tempted to leave a humming chord of her misery or hope on the bleak air. There were too many chairs, assorted in size or shape, disposed around half a dozen small highly polished tables. The walls were plain and smudged in places, as if someone had cleansed them of graffiti. Over the fireplace was a print of Constable's *Hay Wain* and below it on the mantelshelf a glass vase of artificial flowers. In the middle of the room was set a small octagonal table with two facing chairs. In contrast to the informality of the room they looked as if they had been specially arranged. Perhaps a helpful inmate, instructed to see that the room was tidy, had placed them there, seeing every visit as a formal confrontation across an invisible but impregnable grille.

The waiting minutes seemed to stretch for hours. Occasionally footsteps passed the door. It was as cheerfully noisy as school at mid-morning break. Philippa's mind was a turmoil of emotions: excitement, apprehension, resentment, and finally anger. What was she doing abandoned here in this dreary room where the furniture was too clean, the walls too grubby, the flowers artificial? They had a large enough garden, surely they could at least provide fresh flowers. A cell would have been less disquieting to wait in. At least it didn't pretend to be anything but what it was. And why wasn't her mother here, waiting for her? She knew that she was coming, she must have known the time of the bus. What was she finding to do that was more important than being here? Her mind spun with grotesque images. Hair that had once been golden but was now dry as straw, dancing with threaded beads, her mother's face sagging under the weight of make-up, a cigarette hanging from a slack mouth, hands with painted talons stretched out to her throat. She thought: "Suppose I don't like her. Suppose she can't stand me. We've got to spend two months together. I can't get out of it now. I can't go back to Calde-cote Terrace and tell Maurice I made a mistake." She walked over to the window and looked out across the cobbled courtyard at the second set of stables. She would make herself think about the architecture. Maurice had taught her how to look at buildings. This stable block was later than the house; it might even be neo-Georgian. But the clock turret with its swinging golden cock looked older. Perhaps they had re-erected it when the original stables were demolished. They had made a good job of the conversion. But where was her mother? Why didn't she come?

The door opened. She turned round. Her first impression, but so

72

fleeting that the thought and its rejection were almost simultaneous, was that her mother had sent a friend to break the news that she had changed her mind, that she didn't want to meet her after all. It was stupid to have expected so much older a woman. And, at first, she looked so ordinary; a slight, attractive figure in a grey pleated skirt with a paler cotton shirt blouse and a green scarf knotted at the neck. All her grotesque imaginings fled like shrieking demons before a relic. It was like recognizing oneself. It was the beginning of identity. Surely if she had met this woman anywhere in the world she would have known herself to be flesh of her flesh. Instinctively they each slowly took a chair and regarded each other across the table. Her mother said:

"I'm sorry I've kept you waiting. The bus was early. I didn't want to watch out for it in case you didn't come."

Philippa knew now from which parent she had inherited her corn-gold hair. But her mother's hair, shaped to her head like a cap and cut in a fringe above her eyes, looked finer and lighter, perhaps because it was streaked with silver. The mouth, wider than her own, had the same curved upper lip, but it was more resolute, the delicate droop at each corner less sensual. But here was the pattern of her high cheekbones, her slightly arched nose. Only the eyes were different, a luminous grey faintly streaked with green. They held a look of half-startled wariness, of endurance, like those of a patient facing once more the inescapable and painful probing. Her skin might once have been honey-coloured, but now looked clear, almost bloodless. The impression was of a face still attractive, still young, but from which colour had been drained by a perpetual weariness, of watchful eyes which had seen too much for too long.

They didn't touch each other. Neither stretched a hand across the table. Philippa said:

"What shall I call you?"

"Mother. Isn't that why you're here?"

Philippa didn't reply. She wanted to say that she was sorry to have come empty-handed, but was frightened that her mother might reply, "but you've brought yourself." It would be intolerable if their first meeting began with such banality. Her mother said:

"You do understand what I did, why you were adopted?"

"I don't understand, but I do know about it. My father raped a child and you killed her."

It seemed to Philippa that the air between them had solidified, had become the oscillating medium through which their words flickered and spun. Now it trembled, and her mother's face was for a moment blank as if some tenuous link of perception had been broken. She said:

"Did feloniously and with malice aforethought kill one Julia Mavis Scase. It's true, except that they don't use those words any more and it wasn't with malice aforethought. It wasn't meant. But she's just as dead as if it had been. And all murderers tell you that anyway. You don't have to believe it. I don't know why I said it. You must excuse me if I seem socially inept. You are my first visitor for nine years."

"If you tell me, why shouldn't I believe you?"

"But it's irrelevant. You aren't a romantic, are you? You don't look as if you are. You haven't come here with the idea of proving me innocent? You haven't been reading too many crime novels?"

"I don't read crime novels except Dostoevsky and Dickens."

The noise from outside was louder now, the voices had become strident, feet were pounding down the corridor. Philippa said:

"They're a noisy lot, aren't they? It's rather like a boarding school."

"Yes, a boarding school with strict discipline where they take difficult girls off their parents' hands. This part is the old stable block converted into a pre-release hostel. Lifers have to live here for nine months before they let us out. We go out to work. There are a few liberal-minded employers in York with an interest in rehabilitating prisoners. After the prison authorities have deducted a contribution towards our keep and paid out pocket money they bank the surplus. I shall have two hundred and thirty pounds forty-eight pence when I leave. I thought—if you still want me—that the money could go towards the rent of the flat."

"I can pay the rent of the flat. You'll need your two hundred pounds. What do you do? I mean, what kind of job?"

She hoped she didn't sound like a prospective employer. Her mother said:

"I'm a chamber-maid at a hotel. There wasn't much choice of work. Murderers are easier to place than thieves or confidence tricksters, but with unemployment as high as it is the prison has to take what's on offer. But it does mean that I've had my insurance card stamped."

"Hotel work must be boring."

"Tiring, but not boring. I'm not afraid of hard work."

The statement seemed to Philippa out of character, pathetic, almost demeaning. It embarrassed her by its naivety. It was too close to an appeal, the Victorian kitchen-maid desperate to be taken on. Suddenly she thought of Hilda, bending over the kitchen table. The memory of Hilda at that moment was intrusive and disconcerting. She said:

"Do we have to stay in here? It's lovely in the sun. Can't we go outside?"

"If you'd rather. The warden suggested that we might like to walk round the lawn. Visitors normally have to stay in the house, but she's made an exception for you, for us."

A gravel path, bordered with lime trees, circled the immense lawn. It was here that they walked. The gravel glinted in the sun and grated like hot cinders under Philippa's feet. In the distance the bleached skeletons of denuded elms, stricken by Dutch elm disease, stood like pale distorted gibbets against the varying green of oak, beech, horse chestnut and silver birch. Occasionally their black shadows were broken by a path of green sward and she could see tantalizing vistas leading to a circular rose garden, a bulbous stone cherub. The skeleton of a dried beech leaf trembled momentarily on the path before being ground to dust under her feet. Even at the height of summer there were always some dead leaves. Someone somewhere was burning them: there was a sweet, pungent smell redolent of autumn. Surely it was early to be burning leaves. No one burnt leaves in the London parks. This was a country smell, raking memory back to forgotten autumns at Pennington, except that she had never lived at Pennington. The hard boughs of horse chestnut and oak, weighted with summer, the dead leaf, the smoky bonfire tang, the transitory spring sweetness of the lime flowers, all produced in her a momentary confusion, a sense of all seasons coming together in a moment out of time. Perhaps these two months, before she went up to Cambridge, would be similarly lived in a new dimension, not counted against her allotted years. Perhaps she would look back at this visit, uncertain whether it had been spring or autumn, remembering only the discordant scent and sounds, the single dead leaf.

They walked in silence. Philippa tried to analyse her emotions. What was she feeling? Embarrassment? Not that. Comradeship? That was too sturdily complacent a word for the tenuous link between them. Fulfilment? Peace? No, not peace. Here was a balance between excitement and apprehension, a euphoria which had nothing to do with the mind's quietude. Contentment, perhaps. Now at least I know who I am. I know the worst, I shall know the best. Above all, a sense that it was right to be here, that this deliberate pacing, carefully distanced so that the first touch should not be casual, was a ritual of immense significance, an end and a beginning.

She thought for the first time since she had heard it: "I like her voice." It was low, unpractised, tentative, as if English were a language her mother had learned. Words were symbols formed in the mind and seldom spoken. It was strange, thought Philippa, that she would have found it more difficult to live with a whining or grating voice than with the knowledge that this woman had killed a child. Her mother asked:

"What are you going to do? I mean, what job?" She paused. "I'm sorry. That's the kind of question a ten-year-old gets asked and hates answering."

"I've known since I was ten. I'm going to be a writer."

"Are you gathering material? Is that why you're offering to help me? I don't mind. At least I shall have given you something. There's nothing else I've given you."

It was matter of fact, with no hint of self-pity or of remorse.

"Except my life. Except my life. Except my life."

"*Hamlet*. It seems strange now, but I hardly knew Shakespeare before I went to prison. I promised myself that I'd read every play and in chronological order. There are twenty-one. I rationed myself to one every six months. That way I could be sure that they would last out the sentence. You can annihilate thought with words."

The paradox of poetry.

"Yes," she said. "I know."

The gravel path grated Philippa's feet. She said:

"Can't we walk into the garden?"

"We have to keep to this path. Rules. They haven't the staff to hunt people down all over the grounds."

"But the gate wasn't locked. You could all walk out."

"Only into another kind of prison."

Two women, obviously staff, were hurrying across the grass, running gawkily, lurching together. They weren't in uniform, but it was impossible to mistake them for inmates. One had thrown an arm round her companion's shoulder. Their laughter was happy, conspiratorial. Remembering that they mustn't be called warders, Philippa asked:

"The prison officers, how have they treated you?"

"Some like animals, some like recalcitrant children, some like mental patients. I like best those who treat us as prisoners."

"And those two, running across the grass, who are they?"

"Two friends. They always ask to get posted together. They live together."

"You mean they're lovers, lesbians? Is there a lot of that in prison?" She remembered Maurice's snide innuendo.

Her mother smiled.

"You make it sound like an infectious disease. Of course it happens. It happens often. People need to be loved. They need to feel that they matter to someone. If you're wondering about me, the answer is no. I wouldn't have had the chance, anyway. In prison or

76

out, people need someone they can despise more than they do themselves. A child-killer is at the bottom of the heap, even here. Learn to be alone. Don't draw attention to yourself. That way my sort survive. Your father didn't."

"What was he like, father?"

"He was a schoolmaster. He hadn't a university degree. His father, your grandfather, was a clerk with an insurance company. I don't suppose any member of the family has ever been to a university. Your father went to a teacher training college. That was regarded as a great achievement. He taught the senior boys at an inner London comprehensive school until he couldn't stand it any more. Then he took a job as a clerk with the Gas Board."

"But what was he like? What were his interests?"

Her mother's voice was a harsh grate:

"His interest was little girls."

Perhaps the bleak reply was meant to shock, to jolt her into a fresh awareness of why they were here, pacing the gravel together. Philippa waited until she could be sure that her voice was calm. She said:

"That isn't an interest. That's an obsession."

"I'm sorry, I shouldn't have said that. I'm not even sure that it's true. It's just that I don't seem able to give you what you want."

"I don't want anything. I'm not here because of wanting."

But it seemed to Philippa that her question had been only the first of a catalogue of wants. I want to know who I am, I want to be approved of, I want to be successful, I want to be loved. The question, "Then why *are* you here?" hung between them, unasked, unanswerable.

They walked on together in silence. Her mother seemed to be thinking, then she said:

"He liked second-hand books, exploring old churches, roaming city streets, taking a train to Southend for the day and walking to the end of the pier. He liked reading history and biography, never fiction. He lived in his own imagination, not other men's. He disliked his job but hadn't the courage to change it again. He hadn't the courage to change anything. He was one of the meek who are supposed to inherit the earth. He liked you."

"How did he manage to entice her into the house?"

She disciplined her voice, politely interested, as if the enquiry were about some social trivia. Did he take sugar in his tea? Did he enjoy sports? How did he rape a child?

"He had his right hand bandaged. It was quite genuine. He'd grazed it when he fell over a garden rake and it had become septic. He had just come home from work when he saw her, walking home

77

after her Girl Guide meeting. He told her that he wanted a cup of tea but couldn't manage to fill the kettle."

Ah, but that had been clever. He had seen a child coming down that suburban street, walking in the dangerous innocence of childhood. A Girl Guide in uniform. Her good deed for the day. He had used the one ploy that might succeed even with a suspicious or timid child. She hadn't sensed danger where there was a need she could meet, something within her power. She could picture the child carefully filling the kettle at the cold tap, lighting the gas for him, offering to stay and make the tea, setting out his cup and saucer with anxious care. He had made use of what was good and kind in her to destroy her. If evil existed, if those four letters placed in that order had any reality, then surely here was evil.

She was aware of her mother's voice.

"He didn't mean to harm her."

"Didn't he? Then what did he mean?"

"To talk, perhaps. To kiss her. To fondle her. I don't know. Whatever he had in mind, it wasn't rape. He was gentle, timid, weak. I suppose that's why he was attracted to children. I thought I could help him because I was strong. But he didn't want strength. He couldn't cope with it. What he wanted was childishness, vulnerability. He didn't hurt her, you know, not physically. It was a technical rape, but he wasn't violent. I suppose if I hadn't killed her she and her parents would have claimed later that he'd ruined her life, that she could never make a happy marriage. Perhaps they would have been right. The psychologists say that children never get over an early sexual assault. I didn't leave her any life to be spoiled. I'm not excusing him. Only you mustn't picture it as worse than it was."

How could it have been worse than it was, Philippa wondered. A child had been raped and murdered. The physical details she could imagine, had imagined. But the horror, the loneliness, the last terrifying moment; it was no more possible to enter into these by an effort of will than it was physically to feel another's pain. Pain and fear. To experience either was to be aware for ever of the loneliness of the self.

Maurice, after all, had warned her, in one of their short bouts of disconnected talk during those four days when she had been waiting for her mother's reply:

"None of us can bear too much reality. No one. We all create for ourselves a world in which it's tolerable for us to live. You've probably created yours with more imagination than most. Having gone to that trouble, why demolish it?"

And she in her arrogant confidence had replied:

"Perhaps I shall find out that it would have been better for me if

I'd been content with it. But it's too late now. That world has gone for good. I have to find another. At least this one will be founded on reality."

"Will it? How do you know that it won't turn out to be just as illusory and far less comfortable."

"But it must be better to know the facts. You're a scientist—a pseudo-scientist anyway. I thought you held truth to be sacred."

And he had replied:

" 'What is truth', said jesting Pilate, and would not stay for an answer. Facts are sacred, if you can discover them, and as long as you don't confuse them with values."

They had circled the lawn once and were back at the Grange. Rejecting it, they turned slowly and began retracing their steps. She said:

"Have I any relations on my father's side of the family?"

"Your father was an only child. He had a cousin, but she and her husband emigrated to Canada about the time of the trial. They didn't want anyone to know about the connection. I suppose they're still alive. They hadn't any children and they were both middle-aged then. About forty, I think."

"And your side?"

"I did have a brother, Stephen, eight years younger than I, but he was killed in Ireland the first year of the troubles, before he was twenty. He was in the army."

"So my only uncle is dead, and there's no one else?"

"No," she said gravely, unsmiling. "Only me. I'm your only blood relation."

They continued their slow pacing. The sun was hot on Philippa's shoulders. Her mother said:

"They provide tea for visitors, if you'd like a cup."

"I would, but not here. I'll get it in York. How much longer have we?"

"Before the bus? Another thirty minutes."

"What do I have to do? I mean, can you just come to me when you leave, or are there formalities?"

She was careful to keep her eyes on the path, unwilling to face what she might see in her mother's eyes. It was the moment of final offer and acceptance. When her mother spoke her voice was controlled.

"The present plan is for me to go to a probation hostel for women in Kensington. I hated the thought of another hostel, but there wasn't any choice, at least for the first month. But I don't think there'll be any difficulty about coming to you instead. They'll send someone to check that you've actually got a flat and the

79

arrangements have to be approved by the Home Office. The first stage is for you to write formally to the Chief Welfare Officer here. But hadn't you better take a week or two to think about it?"

"I have thought about it."

"What would you normally be doing in these next two months?"

"Probably the same, taking a flat in London. I've left school. I got my Cambridge scholarship last year when I was seventeen. This year I've been taking philosophy and adding to my A-levels just to fill in time. I'm hardly the VSO type—Voluntary Service Overseas. I'm not altering my plans for you, if that's what's worrying you."

Her mother accepted the lie. She said:

"I shall be an embarrassing flat mate. How will you explain me to your friends?"

"We shan't be seeing my friends. If we do run into them, I shall explain that you're my mother. What else do they need to know?"

Her mother said formally:

"Then, thank you Philippa. Just for the first two months I'd be very glad to join you."

After that they spoke no more of the future, but walked together, each with her thoughts, until it was time for Philippa to join the desultory stream of visitors making their way up the wide sun-scorched path towards the gates and the waiting bus.

11

Neither Maurice nor Hilda asked any questions when she got home shortly after half-past eight. Not to ask questions was part of Maurice's policy of non-interference; usually he managed to convey the impression of not being particularly interested in knowing. Hilda, who looked flushed and rather sulky, kept a resolute and sullen silence, enquiring only if Philippa had had a good journey. She glanced fearfully at Maurice as she asked this seemingly innocuous question, and appeared not to hear Philippa's answer. The tone was forced; she might have been speaking to a newly arrived and not particularly welcome guest. During a late dinner they sat like strangers; but strangers, after all, were what they were. It was a night when company would have been a relief, but they drank their vichyssoise and ate their chicken marengo almost in silence. As she finally pushed her chair from the table, Philippa said:

"My mother seems quite glad to share a flat for the next month or so. I'll start looking tomorrow."

The words came out unnaturally loudly, belligerent as a challenge. She was angry with herself that they should sound so forced, that despite her silent rehearsal throughout dinner speaking them aloud had been so difficult. She had never been frightened of Maurice. Why should she start being frightened of him now? She was eighteen, officially an adult, responsible to no one but herself. She was probably as free now as she was ever likely to be. She had no need to justify her actions. Maurice said:

"You won't find it easy to rent a flat at a price you can afford, not in central London anyway. If you need to borrow money, let me know. Don't go to the bank. There's no point in paying interest at the present rate."

"I can manage on my own. I've got the money I saved for my European trip."

"In that case, good luck. You'd better keep your key in case you need to come back. And if you are intending to move out permanently, it would be helpful if we could have as much notice as possible. I could probably find a use for your room."

He made it sound, thought Philippa, as if he were dismissing an recalcitrant paying guest. But that was how he had intended it to sound.

12

On Monday 17 July, shortly after nine o'clock in the morning, Scase rang a number in the city which he had rung every three months for the last six years. But this time the information he requested wasn't given to him. Nor, as usually happened, was it promised for a few days' time. Instead Eli Watkin asked him to call in at the office as soon as was convenient to him. Within half an hour he was on his way to Hallelujah Passage off Ludgate Hill to see a man whom he had last seen six years ago. Then Mavis had been with him; this time he made his way past St Paul's churchyard and into the dark, narrow little alley on his own.

They had waited for three years after the end of the trial before getting in touch with Eli Watkin Investigations Limited. They found the firm's name in the Yellow Pages of the London telephone directory among a list of some dozen private detective agencies, sandwiched between Designers and Diamond Merchants. They spent a day in London visiting each office in turn, trying to assess from the address and outward appearance whether it was efficient and reputable. Mavis had wanted to exclude any agency which accepted divorce cases, but Scase had persuaded her that this was an unnecessary limitation of choice. The task wasn't easy. Mutually supportive and determined as they were, they nevertheless felt themselves on alien and frightening territory. They were intimidated by the smart, impersonal-looking offices of the largest concerns, and repelled by the seediness of some of the smallest. In the end they ventured into Eli Watkin Investigations because they liked the name of Hallelujah Passage, the office exuded a Dickensian atmosphere of cheerful amateurism, and Mavis was reassured and cheered by the window box outside the ground-floor window in which the spears of early daffodils were already beginning to show. They were greeted by an elderly typist, then shown upstairs to Mr Eli Watkin himself.

On their entry into his small, claustrophobic office, they had found him squatting before a hissing gas fire, spooning cat food into three saucers while five squalling cats of varied sizes and hues butted against his thin ankles. A matriarchal tabby sat, paws folded, on top of a bookcase, regarding the mêlée with slit-eyed disdain. When the last of the food had been distributed, she jumped lightly down with a switch of her tail and arranged herself at the third bowl. Only then did Eli Watkin stand up to greet them. They had seen a squat, crumple-faced man with a comb of white hair and heavy-lidded eyes. He had a disconcerting habit of appearing to keep them half closed when speaking, then of suddenly raising them, as if by a conscious effort, to display small but intensely blue eyes. He welcomed them with none of the smarmy condescension which Scase had feared. Nor did he seem at all surprised by their commission. Scase had practised what he intended to say.

"Three years ago a woman, Mary Ducton, was sentenced for life for the murder of our daughter, Julia Mavis Scase. We want to be kept in touch with her. We want to know when she's moved and where, what she's doing, and when she's due to be released. Is that the kind of information you deal in?"

"Well now, it could be. There's no information in the world that you can't get hold of if you're prepared to pay."

"Would it be expensive?"

"Not that expensive. Where is the lady now? In Holloway? I

thought so. Ring me at this number in ten days' time and we'll see what we can do."

"How do you obtain your information?"

"The way one always gets information, Mr Scase. By paying for it."

"This is confidential, of course. There's nothing illegal about it, but we don't want other people to know our business."

"Of course. That is why you pay a little more."

After that they had telephoned Eli Watkin four times a year. On each occasion he would ring back three days later and tell them what he knew. Within a week a bill would come, "to professional services rendered". The amount varied. Sometimes it was as high as twenty pounds, sometimes as low as five. In this way they learned when Mary Ducton came out of her self-imposed isolation and began working in the prison library, when she was moved from Holloway to Durham and from Durham to Melcombe Grange, when she was admitted to the prison hospital for treatment after an assault by three of the other prisoners, when her case was first considered by the Parole Board. Six months ago he had learned from Eli Watkin that she had been given a conditional release date for August 1978.

It was nearly eleven o'clock when he reached Hallelujah Passage. There was still a window box outside Eli Watkin's office, but now it held nothing but caked earth. The door into the passage was open and the ground-floor office, which was empty, was filled with packing cases. The dingy walls had been stripped; there were oblong shapes where once pictures must have hung. The windows were so filthy that the daylight was almost entirely excluded and he had to feel his way across the tattered linoleum to the uncarpeted stairway.

In the upstairs office Eli Watkin awaited him as he had six years ago. The same gas fire hissed away and he recognized the large roll-topped desk and the two battered filing cabinets. There were no cats now, but it seemed to Scase that there hung on the air the sharp, sour reek of their food. But then he wondered whether what he was smelling was mortal sickness. He could recognize Eli Watkin because the bright blue eyes were the same; nothing else was. The hand held out to grasp his was a cluster of loose bones held together by dry flesh. The face was a yellow death's-head from which the eyes blazed with the brilliance of jewels.

Scase said:

"I've called about Mary Ducton. I rang to ask if you'd yet got the actual day of release. You asked me to call."

"So I did, so I did, Mr Scase. There are some things which are best said face to face. Come in now, will you?"

He went over to the first of the filing cabinets and took from the

83

top drawer a buff folder. The drawer seemed otherwise to be empty. The folder was faded but clean, almost untouched. But then, thought Scase, it had only been handled four times a year. Eli Watkin carried it back to the desk and opened it. Scase saw that it contained copies of his bills and small scraps of paper—notes, perhaps, of telephone conversations. There was nothing else. Watkin said:

"The subject is due to be released from Melcombe Grange prison on Tuesday the fifteenth of August 1978."

"To what address?"

"Now that I can't be telling you, Mr Scase. It was to have been to a probation hostel in North Kensington, but there's talk at the prison that the arrangement may be changed."

"When would you be able to let me know? Could I telephone you next week?"

"I shan't be here next week, Mr Scase. By next month the builders will be in converting this place to a coffee and sandwich bar. A little tucked away, I should have thought, to suit the customers, but that's not my worry. I've been paid well enough for the lease. And if you should telephone in six months' time they'll tell you, if there's any-one still here and if they care, that I'm dead. By August the fifteenth I shall be in Mexico. I've waited all my life, Mr Scase, to see the floating gardens of Xochimilco, and I'm off in three days' time. This is the last information I'll be giving you. And you, Mr Scase, are my last client."

Scase said:

"I'm sorry."

There was nothing else that he could think to say. After a moment he asked:

"And you've no idea what town she'll be travelling to?"

"I imagine she'll come to London. They usually do. She lived in Seven Kings in Essex at the time of the murder, didn't she? Likely as not she'll come to London."

"Do you know what time they'll release her?"

"It's usually in the morning. I should plan for the morning if I were you. The morning of Tuesday the fifteenth of August."

Had there been a subtle emphasis on the word "plan"? Scase said:

"It would be helpful to know. I have to see her personally, to hand her a letter from my wife. I promised Mavis to put it into her hand."

"I've promised myself all my life that I'd see the floating gardens. Do you believe in reincarnation, Mr Scase?"

"I haven't thought about it. I suppose it could be a comfort to people who need to believe in their own importance."

"But you can believe in your own importance without myths?"

The swollen lids were suddenly raised and the blue eyes stared at him, unfaded, ironic. He said:

"Killing someone isn't easy, Mr Scase. Even the State has had to give it up. And the State had all the conveniences, you might say; a scaffold, a skilled and experienced operator, the condemned person safely to hand. Are you a skilled operator, Mr Scase?"

He wondered why the words, the implied threat, didn't worry him. And then a glance at that skull, marked out like an anatomist's model with its tributaries of blue veins, at the paper-thin membrane stretched over the jutting bones, told him why. Even the mark of death was enough to make a man virtually harmless. He was already moving away from the petty concerns of the living towards his floating gardens. And what difference did suspicion make? When the murderess was dead he must expect to be the chief, perhaps the only suspect. What mattered was that he should give the police no real evidence, no legal proof. Part of him half believed that they might not look for that proof too assiduously. He said calmly:

"If that's what you believe, aren't you going to warn the police?"

"But that would be unethical, Mr Scase. In my profession I don't often speak to the police, although sometimes they like to speak to me. And you and I have had a long and, I think, fruitful professional relationship. You've paid me well over the years for certain information. What you do with it isn't my responsibility. And I have to catch that plane in three days' time."

Scase said calmly:

"You are mistaken. I have to see the woman, have to hand over a letter, that's all. My wife wanted her to know that we have forgiven her. One can't go on hating for nearly ten years."

"Very true. Do you read Thomas Mann, Mr Scase? A fine writer. 'For the sake of humanity, for the sake of love, let no man's thoughts be ruled by death.' I think I have quoted it correctly, but you get the meaning I'm sure. That will be fifty pounds."

"It's more than I expected. I've only brought forty pounds in cash with me. I've never paid more than thirty before."

"But this is the final payment, and I think you can say that the information is worth it. But we'll say forty. We don't want any cheques, do we?"

He paid over the eight five-pound notes. Eli Watkin folded them into his wallet. He said:

"I don't think we need trouble this time with a receipt. And now we can add your file to the rest of this rubbish. There are quite a number of secrets and a lot of misery torn up in this sack. Perhaps you'll deal with it. The file cover is rather too stiff for my hands."

Scase tore up each scrap of paper, then ripped the file cover into

85

small pieces and shook them into the sack in which the debris of Mr Watkin's small business slid in a restless tide of paper. Last of all they shook hands. Watkin's hand was dry and very cold, but his handshake was surprisingly firm; strong enough, surely, to have torn up the file had he chosen. Scase's last sight of him was of him still sitting at his desk, and looking after him with an amused, benignant pity. But his last words were cheerful enough:

"Don't fall over the dustbins, Mr Scase. Wouldn't it be an inconvenient thing now if you were disabled just at this interesting period of your life?"

That afternoon he telephoned the best known of the local estate agents and instructed them to put his house on the market. The firm said that they would try to send round their Mr Wheatley early next morning. By ten o'clock Mr Wheatley had arrived. He was younger than Scase had expected—not more than twenty, surely—with a sharp, unhealthy-looking face, and was dressed with a desperate respectability, presumably to inspire confidence in the efficiency and probity of the firm. The padded shoulders of his cheap, dark blue suit hung loosely on him as if he had chosen it to allow for growth. But he entered with brisk assurance and was hardly through the door before he began surveying the house with a keen appraising eye. He carried a clip-board and measured each room expertly with a spring measuring tape which he used with a flourish. Walking behind him from room to room, Scase saw that he had a small pustule on his neck. It had broken, staining the top of his shirt collar with blood and pus. He found it difficult to take his eyes off it.

"Well, it's a nice little property, sir. Nicely maintained. We shouldn't have much trouble in getting rid of it for you. Mind you, the market isn't quite what it was six months ago. What price were you thinking of?"

"What price do you suggest?"

He wouldn't, Scase knew, put it higher than he needed to. The commission went up with the price, but what really paid was a quick sale and no trouble. And he wouldn't be valuing it himself for all his pursed lips and air of calculation. His firm would have told him exactly what a reasonably well-maintained semi in Alma Road would fetch.

After a couple of minutes spent slowly pacing from hall to sitting-room, from sitting-room to kitchen, he said:

"You might get nineteen and a half if you're lucky. The garden's a bit neglected and these houses haven't got garages. That always brings the price down. People like a garage. We could start at twenty and be prepared to drop."

"I want a quick sale. I don't mind starting at nineteen and a half."

"It's up to you, sir. Now, what about viewing? Will you be in this afternoon?"

"No. I'll give you a spare set of keys. I'd like you to show people round. I don't want to see them."

"That may hold things up a bit, sir. It's a question of staff, you see. We'd have to try and fit a number of viewers in together. Now, if you could arrange to be home early evenings for, say, a couple of weeks. . ."

Scase thought, let them earn their commission.

"I don't want to see anyone. You can hand over the keys if they sign for them and undertake to lock up carefully. There's nothing here for them to steal."

"Oh, we wouldn't want to do that, sir. Look, if I could tell prospective purchasers that you might take eighteen and a half, or even eighteen at a pinch, I don't think you'll have to wait long."

"All right. Ask eighteen and a half."

"There's a young couple on the books who might be interested at eighteen thousand. They've got two kids and you're handy for the school. I'll see if I can get them over this evening."

"I want a quick sale. Won't they need a mortgage? That takes time."

"There'll be no difficulty there, sir. They've been saving with a building society. I think you'll find that it will all go very easily if they like the house."

Taking one last disparaging look at the meanly proportioned front sitting-room, he added:

"Whoever takes it will probably knock that middle wall down and make one large room. Open it up, like. And the kitchen will need remodelling."

Scase didn't care what they did to it as long as it was quickly sold. He needed the money to finance his enterprise. He and Mavis had always agreed that selling the house might be necessary. He didn't think Mavis had thought beyond the actual deed; at present he wasn't thinking beyond it himself. But the prospect of virtual homelessness, of moving from this snug suburban respectability into and unknown, intimidating world, filled him with a mixture of excitement and apprehension. It would be so easy to hang on, to see the house as a familiar refuge to which he could retreat if the hunt got hard or disappointing. As he followed behind Mr Wheatley, watching the silver measure leap out to record the meagre dimensions of kitchen and hall, the house seemed to him like the lair of some small predator, earth-bound, secret, holding within its brown walls the beast's very smell. In the kitchen he imagined that he could see its spoor on the linoleum, could see under the table a litter of fur and bones.

87

13

Philippa knew that in her search for a furnished, two-roomed flat in central London at a reasonable rent, she was privileged; appearance, age, voice and colour—although no one was so unwise as to hint at race—all were in her favour. She read the truth of her advantage in the appraising eyes and deference of the receptionists and interviewers in the dozen or so flat agencies at which she called. It was an added attraction to them that the lease required was so short—"only the three months before I go up to Cambridge"—and that she didn't want a joint let. The words, "just for the two of us, my mother and me, we want to spend some months together in London before I go up to college and she goes abroad", spoken in her confident, educated voice were, as she well knew, a reassuring guarantee of filial duty and respectability. Any of the agents would gladly have let to her if they had had anything suitable to offer. But short-term furnished leases in inner London were exorbitantly priced for the foreign market, and her tentative suggestion of forty to fifty pounds a week was met with incredulous smiles, shakes of the head, and murmurs of the evil effect of the rent restriction acts. She was made to feel guilty of some deception; she had no right to walk in looking so prosperous and admit to such poverty. Losing interest, the agencies took her name and address and promised nothing.

She followed the same daily routine during the first week of her search. She left 68 Caldecote Terrace after breakfast and spent the morning trudging round the agencies. As soon as the lunchtime editions of the evening paper were available, she bought them and marked the possibilities. The next half-hour was spent in a telephone kiosk where, provided with a supply of coins, she began the frustrating task of trying to contact the advertisers on numbers most of which were either continually engaged or unobtainable. Then came the viewing; flats whose grimy windows overlooked deep wells which no sunlight could ever penetrate; shared lavatories and bathrooms remote from the flat itself and in a state to encourage permanent constipation; furnished flats where the furniture consisted of the landlord's broken rejects, wardrobes whose doors swung perpetually open, cookers with chipped enamel and food-encrusted ovens, tables with scorched tops and uneven legs, and filthy lumpy beds; landlords whose advertisement for a female tenant had less to do with the probable greater cleanliness of the kitchen than with other more elemental needs.

She was soon forced to widen the area of her search. She came to know a different London and she saw it through different eyes. The city was all things to all men. It reflected and deepened mood; it did not create it. Here the miserable were more miserable, the lonely more bereft, while the prosperous and happy saw reflected in her river and glittering life the confirmation of their deserved success. In her week of seeking, unsuccessfully, for a flat in which she could bear, even temporarily, to live, Philippa felt increasingly depressed and rejected. Once, from the security of Caldecote Terrace, she would have seen the meaner streets of north Paddington, Kilburn and Earls Court as fascinating outposts of an alien culture, part of the variety and colour of any capital city.

Now with disenchanted and prejudiced eyes she saw only filth and deformity; the bursting bags of uncollected rubbish, the litter which choked the gutters and blew down the passages of the Underground, the walls defaced by the scribbled hate of extremists of the left and right, the crude obscenities with which the platform posters were embellished, the stink of urine over-laid with disinfectant which rose from the stained concrete of the underground walkways, the ugliness of people. Man, fouling his own habitat, couldn't even behave like a good animal. The alien shrouded bodies crouching on the kerb-side, watching from the open doors, threatened her with their strangeness; the prevailing smells of curry, of herded bodies, of scented women's hair, empha-sized the sense of exclusion, of being unwanted in her own city.

And then on the morning of Friday 28 July, walking down Edgware Road after finding that yet another advertised flat had been taken, she saw down a side road an agency which she hadn't before discovered. The most remarkable thing about the Raterite Accommodation Bureau was that it existed at all, or that, existing, it did any business. If larger, cleaner and more imposing agencies were short of properties to rent or manage, it was strange that this seedy unprepossessing establishment attracted prospective land-lords. The window was patterned with hand-written cards sellotaped to the smeared glass. Most were brown with age; on some the ink had faded to the colour of thin dried blood. The variety of hand-writing and eccentricity of spelling suggested a frequent change of staff and no great discrimination in their choosing. The few clean white cards were intrusive patches of hope which was quickly vitiated by the word "taken" scrawled across those few which, judging from the reasonable rent demanded, had probably never genuinely been on offer.

Philippa pushed open the door and stepped into a small office containing two desks and a row of four chairs against the wall. On one of these an Indian was sitting in patient resignation. Behind the larger of the two desks a flamboyantly dressed woman with red hair and a multitude of clinking bangles sat smoking a cigarette and doing the crossword in the morning paper. She had the look of a woman who has found life recalcitrant since childhood but has finally succeeded, at some cost to herself, in pounding it into shape. At the second desk a younger, blonde woman was listening with careful uninterest to the volubility of a red-faced, bandy-legged man whose suit of checked tweed and natty, feather-trimmed trilby were more appropriate to the Brighton racecourse than to this seedy office.

The blonde shifted her eyes to Philippa, apparently to indicate that she was now prepared to do business. The bandy-legged man, taking the hint, made for the door.

"Well, see you."

"See you," the two women chorused together with a marked lack of enthusiasm.

Philippa said her piece. She was looking for a small, partly furnished, two-roomed flat for herself and her mother in central London for about two months.

"Until I go up to university. There's just the two of us. I don't mind doing something to it if it's basically in good order and fairly central."

"What sort of rent were you thinking of?"

"What sort of rents are there?"

"Depends. Fifty, sixty, eighty, a hundred and more. We don't usually get anything under fifty a week. It's the Rent Act you see. Doesn't pay a landlord to rent when he can't get the tenants out."

"Yes, I know all about the Rent Act. I could pay cash in advance."

The woman at the other desk looked up but didn't speak. The blonde went on:

"Two months, you say? Most landlords look for a bit longer."

"I thought they liked short lets. Isn't that why they let to foreigners because they know they can get them out? I can promise we'll be out by the autumn."

The red-headed woman spoke.

"We don't take promises. There'd be an agreement. Mr Wade, the solicitor round the corner, draws it up for us. You did say cash?"

Philippa made herself look hard into the calculating eyes.

"For ten per cent discount."

The blonde laughed: "Are you kidding? Anything we get to rent furnished we can let without a discount."

The woman at the other desk said:

"What about that two-roomed place with kitchen and shared

bathroom in Delaney Street?"

"It's taken, Mrs Bealing. That young couple with the kid and the baby on the way. They viewed yesterday. I told you."

"Let's have a look at the card."

The blonde opened the top left-hand drawer of her desk and flicked through a card index. The card was passed across. The redheaded woman looked at Philippa.

"Three months' cash in advance. He won't let it go for less than three months. He's asking one hundred and ninety a month. Say five hundred and fifty for the three months, cash down, no cheques. And it's what's called a holiday letting. That means that the Rent Act doesn't apply."

She had just short of one thousand pounds in her bank account saved from birthday presents and holiday jobs. But money, although she never spent it without thought, had never been important to her. She had always believed that she could earn money. Of all her needs, it seemed to her the most easily satisfied. She said with only a moment's hesitation:

"All right. But if it's taken?"

"Please yourself. It's up to you."

The blonde glanced at Philippa with the amused, slightly contemptuous look of a woman who has long given up expecting people to behave well, but can still gain some satisfaction from watching them behave badly. Philippa nodded. The older woman picked up the telephone and dialled.

"Mr Baker? The Raterite Bureau here about the flat. Yes. Yes. Yes. Well, the fact of the matter is that Mr Coates isn't happy. Yes, I know he's in New York. He rang. He doesn't like the idea of your wife managing those narrow stairs, not in her condition. And he doesn't want a let with children. Yes, I know, but I'm the one who makes the decisions and I wasn't here when you came in. And then there would be the pram in the hall. No, it wouldn't be any good writing to him. I don't know where he'll be for the next month or two. Sorry. Yes, we'll let you know. Up to forty pounds a week. Yes. I know, Mr Baker. Yes, we've got all the details. Yes. Yes. I don't think it's very helpful to take that attitude. After all, nothing has been signed."

She took up her cigarette again, and returned to her paper. Without looking at Philippa she said:

"You can view it now if you like. Number 12, Delaney Street. It's at the bottom of Mell Street off the Edgware Road just this side of Praed Street. Two rooms and kitchen. Use of bathroom. The bathroom's shared with the lock-up greengrocery on the ground floor. You won't find anything cheaper, not in central London. It's a

91

snip. It'd be twice the price, but Mr Coates went to New York in a hurry and he wants a short let."

"Is it furnished?"

The blonde said:

"Not so as you'd notice."

"Well, most people like to bring in their own bits and pieces. But it's a furnished letting."

"I'd like to view it now, please."

She signed for the keys, but didn't at once make her way to Delaney Street. It seemed to her that once there the decision would have been made. If she were going to reject the flat she must do so now. She felt the need to stride out vigorously, to co-ordinate thought with action. But the pavement was too crowded; the pressure of bodies, the tangle of pushchairs and trolleys forced her restless feet from the kerb into the stream of traffic. Almost without thinking she turned into a café about a hundred yards down Edgware Road and found a seat at a grubby formica-topped table near the window. A lank-haired waiter in a stained jacket slouched over from the counter and she ordered a coffee. The coffee, when it arrived in a plastic cup, pale, lukewarm and tasteless, was literally undrinkable. Glancing round at her fellow customers who were not only managing to drink it—although with no apparent signs of pleasure—but had actually bought food, over-cooked hamburgers, flabby chips, fried eggs curling brown at the edges and swimming in grease, she reflected that one at least of Maurice's axioms was true: The poor always got worse value pound for pound than the rich.

The window was festooned with wicker baskets of dusty artificial flowers and trailing vineleaves. Against the glittering panorama of the traffic the pavement was heaving with life. From time to time, faces, grey, brown or black, moved momentarily to the glass to study the price list. They seemed to be staring in at her; face succeeded face like a peripatetic jury, mute witnesses of her moral dilemma.

Nothing she could recognize from her past had equipped her to deal with it. She slipped the key ring on her thumb so that the two keys, the Yale which must be for the shared front door, the Chubb for the door to the flat itself, lay cold and heavy against her palm, reinforcing symbolism. Her moral training—indoctrination Maurice would have called it, smiling a self-satisfied acceptance of his own honesty—had been a matter of semantics, of the intellectualization of a comfortable, ethical conformity. You behaved reasonably well to other people in the interest of certain abstractions: good public order, a pleasant life, natural justice—whatever that meant—the greatest good of the greatest number. Most of all, you

92

behaved well to others to ensure that they behaved well to you. The implication was that the clever, the witty, the beautiful or the rich had less need of these expedients; it was the more seemly in them to set an example.

She could find no answer in her schooling. The South London Collegiate was nominally a Christian foundation but the fifteen minutes' corporate worship with which the school started the day had always seemed to her no more than a convenient celebration of tradition, a way of ensuring that the whole school was present when the headmistress read out the day's notices. Some of the girls practised a religion. Anglicanism, particularly High Anglicanism, was accepted as a satisfying compromise between reason and myth, justified by the beauty of its liturgy, a celebration of Englishness; but essentially it was the universal religion of liberal humanism laced with ritual to suit each individual taste. She had never supposed that for Gabriel, professed High Anglican, it had ever been more. The small number of Roman Catholics, Christian Scientists and Nonconformists were regarded as eccentrics governed by family tradition. Nothing that any of them professed to believe interfered with the central dogma of the whole school, the supremacy of human intelligence. The girls, like their brothers at Winchester, Westminster and St Paul's, were conditioned from childhood to a fierce intellectual competitiveness. She herself had been so conditioned from the time of her entry to the lower school. They were marked for success as if with invisible stigmata: the blessed company of the redeemed; redeemed from monotony, from poverty, from inconsequence, from failure. The universities they would go to, the professions they would choose, the men they would marry, were ranked in a hierarchy, unstated but subtly understood. She didn't feel that this was the only world in which she could find a place. She was a writer; all worlds were open to her. But it was the world into which Maurice had raised himself, into which she had been adopted, and she had no quarrel with it. After her foragings among the philistines this civilized city would always open its doors to her, not as an alien but as a freeman.

She supposed that Dame Beatrice, who visited the school once a week to teach moral philosophy, would have had an answer to her dilemma: if asking more questions and discussing their relevance, whether they had, in fact, any meaning, was an answer. She recalled the last weekly essay, which was in itself a diploma of superiority since only the upper sixth attended Dame Beatrice's lectures.

"Act only on that maxim through which you can at the same time will that it should become a universal law. Discuss with reference to Hegel's criticism of Kant's system of moral philosophy."

93

And what relevance had that to the opposing claims to a cheap flat of an ex-convict who was a murderess and a pregnant wife? Except that the pregnant wife had got there first. There was a notice on the board in the school hall. The Chaplain is available to girls in his study by appointment or on Friday from twelve-thirty to two p.m. and on Wednesday from four to five-thirty. A spiritual stud. He was a humourless man and the girls had giggled at the infelicitous wording. But he would, she supposed, have had his answer:

"Behold, I give you a new commandment, that you love one another."

But that wasn't possible by an act of will. Surely the faithful were justified in replying, "But Lord, show us how"? And He, that itinerant man/God, whom no one would have heard of if he had died sane and in his bed, would have had his answer too: "I have."

The café was not the most suitable place for the resolution of a moral dilemma. The noise was appalling and there was a shortage of seats. Harassed women with folded pushchairs and children clutching at their coats were looking for a place. She had sat there long enough. She left a five-pence tip under the saucer of unfinished coffee, dropped the keys in her shoulder bag and set off resolutely down the Edgware Road towards Mell Street.

14

Delaney Street was at the Lisson Grove end of Mell Street, a narrow street with, on the left, a terrace of small shops with living accommodation above. There was a pub at the end, the Grenadier, with a swinging sign of some splendour, then a betting shop, secretive behind painted glass, giving out a low murmur like a hive of angry bees. Then came a hairdresser's, the front of his window strewn with advertisements for hair tonics and lotions, and the back occupied by four dummy heads. The blank dolls' eyes turned upwards in the gaping sockets, and the wigs, dry as straw, gave the heads the look of guillotine victims of some ancient holocaust, needing only a jagged red line around each severed neck to complete the illusion. The door was open, and Philippa could see two customers awaiting their turn, and a wizened old man, comb poised, busying himself with the back of a customer's neck.

A green door with "12" painted in black and a Victorian iron knocker and letter-box was between a junk shop and a greengrocer whose open-fronted shop had once been the ground floor of the house. On the fascia was painted "Monty's Fruit and Veg". Both shops had spilled out on to the pavement. The greengrocer's stall, covered with a mat of lurid artificial grass, was piled with fruit and vegetables, displayed with an eye to artistic effect. An intricate pyramid of oranges gleamed against the dimness of the inner shop; bunches of bananas and grapes hung from a rail above the back of the stall and the boxes of burnished apples, the carrots and tomatoes were arranged in a balanced pattern as if for a church harvest festival. A stocky young man with greasy fair hair straggling to his shoulders, a podgy, amiable face and huge hands, was pouring potatoes from the pan of his scales into the outstretched shopping bag held by the mittened hands of an elderly customer, so well-wrapped against the unkind summer that little of his face was visible between the flat cloth cap and the swathed woollen scarves.

Now that she was here she found herself torn between anxiety to see the flat and a curious reluctance to put the key in the door. It was almost as an exercise in self-control as well as a wish to postpone disappointment that she made herself take stock of her surroundings.

The junk shop looked exciting. Outside there was an assortment of old furniture: four bentwood chairs, two more with broken cane seats, a sturdy kitchen table bearing boxes of paperback novels and old magazines, an ancient treadle sewing-machine, an enamel wash-tub filled with assorted crockery, most of it chipped, and a wooden mangle. Victorian prints and amateur water-colours in a variety of frames rested against the table legs. On the pavement was a square cardboard box of linen in which a couple of young women were rummaging happily. In the shop window every inch of space was occupied. Philippa gained an impression of articles jumbled together, irrespective of merit and, presumably, of price. She could see chipped Staffordshire, delicately painted cups and saucers, dishes and bowls, candlesticks and horse brasses, while an antique doll with a delicate china face and straw-filled bulging legs was perched in the pride of place.

She inserted the Yale key in the lock, aware as she did so of the interested glance of the greengrocer, and found herself in a narrow hall. The hall smelled of apples and loam, a strong rich tang which, she guessed, overlaid less agreeable smells. It was very narrow—too narrow for a pram, she told herself—and obstructed by two sacks of potatoes and a meshed bag of onions. To the right an open door led into the shop; a second, with a glass panel, gave sight of a back yard. She decided to explore this later, although the glimpse of it immediately evoked visions of climbing plants and geranium-filled tubs. A flight of steep, drugget-covered stairs led to a back room on a half landing. She opened the door gingerly and saw that this was the bathroom. The large old-fashioned bath was heavily stained round the waste-pipe, but otherwise surprisingly clean. There was a small wash-basin encrusted with grime and with a slimy face-flannel jammed into the soap dish. The lavatory had a heavy mahogany seat, a high cistern and a chain lengthened by string. Another length of string was stretched across the bath. It sagged with the weight of a pair of jeans and two grubby towels.

She went up a further short flight of stairs to the flat door. The key turned in the Chubb lock without difficulty and she passed into a short hall. After the dimness of the stairway the flat seemed full of light, perhaps because the doors to the three rooms were all open. She moved first into the one at the front which she guessed would be the principal room running the whole width of the house. The curtains were drawn back and a single beam of sunlight shone through the dirty window panes so that the air was iridescent with dancing motes of dust. It wasn't large, she judged about fifteen feet by ten, but was pleasantly proportioned with a carved cornice and with two windows facing over the street. On the left-hand wall was a Victorian grate, its hood was patterned with a border of scallop shells and decorated with a design of beribboned grape vines; above it was a plain wooden overmantel. The grate was stuffed with brown and brittle old newspapers, and the tiled surround was littered with cigarette butts, but the air held no taint of cigarette smoke, only the faint autumnal smell of vegetables and apples. The room was shabby. The paint on the window frames had chipped and flaked to the bare wood. The carpet was a dull green, splodged and ringed in front of the fire as if the occupier had placed his hot cooking pans on the floor. But the wallpaper, patterned in small posies of rosebuds, had faded to a pleasant pinkish brown, and was surprisingly intact, and although the ceiling obviously hadn't been painted for years, there were no ominous cracks, no hanging swathes of lining paper. A long cord with a single unshaded light bulb on the end had been drawn from the middle of the ceiling and stretched over a hook so that the light was suspended over the single divan bed.

The divan was covered with a woollen blanket made of hand-knitted squares in different colours. Philippa drew it back and saw with relief that the mattress was clean, so clean that it looked new. There were two pillows, also new, but no other bedclothes. Between the windows was a small but sturdy oak wardrobe with carved doors. It stood firm when she pulled open the door. Inside were two empty hangers and, folded on the floor, three grey army blankets exuding a

96

smell of moth-balls. The only other items of furniture were a wicker chair with a limp fawn cushion, an oblong table with a centre drawer, and a bentwood rocking-chair with a wicker seat.

The windows were curtained in a coarse unlined linen, slung from wooden hooks on an old-fashioned bamboo curtain rail. They had the creased, grubby look of curtains which had been laid aside, unused, but the material was good. Standing behind them she looked out over the narrow street. Opposite but about thirty yards to the left was another pub, the Blind Beggar. It was a high Dutch-fronted building with the date 1896 painted in heavy curved numerals on an oval plaque under the central gable. The swinging sign, which was competently painted and highly sentimental, was almost certainly the original. It showed a bent white-haired man with sightless eyes being led by a golden-haired child. A narrow passage ran down the side of the building, separating it from a wasteland bordered with a high fence of corrugated iron. It looked like a bomb site which had been neglected since the war but, she thought, more probably it had been cleared for some development which had been thwarted for lack of money. It had been concreted, but the surface had cracked and grass and weeds waist-high had burgeoned in the crevices. Three vehicles had been parked there, a van and two saloons. They had the isolated battered look of ramshackle rejects abandoned in a small oasis of decrepitude. Next to the car park was a second-hand bookshop. The window was half shuttered but two trestle tables outside the shop were bright with the green and orange of old paperbacks. Next came a small general store, the window plastered with notices of special offers. On the corner of Delaney Street and Mell Street was a launderette. As she watched, a black woman came out lugging two plastic bags which she humped on to an empty pushchair. But otherwise the road was empty, lapped in a mid-morning lull.

She turned away from the window and looked round the room again with mounting excitement. Something could be made of it. In her mind's eye she saw it transformed, the grate cleaned and polished, the woodwork painted a gleaming white, the curtains washed. Nothing need be done about the walls, she liked that delicate washed-out pink and brown. The floor would be a problem, of course. She turned back a corner of the carpet. Underneath the solid oak boards were dirty but looked undamaged. The most exciting thing to do would be to sand the floor and then polish it so that the natural oak shone with the simplicity and beauty of wood against the darker walls, but she doubted whether that would be possible. Without the use of a car it would be difficult to hire a sanding machine, and there wasn't very much time. She had never realized before just how important a car could be. But the carpet would have to go. She would rip it out, roll it and get rid of it somehow, and replace it with rugs. The room might in the end be bare, but it would have some grace, some individuality. It wouldn't have what her mind's eye pictured as the dreadful compromise between bleakness and claustrophobic cosiness of a prison cell.

She continued her exploration. At the rear were two rooms, a narrow bedroom and the kitchen. Both overlooked the walled yard and, beyond it, the narrow back gardens of the next street. One or two of them had been carefully tended but most were an untidy conglomeration of ramshackle sheds, dismembered motor bikes, broken and discarded children's toys, washing lines and concrete fuel bunkers. But there was a plane tree at the bottom of the garden opposite the bedroom, providing a green light-filled shield for the worst of the clutter, and at least the view had some human interest.

She decided that the small room would have to be hers. It was too like a cell in its proportions to be suitable for her mother. She sat on the single divan bed and assessed the room's possibilities. There was a fitted cupboard on each side of the iron Victorian grate and the walls had been stripped of paper ready for redecoration. She wouldn't need to buy a wardrobe and it would be a simple matter to apply a coat of emulsion. She liked, too, the pine overmantel. Someone had painted it green but the paint was already peeling. It wouldn't be too difficult to strip and polish it. The window sill was wide enough to hold a plant. She could picture the sill gleaming with white paint, reflecting the green and red of a geranium.

Lastly she went into the kitchen. Here she was agreeably surprised. It was a good-sized room with the sink and teak draining board in front of the double window. The owner had started here with his redecoration and the walls had been painted white. There was a wooden-topped table, two wheel-backed chairs, a small refrigerator and what looked like a new gas stove. She turned on the gas tap and found to her relief that the supply hadn't been disconnected. He must have left for America in a hurry.

After her inspection she relocked the front door and went finally to explore the back yard whose worst horrors had been obscured from the upstairs windows by an overhanging bough of the plane tree. The outside lavatory with its wooden seat and stone floor obviously hadn't worked for years. But at least it didn't smell. The yard was a mess. There was a bicycle against one wall and the other two were piled with rubbish; empty paint cans, a rotting roll of old carpet, and what looked like the dismembered parts of an ancient gas stove. Here, too, were two battered and malodorous dustbins. She supposed that they would have to be dragged into the street for the weekly collection. Something, she decided, would have to be done about the yard, but it would have to wait its turn.

She looked at her watch. It was time that she went back to the agency and confirmed that she would definitely take the flat. She had thirty pounds with her in cash. Perhaps they would take that as a deposit until she could get to her bank and draw out the rest of the rent. Whatever happened, she mustn't lose it now. As soon as the agreement had been signed she would move in and start work. But first it might be prudent to make the acquaintance of her neighbour.

He had just finished serving a customer and was carefully repairing his pyramid of oranges. She watched him for a moment, knowing that he was aware of her but was waiting for her to make the first move. She said:

"Good morning. Are you Monty?"

"Naw. Monty was me granddad. Dead twenty years." He hesitated, then added: "I'm George."

"I'm Philippa. Philippa Palfrey. My mother and I have just taken the upstairs flat."

She held out her hand. After another hesitation he wiped his palm against his side and gripped her knuckles hard. She winced as the bones ground together. He said:

"Marty gone to New York then?"

"He's gone somewhere. I suppose he'll be back. It's only a short-term let for two or three months. I was wondering about the bathroom. They said at the agency that we share it. I thought we'd better settle about the cleaning."

He looked, she thought, a little nonplussed.

"Marty's birds always did the cleaning."

"Well, I'm no one's bird. But as there are two of us and only you, I don't mind taking responsibility for the bathroom, if that's all right by you."

"Suits me."

"We'll do the passage and the stairs, too. Do you mind if I clear up the yard, I mean, just get rid of some of the mess? I thought we might have some pots—geraniums perhaps. I don't suppose it gets much sun with that high wall, but something might grow."

"I keep me bike in the yard."

"Oh, I didn't mean I'd move your bike. Of course not. I'd just get rid of those old paint cans and the bits of iron."

"That's OK by me. That outside WC doesn't work."

"So I found. It hardly seems worth mending it; after all my mother and I won't be monopolizing the bathroom. We can bath out of shop hours. We'll try to keep it clear for you if you can let us know when you want to use it."

"Look love, I pee in the bloody place. It's me bog. I can't tell you when I'm going to be took short, not with the amount of beer I drink."

"I'm sorry. I saw your bath towel there and I thought you might want to bath after you close the shop."

"That's Marty's towel. I bath at home. There's only two things I want to do up there and I can't tell you when I'll want to do them. OK?"

"Well, that's all right then."

They looked at each other. He said:

"Marty OK? Doing all right is he?"

"I haven't the least idea. Considering the rent he's asking, he should be doing fine."

He smiled. Then with the élan of a conjuror his chubby hands picked out four oranges, tossed them into a bag and held it out to her.

"Sample the produce. Monty's best. It's on the house. House-warming present."

"That's very kind of you. Thank you. I've never had a house-warming present before."

The action in its generosity and grace disconcerted and touched her. She smiled at him and turned quickly away, afraid that she might cry. She never cried, but it had been a long and exhausting week and she was at the end of her search at last. Perhaps it was only tiredness and the relief of finding somewhere when she had almost given up hope that made her so ridiculously sensitive to a simple act of kindness. The bag was too fragile for the weight of the oranges and she had to support them on her hands. She looked down at their gleaming pock-marked skin and felt their round solidity resting on her palms. She bore them upstairs slowly and carefully as if they might crack, then rested the bag against the wall while she unlocked the flat door. She had found during her inspection a shallow Wedgwood-patterned bowl in the kitchen cupboard among a miscellany of crockery and half-used tins of coffee and cocoa. She set the oranges in it. Then she placed the bowl precisely in the middle of the kitchen table. It seemed to her that with this action she took possession of the flat.

15

On the following day, Saturday 29 July, Scase took a cheap day return ticket from Victoria to Brighton. He was on his way to buy the knife. He had been born in Brighton, in a small pub near the station, but his return for the first time since his youth had nothing to do with nostalgia. The purchase of the knife seemed to him of immense significance; he had to make the right choice and to make it without risk that his purchase would afterwards be remembered. That meant that he needed to buy it in a large town, preferably some distance from London, and on the busiest shopping day of the week. He would feel at home in Brighton. There were advantages in not having to cope with so important a purchase and at the same time find his way around a strange town.

His first thought was to buy a hunting or sheath knife from a shop which dealt in camping equipment, but when, after anxiously scrutinizing the window, he ventured inside such a shop, there were no knives on display and the thought of actually having to ask for one, and of perhaps being asked by an assistant, anxious to be helpful, for what precise purpose he wanted it, reinforced his feeling that this wasn't the right place. Wandering among the anoraks, the bed-rolls and the camping gear, he did eventually find a selection of jack-knives hanging from a display board, but he thought that the blades might be too short. He was worried, too, that if he had to act in a hurry his fingers might be too weak to get the blade prised open in time. What he wanted was a simpler weapon. But he did find, and buy, at the camping shop another necessary piece of equipment; a strong canvas rucksack in khaki, about fourteen inches by ten with two metal buckles and a shoulder strap.

In the end he found the knife in the kitchen department of a fashionable household store, new since his time. The goods were displayed in racks; stacks of pretty cups and saucers, earthenware casserole dishes, plain, well-designed cutlery and every possible item of equipment for cooking. The store was very busy and he moved with his blood-stained preoccupation among young couples conferring happily over purchases for their homes, families with boisterous children, chattering foreign tourists and the occasional solitary shopper surveying with a discriminating eye the bottles of spices and coffee beans and the jars of preserves. The store seemed to be staffed by pretty girls in summer dresses, much occupied with their own conversations. No one approached him. Customers selected their own items and carried them in the store's baskets to the check-out desk. He would be one of an endless, moving line of people, anonymous, quickly dealt with, not even required to speak.

He took his time at the knife rack, trying them in his hands for weight and balance and for a comfortable feel of the handle in the grasp of his palm. In the end he chose a strong carving knife with a triangular, eight-inch blade, very sharp at the point and riveted into a plain wooden handle. The blade, razor sharp, was protected with a tough cardboard sheath. The sharp point seemed to him important. It was that first deep thrust into her flesh which he imagined might take all his strength and purpose. That done, the final twist and withdrawal would be little more than a reflex action. He had the right money ready, and after standing in a short queue, was through the check-out within seconds.

He had brought with him to Brighton the binoculars which he had bought as his retiring present. He already had at home a street map of London, but there were two other necessities, and both he bought in Brighton. In a chainstore chemist he purchased the small size of the finest protective gloves which they had on display, and, in another large store, a white transparent macintosh. Here, but without bothering to try it on, he selected the largest size. If he were to be adequately protected against what might be a gushing fountain of blood, he needed a protective coat which would reach almost to the ground. He put the gloves in the pocket of the macintosh, then rolled it round the binoculars and the sheathed knife. The bundle fitted easily into the bottom of the rucksack and its wide strap fitted comfortably on his shoulder.

He couldn't be sure why, in the end, he decided after all to visit the Goat and Compasses. Perhaps the reasons were a mixture of the simple and complex; he was, after all, in Brighton and was unlikely to visit here again in the near future, the pub was on his way to the station, he was moving into a new sphere of existence which would distance still further those early traumatic years, it would be interesting to see whether the place had changed. Nothing about it had. It still seemed to crouch under the shadow of the railway arches, a low, dark, claustrophobic pub, liked by its regulars but hardly inviting to the casual passer-by. The wooden-walled public bar was still furnished with the same long oak tables and benches, the walls were still hung with the same maple-framed old photographs of Brighton pier, and groups of sou'wester-clad fishermen before their boats. Opposite and seen through the windows the railway arches still gaped like black menacing mouths. In his childhood the arches had been a place of terror, the lair of the spitting monsters with no necks, whose spittle was death. Always

102

he passed on the other side of the road, not running, in case his padding feet drew their attention, but walking in steady haste, his eyes averted. But then, when he was eleven, he made a pact with them. He used to secrete scraps of his meals, a crust from breakfast, the end of a sausage or a piece of potato from supper, and lay them, a propitiatory offering, at the entrance to the first arch. Returning at night, he would look to see if the offering had been accepted. With part of his mind he knew that the seagulls scavenged there, but when he found that the scraps had gone he went home comforted. But the trains never frightened him. He would lie at night mentally timing their visitation, hands clutching the blanket edge, his eyes fixed on the window, waiting for the preparatory whistle, the approaching rumble, which, almost as soon as he heard it, exploded into a climax of clashing metal and flashing lights while his bed shook under the momentary dazzle of the patterned ceiling.

Sitting there, alone, in the dim corner of the saloon bar with his hands clasped round his glass of lager, he recalled the day when he had first learned that he was ugly. He had been ten years and three months old. His Auntie Gladys and Uncle George were setting out the public bar for the first evening customers. His mother was out with Uncle Ted, the latest of the so-called uncles who came and went in his life, and he was playing alone in the dark little passage between the bar and the sitting-room, sprawled on the floor and taxiing his model bi-plane carefully on to one of the grey squares of the chequered lino. The door to the bar was swinging open and he could hear footsteps, the clink of bottles, chairs being dragged across the floor, and then his uncle's voice:

"Where's Norm? Marge said he wasn't to go out."

"In his room, I suppose. That kid gives me the willies, George. He's right ugly. He's a proper little Crippen."

"Oh come off it! He's not that bad, poor little sod. His dad was no oil painting. The kid's no trouble."

"I grant you that. More healthy if he was. I like a boy with a bit of spirit to him. He creeps around the place like some sodding animal. You got the key to this till, George?"

The voices sank to a murmur. He slid across the floor soundlessly and stole out of the door and up the twisting stairs to his bedroom. There was a rickety oak chest of drawers in front of the window and on top of it an old-fashioned swivel looking-glass, the mirror spotted with age. He hardly ever used it and had to drag the bedside chair across to the chest and stand on it before he saw the thin grubby fingers pressed white against the oak, the toy plane between them, his face rising to confront him, framed in split mahogany. He gazed at himself stolidly, the protuberant eyes behind the cheap

103

crooked spectacles with their steel rims, the straight fringe of dry brown hair, too thin to obscure the rash of spots across his forehead, the unhealthy pallor of his skin. Ugliness. So this was why his mother didn't love him. The realization didn't surprise him. He didn't love himself. The knowledge that he was ugly and therefore beyond the possibilities of love was only the confirmation of something always known but never, until now, acknowledged, taken in with his milk when she thrust the bottle teat between his gums, mirrored in the anxious disappointed face which bent over his, perpetually present in adults' eyes, heard in the whining nag of her voice. It was too inescapably a part of him to be resented or grieved over. It would have been better for him to have been born with one leg or one eye. People might have been impressed by how well he managed, might have been sorry for him. But this deformity of the spirit was beyond pity as it was beyond healing.

When his mother came home, he followed her up to her room.

"Mum, who was Crippen?"

"Crippen? What a question. Why d'you want to know?"

"I heard someone talking about him at school."

"Pity they couldn't find something better to talk about then. He was a murderer. He killed his wife and cut her up and buried her in the cellar. That was a long time ago. In your granddad's time. Hilldrop Crescent. That's where it happened!" Her voice brightened at the wonder of memory's capricious cleverness, then resumed its normal hectoring tone. "Crippen indeed!"

"What happened to him?"

"He was hanged, of course, what do you think happened to him? Give over talking about him, will you."

So he was wicked as well as ugly, and in some mysterious way the ugliness and the wickedness belonged together. When he thought about his boyhood he marvelled at the child's stoical acceptance of this yoked burden of physical and moral repulsion, hardly made more bearable by the knowledge of its arbitrariness, or of his power-lessness to shift the load from his shoulders.

Two things saved him, delinquency and chess. The first had begun in a small way. He had wandered unobserved into the saloon bar early one Saturday morning before opening time. He liked the bar when it was silent and empty: the round tables with their ornate cast-iron legs and stained tops; the wall clock with its swinging pendulum and flower-painted face measuring the silence with ticks which were too soft to be heard except out of opening hours; the smeared glass dome covering the tray holding two of yesterday's sausage rolls, even the smell of beer which permeated the whole house, but which in this smoky brown-clad cabin was strong and potent as a gas; the mysterious dimness behind the counter with its rows of darkly gleaming bottles awaiting the magic moment when the bar lights would be switched on and the liquids would take fire. Venturing behind the bar into this heartland of the forbidden territory, he saw that the till drawer was unlocked and slightly open. Gently he pulled it towards him. And there it was—money; not money in the possession of grown-ups, a symbol of adult power, not a few crumpled notes being stuffed, almost surreptitiously, into his mother's purse in the corner shop, not coins carefully doled out weekly to him to pay for school dinners or his fares. Here was money under his hands, two bundles of notes held together in rubber bands, silver coins, unnaturally bright, looking as heavy as doubloons, coffee-coloured pennies. Afterwards he couldn't recall taking the one-pound note. All he could remember was being back in his own room, terrified, his heart thudding, his back pressed against the door, turning the note over in his hands.

It was never missed, or if it was, he was not suspected. He spent it that morning on a model railway engine, and on Monday, brought it out ostentatiously between lessons, and ran it over his desk top. The boy in the next desk looked at it trying to conceal his envy.

"That's the new Hornby, isn't it? Where d'you get it?"

"Bought it."

"Let's have a look."

He passed it across, feeling a momentary pang at the loss of its smooth brightness. He said:

"You can keep it if you like."

"You mean you don't want it?"

He shrugged his shoulders.

"I mean you can have it."

Thirty pairs of eyes slewed round to witness this marvel. The form bully said:

"Got any more at home?"

"Might have. Why, d'you want one?"

"I don't mind."

But he did mind. Looking into the face he feared, into the greedy little eyes, Norman rejoiced in the knowledge of just how much he minded.

"I'll bring you one next week. Monday maybe."

And that was the end of the persecution and the beginning of a year during which he lived at a pitch of inner excitement, of exhilaration and terror, which he had never experienced since. He didn't again steal from the pub takings. Twice more he stole into the saloon bar in hope, but on neither occasion was the till drawer unlocked.

Part of him was relieved to be spared the temptation. To risk a second theft would have been too dangerous. But with the beginning of summer and the influx of visitors came other and safer opportunities. In his solitary wanderings after school along the promenade or on the beach, his restlessly blinking eyes, so deceptively mild behind steel-rimmed spectacles, grew adept at spotting his chances; a purse casually lain on top of a beach bag, a wallet stuck into a blazer pocket, loose change from paying the deck-chair attendant dropped into the pocket of a coat slung across the back of the canvas. He grew skilful at picking pockets, the tiny marsupial hands insinuating their way under the jacket, into the back trouser pocket. Afterwards, his tactic was always the same. He would wait to examine the spoils until he could be sure that he was unobserved. Usually he would seek the rank-smelling metallic saltiness of the gloom under the great iron girders of the pier, take out the money, then scuff the purse or wallet under the sand. Apart from coins, he took away only pound notes. To proffer anything larger at a local shop would be to invite suspicion. But, perhaps because he worked alone, was so unremarkable, looked so neat and respectable, there never was suspicion. Only once, during the whole of the year, was he in danger of discovery. He had bought a model of a breakdown van and had been unable to resist playing with it in the hall before school. His mother's eye had been caught by the unexpected brightness.

"That's new isn't it? Where d'you get it?"

"A man gave it to me."

"What man?" Her voice was sharp, worried.

"Just a man coming out of the bar. A customer."

"What did you do for it?"

"Nothing. I didn't do anything."

"Well, what did he ask you to do?"

"Nothing, Mum. He just gave it to me, honest. I didn't do anything."

"Well don't, that's all! And don't take toys from strangers."

But in the following autumn, the beginning of his second year at senior school, came Mr Micklewright, a new and enthusiastic young member of staff, with his passion for chess. The school chess club was formed and Norman joined. The game fascinated him. He played every day, needing no opponent since there were published games to work out, strategies which could be developed in secret, books from the public and school library to teach him the subtleties of the various openings. Encouraged by Mr Micklewright's enthusiasm and praise he rapidly became the best player in the school. Then there were the local school competitions, the Southern

Championship, and eventually even a photograph in the *Brighton Evening Argus*, a photograph cut out by his aunt and passed from hand to hand round the saloon bar. That established his fame. From then on he lived the rest of his school life without fear. He stopped stealing because it was no longer necessary for him to steal. Even the spitting monsters deserted the railway arches, leaving nothing but their debris of beer cans, screwed-up cigarette cartons and a brown, mildewed pillow leaking damp feathers against the furthest wall.

On his walk back to the station and his homeward train, he wondered what would have happened to him if he had gone on with the stealing. He couldn't have hoped to have evaded detection for ever. And then what? He would have been officially labelled delinquent; processed through the juvenile justice system; become the unprepossessing object of the machinery of bureaucratic caring. There would have been no respectable career in local government, no meeting with Mavis, no Julie. So much in his life seemed to have depended on that moment when Mr Micklewright set out before his fascinated gaze those mythical warriors whose lives, like his, were governed by such unalterable and arbitrary rules.

When at last he reached home he went to his bedroom and tried on his equipment for murder. He looked at himself in the long wardrobe glass. With the unsheathed knife in his hand, the raincoat hanging in glistening folds from his thin shoulders, he looked like a surgeon gowned for some desperate operation or, perhaps, like the member of a more ancient and sinister priesthood garbed for a ritual slaughter. And yet the image was not wholly terrifying. There was something wrong about it, something almost pathetic. The clothes were right, the naked knife showed the keen edge of fear; but the eyes which met his with their look of mild, almost painful resolution, were the eyes, not of an executioner, but of the victim.

16

On 4 August a probation officer came by appointment to look at the flat. Philippa prepared for the visit with excessive care, cleaning and rearranging the sparse furniture and buying a geranium in a pot to sit on the kitchen window. There was still a lot to do to the flat before it was ready to receive her mother, and only another ten days in which to do it, but she was pleased with her efforts so far. She couldn't remember when she had physically worked harder than during the last week, or with more satisfaction. She had concentrated on her mother's room and it was now nearly ready. The worst job had been taking up the carpet and getting rid of it, but George, hearing her coughing with the dust and struggling on the stairs with the discarded roll, had helped carry it down and had bribed or persuaded the dustmen to take it away. Then she had spent two days scrubbing and staining the floor. She had brought nothing with her from Caldecote Terrace except one suitcase of clothes and the Henry Walton oil. She had hung it above the fireplace in her mother's room where, although it was not in period, she thought it looked particularly good above the newly gleaming fire-hood and the plain but elegant overmantel.

She was glad that she still had some money in reserve. She was surprised how expensive cleaning materials were; how many small items were essential to domestic comfort and how costly they were to buy. The previous owner had left in a box under the sink his set of tools, and after trial and error and much consulting of a book on elementary carpentry borrowed from the Marylebone Road branch of the Westminster library, she managed to make a reasonable job of putting up extra shelves in the kitchen and a coat rack in the hall. She found in the market a cheap batch of old Victorian tiles and fixed them behind the sink. Some of the jobs she particularly enjoyed: painting the woodwork white, with the sun from the open window warming her arms; searching in the local junk shops and in Church Street market for the extra pieces of furniture they needed. One particularly successful buy was two small cane chairs. They were in perfect condition but painted a particularly repulsive green. After a coat of paint and with new patchwork cushions they added a touch of gaiety to the two rooms. George, if he saw her struggling with items of furniture, would temporarily leave his shop and give her a hand. She liked him. They seldom spoke, except when she bought from him the fruit which she ate each day for lunch, but she was aware that there flowed from him a general goodwill. Once he asked when Mrs Palfrey was expected to arrive. She told him on August the fifteenth, but didn't correct the name.

At night she lay on the narrow bed in the back room in an almost sensuous languor of exhaustion, with the window wide open, listening to the rumble and murmur of London, watching the stain of its night life on the scudding clouds, letting herself be gently shaken into sleep by the shudder of the Underground trains running between Marylebone and Edgware Road.

The probation officer was ten minutes late. When the downstairs bell at last rang Philippa opened the door to a tall, dark-haired woman who looked little older than herself. She was lugging a bulging plastic bag from the Edgware Road supermarket and seemed harassed. She said:

"Philippa Palfrey? I'm Joyce Bungeld. Sorry I'm late. The gasket went. I only got back from holiday this morning and it's been one hell of a day. All the eight O'Briens in court together. They're apparently terrified that I may be made redundant so they go out on a family shop-lifting bash every time I'm away just to prove to the authorities that I'm indispensable. Very pleased with themselves they were, grinning in the box like a row of monkeys, but I could have done without it. You weren't thinking of making tea, were you? I've got a throat like a gravel pit."

Philippa made the tea, taking down her two new pottery mugs. Her first visitor. She told herself that she mustn't let resentment at the inspection prejudice her enterprise, and was resolved to counter officialdom with at least a show of docility. The probation officer rummaged in her bag and produced a packet of chocolate wholemeal biscuits. She tore open the package and offered it to Philippa. They munched companionably, sipping hot tea, both perched on the kitchen table.

"Your mother has her own room, has she? I see, in here. I like your picture."

What was she afraid of, thought Philippa—that she and her mother were about to embark on a sophisticated variety of incest? And how could having separate rooms prevent that? She said:

"Don't you want to look at the bathroom? It's on the half landing."

"No thanks. I'm not a sanitary inspector, thank God. You're here; the flat's here; your mother has someone and some place to come to. That's all I'm interested in. I'll write to the prison CWO tomorrow. You should hear in a day or two. I think they're trying to keep to the original release date, the fifteenth of August."

"Will it be all right?" Philippa tried to keep the note of anxiety out of her voice.

"I should think so; why not? But it's finally up to the Home Office. Will you be here much? I mean, I suppose you've got a job?"

"Not yet. I thought we'd get one together; hotel work, waitressing, something like that." She added, with an echo that was only half ironic: "We're not afraid of hard work."

"Then you're the only two people in London who aren't. Sorry. I'm feeling a little sour this afternoon. This would be a lovely job if it weren't for the clients. You go up to Cambridge in October, don't you? What had you in mind then?"

"For my mother? Nothing. I imagine she'll look for a cheaper flat if she can't afford to stay on here, or she could take a living-in job, if she can find one. And there's always one of your post-release hostels."

She thought that the probation officer looked at her a little strangely. Then she said:

"Then she's probably only postponing most of her problems. Still, the first two months are the most difficult for a lifer. That's when they need support. And she did ask to come here. Thanks for the tea."

The visit had lasted for less than twenty minutes, but Philippa thought that Miss Bungeld had seen all she wanted to see, had asked all the questions which it was necessary to ask. Shutting the street door after her and climbing the stairs she could imagine her report.

"The prisoner's daughter is of full age. She is an intelligent and sensible girl and the accommodation for which three months' rent has been paid in advance appears adequate. The licensee will have her own room and the flat, although small and unpretentious, was clean and tidy when I called. Miss Palfrey intends to find a job working with her mother. I recommend that the arrangements be approved."

Book Two

AN ORDER OF RELEASE

1

On Tuesday 15 August, Scase was at York Station beginning his watch by half-past eight in the morning. He had travelled to York the previous evening and had taken a room in a dull commercial hotel close to the station. He could have been lodged in any provincial city. It never occurred to him to visit the Minster or to stroll through the cobbled streets within the city walls. Nothing the city promised could seduce his mind for an instant from the task in hand. He travelled light, carrying only his rucksack, adding nothing but his pyjamas and toilet bag to the sheathed knife, the rolled plastic macintosh, the binoculars and the thin gloves. He was never now parted from the knife and the other impedimenta of murder. It was not that he expected to be able to kill her during the journey to London, a crowded train was hardly likely to afford opportunity, but it had become necessary to him to carry the knife. It was no longer an object of fascination or horror, but a familiar and potent extension of himself; the part which, when he closed his hand round it, completed him and made him whole. Now, even at night, he felt bereft without the drag of the rucksack on his shoulder, without being able to slip his hand under the flap and run his fingers along the cardboard sheath.

It was a convenient station in which to keep watch. From the outside hall an arched passage led through to the small concourse. To the right was the women's waiting-room. He could glimpse through the door a heavy mahogany table with carved legs, a lumpy couch and a row of carved chairs against the wall. Above the unlit gas fire was a nondescript modern print; it looked like a row of fishing nets strung out to dry. The waiting-room was empty except for one very old woman huddled in sleep among an assortment of bulging packages. There was only one entrance to the station concourse and the indicator showed him that the London trains went from platform 8. Beyond it the cavernous arched roof rose from the pale milk-grey pillars with their ornate capitals. There lay over the station the freshness of the early morning redolent with the smell of coffee. It waited in what seemed an eerie and portentous calm for the flood of commuter traffic and the chattering throng of the day's first tourists. Scase knew that, loitering alone so early, he would be conspicuous, but he told himself that it didn't matter. No place was more impersonal and anonymous than a railway station, no one would challenge him, and if they did he would say that he was waiting for a friend from London.

The bookstall was open and he bought a *Daily Telegraph*. A paper would be a quick way of hiding his face when she arrived. Then he settled himself on a bench to wait. He never doubted that Eli Watkin had kept faith with him, that this morning was the day of release. But he began to agitate himself with fears that he might not recognize her, that nearly ten years in prison might have changed her fundamentally or so subtly that she would slip past unnoticed. He took from his wallet the one picture that he had of her, cut from the local paper at the time of the trial. She and her husband had been snapped by a commercial photographer on what looked like a promenade at Southend. It was a photograph of two young people laughing, holding hands in the sun. He wondered how the reporter had managed to get hold of it. It told him nothing, and when he held it close to his eyes the image disintegrated into an anonymous pattern of microdots. It was impossible to connect this face with the woman whom he had last seen in the dock at the Old Bailey.

He had sat alone through every day of the three-week trial of his child's murderess, and by the last day nothing had any longer seemed real to him. It was like living in a dream world confined within the clean claustrophobic courtroom in which the ordinary conventions of life had been replaced by a different logic, an alien set of values. In that surrealist limbo no one except the professionals had any reality. All present were actors, but only those gowned or bewigged moved and spoke with assurance or knew their parts. The two accused sat side by side in the dock, yet distanced, not looking at each other, hardly moving their eyes. Perhaps if each had stretched out an arm their fingers might have touched, but their arms did not move. Touching was not in the script. The searing hatred which had infected him like a fever during the first days after Julie's death, which had driven him out into the suburban streets, walking endlessly, pointlessly, unseeing, desperately striding on to prevent himself from beating his head against those neat suburban walls and howling for vengeance like a dog; all that passed when he looked at their dead faces, since how could you hate someone who wasn't there, who was merely a bit-player, selected to sit in the dock so that the play could go on? They were the most important characters, yet they had the least to do, were the least regarded. They had a look of ordinariness which, in some dreadful way, wasn't ordinary at all; they were shells of flesh from which not only the spirit was missing. If they were pricked, they wouldn't bleed. The members of the jury seemed afraid to meet their eyes. The judge ignored them.

114

He felt that the drama, so muted, so desultory, could have gone on even without their presence.

The court was very full, yet the air had no taste to it, no smell. Time stretched out to accommodate the leisurely charade. Counsel for the prosecution spoke with calm deliberation, his fine voice distastefully reducing horror to an orderly recital of facts. From time to time there was a hiatus when no one spoke, when the be-wigged lawyers would suddenly perk up and watch the judge, and the judge would appear sunk in a private reverie. And then the moment would pass. The judge's pen would move again. Counsel would begin again his slow peroration. The court, almost imperceptibly, would relax.

There was one woman member of the jury from whom he had found it difficult to avert his eyes. Afterwards, whenever he thought about the trial, it was she who dominated his mind. The images of the accused and the judge faded, hers became clearer with the years. She was a stockily built grey-haired woman, wearing upswept diamanté-trimmed spectacles, dressed in a plaid cloak of red, green and yellow, her rolls of tightly curled hair topped with a matching cap. The brim was set straight across her intimidating brow, the crown was bulbous, as if stuffed with paper, the whole topped with a pom-pom in red wool. Like the other jurors, she sat very still throughout the trial, grim-faced under the ridiculous hat, only turning her head like an automaton, betraying no emotion.

Both the accused had been represented by the same counsel who had attempted in a voice of quiet reasonableness to persuade the jury that rape had been sexual assault, and murder manslaughter. The verdicts, when they came, conveyed no sense of climax or release. The judge pronounced the two sentences of life imprisonment with no more than the customary comment that this was a mandatory sentence provided by law. He rose without fuss and the court rose with him. The spectators shuffled out of the public gallery, casting last looks behind them as if reluctant to believe that the entertainment was over. The lawyers stuffed their papers and books into briefcases and conferred. The clerks bustled about the court, minds already occupied with the next case. It had been as undramatic and ordinary as the ending of a parish council meeting. Once there would have been a black cap—not a proper cap, but a small square of black cloth which the clerk would have placed grotesquely on top of the judge's wig. Once there would have been a gowned chaplain and the sonorous "Amen" after the sentence of death. He had felt the need of some such bizarre and histrionic end to this formal celebration of reason and retribution. Something memorable should have been said or done, more worthy of the corporate ritual than the foreman's carefully expressionless voice pronouncing the word "guilty" in response to the clerk's questions, the judge's dispassionate judicial tone. For one wild second he had been tempted to leap to his feet and to cry out that it wasn't over, that it couldn't be over. It had seemed to him that the trial had been less a judicial process than a comforting formality through which all participants except himself had been purged or justified. It was over for them. It was over for the jury and the judge. It was over for Julie. But for him and for Mavis it had just begun.

The station clock jerked away the minutes and the hours. By eleven o'clock he was thirsty and would have liked to buy himself a coffee and a bun at the buffet, but he was afraid to leave his seat, to take his eyes off the entrance. But when at last he saw her, just after eleven-twenty, he wondered how he could ever have doubted that he would know her again. He recognized her at once, and with such a physical shock that he instinctively turned away, terrified that she would feel across the concourse the surging power of his presence. It was impossible to believe that she could be here within yards of him, yet not be struck by the shock waves from that moment of recognition. Surely not even love could so cry out for a response.

He saw that she was carrying a small case, but apart from that he was aware of nothing about her, only of her face. The years dropped away and he was once again in that wood-panelled court gazing fixedly at the dock, but seeing her now with a dreadful knowledge which then he hadn't had; that he could never escape her as she could never escape him, that both of them were victims. He moved behind a rack of paperbacks in front of the station bookstall, bending like a man in a spasm of pain, hugging the rucksack to his body as if his wrapping arms could stifle the potent signals of the knife. Then he became aware that a man carrying an official brief-case was glancing at him with concern. He straightened up and made himself look again at the murderess. It was then that he noticed the girl. In that moment of recognition there was nothing about Mary Ducton that was hidden from him. The girl was a blood relation. He knew with absolute certainty, even without noting the imprint of the murderess on this younger, more glowing face, without consciously deducing that the girl was too young to be her sister and unlikely to be her niece, that this was Mary Ducton's daughter.

The girl proffered one ticket at the barrier together with a slip of paper, perhaps some kind of travelling warrant. The murderess stood back, her eyes fixed ahead like an obedient child under escort. He followed them through the gate and on to platform 8. There was a group of about twenty people waiting for the 11.40 train, and the murderess and her daughter walked some fifty yards farther down

116

the platform and stood alone, not speaking. He dared not make himself conspicuous by detaching himself from the main group. Now, with time to spare and nothing to do, they might well notice him. He opened his newspaper and with his back half-turned towards them, listened for the vibrations of the approaching train. The first part of his plan was simple. He would move unhurriedly and unselfconsciously towards them as the engine drew in, and get into the same compartment. It was important to travel together if he were not to risk losing them at King's Cross. He was glad that the modern inter-city trains had long open carriages. The old-fashioned corridor trains with their single compartments would have been a difficulty. Apart from the fear that the murderess might recall his face even after all these years, the prospect of having to sit opposite them, almost knee to knee, to feel their eyes straying to his face, momentarily intrigued, perhaps, by his ugliness, his isolation, was intolerable.

The train drew in on time. Prudently he stood back to let a family with young children enter before him, but the two corn-coloured heads were plainly in sight. They had moved down the compartment and had seated themselves side by side facing the engine. He slipped into a vacant window seat just inside the door, kept his rucksack on the table in front of him, and took refuge again behind his paper. Once he was seated their faces were out of sight, but, over his paper, he kept a watchful eye on the far door in case they should, after all, decide on a different carriage. But the door was blocked with in-coming passengers and they didn't move.

Almost at once he realized that it had been a mistake to take a window seat. Just before the guard blew his whistle, a family of three, a fat, perspiring couple and their moon-faced teenage son, pushed through the door and settled themselves with grunts of satisfaction into the three empty seats. He sifted himself imperceptibly, disagreeably aware of the warm bulk of the woman urging his thighs nearer to the window. As soon as the train got up speed she opened a bulging plastic bag, took out a Thermos flask and three disposable cups and a plastic sandwich box, and began distributing cheese and pickle sandwiches to her husband and son. A powerful reek of vinegar and cheese hung over the table. He had no room to spread his paper, but he folded it small and pretended an interest in the list of births and deaths on the last page. He hoped he wouldn't need to visit the lavatory. The prospect of asking this hulk of a woman to shift herself intimidated him. But worse was the worry that he might be trapped at the end of the journey, that the murderess and her daughter might slip out of their seats and be gone before he could free himself.

He was hardly aware of the passing of time. For the first hour he sat stiffly, half fearing that the woman would hear the thudding of his heart, would sense the excitement that kept him rigid in his seat. For most of the time he stared out of the window at the bleak landscape of the Midlands, the rain-soaked fields and dripping trees, the alien towns with their blackened back-to-back houses, and the villages, like rejected outposts of a deserted civilization, while beside the track the glistening wires rose and fell. After about an hour the rain stopped and the sun came out, hot and bright, drawing from the sodden fields faint puffs of vapour like a crop of thin cotton wool. Once, by a trick of light, the carriage was reflected in the windows, and he saw a row of ghostly travellers borne through the air, sitting immobile as dummies, their faces cavernous and grey as the faces of the dead. Only once was his attention keenly caught. The train stopped momentarily outside Doncaster and in the brief unnatural calm he saw, in the grass verge, tall strong stalks of cow parsley, bearing their delicate white blossoms like a foam. The flowers reminded him of the Methodist Sunday school to which he had been sent every Sunday afternoon, he supposed to get him out of his mother's way. Every August they had held a Sunday school anniversary service, and the children, by tradition, had decorated the church with wild flowers. It was an ugly Victorian building, its ponderous dark stone eclipsing the fragile beauty of the flowers. He saw again an earthenware jar of buttercups wilting against the pew end, and the cow parsley shedding its white dust over his new Sunday-best shoes. He had sat very still, huddled in his seat lest God should notice him, a Crippen sitting among the blessed, distancing himself from what he had no right to share, terrified he might be seeming to claim it. Sunday school had left him with nothing except that, for the rest of his life, at moments of stress and crisis, biblical texts, not always apposite, would slip unbidden into his mind. Remembering those long-drawn-out, anxiety-filled afternoons, it had never seemed to him a fair exchange.

Once during the journey he turned his eyes from the window and saw the girl coming down the compartment. She passed him without glancing at his table and tugged open the door. For the first time he took note of her and wondered how her existence might affect his plans. He wished her no particular harm. She was, he judged, some two to three years younger than Julie would have been. Julie was dead, she was alive. No other comparison between them was important in the face of that irrevocable alienation. But he doubted whether his gentle, timid daughter would have held herself with such assurance, would have surveyed the world with eyes so calmly confident in their own judgement. He took in every detail;

118

the tight corduroy trousers taut over her thighs, the casually-worn jacket, the leather and canvas travelling bag slung over her shoulder, the thick pigtail of hair. The sheen of the corduroy curving over her inner thighs, the front zip which emphasized the flatness of the stomach and pointed to the gently swelling mound beneath it, had evoked in him as she passed a small leap of sexuality, so long dormant that the gentle disturbance released for a brief moment all the forgotten uncertainties and half-shameful excitements of adolescence.

The girl puzzled him. Try as he would he couldn't remember ever having heard of her at the time of the trial. But then, neither he nor Mavis had been interested in the members of that family except for the rapist and the murderess. They alone had existed and the fact of their existence was an abomination which would one day be purged. He wondered what had been happening to the daughter in the intervening years. She looked well-nourished, prosperous. There was nothing of deprivation in that proud carriage, that assured walk. She had presumably kept in touch with her mother since they were here together; but they didn't look intimate. During the time he had observed them they had hardly spoken. Perhaps this journey was no more than a filial duty to be gratefully relinquished when the murderess was safely delivered at her final destination. Her unexplained and unexpected presence was a slight complication, but no more. But as she passed him on her return journey to her seat, balancing two covered plastic mugs and a pork pie, he noticed that there was a small identity tag attached by a narrow strap to the end of her travelling bag. It was just large enough to hold a visiting card, but the name was covered by a curling leather flap. Suddenly it occurred to him that if he could get close enough to her without attracting attention, perhaps in the crush when they were leaving the train, it might be possible gently to bend back the tag and get a sight of the name. The thought excited him. He spent the rest of the journey staring sightlessly out of the window imagining how it might be done.

It was two-fifteen when the train drew into King's Cross, one minute late. As soon as it slowed he stood up and reached for his raincoat and case. The fat woman grudgingly made way for him and he was one of the first out of his seat. He saw that the murderess and her daughter were making for the door closest to them at the other end of the compartment. He edged his way down the carriage, obstructed now by standing passengers reaching for their bags and struggling into their coats. By the time the two women had reached the doorway he was immediately behind them. There was the usual delay as passengers manoeuvred their luggage through the door and

119

clambered down to the platform, and the women patiently waited their turn. Neither of them looked round. It was far easier than he had hoped. He let his rucksack rest for a moment on the floor then bent down and fumbled with his shoe lace. As he rose his eyes were on a level with the dangling tag. It was the work of a second to lift the covering flap with his small cunning hands. The light was poor but it didn't matter. The name wasn't in small print on a visiting card but written by hand in an elegant black script. P. R. Palfrey.

He hoped that the next stage wouldn't be by taxi. It would be too risky to stand in the queue immediately behind them and, even if he did, he was unlikely to hear their directions. In the library books he remembered from his boyhood the hero leapt into the next cab shouting to the driver to follow the one in front. He couldn't see himself doing that, nor did it seem a practicable ruse in the tangle of traffic outside a major London terminus. But to his relief, the girl led the way down the steps to the Underground. This was what he had hoped. He followed about twenty feet behind them, feeling in his pocket for his loose change. There must be no delay at the ticket office. With luck he might get close enough to hear their destination. At worst he would be able to watch the machine from which they got their tickets. But as long as he again travelled with them all would be well. He felt a surge of confidence and excitement. So far it had been easier than he had dared to hope.

But suddenly the entrance tunnel was clamorous with shouting and the clatter of rushing feet. Another train must have disgorged its passengers, and a crowd of youths had hurled themselves down the steps and were shouting and jostling their way past him, forcing him against the wall of the tunnel and momentarily obstructing his view. Desperately he pushed his way forward and saw again the two pale bobbing heads. They passed the entrance to the Northern and Bakerloo lines and, walking on, eventually turned right down the wide steps leading to the concourse of the Metropolitan and Circle lines. The crowd had swollen here and there was a long queue at the ticket office. The girl didn't join it, nor did she attempt to press through the jabbering crowd of travellers at the ticket machines. Instead he saw with horror that she had bought two tickets in advance and that she and the murderess were calmly making their way through the barrier. And the ticket collector was meticulously looking at every ticket. There was no chance of forcing his way through and to try would only draw attention to himself. He almost fought his way to the first machine. His tenpenny piece seemed to stick to his fingers. His hand was trembling as he pushed it home. There was a clatter as the coin, rejected, fell into the waiting receptacle. He pushed it in again, and this time the machine delivered his ticket. But the air was already loud with the clatter of an approaching train, and as he pushed his way through the crowd at the barrier, the noise stopped. He dashed to the westward platform, the one they had taken, just in time to see the doors of the Circle line train close in his face. Apart from two turbaned Indians, and a tramp laid out asleep on a bench, the platform was empty. Even as he looked up, the train moved, the words "Circle Line" disappeared from the indicator and the Hammersmith train was signalled.

2

Only when he reached Liverpool Street was he aware of hunger. He bought himself a coffee and roll before catching the train home. It was nearly four before he put his key in the latch. The silence of the house received him conspiratorially as if it had been watching for his return and was waiting to share his failure or success. Although it was still early, he felt very weary and his legs ached. But this positive tiredness was a new sensation, different in kind from the lassitude which had dragged his homeward footsteps at the end of each working day, and had made the half-mile trudge from the station a small daily tribulation. He made himself a high tea of sausages and baked beans, followed by a jam tart from a packet of four in the refrigerator. He supposed that he was hungry, certainly he was rapacious for the food. The sausages split and burned under the grill and the gas flared under the saucepan of beans. He ate voraciously, yet he hardly tasted the meal, aware only of a physical need that demanded satisfaction. As he made a pot of tea in the small back kitchen, taking down the blue and white teapot with its patterned band of roses which he and Mavis had bought together on their honeymoon, he felt for the first time some affection for the house, and a tinge of regret that he must leave it. This struck him as odd. Neither he nor Mavis had ever been at home in it. They had bought it because it was the sort of house they were used to at a price they could afford, and because they needed to leave Seven Kings with all its memories and 19 Alma Road had been available. In the suburbs you could buy anonymity by moving three stations down the line, by changing your job. He remembered how they had first been shown over it, Mavis passing listlessly

121

from room to room while the estate agent, desperately trying to evoke some response, had extolled its advantages. At the end of the inspection she had said tonelessly: "It'll do. We'll take it." The man must have been amazed at so easy a sale. They had done little to it in the last eight years, some repainting, new paper in the seldom-used front sitting-room, the minimum structural repairs necessary to preserve their small investment in it. Mavis had worked conscientiously, though without interest, but it had always looked clean. Something about it repelled dust and wear as it repelled intimacy, happiness, love. How strange it was that only now was he beginning to feel that he belonged here, that he would leave something of himself behind its prim laurel hedge. The sense of the house's participation in his enterprise grew so strong that he found himself wondering whether he dared leave it, whether the strangers who would unpack their kettles and saucepans in this kitchen would pause in temporary unease and imbibe from the very air some secret knowledge that here murder had been planned. But he knew that he had to go. The quarry was in London, and in London would be run to earth. And he needed to be free, free even of this new sentience between him and the house, free of personal belongings, however meagre, free to begin his search, moving unrecognized and rootless amongst strangers.

And he knew now where he must look. When he had drunk his tea, he opened his map of London and the chart of the Underground and placed them side by side on the table. They had travelled westward on the Circle line. He counted up the stations. St James's Park was about half way, so that for any station beyond that it would have been more sensible to travel in the opposite direction. Victoria was out. They would have taken the Victoria line direct. Similarly, he could eliminate South Kensington and Gloucester Road since both were on the Piccadilly line and could be reached direct from King's Cross. That meant that they had almost certainly got out at one of the eight stations between King's Cross and High Street Kensington. It was possible, of course, that they had alighted at Baker Street or Paddington and changed lines or taken a British Rail train out of London. But the thought didn't worry him. He didn't believe for one moment they were in the country. It was in the vast anonymity of the capital that the hunted felt most secure. London, which asked no questions, kept its secrets, provided in its hundred urban villages the varied needs of ten million people. And the girl was no provincial. Only a Londoner would have stridden with such confidence through the complexities of King's Cross Underground Station. And she had bought the tickets in advance.

That meant, surely, that she had travelled up to York early that morning. No, they were in London all right.

On his larger map he traced the route of the Circle line. Bloomsbury, Marylebone, Bayswater, Kensington. The districts were unfamiliar to him, but he would get to know them. And the day hadn't been unsuccessful after all. He knew now that she had a daughter, and he knew the name of that daughter. She had changed it to Palfrey from Ducton by deed poll, adoption or marriage. But she hadn't, he remembered, been wearing a wedding ring. He had been thwarted by one small piece of ill-luck, the fact that she had troubled to buy the Underground tickets in advance. Unless they were in a hurry, and they hadn't walked as if they were in a hurry, that could only mean that she wanted to spare her mother the possible trauma of being crushed among crowds while she waited at the ticket office. If so, it suggested a concern that he hadn't expected. And if the girl were concerned for the murderess, then they might stay together, at least for a time. That surely increased his chances of finding them. If all else failed, the daughter might yet lead him to the mother. He wrote the names of the eight stations in his diary in his careful copperplate, then stared at them as if they were a conundrum and he could will the letters to move and shuffle and, at last, click into place and spell out the address he sought.

Tomorrow he would move into the next phase of the enterprise. He would make a direct effort to trace the murderess through her daughter. Even if they weren't still together, to know where the daughter lived would be a definite gain. He went into the hall and dragged out the L–R London telephone directory. There was no Palfrey, P. R., listed, but that wasn't particularly significant. If she had been adopted the number would be shown under her father's initials. The first step would be to telephone all the seven Palfreys listed in the London directory. It was an obvious ploy, more sensible than perpetually riding the Circle line or walking the squares of Bloomsbury or Kensington; but he would have to think of a plausible excuse, a reason for ringing those seven strangers which wouldn't sound suspicious. Suppose the girl herself came to the telephone, what was he to say? It was vital that the murderess shouldn't suspect that she was hunted. If he frightened her into flight, into changing her name, he might spend a lifetime in tracing her only to fail at last. He was twenty years older than she was. Death had robbed Mavis of revenge, it might even rob him.

And then, as he sat in the quietness of the kitchen, his hands cradling the cup of tea, the idea came to him. It fell into his mind like a minor act of creativity, as if it had always existed in its simplicity, its rightness, waiting the moment until it could slip into

123

his mind. The more he examined it, the more faultless it seemed. He was surprised that he hadn't thought of it earlier. He went to bed impatient for the morning.

3

Her mother walked into the room and stood still. She seemed afraid to speak, only her eyes moved. The room seemed to have shrunk since Philippa left it. The newly stained wooden boards, the faded rugs, the unmatched chairs, did they look too makeshift, too cheap a compromise? Had she glorified them in her own eyes?

"You like it?" She was irritated to hear the note of anxiety in her voice. She had done her best with the place. Presumably it was better than a shared room in a hostel. And it was only for two months.

"Very much." Her mother smiled, a different smile from the one with which she had greeted Philippa that morning. This time it reached her eyes.

"It's lovely. I didn't expect that it would be as attractive as this. You were clever to find it. And you must have worked hard."

Her voice shook, and Philippa saw that her eyes were too bright. And she looked very tired. The journey, the pressure of people must have been a strain. Terrified that the unshed tears would fall, she said quickly:

"I enjoyed myself. It was fun rummaging around the market. The greengrocer, George, helped me up with some of my finds. The picture is the only thing I've got from Caldecote Terrace, a Henry Walton. He was an eighteenth-century painter. Some of his work is too sentimental for my taste—almost Victorian—but I like that picture. I thought that it would look good in that light and against the wallpaper. But you don't have to keep it there."

"I should like it to stay, unless you want it in your room. Where are you?"

"Here, next to the kitchen. I've got the quietest room and the better view. You've got the sun but more noise. We can change if you'd rather."

They went into the back room. Her mother walked to the window and stared out over the patch of yard and the narrow strips of cluttered gardens. After a few minutes she turned and looked round the room.

"It doesn't seem fair for me to have the larger room. We could spin a coin."

"But I've had the larger room for the last ten years. It's your turn now."

She wanted to ask: "Do you think you can be happy here?" But the question seemed a presumption with its implication that she —Philippa—had happiness within her gift. It was new to her, this carefulness with words, this sensitivity to their power to wound. It should have caused a constraint between them, but it didn't. She said:

"Come and see the kitchen. I've put the television there. We can carry our easy chairs in there if we want to watch."

Hilda had said, resentfully:

"You'll have to hire a colour telly. She'll have got used to that in prison. Lifers get these extra privileges. She won't be satisfied with black-and-white."

They went back together into the front room. Philippa said:

"I thought we might take about ten days' holiday before we start thinking of a job. We could look at London, or have some days in the country if you prefer."

"I'd like both. Only there's one thing. I don't think I'll be much good going about on my own for a week or so. At least not in crowds."

"You don't have to be on your own."

"And could we buy some clothes first? I've only got what I'm wearing and one pair of pyjamas. I thought I could spend about fifty pounds of my two hundred. Then I could get rid of these things in the case. I don't want anything here which I had in prison."

"That'll be fun. I like buying clothes. The sales are still on in Knightsbridge and we might get something good quite cheaply. We can get rid of what you've got in Mell Street market."

They could get rid of the case there too, although Philippa doubted whether any of the stallkeepers would give more than a few pence for it. Better still, they could chuck it in the canal. It was a cheap fibre case, already scruffy at the corners. Her mother placed it on the floor, then, kneeling, opened it. She took out a pair of white cotton pyjamas and placed them on the bed. The only other objects in the case were a draw-string toilet bag and a manilla envelope. She handed it to Philippa, looking up into her face.

"This is the account I wrote in prison of what happened to Julia Scase. Don't read it now, wait a day or two. And I don't want to know when you've read it. While we're living together I know that

125

you've a right to ask questions about the crime, about me, about your past. But I'd rather that you didn't. Not yet, anyway."

Philippa took the envelope. Maurice had said:

"Lifers, murderers, have to justify themselves. I'm not talking about political murderers, terrorists—they don't have to waste mental energy fabricating excuses. They get their justification like their political philosophy, second-hand and ready made. I'm talking about the ordinary lifer, and most of them are ordinary. Murder is the one crime for which there can't be any reparation for the victim. We're all conditioned to regard it with particular abhorrence. So murderers, unless they're psychopaths, have to come to terms with what they've done. Some of them persist in claiming that they're innocent, wrongly convicted. Some probably believe it."

She had said:

"Some may be innocent."

"Of course. That's the irrefutable argument against capital punishment. A fair number take refuge in religious confession, officially recognized contrition if you like. There's a beautiful simplicity in claiming that you're assured of God's forgiveness, it puts your fellow humans at a moral disadvantage if they obstinately persist in unforgiveness. And of course there are plenty of eminent people happy to assist you in your emotional wallowings. I'd probably opt myself for conversion in the circumstances. Then there are the excuses based on mental instability, provocation, deprived background, drunkenness, the common stuff of any defending counsel's plea in mitigation. A few of the more robust spirits probably claim justifiable homicide, the victim got no more than he deserved. Your mother has survived nine years in prison on the one charge that the other women there can't ever forgive. That means she's tough. She's probably intelligent. Whatever story she decides to tell you will be plausible and, once she's met you, I've no doubt it will be tailored to what she decides are your particular psychological requirements."

"Nothing she tells me can alter the fact that she's my mother."

And he had said:

"So long as you remember that that is probably the least important fact about her."

She put Maurice out of her mind. There was no hurry about questions. She could begin to learn who she was without an inquisition. After all, they were to have two months together. She said:

"I haven't any rights. We're here together because that's what we both want. It suits us both. You're not demanding to know what my life has been during the last ten years."

She added, with deliberate lightness:

126

"There are no obligations except those which sharing a flat necessarily implies—cleaning the bath after use, doing one's share of washing-up."

Her mother smiled.

"From that point of view I'll probably suit. Otherwise I think you could have chosen more wisely."

But there was no question of choice. While her mother went to wash Philippa took the envelope into her bedroom and shut it in her bedside drawer. She had been asked to wait before reading it. She would wait, but not for long. She felt triumphant, almost exultant. She thought: "You're here because you're my mother. Nothing in life or death can alter that. It's the only thing about myself I can be sure of. In your uterus I grew. It was your muscles that forced me into the world, your blood which first bathed me, and it was on your belly where I first took my rest." Her mother liked the room, was glad to be with her. It was going to be a success. She wouldn't have to return to Maurice and confess failure. He would never be able to say "I told you so."

4

The only post next morning was a letter from the house agent to say that the young couple had obtained their mortgage and that contracts were being drawn up. He read its turgid professional jargon without surprise or particular gratification. The house had to go. Apart from the fact that he needed more money than he had been able to save from a modest salary, he couldn't imagine himself returning to it after the murder. There was nothing in the house that he wanted, not even a photograph of Julie. Mavis had destroyed them all after her death. He would take with him enough clothes to fill one suitcase. The rest of his belongings and the furniture he would sell through one of those firms which advertised that they cleared houses. He supposed that they were called in after the deaths of the old and lonely to dispose of the detritus of unregarded lives and to save the executors trouble. It pleased him to think of moving thus unencumbered into his unknown future, so much alone that if he fell under a bus there would be no one in the world with any responsibility for him, no one who need assume the obligations of

127

grief. He would lie, shrouded and docketed in the public mortuary while the police searched for a next of kin, someone to authorize the disposal of this embarrassingly redundant corpse. To move into this nothingness seemed to him a promise of an intoxicating and limitless freedom. As he boiled his breakfast egg and stirred powdered coffee into his cup of hot milk, it occurred to him that he had become more interesting to himself since he had started out on his enterprise. Before Mavis's death he had been like a man treadmilled on a moving staircase, walking but not advancing, while on each side of him bright images of a synthetic world, blown-up photographs, montages of life moved steadily in the opposite direction. As they passed he was programmed to perform certain actions. At daybreak he would get up and dress. At half-past seven he ate breakfast. At eight o'clock he set out to work. At eight-twelve he caught his train. At midday he ate his sandwiches at his desk. Home again in the evening, he would eat his supper in the kitchen with Mavis, then sit watching television while she knitted. Their evenings had been dominated by the television programmes. For some of her favourites through those bleak years, 'Upstairs Downstairs', 'Dixon of Dock Green', 'The Forsyte Saga', she had even taken some trouble with her appearance. She no longer changed to please him or to go out with him, but she put on a different dress and even applied make-up for these bright ephemeral images. On those evenings they would have supper on a tray. It hadn't been an unhappy life. He hadn't felt any emotion as positive as unhappiness. But now, on the shoulders of the dead, he had hoisted himself into a different air, and although it stung his nostrils, at least it gave him the illusion of living.

Sitting in the train as it flashed through the dull, familiar stations of the eastern suburbs, his rucksack on his shoulder, he reflected that it was an odd and interesting quirk of his new character that he should need to make this particular journey at all. His plan stood an equal chance of success if he stayed at home and rang the Palfrey numbers from the anonymity of his front hall. The lie he was proposing to tell wouldn't be more believable because it would be supported by contrived verisimilitude, yet he knew that every detail would have to be right if he were to succeed. No one was going to challenge him, no one would check up on his story, or demand confirmation, yet he was compelled to act, as if by meticulous attention to every small part he could somehow confer the authority of truth on the whole.

From Liverpool Street he took the Central line to Tottenham Court Road and walked down Charing Cross Road. He had decided that Foyle's Bookshop would be the best for his purpose because it was the largest. The book he chose had to be valuable enough to be worth taking trouble about, but not so valuable that an honest finder would naturally take it to a police station. Non-fiction, he reasoned, would be more appropriate than fiction, and after some thought he selected from the shelves Pevsner's first volume on the buildings of London. The girl at the cash desk seemed hardly to look at him as she gave him his change.

Then he walked to Shaftesbury Avenue and took a number 14 bus to Piccadilly Circus. He gave the conductor a pound note for his fare since he knew he would need plenty of small change. At Piccadilly he shut himself up in one of the telephone booths. In the address pages of his pocket diary he wrote in pencil the initials and telephone numbers of all the subscribers listed under the name Palfrey, grateful that the girl had such an uncommon name. None of the Palfreys were shown as "Miss" but that didn't surprise him. He had read somewhere that to advertise that you were a woman was to invite obscene telephone calls. When the eight numbers had been listed he printed in pencil the words "Miss P. Palfrey" on the book-shop bag. No one would ever see it, yet he took care to form the letters in large uneven strokes, as different as possible from his own hand. Then, before raising the receiver, he rehearsed mentally the words he was to say:

"Excuse me for troubling you, but my name is Yelland. I've found a book left on a bench in St James's Park. It was bought at Foyles and it's got the name 'Miss P. Palfrey' written on the bag. I thought it was worth telephoning to try and trace the owner."

The first call was answered by a gruff male voice which told him peremptorily that there was no Miss Palfrey at that address. "Drop it in at a police station," it commanded, and promptly rang off. He knew that this first attempt hadn't been altogether successful; even to his own ears his voice had sounded false and strained. Perhaps the listener had thought that he was a new breed of con man or was hoping for a reward. He put a cross against the name and dialled the second number.

He was almost relieved when there was no reply. He put a query against the number and dialled again.

The third call was answered by a woman, presumably a maid or an au pair, who spoke in a strong foreign accent and told him that "Madam is shopping at 'arrods." He explained that he wanted a Miss Palfrey, not Mrs Palfrey, only to be told again: "Madam is not at 'ome. She is at 'arrods. Please to ring later." He put a query against this number too, although he had little doubt that it wasn't the one he was seeking.

The next number rang for twenty seconds, and he had almost

I   129

given up when the receiver was at last lifted, and he heard a harassed female voice raised to make itself heard against the shrieking of a young child. The sound was as piercingly sustained as a train's whistle. Obviously she was holding the child in her arms. He sensed her impatience with his story, and when he was half way through she broke in to say briefly that her daughter was only six and wasn't yet buying books, let alone leaving them on park benches. "Nice of you to bother, though," she added, and hung up.

He dialled the next number. The call was frustrating. It was answered by yet another female voice, but this had the high monotonous pitch and the quaver of extreme old age. It took a long time before she comprehended his message, then he had to hang on, putting in extra coins, while she held a long conversation with her sister who was called Edith and who was presumably deaf since the conversation was carried on in shouts. Edith disclaimed any knowledge of the book, but her sister was reluctant to ring off, feeling, apparently, that she now had some personal responsibility in the matter.

His stock of small change was getting low. The next name was listed as Palfrey, M. S. The address was 68 Caldecote Terrace, S.W.1. Once again a woman answered. The voice sounded tentative, apprehensive even. She repeated the number carefully as if it were unfamiliar. He said his piece and almost at once he knew that this was it. He ended:

"Perhaps I could have a word with Miss Palfrey?"

"She isn't here. I mean, my daughter isn't at home at present."

This time there could be no doubt of it. The voice held the breathy rising cadence of fear. He felt a surge of confidence, almost of exhilaration. He said:

"If you could give me her address, I could write or telephone."

"Oh, I couldn't do that! And they're not on the phone. But I'll tell her about the book if I see her. Only I don't think I shall be seeing her. What did you say it was called?"

He repeated the title.

"It sounds like Philippa. I mean, she does like books about buildings. Perhaps you could post it here and I'll send it on. Only there's the postage. I know she would send the money to you if you enclosed your address. But then it may not belong to her."

There was a silence. After a few seconds he said:

"Perhaps I'd better return it to Foyle's. They may know who it belongs to. And perhaps your daughter will think to enquire there first."

"Oh yes, yes! That would be best. If Philippa telephones or calls in I'll tell her what you've done. Thank you for taking so much trouble. I think she's probably showing her—her friend—round London. She may need the book. I'll send her a postcard and tell her about your call."

Relief made her sound suddenly effusive. He replaced the receiver and stood for a moment with his hand pressed down on it. The feel of the instrument, warm and sticky, conveyed an almost physical certainty. He knew now where her daughter lived. He knew that she was adopted. He knew that they were still together since the woman had used the plural tense. He knew what the girl's name was. Philippa Palfrey. Philippa R. Palfrey. Somehow the fact of knowing the name seemed more significant than anything he had learned so far.

5

His map showed him that Caldecote Terrace lay on the fringes of Pimlico, south-east of Victoria and Ecclestone Bridge, and he walked there from Victoria Underground down a side road flanking the main station. In distance it wasn't far from his old office, but it was the other side of the river and could have been a different city. It was a cul-de-sac of converted but unspoilt late eighteenth-century terraced houses which lay off the wider and busier Caldecote Road. He walked into it resolutely, but uneasily aware that this was not a street in which he could safely loiter, that the tall, immaculately curtained windows might conceal watching eyes. He felt like an interloper entering a private precinct of orderliness, culture and comfortable prosperity. He had never lived in such a street and knew no one who did; yet he indulged his preconceptions of how such people lived. They would affect to despise the smartness of Belgravia; would enthuse about the advantages of a socially mixed society, even if the mixing didn't actually extend to sending their children to local schools; would patronize as a duty the small shopkeepers in Caldecote Road, particularly the dairy and the delicatessen; and would haul off their friends to drink at the weekend in the saloon bar of the local pub where they would be heartily affable to the barman and resolutely matey to the other customers.

He made himself walk down one side of the street and then up the other. The sense of being a trespasser was so strong that he felt he walked in an aura of guilt. But no one challenged him, no front door opened, the curtains didn't move. The street struck him as being peculiarly different from others; then he realized that it was because no cars were parked at the kerb and there were no residents' parking signs. So these desirable homes must have garages at the rear where once the mews had stabled horses. Momentarily the thought depressed him. It would be impossible to watch two exits to number 68, and if Mrs Palfrey customarily drove rather than walked or took public transport, he didn't see how he would be able to tail her. He hadn't thought of a car. But optimism reasserted itself. Single-mindedness, he had discovered, brought with it stamina and self-assurance; it also brought luck. He was here. It was right that he should be here. He knew where the girl lived and where her family lived. Sooner or later she or they would lead him to Mary Ducton.

As he gained confidence in his right to be walking down the terrace he observed the houses more closely. The street had an impressive uniformity; the houses were identical except for variations in the patterns of the fanlights and in the wrought-iron tracery of the first-floor balconies. The front railings guarding the basements were spiked and ornamented at the ends with pineapples. The doors, flanked with columns, were thoroughly intimidating, the brass letter-boxes and knockers gleamed. Many of the houses were festive with window boxes; geraniums flared in discordant pinks and reds and trails of variegated ivy curled against the stone façades.

He reached the end of the terrace and crossed the road to the even-number houses. Number 68 was at the top end of the street. It was one of the few houses without window boxes or tubs before the door, uncompromising in its elegance. The door was painted black. The basement kitchen was brightly lit. He walked slowly past, glancing down, and saw that it was occupied. A woman was sitting at the table eating her lunch. There was a tray in front of her with a plate of scrambled eggs, and she was glancing as she ate at the flickering image of a black-and-white television set. So the Palfreys had a maid. He wasn't surprised to see her. He would have expected that girl in the train to have come from a home where they kept a maid, to have lived in just such a house as this, that golden girl who had walked past him down the swaying carriage of the train with the arrogant sexuality which spoke to him, to all the old, the poor, the unattractive: "Look at me, but don't touch. I'm not for you."

He returned to Caldecote Road, his mind still occupied with the problem of keeping a watch on the Palfreys' house. The road was in marked contrast to the terrace, a disorderly muddle of shops, cafés, pubs and the occasional office, typical of an inner London commercial street from which any glory had long departed. It was a bus route, and small disconsolate groups of shoppers, laden with their baskets and trolleys, waited at the stops on either side of the road, while the number of cars and lorries adding to the congestion suggested that this was a popular route to the Lambeth and Vauxhall bridges. Here, if not in Caldecote Terrace, he could loiter in safety.

Then he noticed the two hotels. They were on the opposite side of the road, facing down the terrace, two large stuccoed Victorian houses which had survived change, war, decay and demolition and now stood alone, shabby, the stucco peeling, but still grandiosely intact between a car salesroom and the vulgarly ostentatious fascia of a supermarket. From any of the front upper windows he would be able to train his binoculars on the door of number 68; here he would be able to sit in comfort to watch and wait. Here he would have time to think and plan his strategy, freed from the fear of discovery, the tedium and exhaustion of perpetually loitering in the street.

The names might have been chosen to emphasize that neither hotel had any connection with the business next door. The left-hand one was called Hotel Casablanca, its neighbour the Windermere Hotel. The first, less reassuringly named, looked the cleaner and more prosperous and would, he judged, give a slightly better view down Caldecote Terrace. The outer door was open and he stepped into a porch with a framed Underground map on the left wall and a mirror advertising ale on the right. He pushed through an inner door, patterned with overblown facsimiles of credit cards, and was met by the concentrated smell of food, cigarettes and furniture polish. There was no one on duty and the hall was empty except for a young woman seated at a small telephone switchboard behind the reception desk. A brown smooth-haired bitch was sleeping at her feet, its slack pimpled belly flopped over the chequered tiles, its paws gently curving. It took no interest in Scase's arrival except to peer at him briefly through a slitted eye before closing it again and nudging its head closer to the girl's chair. A white guide-dog harness was slung on a hook on the side of the switchboard. She turned as soon as she heard the swing of the inner door, and her sightless eyes, blinking rapidly, seemed to search the air above his head. In one socket the eyeball, retracted and upward-turned, was only half-visible under the lid. The other eye was covered with a milky film. She was slight with a gentle eager face, her straight light brown hair drawn back and fastened behind her ears by two circular blue slides. He wondered irrelevantly why she had chosen blue, how such a decision could be made, what it must mean to be deprived of the petty vanities of choice. He said:

133

"I'm looking for a room. Do you know if there are any vacancies?"

She smiled, but in the absence of any kindling light or warmth from the dead eyes the undirected smile seemed fatuous, meaningless. She said:

"Mr Mario will be here in a moment, if you will ring the bell, please."

He had seen the push-button bell on the counter, but hadn't liked to press it since she might have thought that he was impatient for a service which she was powerless to give. It gave out a strident ring. A minute later a short swarthy man in a white jacket appeared through the door to the basement stairs. Scase said:

"I wondered if you'd got a vacant room, one at the front. I don't like being at the back. I've retired and I'm selling my house in the suburbs and looking for a flat in this area."

This explanation was received with total uninterest. Presumably, if he had explained that he was an IRA terrorist looking for a safe hideout there might have been some response. Mario ducked under the counter hatch and flipped open a grease-stained register. After a brief pretence at consulting it, he said in a voice which was almost entirely Cockney:

"There's a top front single. Ten pounds a night, bed and breakfast, payment in advance. Dinner's extra. We don't do lunches."

"I'll have to go home for my things."

He had read somewhere that hotels were suspicious of guests who arrived without luggage. He said:

"Could I take it from tomorrow?"

"It'll be gone by then. This is the busy season, see? You're lucky to get a vacancy."

"Could I see it, please?"

The request was obviously regarded by Mario as eccentric, but he took a key from the board and pressed the lift button. They were slowly carried up together in cranking, claustrophobic proximity to the top floor. He unlocked the door, then left abruptly, saying, "See you downstairs at the desk, then."

As soon as the door closed behind him, Scase went over to the window. He saw with relief that the room was ideal for his purpose. The view from a lower floor would have been constantly obstructed by buses and lorries; here at this meanly proportioned window under the eaves he was high enough to look down unimpeded over the traffic into Caldecote Terrace. Mario had taken the key away with him but there was a bolt on the door. He shot it, then took the binoculars from his rucksack. The door of number 68 trembled, opaque as if seen through a heat haze. He steadied his hands, adjusted the focus and the image leaped at him, gleaming, sharp

134

edged and so close that he felt that he could stretch out his hands and stroke the glistening paintwork. The binoculars ranged over the façade of the house from window to window, each secretive behind the white veil of its drawn curtains. On the balcony there was a twist of paper, blown up, perhaps, from the street. He wondered how long it would lie there before someone found it and swept it away, that single flaw on the house's perfection.

He put away the binoculars and explored the room. He supposed that he ought not to linger too long; it might seem suspicious. Then he told himself that Mario was unlikely to worry. What, after all, was there to steal or damage in this bleak, impersonal, comfortless cell? He didn't wonder that Mario had left him so promptly, avoiding explanation and excuses.

The floor was covered with a scrappy fawn carpet on which all the previous occupants seemed to have deposited their mark; a spatter of tea or coffee by the bed, more-sinister-looking stains under the wash-basin. In one corner a larger area of dampness mirrored a similar stain on the ceiling where the roof must have leaked. The bed had a plain wooden headboard, presumably so that the occupant shouldn't be tempted to strangle himself with his tie from the bedrail. A large wardrobe stood unsteadily against one wall, its door swinging ajar. An over-sized dressing-table in veneered walnut with a spotted mirror occupied the darkest corner. There were some compensations. The bed, when he sat on it, was comfortable enough; a glance showed that the sheets, although crumpled, were clean. He turned on the hot tap and after some minutes of gurgling and erratic flow the water spurted hot. These were small bonuses. He was glad of them but they weren't important. He would have slept as well on a hard bed and been happy to wash in cold water. The room had all that he asked, the view from the window.

And then he noticed the bedside locker. It was a sturdy oblong box in polished oak with one shelf and a cupboard underneath and with a wooden roller at one side for a towel. He recognized it. He had seen one before. It was an old hospital locker, probably part of a job lot, sold off by some hospital management committee when the wards were upgraded. What could more appropriately find a place in this room for human rejects, furnished with rejects? When he opened the cupboard the smell of disinfectant rose up strongly, working like a catalyst on memory. His mother, dying at last and knowing that she was dying, twisting her head restlessly on the pillow, the dyed hair, that last vanity, grey at the roots, the sinews of her wasted neck stretched like cords, her fingers sharp as claws scraping the coverlet. He heard again her querulous voice:

135

"I've had no bloody luck in my life, by God I haven't. No bloody luck at all."

He had tried to make some gesture of comfort by straightening the pillow, but, impatiently, she had pushed his hand aside. He had known that he was part of the bad luck, that even on her deathbed nothing he did or said could please her. What, he wondered, would she think if she could see him here now, could know why he was here. He could almost hear her scorn.

"Murder! You? You wouldn't have the guts. Don't make me laugh."

He left the room, closing the door carefully and quietly behind him as if her wasted body, uncomforted, lay there on the bed. He wished that the hotel had provided a different type of bedside locker. But otherwise the room would do very well indeed.

6

Philippa had always thought that if one were forced to share a flat it would be easier with a stranger than with a friend. And this stranger was so orderly, so quiet, so undemanding; was accommodating without being subservient, was capable about the flat without being obsessional. It was extraordinary how easily they established their shared routine. Philippa awoke now to sounds and smells that quickly became so familiar that it was difficult to believe that they were new. Her day began with the soft rustle of her mother's dressing-gown, with a cup of tea silently placed on her bedside table. Maurice had occasionally brought up her morning tea at Caldecote Terrace. But that was in another country and, besides, that wench was dead. She prepared their breakfast of cereal and boiled egg while her mother cleaned the flat, and then they sat together over their coffee, map spread, planning each day's excursions. It was like showing London to a foreign visitor, but one from a different culture, even a different dimension of time; an intelligent, interested tourist whose eyes surveyed the sights presented for her edification with pleasure, sometimes with delight, but who seemed to be looking beyond them, attempting to reconcile each new experience with an alien, half-remembered world. She was a tourist who was wary of the natives; anxious not to draw attention to herself by any solecism of taste;

sometimes confused about the currency, mixing the tenpenny and fifty-pence piece; momentarily disconcerted by space and distance.

Watching her, Philippa thought: she's like a woman who suffers simultaneously from claustrophobia and agoraphobia. And she was a visitor whose native country must be thinly populated since she was so frightened of crowds. London was packed with tourists, and although they set out early and avoided the most popular tourist haunts, it was impossible to avoid the crush of bodies at bus stops and tube-station platforms, in shops and subways. Either they lived as hermits, or they contributed to and endured the hot, chattering, polluting pressure of humanity, breathed air which, on the warmer airless days, seemed to have been exhaled from a million lungs.

She discovered that her mother liked and had an instinctive appreciation of pictures; it was a discovery, too, for her mother. It pleased her to believe that her own pleasure in painting was inherited, enhanced by, but not the result of Maurice's careful tutelage. They became almost obsessive tourists during their first week together, setting out early with a packed lunch to be eaten on park seats, on river steamers, on the top deck of a bus, in the secret squares and gardens of the city.

She thought that she knew the exact moment when her mother had voluntarily taken upon herself the burden of happiness. It was the evening of their third day together when they threw the things she had brought with her from Melcombe Grange into the Grand Union Canal. In the morning they had taken a bus to Knightsbridge and had fought their way into one of the sales. Watching her mother's face as the horde of bodies pressed upon them, Philippa surprised in herself an emotion too close to sadism to be comfortable. They could have shopped perfectly well in Marks and Spencer in Edgware Road, getting there at nine-thirty before the crowd of tourists arrived. Had it been entirely because of a wish to see her mother in expensive clothes that she had led them to this mêlée? Hadn't it been in part deliberate, a test of her mother's courage, perhaps even the half-shameful pleasure of observing with detached interest the physical manifestations of pain and endurance? At the worst moment, the crush at the foot of the escalator, looking at her mother's face, she had been suddenly afraid that she was going to faint. She had taken her mother by the elbow and urged her forward; but she hadn't held her hand. Not once, not even in that bleak sitting-room at Melcombe Grange, had there been a touching of each other's fingers, a meeting of flesh.

But she had been pleased with their bargains; a pair of fawn linen trousers, a jacket to match in fine wool, two cotton shirts. Trying them on again once they were home, her mother had turned to her

137

with a curious look, half rueful, half resigned, which seemed to ask: "Is this what you want? Is this how you see me? I'm attractive, intelligent, still young. I have to live the rest of my life without a husband, without a lover. So what are these clothes for? What am I for?"

Afterwards she had sat on the bed and watched while her mother packed her case. Everything that she had brought with her from prison went in; the suit in which she had travelled to London, her tights, her underclothes, her shoulder bag, even her toilet articles and pyjamas. It was an extravagance thus to relinquish even the small necessities of living, all of which would have to be replaced; but Philippa didn't check her. It was an extravagance necessary to both of them.

They set out for the canal half an hour before the tow-path was due to be closed to the public, and walked in silence, her mother carrying the case, until they reached an unfrequented stretch of the path overshadowed by trees. It was a warm, heavy evening of low cloud. The canal, rich and sluggish as treacle, slipped undisturbed under the low bridges and seeped into the moist fringes of the bank. A crowd of midges danced above the water, and single leaves, dark green, still glossy with the patina of high summer, floated slowly past on the sluggish stream. The air was rich with a rank river smell overlaid with loamy earth and spiced with the drifting scent of lawn cuttings and roses from the high gardens above the canal. The birds were silent now, except for the occasional distant cry, plaintive and alien, from the zoo aviary.

Still without speaking, Philippa took the case from her mother and hurled it into the middle of the stream. She had first glanced each way to make sure that the tow-path was empty, but even so the splash as the case hit the water sounded so like a falling body that they simultaneously glanced at each other, frightened that someone from the road must have heard. But there were no calling voices, no running footsteps. The case rose slowly, slid along the greasy surface of the water, then reared itself like a sinking ship, toppled and was gone. The circle of ripples died.

She heard her mother give a little sigh. Her face, stained by the green shadows, was extraordinarily peaceful. She looked like a woman in a moment of mystical exultation, even of religious ecstasy. Philippa felt an almost physical relief, as if she had flung away something of herself, of her past, not the past which she knew and recognized, but the formless weight of unremembered years, of childhood miseries which were not less acute because they lurked beyond the frontier of memory. They were gone now, gone for ever, sinking slowly into the mud. She needn't bother any more to try to recall them, nor fear that they might leap out of her subconscious to confuse and terrorize her. She wondered what her mother was thinking, she whose past, seared on so many memories, documented between the buff covers of official files, could not so easily be flung away. They stood in silence at the water's edge. Then the spell broke. Her mother turned to her. Her face relaxed into the smile of a woman released from pain into peace. It was almost a grin of pleasure. But all she said was:

"That's done. Let's go home."

7

That night she decided that she had waited long enough; it was time to read her mother's account of the murder. But now that the moment had come she found herself reluctant to take the manuscript from her drawer. Almost she wished that her mother hadn't handed it to her, that she could have been spared this new moment of decision. She wished it read; yet dreaded to read it. There was nothing to prevent her from destroying it, but that was unthinkable. It was here; she had to know what it said. She asked herself what was holding her back. Her mother had told her the bare facts on that first visit to Melcombe Grange. Nothing in that waiting foolscap envelope could alter those facts, nothing could extenuate or excuse them.

The night was warm and she lay rigidly under a single blanket staring at the pale haze of the open window. Her mother's window must be open too. She could hear the faint rumble of traffic along Lisson Grove and the occasional shouts and laughter of revellers outside the Blind Beggar. Through her own window there wafted a warm summer smell of flowers and earth as if there lay outside all the richness of a country garden.

There was no sound from her mother's room but she waited to put on her bedside light until the last shouts from the pubs had died away and the street was finally quiet. It seemed to her important that she shouldn't begin reading until she could be sure that her mother was asleep. Then she switched on the lamp and slowly drew the envelope from the drawer. The manuscript was written in her mother's firm, upright, but rather difficult hand on heavy, closely lined paper with a red margin. Her mother had written only on alternate lines. The careful handwriting, the official-looking, very clean paper and the red margin gave the manuscript the look of an affidavit or of an examination script. It was written in the third person:

After she had been in Holloway for five years a new prisoner, a woman who had run a prostitution and extortion racket, standing beside her at the library shelf and looking at her with slant-eyed malice, had whispered:

"You're one of the Ductons, aren't you? I read about you in a book I got from the public library: *Fifty Years of Murder 1920–1970*. It was a kind of encyclopaedia of murder, the most notorious cases. You were under D in the Child Killer section. The Ductons."

It was then that she realized that she wasn't a person any more. She was a Ducton, categorized by crime, partner in an unholy alliance, indissolubly linked by infamy. But she was surprised that the compiler had thought them worth including. They hadn't seemed notorious at the time, only a commonplace pair of bunglers, putting up a particularly poor fight in a trial which hadn't attracted much publicity, hadn't been able to compete with the suicide of a pop star or the sexual indiscretions of a minister of the Crown. The author must have had to scrape the barrel to pad out his chapter on child-killers. She could guess what he had written under their entry. She herself had browsed through just such an encyclopaedia of death.

"Martin and Mary Ducton, who were convicted in May 1969 of the murder of twelve-year-old Julia Mavis Scase both came from respectable, upper-working-class parents. Ducton was a clerk at the time of the murder, and his wife worked as a hospital medical records clerk. She was studying in her spare time for an external university degree and had some pretensions to culture. She is generally considered to have played the leading part in the child's death."

She had other pretensions too, to happiness, to achievement, to a different life for them both. And it was true that she took the lead. She always took the lead, even in their joint destruction.

After that meeting she decided to write the truth about the crime, except that the truth was as shifting as her feelings, as unreliable as memory. It was like a butterfly. You could catch it and kill it and pin it down on a board with every delicate detail, every nuance of colour displayed. But then it wasn't a butterfly any more. She thought that the imagery was pretentious; but then she had pretensions.

At the trial she had sworn to tell the truth, the whole truth and nothing but the truth. She had nearly added "So help me God" but that wasn't written on the card. Only in fiction, apparently, did witnesses speak those words. There had been a little pile of holy books on the ledge of the box. The clerk, who was gowned like a verger, had handed her the Bible. She wondered what would happen if he gave her the wrong one, the Koran perhaps. Would she have to give her evidence all over again? The Bible was black and she took it with distaste because it was contaminated with the sweat of murderers' hands and she knew that they hadn't bothered to disinfect it. That was almost all she remembered of the trial. These facts are the truth.

She remembered coming home a little later that evening because the gynaecological clinic at the hospital where she worked had been busier than usual and she wasn't free until after six. It was very cold even for January. A thin fog writhed round the street lamps and crept into the front gardens truncating the trees so that they seemed to move uprooted in majestic inconsequence, surpliced in white mist. As soon as she opened the front door she heard the child crying. It was a high desolate wailing, not loud but continuous and piercing. At first she thought that it was a cat. But that was ridiculous. She was the last woman to mistake the cry of a child.

And then she saw her husband. He was standing half way up the stairs looking down at her. She could remember everything about that moment, the thin wailing of the child, the warm familiar smell of the hall, the patterned wallpaper and the break at the join where she hadn't managed to match it accurately, her husband's eyes. She remembered most his look of shame. There had been terror there, too, and a desperate appeal. But what she remembered was the shame. She could never afterwards remember what they said. Perhaps they didn't speak. It wasn't, after all, necessary. She knew.

There is no rehearsal for a murder trial. You have to get it right first time. There are no explanations, only deceptively innocent questions to which the most dangerous response can be the truth. She could only recall one question to her in the witness box from the prosecuting counsel and her reply to that had been fatal.

"And what had you in mind when you went upstairs to the child?"

She supposed that she could have said: "I wanted to see that she was all right. I wanted to tell her that I was there and that I'd take her home. I wanted to comfort her." None of the jury would have believed her, but some of them might have wished to believe her. Instead she told them the truth.

"I had to stop her crying."

Childhood is the one prison from which there's no escape, the one sentence from which there's no appeal. We all serve our time. She was eleven when she realized the truth, that her father didn't beat her and her brother because he was drunk; he got drunk because he enjoyed beating them and that was how he found the courage to do it. When he came home at night her brother would begin crying even before they heard his heavy feet on the stairs and she would slide into bed with him trying to stifle the noise in her arms, hearing the lurching feet, her mother's expostulatory whine. She learned at the age of eleven that there was no hope, only endurance. She endured. But for the rest of her life she couldn't bear to hear a child crying.

Murderers often excuse themselves by claiming that they can't remember exactly what happened. Perhaps it's true. Perhaps the mind mercifully erases what it can't bear to recall. But she could remember so much horror. Why then should this particular moment be a blank? She must have tried to shake the child into silence. She must have lost her temper with this wailing stupid girl who hadn't, after all, been seriously hurt, who surely had been warned that she shouldn't go with strange men, who hadn't even the sense to stop crying and get out of the house and keep quiet. At the trial the pathologist described the post mortem findings. Death had been by throttling; the neck was bruised with the marks of human hands. They must have been her hands. Who else's could they have been? But she couldn't remember touching the child, nor could she remember the moment when what she was shaking was no longer a child.

After that, memory was like a film rolling on with only a few moments when the picture was lost or no longer in focus. Her husband was in the kitchen. She saw that there were two cups and the teapot and milk jug on the kitchen table. For one moment she had a ridiculous thought, that he was restoring them with tea. She said:

"I've killed her. We must get rid of the body."

He accepted the brutal statement as if he already knew, as if she was telling him the most commonplace of facts. Perhaps he was so petrified by horror that no new horror could touch him.

He whispered:

"But her parents. We mustn't hide her. We can't let them go on hoping, wondering, praying that she's all right."

"They won't be left hoping for long. We won't take her very

far, just to the edge of Epping Forest. The body will be found soon enough. But it mustn't be found here."

"What are you going to do?"

Fear sharpened her wits. It was like fabricating a plot. All the details had to be right. She considered, discarded, contrived. They would use the car. The body would be put in the boot. But it would have to be wrapped. If they were suspected, the car would be searched by forensic scientists. They would find traces of the child, hair, dust from her shoes, a thread of cloth. A sheet would do to cover her, a clean, ordinary, white terylene and cotton sheet from her airing cupboard. She always washed them at the launderette. There would be no laundry mark to betray them. But it would be difficult to dispose of a sheet; they would have to bring it back in the car for washing. Plastic would be better, that long plastic bag in which her winter coat had come back from the cleaners. No one would be able to trace it to her, and after they had disposed of the body it could be screwed up and left in any public litter basket. But they would need an alibi for the time of death and that meant speed. They must start now, at once. She said:

"We'll take back our library books. I'll ask for the new Updike; it's still on the reserve list. That means that the girl will remember us if the police check up. Then we'll go to the cinema at Manse Hill. We'll have to do something there to make the box-office girl notice us. I'll find I haven't enough money and ask you for some. We'll argue about it. No, better still, I'll accuse her of cheating me over the change. That means paying with a five-pound note. Have you got one?"

He nodded.

"I think so."

He tried to take out his wallet. His hands were shaking as if he were palsied. She put her own hand into his jacket pocket and found it. In the note compartment there was a new five-pound note and a couple of crumpled pound notes. She said:

"We'll only stay in the cinema for about half an hour. Once we're through the foyer we'll take our own tickets and separate. If the police do suspect us they'll be asking people if they saw a couple leaving. They won't expect us to be apart. And we'd better sit at the end of different rows, not next to anyone. It shouldn't be difficult. There won't be many people there on a night like this. But you must keep your eyes on me. As soon as I get up to leave slip out after me. We'll go out by the side entrance, the one that leads straight on to the car park. Then we'll drive to the forest."

He said:

"I don't want to sit away from you. I don't want us to be parted. Don't leave me."

He was still shaking. She couldn't be sure that he had understood. She wished that she could do it all alone, that she could help him to bed, tuck him in with a hot water bottle, cosset him like a grieving child. But that wasn't possible. He, more than she, must have an alibi. She couldn't leave him alone in the house. They had to be seen together. Then she remembered the brandy, the miniature bottle she had won at the hospital Christmas party. She had been saving it for some unspecified emergency. She hurried to the pantry and poured the brandy into a glass. When she smelled it she knew how much she needed it. But there were only a couple of mouthfuls in the bottle, not enough to do good to two of them. She took it to him. She switched on the third bar of the electric fire.

"Drink this, darling. Try to get warm. Stay here, I'll call you when I'm ready."

She was amazed at how clearly her mind was working. Before she went upstairs she put the front door on the latch. She went outside and unlocked the boot of the car. The road was deserted. The nearest street light, ten yards away, was a yellow haze in the freezing mist. All the curtains of number 39 were drawn; behind them the dark and empty rooms waited for their new owners. At number 43 only the front downstairs room was lit. Here, too, the curtains were drawn but they couldn't muffle the gusts of laughter from the television comedy show. The Hicksons, inveterate viewers, were settled for the evening.

She took the plastic bag from the hanger in the cupboard under the stairs. Her coat still smelled of cleaning fluid. She wondered whether this familiar pungent smell would always be associated for her with this night. Then she thought of gloves. There was a pair of thin washing-up gloves hung over the taps of the kitchen sink. She hated to work in thick gloves. She put them on. Then she went upstairs.

The bedside lamp was on beside the double bed, the curtains were drawn. It was as if she saw the child for the first time. She lay sprawled on the bed, her left arm flung out, the fingers curving. Her blue knickers were down to her knees. She looked very peaceful. Her spectacles had been shaken off and lay separately on the counterpane. They looked ridiculously small, a delicate contraption of glass and wire. The woman picked them up and felt in the pocket of the child's coat for the case. It wasn't there. She felt a moment of panic as if it were vitally important that the spectacles were kept safe. Then she noticed a small black shoulder

144

bag on the floor. She picked it up. It was made of cheap plastic and looked very new. Perhaps it had been bought specially to go with her Guide's uniform. Inside was a handkerchief, still folded, a Girl Guide diary, a pencil, a small purse containing a few coins, and a red spectacle case. The woman folded the spectacles into the case. Then she opened the diary. The hand was childish, printed letters linked with straight lines. Julia Mavis Scase, 104 Magenta Gardens. She wondered why the child had taken this long way home. Surely it would have been quicker to go across the recreation ground. And if she had gone across the recreation ground she wouldn't be lying here dead. They were a full mile from Magenta Gardens. It might be a day or two after the body was found before the police started their door-to-door enquiries here, and every day would make them safer.

She took the child's coat and the Girl Guide beret and placed them on the body. Gently she pulled up the knickers. Then she drew the long plastic bag carefully over the child, twisting it above her head. Seen through the transparent sheeting her face, unspectacled, the lids closed, was transformed, delicate, beautiful even, but unreal. The lips were slightly parted showing the moist gleam of the thin metal brace across her teeth. A blob of saliva hung on it like a pearl. She looked like a doll gift-wrapped for Christmas, a present for a good girl. When the woman lifted the body in her arms she could feel its warmth through the thin plastic.

The child was heavier than she had expected. The weight dragged at her arms and stomach muscles. It would have been easier to have slung the burden over her shoulder. Wasn't that how they taught you to carry an unconscious person from a burning house? But she found she couldn't do it. She had to carry the child in her arms gently, as if this were a sick and sleeping baby who must not be awakened. Words came into her mind. She is not dead, but sleeping. She wanted to pray: "Oh God, help us, please help us. Please make it all right." But that wasn't possible. She had put herself beyond the power of prayer. No one, not even God, could make it all right for them ever again.

Their car was a red second-hand Mini. They had only had it for six months. They had been able to save up for it because she worked. Even so, their Sunday trips to the sea with Rosie had had to be rationed. She was an unpractised driver, unused to fog. She drove very slowly, knowing what it could mean if they were in an accident, were stopped by the police. He sat beside her, propped up like a corpse, eyes staring ahead through the wind-screen. She had wound his thick scarf round his neck, half obscuring his face; but she couldn't hide his eyes. Neither of them spoke. Sometimes she murmured foolish sibilant reassurances as one might to a fractious horse. From time to time she took her left hand from the wheel and laid it on his. But she had made him wear his gloves and she didn't know whether those stiff wool-encased fingers were aware of her touch.

The lights of the library windows shone through the fog. Although this was a branch she often used, she hadn't driven there before and was unsure where to leave the car. She turned carefully to a side road and saw two cars parked at the kerb. She stopped the Mini carefully behind them. Then she told him what to do. He nodded. She didn't know if he had understood. She pushed open the library door and was met by the familiar warm effluence of books and floor polish underlaid by the sour smell emanating from the adjacent reading-room where the old men, swathed in their decaying overcoats, sat all day slumped over the newspapers, taking refuge from loneliness and the cold. She could see through the glass partition that three of them were still there. She envied them because they were alive and Martin was dead. That was the only moment during the night in which she was for a second disorientated, the child forgotten, thinking that it was his body huddled there in the boot of the car. But he was walking dead at her side.

She went up to the counter with the three books she had brought with her to return. He remembered her instructions and went over to the nearest fiction shelf. She called out to him:

"There's no time to choose new books, darling, if we're going to get there in time for the big film. I'll just put in my card for the Updike."

He seemed not to have heard. He stood there stiffly facing the shelves like a dummy in a shop window. There was only one person in front of her, a determinedly bright middle-aged woman apparently returning library books for her invalid mother. The girl librarian listened impassively as she sorted out the tickets while the woman gabbled on about the books she was returning, her mother's health, the books she hoped to take out. She must have been a frequent visitor. Perhaps returning library books was the only chance she got of a little freedom. The librarian said "Thank you, Miss Yelland" as she handed over the three tickets.

And now it was the woman's turn. She asked to be placed on the waiting list for the Updike and filled up the card with her name and address in bold capitals. She was surprised that her hand could be so steady. She took a lot of trouble over forming the letters, bold and black against the white card. If the police did check up, surely no one could believe that these firm letters had been penned by anyone under stress. Then she went over to her husband. He seemed rooted to the ground and she had almost to lead him to the door and out to the car.

And here, again, the film ceased to roll, the pictures were lost. The worst part of the drive must have been circling the round-about where five roads met at Manse Hill. But she must have managed that without incident because the next thing she remembered was parking the car in front of the cinema. The car park was more crowded than she had expected, but that was a good thing. It meant that the cinema would be fairly full, that their departure would be less likely to be noticed. She was able to find a parking space close to one of the side exits. When she switched off the engine the silence was almost frightening. They sat together in the fog-shrouded car and she told him again what to do. She said: "Darling, do you understand?" He nodded, but he didn't speak. They got out of the car and she closed his door for him. The fog was thicker now. It rose and fell like a malignant gas, spilling in glutinous dollops from the high street lamps. They waded through it, knee-deep, to the foyer.

The last programme must have begun. There were only two people in front of them at the box office. When her turn came she asked for two eight-and-sixpennies and handed over the five-pound note. She took her change and propelled him a little ahead of her letting one of the four one-pound notes drop from her hand. Then she turned and went back to the box office. She said:

"I think I'm a pound short. There are only three here."

The woman said stolidly:

"I gave you four, madam. You saw me count them out."

"There are only three here."

The woman repeated:

"You saw me count them out, madam," and turned to the next customer.

She moved away from the box office, then said loudly:

"I'm sorry, I must have dropped it. It's here on the floor."

The whole episode struck her even at the time as unreal, artificial. The woman in the box office shrugged her shoulders. They moved together across the foyer to the entrance to the stalls. She tried to hand him his ticket, but he wouldn't take it, pretending not to notice her nudging hands. But she knew that he couldn't face sitting apart from her. They would have to stay together.

They stepped into what seemed an immensity of warm-scented blackness. Only the screen was alight, blazing with colour and noise. It was a James Bond film and it must just have begun. She followed the pinpoint of light from the usherette's torch down the centre gangway, one hand behind her clutching at his coat. They were shown into two seats at the end of a row. This wouldn't do. She wanted to slip out from the side entrance, not to walk again up the centre aisle. After they had sat for about ten minutes she whispered to him and took his hand. Together they slipped out of their seats and she led him forward towards the screen until her eyes, more accustomed now to the darkness, could discern a sparsely occupied row. There were only three couples, all seated near the central gangway. They pushed their way past them muttering apologies and took their seats at the far end of the row, almost immediately opposite the red exit sign.

She made herself wait nearly half an hour before she gave him the sign. It was an exciting point in the film; the background music was rising to a crescendo, the screen was full of hurling cars and screaming mouths. In the rows in front of her every face was turned to the screen. She gave a pull on his hand and half rose to her feet. He followed her and they were out through the door. There was a short flight of concrete steps, then she was pushing at the bar of the final door, the cold fog swirled in their faces, and they were in the car park. She felt in her coat pocket for the keys. They weren't there. And instantly she knew. She had left them in the car. Clutching his hand she dragged him with her as she raced through the fog to where she had parked the Mini; but she knew what she would find. The two painted white lines enclosed emptiness. The Mini had gone.

And after that the film of memory broke again. They must have walked for three hours, hand in hand, trudging onwards through the fog towards the forest. Her next memory was of a narrow road stretching straight and unlit between the trees.

The night was icy cold and very still. On each side of the road the forest stretched ahead of them, shrouded in mist. She thought she could hear from it a gentle persistent dripping, slow and portentous as drops of blood. In her imagination it stretched for ever, exuding its black miasma, dropping terror from the tangled bushes, the high leafless boughs, oozing a slow contagion from the slimy trunks. She could see their breath, small puffs of white smoke, leading them onwards. There was no other sound, only the endless ring of their feet on the tarmac. Occasionally they would hear the purr of an approaching car. Instinctively they would step into the darkness of the trees until it passed in a sweep of light, carrying ordinary people, perhaps on their way to a party or driving home late after a long day, happy people with nothing

148

to worry about except mortgages and sickness, their children, their marriages, their jobs.

And then, suddenly, he stopped. He said, his voice dull, utterly defeated:

"I'm tired. Come with me into the forest and we'll find somewhere to sleep. I'll cuddle you. You won't feel the cold. We'll be together. We need never wake up ever again."

But she failed him. She wouldn't go with him. In the end he pleaded, almost cried, but still she refused. She made him turn with her, defeated, and begin the slow trudge home. Ever since earliest childhood she had been terrified of the forest. It wasn't the forest of primary-school fairy tales, the wail of a hunting horn calling through dappled glades, paths regal with stags. This was a mush of corruption, the place where her father had threatened to lose her if she screamed, the dumping ground for murdered bodies. In her childish imagination the sluggish streams ran with blood.

And it wasn't only the terror of the forest. She didn't share —she never had shared—his pessimism. Life for him was fundamentally tragic, a series of days to be somehow got through, not a privilege to be rejoiced in but a burden to be endured. He was always surprised by joy. The thought of death held no anguish for him; it was life which called for courage. But she was different. Nothing but intolerable pain or utter despair could make her kill herself. The heart of her personality was buoyant with optimism, all her life she had been nourished by hope. She hadn't survived the miseries of her childhood to die so easily now. She told herself that all might yet be well. The car thieves might never open the boot; why should they? The car wasn't worth stealing for its own sake. That meant that they wanted it just for the ride and would abandon it when they had finished with it. In time the police would find it and examine it. But tracing the car to them didn't make her a murderess. The rapist—anyone—could have stolen it from outside their door. All they had to do now was to make their way home, wait for the morning, and report it missing.

But in her heart she knew that the hope was false. Once the car was found they would be the chief suspects. They would be asked about their movements that evening; the call at the library, the argument over the cinema tickets. They would be asked how they had travelled to the cinema. There was no direct or easy bus route. And they couldn't reply that their car had been stolen from outside their house. Why then hadn't they reported the theft before they left the house? She knew that Martin wouldn't be able to stand up to this early and probing questioning. She had banked on having several days before the police got around to him and, even then, with nothing to connect them with the crime, it would only have been a routine door-to-door visit. Nothing was known against him. Now everything was changed. The plastic bag would be traced to the local dry-cleaners. Her recent visit there would be discovered.

And so they trudged home together to the waiting police cars standing already outside the house, to the watching eyes from the houses across the road, to the knowledge that, never again, would they be alone together.

The terrors of the forest were imaginary. All the terrors to come would be real. If she had cared enough she could surely have taken his hand and let him lead her into the darkness under the trees. She could have conquered panic in his arms. Always she had been the stronger. It was to her he had looked for support, for comfort, for reassurance. Wasn't that, after all, why she had married him, because he was a man who had none of the qualities which her father had taught her belonged to manliness? Now, and for the first time, he had asked her to trust to him. He had wanted it that way, wanted to lie in the darkness with her, comforting her into death. But because of her childhood terrors she failed him. She withheld from him the right to die with dignity in his own way and in his own time. She condemned him to the trial, the dock, the torture of those eighteen months in prison before death released him. She had heard what prisoners did to child molesters. She had lived through those eighteen months separated from him, unable to comfort him, unable to tell him that she was sorry. The child's death hadn't been willed; she told herself that she couldn't have prevented that act of violence. The child had been murdered by the child she had once been. But this desertion of him at the end had been voluntary.

I should have died with him that night. He was right, there was nothing else for us to do. That was the real sin, the failure of love. "Perfect love casteth out fear." It didn't need a perfect love not to fail him then. It only needed a little kindness, a little courage.

And there the manuscript broke off. When she had finished reading Philippa turned off the light and lay very still, her heart pounding. She felt sick and at the same time faint. She got up and sat on the edge of her bed for a moment then made her way over to the window and leant out, breathing great gulps of the sweet-smelling air. She didn't ask herself how much of the story she believed. She didn't judge it as writing or as description. She couldn't distance herself from it any more than she could distance herself from the woman who had written it. She knew that she wouldn't tell her

150

mother that she had read it and that her mother wouldn't ask. This was all that she would ever be told about the murder, all she would ever know or need to know. After ten minutes of silently gazing at the night sky she put the manuscript back in her drawer and went back to bed. Only then did she wonder where she had been that night.

8

He returned that same evening and took possession of his command post. Next morning he breakfasted as soon as the dining-room was open at half-past seven, and by eight o'clock he had begun his watch. He sat at the window on the one chair, the binoculars resting on the ledge, the door bolted. At his side he placed the open rucksack ready to slip the binoculars inside and to hurry downstairs once Mrs Palfrey was sighted. It would take too long to go down by lift; he would have to move fast if he were to keep her in sight.

At nine-fifteen precisely a tall, dark-haired man carrying a brief-case left number 68. This, presumably, was Mr Palfrey. He had the businesslike air of a man with his morning planned, and Scase didn't believe that it included calling on the murderess or her daughter. His first conviction had never wavered; it was the woman whose frightened voice he had heard over the telephone who would eventually lead him to them.

At nine-forty-five the maid appeared, bumping a shopping trolley up the basement steps. Then no one left or arrived until she returned two hours later, pulling its laden weight after her and manoeuvring it carefully through the iron gate. He went out and lunched on coffee and sandwiches at a coffee bar down a side street within fifty yards of the hotel, and was back at his post at a quarter to two. All the afternoon he kept watch but no one appeared. The man returned home shortly after six and let himself in at the front door.

He broke off his watch again at seven o'clock for dinner, but was back at the window by eight, and stayed there until the light faded, the street lights came on and, at last, it was eleven o'clock and then midnight. The first day was over.

And this was the routine of the next three days. The man left at nine-fifteen precisely in the morning. The maid, usually with her trolley, was out of the house by ten. It was on the following Monday, tempted by the sun, by the need for exercise and by frustration, that he decided to follow her. He had some idea that he might get into conversation, might at least learn whether Mrs Palfrey was at home, might even think of some excuse for asking her where the girl had gone. He didn't know how he would approach her, or what he would say, but the instinct to follow her was suddenly so immediate, so strong, that he was down the stairs and in the street almost as soon as she had reached the corner of Caldecote Terrace.

The first shop she visited was a local newsagent to pay the paper bill. And here the newsagent greeted her by name, and he knew who she was. He was irritated with himself; the facile assumption which had taken her for a maid had wasted three days. Glancing at her as he pretended to hesitate over his choice of newspaper it was difficult to associate this slight, depressed figure, this anxious face, with the confident girl he had seen in the train, or to see her as mistress of number 68. When she had settled the bill, he bought a *Daily Telegraph*, then followed her at a careful distance to her next call, the butcher. Here there was ham on the bone on display in the window, and he decided to buy a quarter of a pound and lunch on it in his room. He joined the queue behind her and waited patiently while she selected a shoulder of lamb. For the first time he saw her animated. The joint was displayed for her inspection and she and the butcher, confederates in expertise, contemplated it with loving care. She asked for it to be boned and he bore it off willingly, leaving his assistant to serve the queue while he obliged this discriminating customer.

After he had bought the ham he followed her through squares of stuccoed Victorian houses to a street market. Here she moved slowly from stall to stall, eyeing the produce with what seemed to him excessive anxiety, surreptitiously pressing the tomatoes and pears. Lastly she visited a delicatessen. He stood on the pavement, pretending an interest in the shrivelled fingers of dried sausages while she bought smoked salmon, watching while the shopkeeper laid his long knife against the pink flesh, and held drooping over the blade the first rich transparent slice for her inspection. Scase had never tasted smoked salmon and the price on the half fish displayed in the refrigerated window appalled him. They ate well, the Palfreys. The Ducton girl had done well for herself. On impulse he followed Mrs Palfrey into the shop and bought two ounces. He would eat them before dinner in his room and discover what this unknown delicacy tasted like, knowing that her tongue would experience the same sensation, that these two slivers of veined flesh would bind them closer together.

And this was the pattern of his life for the next ten days. Pimlico was her village, and it became his, bounded by Victoria Street and

Vauxhall Bridge Road, two flowing thoroughfares like unnavigable rivers over which she never ventured to pass. Twice a week she would walk to the Smith Street branch of the Westminster Library to change her books. He would go into the reading-room and pretend to occupy himself with periodicals while he watched her through the glass partition moving from shelf to shelf. He wondered what books she bore back to solace her in that basement kitchen. It seemed to him that she carried with her a climate of anxiety and loneliness, but it didn't affect him. He couldn't recall any recent time in his life more free from strain. She was easy to trail. Her preoccupations were personal and secret; she seemed hardly to notice the life around her except as it related to shopping and food. But he had no sense of hurry or of time wasted. He knew that this was where he was meant to be. In the end, before long, she would lead him to them.

The weather became warmer, the sun less fitful. On these high summer days she would take a sandwich and fruit to eat on one of the benches in the Embankment Gardens where the boughs of the plane trees dragged to sweep the water with their leaves. He had got into the habit of carrying a packed lunch himself, bought from a delicatessen in Caldecote Road, to be eaten either in a park or at the window of his room. They would sit distanced by twenty or thirty yards on their separate benches and he would watch as she stared over the parapet at the gritty fringes of the Thames, plumed with gulls, at the great barges as they grunted upstream, slapping the tide against the embankment wall. After she had eaten she would feed the sparrows, crouching patiently for as long as fifteen or twenty minutes with the crumbs on her outstretched palm. Once he did the same, and smiled when, after a few minutes of patient waiting, the sparrow fluttered down and he felt the commotion of its frantic wings and the scrape of its tiny claws on his palm. One warm turbulent morning when the high tide heaved in the throes of a spent and distant storm, she brought with her a bag of crusts to feed the gulls. He watched while she stood at the parapet, hurling the bread with stiff ungainly jerks of her arm. The rushing air was suddenly white with wings, spiked with beaks and claws, clamorous with high, desolate screams.

He was surprised how quickly he came to feel at home at the Casablanca. The hotel had few comforts, but it had no pretensions. There was a small and over-crowded bar in a room off the dining-room and most evenings he would take a single dry sherry before his dinner. The meals were predictable: eatable, but only just. But occasionally the standard varied. It was as if the cook were engaged in a private game, judging when the customers were on the point

153

of revolt and then confounding them with a dinner of surprising excellence. But usually little cooking had been done. Scase was familiar with the taste of all the soups; he had opened these tins himself. The prawn cocktail consisted of tinned prawns, hard and salty, smothered with the cheapest of bottled dressing and reposing on a limp lettuce leaf; the pâté maison was commercial liver sausage; the potatoes were invariably served mashed since they were reconstituted from a packet. All his senses were sharpened since he had set out on his enterprise; he noticed these things now, but they didn't bother him.

The Mario who had booked him in seemed to run the place. Scase saw no one else in authority. The other staff were part-time, including Fred, an elderly cripple who spent all night dozing in an armchair behind the counter and whose job it was to let in guests who arrived back after twelve-thirty. The regular clientele were mostly commercial travellers. With some of them Mario was friendly, joining them, white-jacketed, at their table for long intimate conferences. Their common interest was apparently betting. Lists and evening papers were consulted and money changed hands. But most of the trade was foreign package-tours from Spain. With the weekly arrival of the morning coach the hotel came alive. Mario, galvanized into frantic activity, immediately became Spanish in speech and gesture; the hall was blocked with luggage and chattering tourists; the lift invariably broke down and Coffee, the bitch, quivered with excitement.

The hotel was ideal for his purpose. No one bothered about him, no one was curious. The only way in which a visitor could attract interest at the Hotel Casablanca was by failing to settle the bill weekly in advance and in cash. If he felt the need for conversation, a brief craving for the sound of a human voice directed at himself, he would stop to chat to the blind girl. He learned that her name was Violet Tetley and that she was an orphan who had been educated in a residential school for the blind and now lived with a widowed aunt in a council flat off the Vauxhall Road. In exchange he told her nothing about himself except that his wife and only child were dead. She was the only person to whom he felt he could safely talk. Whatever her private imaginings of him might be, he knew that all his secrets, his past, his present purpose, even his ugliness and his pain, were safe from any probing by those sightless eyes.

On Friday morning, 25 August, he was led by Mrs Palfrey across the newly created piazza and into the cool, incense-sweet immensity of Westminster Cathedral. He saw that she didn't dip her fingers in the stoup of holy water; that she hadn't, apparently, come to pray. This visit was just one more way of killing time. He

154

followed her, attaching himself unobtrusively to a party of French-speaking tourists, as she wandered between the great square marble pillars, paused to survey each of the side chapels, bent to stare with repugnant fascination at the silver-encased body of St John Southworth, small as a child in his glass case.

He had never before been in the Cathedral and its red-brick-bounded Byzantine exterior hadn't prepared him for the wonder which lay beyond the west door. The rough unadorned bricks climbed upwards from great pillars of smooth marble, green, yellow, red and grey, to the black curving immensity of the domed roof. It hung suspended above him, darkness and chaos given a form and substance, and he felt that he crawled crab-like beneath its mystery. The completed Lady Chapel, gleaming with gold mosaics, pretty and sentimental, meant nothing to him. Even the smooth beauty of the marble pillars served only to draw the eye upwards to that curving wonder of the roof. He hadn't expected to be so excited by any building. When the act was done, he would come back and walk here again. He would look up at that dark void and find a comfort which he would gain from no lighted candles, no stained glass. There would be other buildings to explore, perhaps even other cities to visit. There could be a life, solitary though it might be, that was more than mere existence. But now even to experience this wonder pricked him with guilt. He remembered the prick of the sparrow on his palm. That, too, had been a moment very close to joy. But to feel joy while Mary Ducton was still alive was a betrayal of the dead. Already he felt that he was being seduced by routine into a complacent lethargy. He would wait for only one more week. If in that time he hadn't been led to the murderess, if the girl Philippa still hadn't returned to Caldecote Terrace, then he would have to think of a plan, however desperate, to trick Mrs Palfrey into betraying to him where they were.

9

When the ten days of freedom which they had promised themselves were up and it was time to look for a job, they avoided the Government Job Centre in Lisson Grove, which was too intimidatingly a reminder of officialdom, and searched instead in the evening papers and on the display boards outside newsagents. They found the advertisement for kitchen staff/waitresses at Sid's Plaice off Kilburn High Road pinned to a board outside a stationer's shop at the north end of the Edgware Road. The advertisement said helpfully "take 16 bus and alight Cambridge Avenue". It added that the wages were one pound an hour plus food. They calculated that if they worked six hours a day for five days their living expenses should be comfortably covered. One free fish meal a day would be a bonus.

Sid's Plaice was a double-fronted fish-and-chip shop with café attached, and looked and smelled reassuringly fresh. Sid himself, whom Philippa had pictured as small, swarthy and greasy, was discovered to be a blond, ruddy-faced, amateur boxer. He himself worked behind the counter, simultaneously directing operations on both sides of his establishment, crashing down the lid of the fish-fryer, plunging the wire baskets of chips into the sizzling fat, joking with customers at the counter as he wrapped their orders in grease-proof and newspaper, bawling demands at the kitchen staff and slapping fish and chips on plates to be shoved at the waitresses who regularly pushed their heads through the serving hatch and yelled out their orders. The din, to which Sid and his staff were apparently impervious, was constant and appalling. Philippa early decided that customers needed strong nerves although not necessarily a strong stomach to dine at Sid's Plaice.

Sid's girls took it in turn to wait at the tables, if taking the plates from the hatch and dumping them in front of the customers at the formica-topped tables could be described as waitress service. The job was preferred to washing-up, since there were the tips. Sid explained that most customers left something, and there was always the hope of unintended generosity from a visitor or recently arrived immigrant confused about the value of English money. This flexible use of his female labour, which saved him the expense of employing two categories of worker, was described by Sid as "mucking in together like one big happy family".

He took on Philippa and her mother with alacrity, and if he were surprised that two apparently educated women were actually seeking work in his shop, he didn't show it. Philippa told herself that this was a place of work where she could be in no possible danger of meeting anyone from her past life, and where no questions would be asked. She was wrong in that; questions were perpetually asked by her fellow workers, but no one cared whether the answers were true.

There were three other washers-up on the evening shift: Black Shirl, Marlene and Debbie. Marlene's hair, spiked and dyed bright orange, looked as if it had been hacked off by shears. Two moons of bright red decorated each cheek, but Philippa was relieved to see that she had apparently jibbed at piercing her ear lobes with safety pins. Her forearm was covered with tattoos, two intertwining hearts pierced with an arrow and surrounded by a garland of roses, and a sixteenth-century galleon in full sail. It fascinated Debbie who was happy to wipe up dishes for Marlene all evening so that she could see it sinking and rising in the detergent.

"Make it sink. Go on, Marl! Make it sink," she would plead, and Marlene would plunge her arms in the detergent foam and let the bubbles froth around the little craft.

In the damp and ill-equipped kitchen behind the café, with its two sinks, they worked in pairs. They talked incessantly, usually about the previous night's television, their boyfriends, shopping up West. They were given to extraordinary swings of mood and terrifying bursts of temper. They walked out frequently, demonstrating a pathetic and fiercely guarded if illusory independence, and walked in again a few days later. They complained about Sid behind his back, and were alternately surly and outrageously flirtatious to his face. They discussed his alleged sexual inadequacies in anatomical detail and at length, although it was obvious to Philippa that all Sid's energies were spent on the business, his occasional amateur boxing bouts, racing his greyhound and keeping Mrs Sid happy. This lady, of a formidable smartness and vulgarity, appeared briefly once a day in the chippie, apparently to remind Sid and warn the others that she existed. Poor Sid, thought Philippa. He would probably have been afraid of his female helots if they had had enough sense to organize a united confrontation. But they waged their war of attrition with cunning and some success. They regularly stole small quantities of food from him, bread, butter, sugar and tea, and he knew they did. Perhaps this was regarded by both sides as one of the perks of the job; but Philippa saw that he took no chances with his till, which was closely guarded.

Debbie, waif-like, with pale transparent skin, looked as if her life were subcutaneously draining away. Her nose and fingers were perpetually pink-tipped, her anxious eyes swam in red pools and even the ridges of her ears, ragged as if they had been nibbled, looked about to ooze blood. She spoke in whispers and crept about the kitchen bestowing indiscriminately her sweetly inane smile. But it was Debbie who was the most violent. Sharing a sink with Philippa, Black Shirl said:

"She knifed her ma when she was twelve."

"You mean she killed her?"

"Bloody near thing. They put her in care. But she's all right now as long as you don't let her near your feller."

"You mean she'd knife him?"

Black Shirl roared with laughter.

"Naw. She'd fuck 'im. She's terrible she is. Lord, that girl, she's terrible!"

Mechanically taking plate after plate from Shirl's hands, Philippa thought that if her father had encountered Debbie instead of Julia Scase, he would be alive now. There would have been no rape, no murder, no adoption. His only problem would have been to get rid of her, to stop another visit; but ten shillings and a bag of sweets would probably have done the trick. It was his bad luck to have met instead Julia Scase, that dangerous mixture of innocence and stupidity.

All three treated her mother with wary respect, perhaps because she was older, perhaps because there was something inhibiting about her quiet composure. Unlike Philippa, she seemed undisturbed by the irrational explosions of violence. Once when Debbie, washing a carving knife, suddenly pointed it at Marlene's throat, she succeeded in persuading the girl to hand it over with no more than a quiet, "Give it to me, Debbie." But they were curious about her. One night, when her mother was on waitress duty and Marlene and Philippa were sharing a sink, Marlene said:

"Been in the bin, has she, your ma? You know, a mental hospital?"

"Yes, she has. Why did you ask?"

"You can allus tell. My auntie was the same. You can tell by the eyes, see. All right now, is she?"

"Oh yes, she's fine. The doctor said she mustn't be under any strain. That's why we took this job. It isn't exactly stimulating, but at least you can put it behind you when you go home."

This was accepted in silence. They all had excuses for lowering themselves by condescending to take Sid's job. Black Shirl, sloshing suds at the next sink, said, belligerent, suspicious:

"Why do you speak posh?"

"It's not my fault. My uncle looked after me when I was a kid, after my dad died. He and my aunt were particular. That's why I ran away. That and my uncle trying to get into bed with me."

Marlene said:

"My uncle did that to me, too. I didn't mind. He was all right. Used to take me up West Saturday nights.

Black Shirl said:

"Went to a posh school then, did you?"

"I ran away from that too."

"Got a place have you? You and your ma?"

"Oh yes, just a room. But we won't be stopping there long. My boyfriend is buying a flat for us."

"What's his name, your boyfriend?"

158

"Ernest. Ernest Hemingway."

The name was received in a disparaging silence. Marlene said:
"You wouldn't get me going out with a feller called Ernest. My granddad was Ernest."

"What's he like?" asked Black Shirl.

"The outdoor type really. He shoots and hunts a lot. And he likes bulls. Actually, he's getting rather a bore."

She enjoyed fabricating the lies and soon learnt that they were infinitely credulous. Either nothing was too egregious to be unbelievable, or they didn't greatly care. Their own lives were made tolerable by fantasy; they had none of the pettiness which would grudge it to others. What did worry them, as it obviously did Sid, was the fact that she and her mother had presented their National Insurance cards for stamping. All the girls working in the chippie were drawing unemployment benefit. They felt vaguely threatened by this orthodoxy. Philippa found it necessary to explain:

"It's my probation officer. He knows I'm working. I can't put anything across on him."

They looked at her pityingly. Probation officers were admittedly less gullible than local authority social workers, but this unreasonable docility lowered her in their eyes. Not by such naivety did one survive in the urban jungle. Often she smiled to herself, remembering that Gabriel believed, or claimed to believe, that the weak, the sick and the ignorant preyed on the strong, the healthy and the intelligent. He could have found evidence enough at Sid's Plaice. But Philippa, bent over the sink, her back aching, her skin sodden with steam, told herself that Gabriel's world could well survive the pathetic depredations of Marlene, Debbie and Black Shirl.

Two vivid and contrasting mental pictures came frequently into her mind: Gabriel calling for her one bright Saturday morning in the summer term, swinging himself out of his Lagonda, running up the steps of number 68, his cashmere sweater slung from his shoulders; Black Shirl humping to a corner of the kitchen the great bag of washing for her five children which she would wheel in a pram to the launderette on her way home. Perhaps Maurice's mind was patterned with equally vivid images, contrasts which had made him a Socialist and which, even now, kept him one, despite the knowledge, which surely he shared, that his creed would merely transfer the Lagonda to an owner equally, if differently, privileged and that there was no economic system in this world which would transfer the Lagonda to Shirl and the washing and the five children to Gabriel.

Once, when walking to the late-night bus, her mother asked:

"You don't think we exploit them?"

"How? Considering we get through twice the washing-up at our

159

sink that they do at theirs, you could argue that they exploit us."

"I suppose I mean that we pretend to be friendly, to be one of them, but back home we talk and laugh about them as if they're objects, interesting specimens."

"But they are interesting specimens, more amusing and interesting than any we'd meet in the typical office. If they don't know how we talk about them does it matter?"

"Perhaps not to them. It might to us."

After a few seconds silence, she said:

"Are you going to write about them?"

"That hadn't occurred to me. That isn't why we took the job. I suppose I'll file them in the subconscious until I need them."

She half expected her mother to ask, "Will you file me there too?" But she said nothing, and for a little time they walked together in silence.

In the bus, her mother asked:

"How long do you suppose we ought to stay at Sid's?"

"As long as we're happy to live on fish and chips. I admit I sometimes wonder if they've any vacancies for washers-up at L'Ecu de France."

"Is that where you used to eat?"

"Only on special occasions. That and the Gay Hussar and Mon Plaisir are Maurice's favourites. Bertorelli's was for every day. I used to meet him there for lunch sometimes. I love Bertorelli's."

She wondered whether Maurice still ate there, and if Signor Bertorelli ever asked for her in that other world. Her mother said tentatively:

"We could stay for another week or so, perhaps, if you're not too tired or bored. I don't mind the fish. I rather like it."

"I'm not in the least bored. And we can change jobs as soon as we are. We've got our cards nicely stamped up, and I suppose Sid would give us a reference if we twisted his arm. He doesn't give many bills, have you noticed? Two-thirds of his business is on a cash, no-tax basis. I daresay we'd only have to whisper that and he'd happily give us a year's pay in lieu of notice."

"I don't think we ought to do that. He's been decent to us."

"I was only joking. Anyway, we're free to go when we like. That's the fun of it. Just let me know when you're tired of fish."

160

10

Their freedom did, indeed, seem to be limitless, stretching out in concentric waves from those three small rooms above Monty's Fruit and Veg to embrace the whole of London. The freedom of the city: of the lumpy grass under the elms of St James's Park where they would search for a spare length of grass among the knapsacks of the prone tourists, and lie on their backs, staring up through a dazzle of shivering green and silver and listening to the midday band concert. There would be a circle of deck chairs round the bandstand and here the regulars would sit having taken their seats early: large ladies from the suburbs and the provinces with their sandwiches, their summer hats, their plump, ringed fingers guarding bulging handbags on comfortable laps. When the drizzle began they would rummage in their bags and spread macintoshes over their knees, unfold a concertina of thin plastic to cover their hats. Having paid their money for a deck chair, the vagaries of an English summer couldn't cheat them of their forty minutes of crashing brass, the red-braided uniforms, the conductor's brisk salute.

But for Philippa and her mother, despite these almost daily excursions, the core of their joint life lay in Delaney Street and Mell Street. Philippa told herself that she couldn't have found a better part of London in which to be anonymous. The district had a life of its own, but it was one in which the sense of community was fostered by seeing the same familiar faces, not by enquiring into their business. Delaney Street was a quiet cul-de-sac inhabited chiefly by the middle-aged or elderly living above their small family shops. It had something of the atmosphere of a self-sufficient, ancient and sleepy village, a sluggish backwater between the great surging rivers of the Marylebone Road and the Edgware Road. Many of its occupants, like Mr and Mrs Tookes at the junk shop, and the two eccentric Miss Peggs who spent their time perambulating in Mell Street, leading a string of small discouraged dogs, had been born in the street as had their parents before them. They formed a select and secretive coterie, much given to standing in each others' doorways, apparently wordlessly communicating, seeming to huddle themselves against the cold even on the warmest day, and viewing with dispassionate, amused or ironic eyes the casual visitors or newcomers, like natives viewing the arrival of yet another wave of credulous and soon to be disillusioned settlers. Their chief preoccupation was the rumour and threat of a local authority development which would

L

sweep their world away. They stared across at the corrugated fence of the wasteland with hard but troubled eyes. Philippa, always curious, got to know a little about them by casual discreet questions to George. She might have learned more had she and her mother drank in the Blind Beggar, but they thought it prudent to keep apart; one could not patronize the local pub for long and remain private. But they felt accepted in the street. Their neighbours were always polite and sometimes friendly. They watched, occasionally they smiled, but they asked no questions.

Saturday was market day in Mell Street. By nine o'clock the police van had arrived, the barriers had been dragged out and were in place and the street was closed to through traffic. It was a small, intimate, bustling market, cosmopolitan but at the same time very English. The bargaining was carried out with humour and good nature, and occasionally in the old money. Early in the morning the seller of second-hand rugs and carpets wheeled up his great wooden barrow and patterned the road with his wares. Uninhibited and unrebuked, the shoppers walked over them. The tarmac itself became festive. Later the market took on something of the atmosphere of an eastern souk when the brass-seller arrived to set out his jangling pots, and a Pakistani who sold cheap jewellery hung across his stall a swinging curtain of wooden beads. On the material stall lengths of brightly patterned cloth were spun from the great bales; the vendors of kitchenware, fruit and vegetables, fish and meat, flowers and plants, bawled out their wares; the air was sickly with the smell from the hot-dog stall; and at a corner of the street a thin gentle-faced boy wearing a button, "Jesus loves me", patiently held out his pamphlets to the unregarding crowd. Cats looped among the wooden trestles, stretched themselves and curled voluptuously on the woollen jumpers which spilled from the second-hand clothes stall while, outside the shops, the bright-eyed dogs quivered with excitement or crouched gently groaning, their eyes half closed against the sun. Philippa and her mother rummaged among the clothes stalls for hand-knitted woollens, some of them too worn to be used. Her mother would later unpick, then skein and wash the wool. There seemed always to be crinkled loops of wool drooping across the bath to dry. The boxes of odds and ends placed at the sides of the stalls yielded their treasures, including a tea-cloth of hand embroidered linen which they mended, washed and starched and used ceremoniously for Saturday afternoon tea.

Behind the stalls were the small shops: the old-fashioned draper where one could still buy woollen combinations and sleeved vests, and where the pink lace-up corsets hung in the window, their strings dangling; the Greek delicatessen smelling of syrup and sharp

162

Mediterranean wine; the small general store, clean, sweet-smelling, perpetually dark, with a bell on the door where old Mrs Davies shuffled in from the shadows to serve them with milk, butter and tea; the larger of the half-dozen junk shops whose cluttered interior they would penetrate through to a back yard piled with old furniture and fitted along one wall with racks where a miscellany of crockery, pans and pictures offered the chance of a find. Here it was they uncovered two uncracked cups, one early Worcester, one Staffordshire, with chipped but matching saucers, and an agreeably shaped grime-covered dish which, after washing, was revealed as blue and white seventeenth-century Swansea pottery. It was like playing at housekeeping; the re-enactment of the innocent childhood games which neither of them had known.

Philippa had still learned almost nothing of her mother's past. From time to time they would talk briefly about her life in prison, but nothing about the crime and nothing about their earliest and shared years. Philippa asked no questions. She told herself that P. L. Hartley was right; the past was another country and they could choose whether to visit there. Her mother didn't choose and she had no right to compel her, vulnerable as she was, to travel that stony road. She had been given the account of the murder; she told herself that, for the present, it must be enough. She couldn't use her possession of the flat, her companionship, her defence against the noisy intrusions of this new world to purchase a confidence which wasn't freely offered. There was no commitment and that meant no commitment on either side. But she found that she was visualizing less and less a future in which they would be completely apart. She had virtually compelled her mother to share a flat with her because she needed to discover her own identity. She was discovering it, and in ways which she had neither expected nor planned. Discovering her mother's identity was another matter and it could wait. There was no hurry to explore the past; experiencing the present was interesting enough, and they had, after all, their whole lives before them.

11

After a fortnight her mother's probation officer came to the flat. Philippa knew that the visit was inevitable, a condition of her mother's licence, yet she prepared herself to dislike him. He had written to say when he would arrive, and she arranged to take their sheets to the launderette, ostensibly so that her mother and he could talk in private, but really in the hope of avoiding an introduction. But when she returned and put the key in the lock she could hear her mother's voice, clear, ordinary, even animated. He was in the kitchen, drinking tea from a mug. She found herself shaking hands with a mild-eyed, stocky young man with a russet, tangled beard and balding head. He wore blue jeans and a fawn sweat-shirt. His sandalled feet were brown and surprisingly clean. Everything about him was clean. Some of Maurice's colleagues dressed with just such informality, but with them it was an ostentation, a desire to demonstrate their solidarity with their students. She felt that this man dressed to suit himself. Her mother introduced him but her mind blocked the words from her consciousness. She wanted none of him, not even his name.

He had brought with him an African violet which he had grown himself from a cutting. Watching him help her mother to pot it, she knew that she resented him, resented her mother's docile acceptance of this mild but degrading surveillance, resented his intrusion on their privacy. And she knew herself to be jealous. She was looking after her mother. They were looking after each other. They didn't need the bureaucratic, carefully rationed caring of the State. Later during the visit, when he and her mother had been discussing the pots of herbs growing on the kitchen window, and her mother had gone to find a pencil and paper to write down some of the names, she said:

"Don't you think that after ten years society could leave my mother alone? She isn't a danger to anyone; you must know that."

He said gently:

"Licence has to be the same for everyone. The law can't make fish of one and fowl of the other."

"But what good do you hope to do? Not to my mother; I know the answer there. What good do you do for your more ordinary clients? You do call them clients, don't you? I mean, you are a kind of emotional bank manager."

He ignored the last question and answered the first.

"Not much. It's more a question of not doing them harm, trying to help them not to do themselves harm."

But what exactly do you do?"

"The Statute says 'advise, assist and befriend'."

"But you can't befriend someone by Act of Parliament. How could anyone, even the most deprived, be satisfied with or deceived by that kind of friendship, a spurious second-best?"

"Second-best is all that most people ever have. People manage with very little; friendship as well as money. I rely on their good will more than they do on mine. Your parsley's doing very well. It won't grow for us. Did you start this from seed?"

"No. It's a root we got from the health-food shop in Baker Street."

She picked a small bunch for him, glad to give an exchange for the violet. That way they needn't feel under an obligation to him. He took the parsley, and washing his handkerchief under the hot tap of the kitchen sink, rinsed it with cold water and folded the leaves carefully inside it. His hands were large, snub-fingered. He used them gently, unfussily. When he bent over the sink his sweat-shirt rode up to reveal a few inches of smooth flesh, brown and speckled as an egg. She felt a sudden desire to touch it, and found herself wondering what he would be like in bed. Gabriel had made love as if he were a ballet dancer, narcissistically preoccupied with his body, every movement an exercise in control. He performed as if thinking, "This is a necessary, unaesthetic business; but see how I contrive to give it grace." She thought that this man would be different, gentle but direct, free of pretence, free of guilt. After he had wrapped the parsley, he said:

"Mara will be glad of that. Thanks."

She supposed that Mara was his wife or girlfriend. She knew that if she had asked he would have told her; but he never volunteered information. He seemed to view himself and his world with common-sense detachment, accepting kindness at its face value, as if kindness was a common currency of life, answering questions simply, as if unaware of the devious motives from which they sprang. Perhaps in his job it was necessary for survival to take people at their face value too. He hadn't reacted to her obvious antagonism, yet he didn't give her the impression that he was exercising any particular control. She thought that his attitude could be summed up: "We're all of the same blood, and we're in the same shipwreck. Recriminations, explanations, panic are all a waste of time. Safety requires only that we act towards each other with love."

She was glad when, at the end of the visit, he said to her mother:

"In about a month's time then. Perhaps you'd rather go back to seeing me at the office. I'm out visiting or in court most days, but you'll find me there Tuesdays and Fridays, nine to twelve-thirty."

She was glad that he wasn't coming back, that the flat would once again be their own. Apart from George, when he had helped her lug up some furniture, and Joyce Bungeld's brief visit, he was the only other person who had set foot in it. She felt, too, that she wasn't ready yet to cope with someone who might—intriguing and unsettling thought—be naturally good.

12

In the evenings at weekends, or on Mondays when they didn't work, they often watched television together, carrying the two basket chairs from their bedrooms into the kitchen. Watching television was something of a novelty for Philippa. Working for her O- and A-levels and the Cambridge scholarship had taken most of her time, and the television at Caldecote Terrace was seldom switched on. Maurice, like a number of pundits who never refused an invitation to appear, affected to despise all but a few minority-taste programmes. Now she and her mother became mildly addicted to the risible awfulness of a family drama series in which the characters, apparently physically and mentally unscathed by the traumas of the last episode, were resurrected weekly, freshly coiffured, their wounds healed and scarless, for yet another emotional and physical bloodbath. Such a convenient ability to live for the moment with its subliminal message that the past could literally be put behind one had much to recommend it. There ought, she thought, to be a word coined to describe the frank enjoyment to be had from the reassuring second-rate. And that was how, switching the set on too early, they caught the last ten minutes of Maurice's encounter with the Bishop.

Maurice looked relaxed, perfectly at home in this his milieu, swivelling gently in the aggressively modern chair of chrome and black leather, one leg thrown lightly over the other. Philippa recognized the pattern of his socks, the discreet arrow pointing the ankle, the gleam of hand-made leather shoes. He was particular about his clothes. The Bishop, stiffly upright in the twin chair, looked less comfortable. He was a large man. His pectoral cross, insignificant in thin silver, rested crookedly against the episcopal purple. She despised him for this timid affirmation of faith. A talisman, if one went in for these things, should be heavy, beautiful and worn with panache. He had obviously been trapped into fighting on his weakest ground and his heavy face wore the embarrassed, slightly ashamed and conciliatory half-smile of a man who knows that he is letting down the side, but hopes that no one but himself will have noticed it.

Maurice was in excellent form. She anticipated each of the well-remembered mannerisms, the sudden twitch of the left shoulder, the lift of the head away from his opponent, the sudden clasp of his bony hands over the right knee and the hunching of the shoulders as if he were bending his mind to the nub of the argument. None of these antics had anything to do with nervousness. They were the extrovert pantomime of the interaction of mind and body, both too restless to be confined within this trendy contraption of steel and leather, the enclosing cardboard walls with their carefully designed title for the series, "Dissent". His voice was reedier than normal, a pedant's voice.

"Well, let's just recapitulate what you're asking us to believe. That God, whom you say is a spirit, which I take to mean is incorporate—doesn't one of your creeds say without shape, form or passions?—has created man in His own image. That man has sinned. I won't hold you to that fable of some celestial Kew Garden and forbidden Cox's Orange Pippin—let's use your own words, that he's fallen short of the glory of God. That every child coming into the world is contaminated with this primeval sin through no fault of his own. That God, instead of demanding in expiation a bloody sacrifice from man, sent His only son into the world to be tortured and done to death in the most barbaric fashion in order to propitiate His Father's desire for vengeance and to reconcile man to his creator. That this son was born of a virgin. Incidentally, you told us last week that sex was somehow sacred because ordained by God, and I confess to finding it curious that He despised the orthodox method of procreation which He Himself devised and presumably approves. We are asked to believe that this miraculously born, God-made-man lived and died without sin to atone for man's first disobedience. Now we may not have a great deal of historical evidence about the life of Jesus of Nazareth, but we do know quite a lot about Roman methods of capital punishment. Neither you nor I, I'm happy to say, has witnessed a crucifixion, but we can agree that as a method of execution it was agonizing, degrading, slow, bestial and bloody. If you or I actually saw a victim being hauled on to that cross and could get him down—provided, of course,

167

that we didn't risk anything by interfering—I don't think we could prevent ourselves from trying to save him. But the God of Love was apparently content to let it happen, indeed, willed it to happen, and to His only son. You can't ask us to believe in a God of Love who behaves less compassionately than would the least of his creatures. I no longer have a son, but that is hardly my idea of parental love."

Her mother got up and, without speaking, turned down the sound. She said:

"What does he mean, he no longer has a son?"

"He did once, but Orlando was killed in a road accident with his mother. That's why Maurice and Hilda took me on."

It was the first time that her adoptive parents had been mentioned between them and she waited, curious to see if this was the moment when their silence would be broken, whether her mother would ask about those lost ten years, whether she had been happy at Caldecote Terrace, where she had gone to school, what kind of life she had led. But she only said:

"Is that how he brought you up, as an atheist?"

"Well, he told me when I was about nine that religion was nonsense and that only fools believed it and then made it clear that I must think its tenets out for myself and make up my own mind. I don't think he has ever been a believer."

"Well, he believes now, or why does he hate God so much? He wouldn't be so vehement if the Bishop were inviting him to believe in pixies or the theories of the flat-earthers. Poor Bishop! He could only win by saying things that he'd be too embarrassed to utter and which neither the BBC nor the viewers—especially the Christians— would in the least wish to hear."

What things? she wondered. She said:

"Do you believe?"

Her mother answered:

"Oh yes, I believe." She glanced towards the screen where Maurice, still articulating, had been reduced to a silent and ridiculously posturing cypher. "The Bishop doesn't know for certain, but loves what he thinks he believes. Your father knows and hates what he knows. I believe, but I can't love any more. He and I are the unlucky ones."

Philippa wanted to ask: "What do you believe? What difference does it make?" She felt the mixture of excitement, curiosity and apprehension of someone putting a first tentative foot on dangerous and uncertain ground. She said:

"But you can't believe in hell."

"You can once you've been in it."

"But I thought anything is forgivable. I mean, isn't that the whole

168

point of it? You can't place yourself beyond the mercy of God. I thought Christians only had to ask."

"You have to believe."

"Well, you do believe, you've just said so. That's lucky for you. I don't."

"There has to be contrition."

"What's so difficult about that? Feeling sorry. I should have thought that was the easiest part."

"Not sorry because you did something and the results have been unpleasant for you. Not just wishing that you hadn't done it. That's easy. Contrition means saying 'I did that thing. I was responsible.'"

"Well, is that so difficult? It seems a fair exchange if you can get instant forgiveness and eternal life thrown in for good measure."

"I can't spend ten years explaining to myself that I wasn't responsible, that I couldn't have prevented myself doing what I did, and then when I'm free, as free as I'll ever be, when society thinks I've been punished enough, when everyone has lost interest, then I can't decide that it would be pleasant to have God's forgiveness as well."

"I don't see why not. Remember Heine's last words: '*Dieu me pardonnera, c'est son métier.*'"

Her mother didn't reply. Her face had the closed withdrawn look of someone who finds the conversation painful or distasteful. Philippa went on:

"Why don't you like talking about religion?"

"You've managed very well without it so far."

She glanced towards the television set, then suddenly rose and switched it off. The Bishop's benign, embarrassed face dissolved into a diminishing square of light. Then another and more personal thought fell into Philippa's mind. She asked:

"Was I christened?"

"Yes."

"You never told me."

"You never asked before."

"What did you call me?"

"Rose, after your father's mother. Your father called you Rosie. But you know that your name is Rose. It's on your birth certificate. Before your adoption you were Rose Ducton."

"I'll make the coffee."

Her mother seemed about to speak, then changed her mind. She went out of the kitchen and into her own room. Philippa took down the two mugs from the kitchen shelf. Her hands were shaking. She put them on the table and tried to fill the kettle. Of course she had known that her name was Rose, had known it as soon as she had

169

opened that innocuous-looking official envelope and had taken out her birth certificate. But then it had been just another label. She had hardly taken it in, except to notice that Maurice, in relegating it to second place, had nevertheless allowed her to retain something from her past. The edge of the kettle rattled against the tap. Carefully she placed it on the draining board and stood bent, clasping the cold edge of the sink as if fighting nausea. Rose Ducton. Rosie Ducton. Philippa Rose Palfrey. A row of books with Rose Ducton on the spine. It was a trisyllabic cypher, having nothing to do with her. I baptize you in the name of the Father and of the Son and of the Holy Ghost. A trickle of water running over her forehead. It could hardly have been of any real importance since Maurice could wipe it away with a stroke of his pen. Where, she wondered, had she been christened; in that dull suburban church in Seven Kings under the stunted travesty of a spire? Rose. It didn't even suit her. It was a name in a catalogue; Peace, Scarlet Wonder, Albertine. She had thought that she had got used to the knowledge that nothing about her was real, not even her name. Why, then, was she so shaken now?

She had control of the trembling now and, careful as a child entrusted with an unfamiliar task, she filled the kettle. Rose. It was strange that her mother hadn't once called her by that name, hadn't once inadvertently let it slip, the name which, after all, she had chosen, or at least had accepted for her baby, the name which she had used for eight years, the name which she must have had in mind during the last ten years of solitude and survival. If she believed in God, that strange eccentricity which she Philippa—she Rose— would have to explore, she must have used that word in her prayers, if she did pray. God bless Rosie. It must have taken a disciplined effort from their first meeting always to remember to call her Philippa. Every time she spoke that new Maurice-bestowed name she was playing a part, being less than honest. No, that wasn't fair. And it was stupid to mind so much. What did it matter? But she wished that her mother had, just once, forgotten to be careful and had called her by her right name.

The loneliness descended on him soon after breakfast, as dragging and exhausting as a physical weight. It was the more disturbing because it was so unexpected. Loneliness was a state he had got used to since Mavis's death and he hadn't expected to feel it again as a positive emotion nor to be visited by its sad aftermath of restlessness and boredom. By eleven o'clock Mrs Palfrey hadn't appeared and he thought it now unlikely that she would. It had been the same last Sunday. Perhaps this was the day when they went out together, leaving by car from the carriage road at the back of the terrace which his investigations had shown led to a row of garages. Without her to follow there was little chance of shaking off this weight of ennui. His life had become so linked with hers, his routine tied to her daily perambulations that, when she didn't appear, he felt deprived as if of her actual company.

The hotel was full; a new package-tour of Spaniards had arrived on Saturday evening and service for the rest of the guests was perfunctory. The dining-room was a jabber of excited voices, the hall obstructed with their luggage. Mario gabbled, gesticulated, rushed frantically from reception desk to dining-room. Glad to get away from the crush, Scase had settled himself early at his bedroom window with his binoculars trained on number 68, but with no real hope of seeing her. It was a morning of alternate rain and sunshine. Fierce and sudden squalls slashed at the window, then as suddenly ceased; the nudging clouds parted and the pavement steamed as the sun reappeared, hot and bright. By half-past eleven restlessness got the better of him and he went downstairs in search of coffee. Violet was at the switchboard as usual, the dog at her feet. Needing to hear a human voice, he said something to her about the pleasure of seeing the sun, then stopped appalled at his tactlessness. He should have said feeling the sun. She smiled, her sightless eyes seeking the echo of his voice. Then to his surprise he heard himself say:

"I thought of going to Regent's Park this afternoon to look at the roses. You go off duty at midday on Sunday, don't you? Would you and Coffee care to come?"

"That would be nice. Thank you. We'd both like it."

Her hand found the dog's head and pressed it. The animal stirred and pricked its ears, bright eyes fixed on her face.

"And would you like to have some dinner first? Lunch I mean?"

She flushed and nodded. She seemed pleased. He saw that, under her fawn woollen cardigan, she was wearing what looked like a new summer dress in blue cotton. After he had spoken she stroked the skirt gently with both hands and smiled as if glad that she had taken the trouble to put it on. He told himself that having committed one folly, he had now embarked on a second. But it was too late now to draw back and he didn't really want to. Then he wondered where he would take her for luncheon. There was a small sandwich bar off Victoria Street which he used occasionally during the week but he wasn't sure whether it would be open on a Sunday. It was very clean but not at all smart. Then he remembered that the shabbiness of its cramped partitions wouldn't matter since she couldn't see them, and was ashamed that the thought had entered his mind. It was wrong to cheat her just because she was blind. He must try to make the occasion special for her. After all, she would be doing more for him than she knew. And she would be the first woman other than Mavis whom he had taken out since the day of his marriage. Admittedly she was blind. But then, if she hadn't been blind, she wouldn't have accepted his invitation. He remembered that there was an Italian restaurant fairly close to the station. Perhaps that would be open on Sunday. At least Coffee wouldn't be any problem. Children, he had noticed, were seldom welcome, but nobody minded a guide-dog.

The day brightened for him. It was time he took a day off, time too that he walked and talked with another human being. He made arrangements with her to call for her at the desk just before twelve and went back to his room. As he unlocked his room door it struck him that there would be little point this morning in taking with him his rucksack with the accoutrements of murder and he wondered whether it would really be safe to leave it in his locked room. But the rucksack had become almost part of him. He felt that he would walk strangely without its familiar weight on his right shoulder. And why shouldn't he take it? It occurred to him that he had by impulse chosen the best possible person as companion on his walk. She wouldn't wonder what he was carrying in the rucksack. She wouldn't ask. And after the killing, if things did go wrong and the police traced him to the Casablanca, she was the one person they wouldn't ask to identify him.

14

After breakfast, on 27 August, their second Sunday together, her mother said abruptly:

"Do you mind if we go to church?"

Philippa, surprised, managed to respond as if this were the most usual of requests. She had gone through a phase of sermon tasting and felt herself as well qualified to recommend a church for its service and music as she was to discuss its architecture. She enquired what her mother had in mind: the ordered ceremonial and beautifully balanced choir of Marylebone parish church? High Anglican Mass at All Saints', Margaret Street, in a dazzle of mosaics, gilded saints and stained glass? The Baroque splendours of St Paul's? Her mother said that she would like somewhere quiet and close, so they went to the eleven o'clock Sung Eucharist in the cool, uncluttered interior of Sir Ninian Comper's St Cyprian's where an all-male choir sang the liturgy in plainsong from the balcony, a gentle-voiced priest preached an uncompromisingly Catholic sermon and the incense rose pungent and sweet, clouding the high altar. Philippa sat throughout the prayers, but with her head slightly bowed since she had, after all, chosen to be there and politeness dictated at least a token compliance. They hadn't compelled her in; why make an offensive parade of unbelief when neither belief nor disbelief mattered? And it was, after all, no hardship to listen to Cranmer's prose, or as much of it as the revisers had left unmutilated. From these sonorous, antiphonal cadences Jane Austen, on her deathbed, receiving the sacrament from her brother's hands, had taken comfort. That fact alone was enough to silence irreverence. Watching her mother's bent head and clasped hands, she wondered what communication she was making to her god. Once she thought, "Perhaps she's praying for me" and the idea was obscurely gratifying. But although she herself couldn't pray, she liked to sing the hymns. The sound of her soaring voice always surprised her. It was a rich contralto, deeper than her speaking voice, unrecognizable as her own, the expression, it seemed, of a part of her personality unrestrained and unpredictable, only released by poor metric verse and cheerfully nostalgic school-assembly tunes.

Her mother didn't move forward to the altar when the time came for the faithful to eat and drink their god, and she slipped out, Philippa following, during the last hymn. That way, as Philippa realized, there could be no risk that the priest or members of the congregation would introduce themselves, or try to make the strangers feel welcome. Whatever this strange, unsacramental, religious life meant to her mother, it could never include coffee in the parish room, or cosy valedictory gossip in the porch; and for that, at least, she could be grateful. Closing the porch door behind them softly as the last hymn drew to its close, they decided not to bother with cooking lunch, but to stay out as long as possible while the weather was fine. They would find themselves somewhere cheap to eat in Baker Street, then spend the afternoon in Regent's Park.

Although they lived so close, it was the first time that they had visited the park. The early morning rain had stopped and high sunlit clouds drifted imperceptibly across a sky of clear blue which deepened to mauve over a cluster of distant trees across the lake. The geraniums and ivy planted each side of the metal bridge trailed down to the water and the rowers laughed, rocking their skiffs as the fronds brushed their faces. The park was coming to life after the rain. Deck chairs, stacked under the trees for shelter, were brought out again; their legs sank into the moist grass as little family groups settled into them to contemplate rose beds, distant vistas and the comforting proximity of toilets and the coffee-house. Staid Sunday promenaders paced with their leashed dogs between the lavender and the delphiniums, and the queue at the coffee-house lengthened. In Queen Mary's rose garden the roses, plumped by the rain, held the last drops between delicate streaked petals: pink Harriny, bright yellow Summer Sunshine, Ena Harkness and Peace.

While her mother wandered among the bushes, Philippa sat on one of the benches under a great swag of small white roses and took from her shoulder bag the pocket edition of Donne's poems picked up for ten pence from a stall in the market. The roses swung gently above her head, thick as May blossom, dropping their sweetness and an occasional shower of small white petals and golden stamens on to the clovered grass. The sun was warm on her face, inducing a gentle lethargic melancholy. She couldn't remember when last she had visited Queen Mary's rose garden, perhaps never. Maurice preferred buildings to nature, even nature as disciplined, organized and formally displayed as Regent's Park. There was one rose garden which she could remember, but that had been at Pennington and her imagined father had been there, coming towards her through the enclosing circle of green. Odd that so clear a memory, scent, warmth and mellow afternoon light, recalled with peculiar intensity, almost with pain, should be nothing but a childish fantasy. But this garden, this park were real enough, and Maurice was right about architecture. Nature needed the contrast, the discipline of brick and stone. The colonnades and pediments of John Nash's terraces, the eccentric

174

outline of the zoo, even the technical phallus of the Post Office Tower soaring above the hedges, contributed to the park's beauty, defined it and set its limits. It would, she thought, be intolerable to contemplate this lush perfection stretching to infinity, a never-ending, corrupted Garden of Eden.

She lowered her eyes from contemplating the swinging roses to watch her mother. She was always watching her mother, who had, she supposed, exchanged one kind of surveillance for another. She was smelling an orange-red rose, cupping the flower gently in her hand. Most of the rose worshippers closed their eyes to savour the scent; she opened hers wider. She had a look of intense concentration, the facial muscles drawn and taut as if racked with pain. She was standing a little apart, quite motionless, oblivious of everything except the rose resting in her palm.

It was then that Philippa saw the man. He had come up the sloping path from the lake, a small, spectacled, grey-haired man, solicitously accompanying a blind woman with a coffee-coloured guide dog. His glance fell on her, their eyes met and instinctively, and out of the lazy pleasure of the moment, she smiled at him. The result was extraordinary. He stood transfixed, eyes widened, in what seemed a second of incredulous terror. Then he turned abruptly away and, taking the woman by the elbow, almost forced her back down the path and towards the lake. Philippa laughed aloud. He was a plain little man, ordinary but not repulsive, and surely not so plain that no woman before had ever spontaneously smiled at him. Perhaps he thought that she was trying to pick him up, a summer temptress lurking under the swinging roses. She watched the odd couple out of sight, wondering about their relationship, whether he was the girl's father, what excuse he was giving her for so abruptly hurrying her away. Then she thought that she might have seen him somewhere before, but the memory was elusive. His, after all, was hardly a memorable face. But the feeling that she ought to have recognized him was frustrating. She bent her eyes again to her book and put him resolutely out of her mind.

15

Violet Tetley said, her voice sharp with anxiety:

"What is it? What happened? Are you all right?"

His grip must have tightened painfully on her elbow. Or was it that she had smelled the sudden reek of excitement and fear? People said that the blind had an extra sense. He slackened his pace.

"I'm sorry. Nothing's wrong. It's just that I saw someone unexpectedly, a man I used to work with in the accounts office. I didn't want to have to talk to him."

She was silent. It occurred to him that she might think that he was embarrassed to be seen with her, and he added quickly:

"I've never liked him. He was rather officious, a bit of a bully. You know the kind. I didn't want him to see me. I didn't want to have to speak to him."

She said gently:

"He must have made you very unhappy."

"Not really. Not too unhappy. But it was a shock seeing him so unexpectedly. I thought that part of my life was behind me for good. There are some rather nice yellow roses in this bed. I'll find the label and tell you what they're called."

She said:

"They're called Summer Sunshine."

It had been hard to keep his voice steady. He felt sick with disappointment. They were there together. He had seen the murderess bending over one of the rose bushes in that second as he turned abruptly away. He had found them at last and he was helpless, tied, prevented from following them. And it was an ideal opportunity. Like the girl, he could have found a seat and sat there innocently in the sun watching them. The park was getting more crowded every minute. When at last they decided to leave for home nothing would have been easier than to tail them, one anonymous man among the crowd. He could even have used his binoculars if necessary. Many of the tourists wore them and trained them occasionally on the more exotic waterfowl. Time, place, chance were all in his favour and he had to let them go. For a moment he toyed with the idea of deserting Violet, making some excuse, planting her on a seat and promising to return. But he couldn't do it, and he was ashamed of the impulse. And after all, he had to return to the hotel and so did she. She would expect some explanation of his desertion and there was none he could give. But, worst of all, Philippa Palfrey had seen him, had actually smiled at him, might recall his face if she saw him again.

The smile, in its spontaneity, its openness, its frank asexual comradeship, had appalled him. It had seemed too like an invitation to a shared happiness in the warmth of the day, the scent of the rose-drenched air, the physical joy of living; an acknowledgement of a common humanity, a kinship of pleasure which he repudiated, most of all from her. But had it been as simple as that? As they made their slow way back to the hotel, not speaking, he tried to recall that moment from which he had turned away with such instinctive horror. Surely he couldn't have been mistaken? It had been a smile of spontaneous pleasure, nothing more. She couldn't have known who he was, couldn't have guessed his purpose. Surely it was madness to persuade himself even for a moment that what he had seen had been a smile of complicity, of shared knowledge?

But one thing was certain. It had spoilt the day for Violet Tetley. It had started so well. She had enjoyed her meal and they had been happy together in the park. He had found himself talking to her without strain. But that was over. Even Coffee lurched along beside them, dejected, tail drooping. And he had learned his lesson. From now on he must learn to bear his loneliness. To move, however cautiously, into the ordinary world of friendship, of caring, of shared confidences, could be fatal. He was totally alone and that was how it must be. He must keep himself unencumbered for the task in hand.

16

And then, at last, on Thursday 31 August, she led him to them. The day had started like any other with himself at his room window, binoculars trained on the door of number 68. Mr Palfrey left as usual at quarter-past nine. He noted the time on his wrist-watch. It wasn't important, but he had grown into this habit of timing every move as if he were a fictional spy. Three minutes later he saw the woman. At once it struck him that there was something different about her, and he saw that she wasn't carrying her string shopping bag or trundling the trolley. All she had with her was a large old-fashioned handbag. She wore a fawn-coloured coat, undistinguished in cut, and a little too long for fashion, instead of her usual cardigan, and her face was obscured by an immense headscarf patterned in blue and white. There was only a gentle humming wind and the day wasn't cold; perhaps she wanted to keep her hair tidy. Most surprisingly, she was wearing fawn gloves, a touch of formality which reinforced his impression that this outing was different, that some attempt had been made at smartness.

He grabbed his rucksack and followed quickly. She was only fifty yards ahead and he saw that she was making her way towards Victoria. As he followed her across Eccleston Bridge and down the side of the station he worried in case she intended to join the queue for taxis at the front entrance and was relieved when she turned instead down the entrance to the Underground. She took a ticket from the thirty-five-pence machine. He found that he hadn't a fivepenny piece and there were two young tourists, rucksack laden, who, pushing ahead of him, had already inserted ten pence and were taking their time over finding the necessary coins. But he had two tenpenny pieces ready in his hand. He inserted them quickly in the next machine and was able to follow a few yards behind her through the barrier and down to the Victoria line.

He kept as close behind her on the escalator as he dared, afraid that she might just catch a train; but he heard with relief a receding rumble before either of them reached the platform. The next came quickly, and the carriage was only half-full. He took a seat close to the door, but distanced from her. She sat very still, unrelaxed, her eyes fixed on the opposite advertisements, feet together, gloved hands in her lap. She looked tense, preoccupied. Was it his imagination that she was bracing herself for some ordeal, rigid with the self-absorption of a victim on her way to a dreaded medical examination or a crucial interview?

She changed at Oxford Circus and he followed her on the long track to the north-bound Bakerloo line. Never once did she glance behind her. She got out at Marylebone and he followed her up the escalator clutching the fifty-pence piece in his hand and suddenly worried that the collector might be desultory in giving him change for the outstanding fare. But all went well. The thirty-five pence were speedily and nonchalantly pressed into his hand and he was through the barrier before she was half way across the concourse of Marylebone Station. Again, to his relief, she ignored the queue of three or four people at the taxi rank and made her way north towards Marylebone Road.

Here he let himself fall back a little. The crossing lights were against her and a solid stream of vehicles in both directions blocked her way. He guessed that it might be some time before the lights

178

changed and he didn't want to stand close to her, the two of them alone at the crossing signal. But it was important to cross when she did. If he lost the lights there might be several minutes in which she could be lost in the criss-cross of streets south of the great divide of Marylebone Road. But again, all went well. He was only a few yards behind her as they crossed together, but she seemed unaware of his presence. She turned into Seymour Place.

And here was her destination, an imposing stone building with an elaborately carved coat of arms above the cornice. A name-plate told him that this was the Inner London Juvenile Court. Mrs Palfrey disappeared through the open double green door through which there came a babble of childish voices as piercingly discordant as a school playground. He walked on pondering his next move. Obviously she was neither a delinquent nor the mother of one. He knew that she didn't work here. That meant that she must be either a witness or a juvenile magistrate. The latter seemed to him un- likely, but in either case he had no way of knowing when she would emerge. At last he went resolutely inside and asked the policeman on duty if he could watch the proceedings. The answer was a polite no; the general public were not admitted to a juvenile court. He said:

"A friend of mine, a Miss Yelland, is one of the witnesses. I forget the name of the case, but I said I'd meet her here when it was over. When are they likely to finish?"

"Depends on the list, sir. And there's more than one juvenile bench sitting. If it's a defended case she could be here a long time. But they should all be through by mid to late afternoon."

He returned to the Marylebone Road. There was a seat beside the bus stop and he sat there to consider his next step. Would there be any point in killing time until Mrs Palfrey left at the end of the day? On reflection he decided that this was what he must do. After all, if what he believed were true, and the murderess and the girl were living together in this area, somewhere near to Regent's Park, Mrs Palfrey was reasonably close to them for the first time since he had been trailing her. There was always the chance that she would visit them on her way home. He would return in the late afternoon and wait for her to come out. It wouldn't be an easy doorway to keep watch on. There were no convenient bookshops opposite in which he could pretend to browse. He would have to return in good time and then walk slowly up and down Seymour Place, never out of sight of the courtroom entrance, yet never loitering so close that his presence would arouse interest. The slow parade, the need for constant watchfulness, would be tedious, but it shouldn't be too difficult to avoid suspicion. This was no village street with peering

179

eyes behind the curtains. As long as he kept quietly walking, crossing the road from time to time at the traffic lights, it was unlikely that his comings and goings would be noticed. And what if they were? He told himself that he was getting unnecessarily careful. There were only three people from whom he must keep his presence secret and one of them was inside that building. In the meantime he decided to spend a couple of hours in the public library on Marylebone Road—the girl was someone who bought books and might even turn up there—and then walk in Regent's Park and revisit the rose garden. There was sure to be a place in upper Baker Street where he could buy a sandwich and coffee for lunch. He looked at his wrist-watch. It was now nearly ten o'clock. Shifting his rucksack more firmly on his shoulder he turned right towards Baker Street.

17

She had never really wanted to sit on the juvenile Bench, but Maurice had suggested with the persuasive force of a command that she ought to have what he described as 'some interest outside the kitchen', and the wife of one of his colleagues, herself a magistrate, had suggested the juvenile Bench and had put her name forward. Maurice had said:

"You ought to be able to make a useful contribution. The Bench is stolidly upper-middle class, self-perpetuating. They need shaking out of some of their comfortable misconceptions. And most of them haven't an idea what sort of lives their clients lead. You'll bring to the job a different experience."

He meant, she knew, that she could bring to the job the experience of living in a small terraced house in the poorer part of Ruislip, of a comprehensive school education, of being the only child of working-class parents who hung their window curtains patterned side outward because what determined conduct and comfort was what the neighbours thought, whose highest ambition for her had been a job as a bank clerk, who saved up to take their annual holiday in the same boarding house at Brighton.

Sitting on the left of the chairman under the royal coat of arms, none of it seemed particularly relevant. Lady Dorothy, with whom she usually sat, brought to the job the experience of living in Eaton

Square with weekends in a converted seventeenth-century rectory in Norfolk. Yet Lady Dorothy, if she didn't share the lives of the children and parents who stood before her in varying attitudes of resignation, sullenness or fear, seemed to have no difficulty in sharing their feelings. She dealt with them with a brisk common sense, tempered with more sensitivity than her heavy tweed-clad body and gruff arrogant voice would suggest. Scanning the social enquiry report with its mention of a common-law husband in prison, of too many children and too little of everything else, she would lean forward and say briskly to the mother of the boy before her:

"I see your husband's not at home at present. That must make it hard for you with four boys. And this office cleaning job you're doing at Holborn; that's a long journey for you. How do you go? On the Central line?"

And the woman, apparently sensing an interest and compassion which the voice certainly didn't convey to Hilda, would crouch forward eagerly on the edge of her chair and pour it all out as if the courtroom had suddenly emptied and there was no one there except herself and Lady Dorothy: how that, yes, it had been hard, and that Wayne was a good boy at home only he missed his dad and had got in with the Billings gang, and how he wouldn't go to school because of the bullying and she'd tried taking him but it meant losing an hour's pay because she was supposed to start work at eight o'clock and, anyway, he only ran off again after the roll had been taken, and how her journey was all right except that she had to change at Oxford Circus and it was expensive because the tube fares had gone up and it was no use going by bus because they weren't all that reliable in the mornings.

Lady Dorothy would nod as if she had spent all her life changing at Oxford Circus to get to her cleaning job at Holborn. But some communication passed between them. An impulse of sympathy, if unspoken, was acknowledged and understood. The woman felt better at the end of it, and so, she supposed, did Lady Dorothy. Hilda remembered having overheard the words of a fellow justice:

"She treats them all as if they were the wives of her father's gamekeepers, but it seems to work."

But what made every sitting of the juvenile court a long-drawn-out purgatory for Hilda was not her inadequacy as a Justice—she was used to inadequacy by now—but her terror of blushing. It was worse some days than others, but she could never hope entirely to escape its anguish. At some stage in the proceedings, early or late, she knew that it was going to happen, that nothing could stop it; not will-power, not desperate prayer, and not the pathetic expedients

181

she had devised to try to conceal it: the hand casually held up to shield her forehead as if in deep thought, the studious examination of her papers so that the hair hung over her cheeks, a paroxysm of simulated coughing, her handkerchief held to her face. She would feel first the clutch of fear at the heart, as physical as pain, and then it would begin, the burning flush spreading over her neck, mottling her face and forehead, a scarlet deformity of shame. She felt that every eye in the courtroom was fixed on her. The child with his parents, fidgeting in his chair, the clerk lifting his head from the court register to stare in wonder, the social workers watching with their pitying professional eyes, the chairman briefly pausing to glance at her before averting his eyes in embarrassment, the attendant police, stolidly gazing at her with their dead, controlled faces. And then the red pulsating tide would recede, leaving her momentarily as cold and cleansed as a wave-scoured beach.

Today she had managed to get through the morning session without too much trauma. The court rose at one and it was then the custom for the three magistrates to lunch together at a small Italian restaurant in Crawford Street. This morning her fellow magistrates were Group Captain Carter and Miss Belling. The Group Captain was a grey-haired, stiff-moving punctilious man who treated her with an old-fashioned courtesy which she could sometimes mistake for kindness. Miss Belling, forthright and keen-eyed behind her immense horn-rimmed spectacles, was the senior English mistress at one of the outer London comprehensive schools. She made Hilda feel like a not particularly bright fourth-former, but as this accorded with her private view of herself she didn't resent it. Neither of them was particularly frightening and she might almost have enjoyed her lasagne and beaujolais if she hadn't been worried in case the Group Captain, always punctilious in enquiring about her family, should ask what Philippa was doing.

But the first case on the afternoon list had only been in progress for about twenty minutes when she felt the quickening drum of her heart and immediately the scarlet tide surged over her neck and face. She was holding her handkerchief in her lap and now she raised it to smother her mouth and nose, pretending to stifle an irritating spasm of coughing. During the morning session and in the intervals at lunch her restless hands had tangled the handkerchief to a moist rag. Now it smelled rankly of sweat, meat sauce and wine. As she hacked away, the simulated cough sounding unnatural even to her own ears, the social worker giving evidence hesitated, glanced at the Bench, then went on speaking. Miss Belling in the chair, without glancing at Hilda, pushed across the carafe of water. Hilda reached for the glass, her hands shaking. But as the water, stale and lukewarm, slid over her tongue she knew that the worst was over. This had been a mild attack. The scarlet tide was receding. She would be all right now until the session ended, all right until the next time.

Crumpling the handkerchief into her lap, she looked up and found herself staring into a pair of terrified eyes. At first she thought that the girl sitting alone two feet from the bench was the juvenile defendant. Then she remembered. This was a care case based on allegations of ill-treatment and the girl was the baby's mother. She was a wan-faced, lanky teenager with blonde straggling hair and a sharp narrow nose above a mouth whose top lip was full and curved, the lower slack and almost bloodless. She wore no make-up except for a smudged black line round her eyes. The eyes themselves were remarkable: large, grey and widely spaced. They looked into Hilda's with a desperate appeal.

For the first time Hilda noticed the incongruity of her dress. Someone must have advised her to wear a hat to court. Perhaps the wide-brimmed straw with the bunch of cherries with crushed and faded leaves drooping from the side of the brim had originally been bought for her wedding. She wore a faded fawn cotton top, faintly patterned with some slogan which had been washed out, above a short black skirt. On the top was pinned a metal brooch in the shape of a rose. It dragged at the thin cotton. Her legs were bare, the knees scabbed and knobbly as a child's. On her feet she wore sandals with thick cork soles and plastic straps wound round her ankles. She was nursing a bulging black handbag, old-fashioned in shape and very large, clutching it desperately to her chest as if afraid that one of the magistrates might leap from the bench and snatch it from her. And still her eyes gazed unwaveringly at Hilda. The fixed stare conveyed nothing but a wordless cry for help, but Hilda was aware of a more complicated and personal communication, an impulse of painful pity. She yearned to lean over the bench and stretch out her hands to the girl, to get out from her seat and fold the rigid body in her arms. Perhaps in that impossible embrace both of them would receive comfort. She too was under judgement, officially deemed incompetent, bereft of her child. Her lips cracked in an inadmissible smile. It wasn't returned. The girl— she looked little more than a child—was too petrified to respond even to so timid and suspect an attempt at friendship.

She seemed not to be listening as the local authority social worker continued her evidence. Her child, a ten-week-old boy, was now in a home under an interim care order and the local authority were applying for a second interim order while they prepared their case for the final hearing. At the end of the submission Miss

Belling turned first to Group Captain Carter and then to Hilda. She whispered:

"We renew the interim care order then, for another twenty-eight days. That should give the local authority time to prepare their case."

Hilda didn't reply. Miss Belling said again:

"We make an interim care order, then?"

Hilda found herself saying:

"I think we ought to talk about it."

With no sign of irritation, Miss Belling informed the court that the magistrates would retire. Surprised, the court shuffled to its feet as Miss Belling led her colleagues out.

Hilda knew that there was nothing she could do or say which would make any difference, that this sick confusion of pity and outrage was futile. They had to protect the baby. The machinery of justice—majestic, well-meaning, fallible—would roll inexorably onward and there was nothing that she could do or say to halt it. And if it were stopped, then perhaps the baby might be harmed again, might even die. In the dull claustrophobic retiring room her fellow justices were patient with her. After all, she hadn't given them any trouble before. Group Captain Carter attempted to explain what she already knew.

"We're only proposing a twenty-eight-day interim care order. The local authority won't be ready with their case for another three or four weeks. We must continue to protect the baby in the meantime. Then it will be for the court to decide what order to make."

"But they took her baby away from her six weeks ago! Now she's got to wait another four weeks. And suppose they don't let her have him back even then?"

Miss Belling said with surprising gentleness:

"It's the court that will decide that. It's us, not some anonymous they. The child is being protected under an interim care order. That expires tomorrow. I don't think we can just ignore the local-authority application for a second interim order; in effect that would mean sending the baby home. It's too big a risk. You heard the medical evidence, the round burns on the inside of the thighs suggestive of cigarette burns, the healed broken rib, the bruises to the buttocks. Those weren't caused accidentally."

"But the social worker said that the husband had left home. He's walked out on them. If he's the one responsible then the baby will be all right now."

"But we don't know whether he was the one responsible. We don't know who ill-treated the baby. It isn't our job to establish that

184

in law. We aren't an adult criminal court. It's our job to consider the welfare of the child. We must continue to protect him until the substantive care proceedings."

"But then she'll lose her baby completely, I know she will. He's only ten weeks old and they've been parted for six weeks. And who's going to talk for her?"

Miss Belling said:

"That's what worries me about these cases. Until the Government implements section sixty-four of the Children Act 1975 there's no chance of a mother in her situation having a lawyer from legal aid to look after her interests. The child gets the lawyer, not the parent. It's a scandal that section sixty-four hasn't been implemented. There ought to be some procedure for looking at Acts of Parliament which are never brought into force, or which are delayed as long as this. But that's not our concern. There's nothing we can do about it. What we have to do now is decide whether there is sufficient evidence to justify us making an interim order. I don't think we have any real choice. We can't prevent the husband from returning home any time he chooses; presumably the girl wants him to come home. And even if she didn't ill-treat the child herself, she was obviously powerless to prevent him from ill-treating it."

Hilda whispered:

"I wish I could take her and the baby home with me."

She thought of Philippa's room, so clean and empty. Philippa hadn't wanted it, had rejected it, but the girl would be safe and happy there. They could put the cot under the south window where it would get the sun. The girl looked as if she needed feeding up; it would be lovely to cook for someone who was really hungry. She heard Miss Belling say:

"You must try and remember what you were told when you were trained. The juvenile court isn't a welfare tribunal. The local authority has the job of looking after the child. We must act judiciously, within the law, within the rules."

When they had resettled themselves on the Bench and Miss Belling had briefly announced the expected decision, Hilda didn't again meet the girl's eyes. She was only aware that one moment the skinny figure clutching the outsized bag was standing like a condemned prisoner to receive sentence, and the next moment was gone. For the rest of the afternoon she made herself attend assiduously to every case. They passed before her, the sad procession of the inadequate, the criminal, the dispossessed. She read each social enquiry report with its catalogue of poverty, fecklessness, misery and failure and felt the increasing weight of her own powerlessness, her own inadequacy. After the session had ended, and as she stood

185

alone in the sun outside the court house, she felt a sudden and overwhelming need to find Philippa, to see that she at least was all right. She wanted to speak to her. She knew that this wasn't possible. Philippa had made it plain that the break, however temporary, had to be complete. But she knew where they were, and Delaney Street was so very close. It wouldn't hurt just to have a look at the outside of their flat, find out exactly where they were.

She walked as usual with her eyes down, carefully avoiding the lines between the paving stones. She had known since early childhood that to step on the line was bad luck. She wondered whether this might be an unpropitious time to risk visiting Delaney Street. If they were both working, and surely they were, they might be coming home about now. It would be dreadful if she ran into them. Philippa would think that she was spying. She had been so insistent that she wanted to be private. No one was to be told where they were, no one was to call. She had only given Hilda the address so that her letters could be sent on, and so that they could contact her in an emergency. What kind of emergency, Hilda wondered. How ill would Maurice have to be before that counted as an emergency? She didn't believe that she herself would ever count. She prayed: "Please God, don't let them see me." Her life was punctuated by such desperate and irrational petitions. "Please God, make the crème brûlée a success." "Please God, help me to understand Philippa." "Please God, don't make me blush this session." "Please God, make Maurice love me again." The crème brûlée was invariably a success, but she could have managed that on her own. The other petitions, those extravagant demands for love, went unheard. It didn't surprise her. She had stopped going to church after her marriage and she could hardly expect her prayers to be answered when it was so apparent that she feared Maurice more than she feared God.

She made her way towards Marylebone Road without noticing the silent watcher about twenty yards down on the opposite pavement who hurried his footsteps so that he caught the traffic lights, crossed the road with her, and followed her at a careful distance past Marylebone Station, across Lisson Grove, and up Mell Street.

18

So he had found them at last. He stood looking down Delaney
Street, outwardly composed, the mild eyes blinking behind his
spectacles, but he could have reared his arms and shouted in
exultation. A part of him, some memory of that boy who had knelt
in the Methodist Chapel at Brighton, wanted to kneel now, to feel
his knees pressing the hard pavement. He had been right, they were
in London. They were here, within yards of where he stood, living
in a flat above a greengrocer's shop at number 12. Here less than ten
minutes ago he had seen Mrs Palfrey loiter, look up, walk quickly
past the shop, retrace her steps, look up again. If she had been an
agent provocateur paid to lead him to his quarry, she couldn't have
improved on that mime of betrayal. After about two minutes of
this pacing she had bought two oranges from the stall, her eyes
slewing up to the flat windows, afraid perhaps that they might
appear. He wondered why she was so nervous. Had the girl perhaps
insisted on privacy? What exactly was the relationship between her
and her adoptive parents, if adopted she had been? But of course
she had been adopted. There could be no doubt that she was the
murderess's daughter, and no doubt either that her name was now
Palfrey. Perhaps her adoptive parents had disapproved of her
leaving home. He felt a surge of fresh excitement when it occurred
to him that this tentative visit by Mrs Palfrey might be the first
step to a reconciliation. If the girl went back to Caldecote Terrace
and abandoned the murderess to live alone here then his task would
be easy.

After buying the oranges she had walked more quickly than usual
up Mell Street to the Edgware Road and had stood in the queue for
the 26 bus to Victoria. She was on her way home. He need follow
no longer. He had almost run back to Delaney Street, terrified that
he might miss the sight of them, the confirmation that they were
really here. But, standing at the corner of the street and looking
down its drab length, he had no doubt. The intoxication of triumph
and fear was familiar. He felt again the sick excitement of the ten-
year-old boy standing on the wet sands under Brighton pier with the
roar of the sea in his ears, holding in his small hands the spoils
of his latest theft. Then, as now, he felt no guilt. It was extraordinary
that during the years of innocence he had lived under a perpetual
burden of guilt; paradoxically, only when he became a thief
had that weight lifted. It was the same with Julie's death. He knew

that when he drove the knife into Mary Ducton's throat he would drive out guilt from his mind for ever. He had no way of telling if he could free Mavis's spirit; he only knew how he could free his own.

And then they appeared. The sight of them was less traumatic than when he had seen them in Regent's Park, and he was better able to control himself. The girl shut the front door, saying something to her mother, and they both turned towards Mell Street. They were casually dressed, both wearing jeans and jackets; the girl had her travelling bag slung over her shoulder. He turned quickly to the right up Mell Street, judging that they would be on their way to Baker Street and the West End. But, glancing back, he saw that they were taking the same path and were only about forty yards behind him. He turned quickly down a side street and loitered there until he had seen them pass.

Back in Delaney Street he surveyed it like a strategist. Now that he knew they weren't there to observe him he could take his time. The problem was to know where, without attracting attention to himself, he could safely keep watch. The pub, the Blind Beggar, was an obvious possibility, quickly rejected. In a small London pub all the regulars were known to the publican and each other; a new and frequent customer would be noticed. They wouldn't force themselves on him; nowhere would he be safer from intrusion. But when the body was discovered he would be bound to be among the suspects. If he had to kill here on the murderess's home ground, the police would come with their photographs and questions. And depending on whether the publican and his customers had reason to oblige the police, someone sooner or later would talk. Besides, he drank very little and the prospect of sitting there in the fumes of tobacco and beer under the curious glances of the regulars, trying to make his pint last, repelled him. And it wouldn't really do as a vantage point. Like all Victorian pubs, he saw that little could be glimpsed of the interior from outside. Short of standing up and peering over the ornately painted glass, he would see nothing.

The bookshop next to the pub and the junk shop adjacent to the greengrocer's both afforded an opportunity to browse and loiter. But, here again, he would be noticed and remembered if he became too frequent a visitor. Perhaps the launderette was the best bet. The prospect of burdening himself with his small supply of spare clothes for frequent and unnecessary washings was a disadvantage; but then he told himself that he needn't wash anything. Once the launderette was reasonably busy, he had only to sit there patiently like the others with his plastic bag and newspaper, and it would be assumed that his washing was either being pounded in one of the washing machines, or was revolving in a drier. During Mavis's illness he had taken their sheets to the local launderette. He knew that it was common practice for people to come and go, shopping or visiting the pub until their washing was ready. But here too he would have to be careful. It was a less likely place for the police to make their enquiries, but he couldn't sit there day after day. It was a place, though, where the woman herself or her daughter might well come. Surely they would use a launderette so conveniently close.

More and more it seemed to him that he ought to try and get access to the flat. He walked slowly but purposefully down that side of the road and noticed the lock. It was a simple Yale, one of the easiest to force. The greengrocer's shop occupied what had obviously been the front room of the original house. He saw that there was a door at the side of the shop which must lead into the downstairs hall and that this, too, was fitted with a Yale.

He went across to the second-hand booksellers and began to look through the four trays of paperbacks set out on trestles. Suddenly it occurred to him to wonder why he was here, why he hadn't followed the murderess and her daughter. He had his knife with him. What had prevented him from following them and seizing his opportunity? It had been done before. He had read about it in newspapers often enough: the crowded pavement, the press of bodies at the tube station entrance, the silent attacker slipping in his knife and making his escape before the onlookers, embarrassed, then puzzled and finally horrified, realized what had happened. It was partly, he decided, that it had all been too sudden, too unexpected. Psychologically he wasn't yet ready for the kill. His mind had been preoccupied with the problem of tracking them down; he had not yet turned his thoughts to the deed itself. But there was something more important—that wasn't how it was meant to be, a sordid street crime, public, hurried, clumsy, perhaps even botched. That wasn't how he saw it. In his imaginings he and the murderess were alone together. She was lying on a bed asleep, her neck stretched out, the pulse beating. The execution, the plunge of the knife into her throat, would be unhurried, ceremonious, a ritual of justice and expiation.

The bookshop was a good place to loiter. A small part of the window obscured from within by the back of a bookcase acted as a mirror. Lifting his eyes from the grubby copy of *A Farewell to Arms* which he was pretending to study, he saw that the greengrocer was closing his shop, lugging the sacks of onions and potatoes to the back, piling up the boxes of tomatoes and lettuces, demolishing the careful pyramids of apples and oranges, and dragging the green artificial grass from the front trestle table. Scase put down his book and sauntered across the road to the junk shop. Here part of the pavement was piled with the cheaper items, a wood-topped desk

189

with all the drawers missing, two cane-bottomed chairs with the seats sagging and split, a tin bath piled with cracked crockery. On the desk was a cardboard box almost filled with a tangle of old spectacles. He rummaged among them, picking out one or two pairs to hold before his eyes, as if testing the vision. Through a distorted haze he saw the greengrocer take off his fawn working coat and replace it with a blue denim jacket from a peg at the back of the shop. Then he disappeared for a second and came back with a pole with a hook on the end and clanged down the metal front to the shop.

A few seconds later he came out of the front door, shut it firmly behind him and made his way up Delaney Street. So he didn't live above the shop. But he would still need a key to the Yale lock on the front door since the shop front had been locked from the inside and there was no other way he could get in to open up the premises except through the front door. He would keep the key on him, perhaps on a ring with others, perhaps in the pocket of his jacket. He had been wearing tight-fitting jeans with two back pockets, both lying flat against the curve of the buttocks. There had been no key there. Almost automatically Scase picked up one pair of spectacles after another and turned them over in his hands. Perhaps it might be worthwhile buying a pair or two if he could find some which weren't too distorting to his vision. A change of spectacles would alter his appearance. He had never before thought of disguise, since it seemed an art beyond his capacity. But there was one skill he knew he had. It was many years since he had exercised it but then it had never once let him down. He didn't think it would let him down now. He could pick pockets.

The exhilaration of knowing that he had found them at last was so intoxicating that he could hardly bear to leave Delaney Street. But the door of number 12 was locked against him, there was nowhere he could safely conceal himself and he needed to get back to the safety and anonymity of his attic room, needed time to rest and think and plan. Before leaving he walked for the last time down the street, surveying the possibilities. It was then that he noticed the narrow passage which led down the side of the Blind Beggar, and which was flanked by the grimy brick wall of the pub and by the corrugated-iron fence about seven feet high which surrounded the acre of weed-infested wasteland. He saw that the panels which faced Delaney Street, rusting, the concrete supports no longer firmly upright, had sagged apart in places producing slits from which it would be possible to keep watch on the street. The problem was to gain access to the wasteland and to check that there were no high windows in surrounding buildings from which the vantage point could be observed.

He glanced quickly up and down the street, then stepped into the passageway. If challenged he would have a credible excuse ready; he would say apologetically that he was looking for a lavatory. He quickly saw that this explanation would have more plausibility than he had realized. The passage led to a small yard smelling strongly of beer and less strongly of urine and coal dust. To the right was the back door of the pub and in front of him an outside coal store, now disused, and a wooden door with a slit at the top and bottom on which the word "Gents" had been crudely painted.

He darted into the lavatory and shut the bolt. Through the top slit he could see one dingy and heavily curtained upstairs window at the back of the pub, and could examine the fence. Here it was even less secure than in the front, and the gap between two of the panels was, he thought, sufficiently wide to enable a slim man to force his way through. After dark it could probably be done with some safety, despite the old-fashioned lamp which projected on brackets at the corner of the pub wall. But this was late summer, a miserably cold and disappointing summer but the light still lasted well into the evening. Unless there were no upper windows over-looking the wasteland, his time of observation might have to be restricted to the hours of darkness.

The huge wooden seat almost engulfed him. It must have been here as long as the pub itself. He slid his thin buttocks to its edge and crouched there, keen as a cornered animal, all his senses alert. There were no voices from the house. He could hear no footfalls, no shouts from Delaney Street and even the rumble of traffic passing down Mell Street was muted. The reek of disinfectant was pungent as a gas. A thin drizzle had begun to fall and the wind was rising, blowing a mist through the slit of the door, obscuring his spectacles. He took out his handkerchief to wipe them and saw that his hand was shaking. He thought it strange that this particular moment, closeted as he was in safety, unobserved, should be so traumatic. Perhaps it was a delayed reaction to the shock of finding them at last.

It was time to go. Having made up his mind he left the shed swiftly and with his shoulder pressed against the most vulnerable panel of the fence. It gave slightly. With his hand he pulled the second panel forward, aware of the sharp edge of the metal biting into his hand. The gap widened. He slipped through, the rucksack under his arm.

It was like stepping into a garden. As he worked his way round in the shadow of the fence the weeds were almost waist-high. They looked so fragile with their small pink flowers, yet they had forced their way through this impacted earth, in places splitting the concrete. Where they were highest he paused to survey the wasteland. It was better for his purpose than he had dared to hope. There was only one

191

gate. This faced Delaney Street and he could see that it was barred and padlocked. Once there had been a row of houses there, now demolished, he supposed, for redevelopment, and in front of him was a blank windowless wall where the neighbouring house had been sliced away. There were no windows in the side wall of the Blind Beggar and the area was bounded on the fourth side by a glass and concrete building which looked like a school. He might possibly be seen from its upper windows, but the building would be empty after school hours unless, of course, it was used for evening classes. But surely not in summer? He would have to find out.

Then he realized that it might not be necessary. He could be in luck. Two decrepit vehicles, a battered van and the chassis of a car, wheel-less and with its left door hanging loose, had been parked or dumped within a few yards of the Delaney Street boundary. They could shield him from any prying eyes from the school if only they were in the right place, standing against a part of the fence where the panels weren't completely joined. Even so, vision would be restricted. Ideally he needed to be exactly opposite the door to number 12. He worked his way towards them, still keeping close to the iron fence as if its height and corrugated surface could somehow confuse an onlooker and make him invisible.

He quickened his pace as he approached the van, the first of the abandoned vehicles, resisting the urge to run for its comforting cover. When at last he reached it, he stood panting with relief, eyes closed, back pressed against the fence. After a few seconds he made himself open his eyes and look round the wasteland. It was still deserted but more desolate now as the drizzle turned to a slanting rain and the clumps of weeds strained against the fretful, changeable wind. Then he turned to examine the fence. It was as he had hoped; there was a gap just below eye-level. It wasn't exactly opposite the greengrocer's shop, but it was close enough and the gap sufficiently wide to give him an uninterrupted view.

He stood there, legs slightly bent, arms wide, fingers clutching at the curve of the iron, staring at the closed door of number 12, watching and waiting. The rain fell steadily, soaking his shoulders, running in rivulets under his jacket collar. He tried to wipe his streaming spectacles but his handkerchief was quickly soaked. The street lamp at the corner of Delaney Street was switched on, laying a shivering gleam on the wet pavement. Somewhere a church clock struck the quarters, the half-hours, the sonorous chimes of nine, ten and eleven o'clock. The swish of passing cars down Mell Street became less frequent. The noise from the pub grew, became raucous, then faded with a clatter of departing feet and the last valedictory shouts. And still they didn't come. From time to time he stretched himself upright to ease the intolerable ache of shoulders and legs, but bent his eyes again to the gap whenever he heard a footfall. It was half-past eleven before they returned home. He watched them—both, it seemed, drooping a little with tiredness—as the girl felt in her bag for her keys. They spoke together easily, casually, as she pushed the door open. And then they were inside and it closed behind them. A few seconds later the two windows on the first floor became oblongs of pale light. Only then, so cramped that he could hardly move, aware for the first time of hunger, of his jacket and shirt heavy as wet poultice against his back, he forced himself once more through the gap in the fence and made his painful way to Baker Street station and took the Circle line to Victoria.

19

When Maurice got home late that afternoon the kitchen, although lit, was empty. He found Hilda in the garden. She was standing at the wrought-iron table arranging a cut-glass bowl of roses. It was a shallow, crudely shaped bowl and it took a second or two before he could remember how they had come by it. Her parents had given it to them as a wedding present. He could picture them conferring anxiously over it, spending more money than they could afford. He remembered, too, that his mother had owned one very like it. He had never been trusted to help wash it up. She had made trifle in it for Sunday tea, a layer of bought sponge cakes covered with jelly and topped with thick synthetic custard. This bowl was filled with crumpled wire to hold the roses. As Hilda forced in each stem the wire scraped against the glass, setting his teeth on edge. The roses had been picked too late and over-handled. Surely Philippa, when she did flowers for the drawing-room, always cut them early in the day and left them in the cool, standing in water. These lay in a flabby heap on the table, their heads already drooping, their stems lax. Suddenly he decided that he didn't like roses. It was a surprising discovery to make at this particular moment and after so many years. They were an over-praised flower, soon blowzy, their beauty depen-dent on scent and poetic association. One perfect bloom in a speci-men vase placed against a plain wall could be a marvel of colour and form, but flowers ought to be judged by how they grew. A rose garden always looked messy, spiky recalcitrant bushes bearing mean leaves. And the roses grew untidily, had such a brief moment of beauty before the petals bleached and peeled in the wind, littering the soil. And the smell was sickly, the stuff of cheap scent. Why had he ever imagined that it gave him pleasure?

Hilda, dissatisfied with her arrangement and pulling out the stems to start again, had pricked herself. There was a bead of blood on her thumb. "Died of a rose in aromatic pain." Browning or Tennyson? Philippa would have known. While his mind was tracing the source of the quotation, she said peevishly:

"I miss Philippa doing the flowers. It's too much, cooking the meal and trying to make the table look nice."

"Yes, Philippa had a pleasant decorative sense. Are those for tonight?"

Immediately she looked up at him, defensive, worried.

"Won't they do?"

"Isn't the arrangement too large? People need to be able to see each other over the flowers. You can't talk to someone you can't see."

"Oh, talking!"

"Talking is what a dinner party's about. And they smell too strong. We want to smell the food and wine. Roses on the dinner table confuse the senses."

She said with the note of sulky truculence which he found particularly irritating and which he had heard more frequently since Philippa's departure:

"I don't seem to be able to do anything right."

"Right? Right for whom?"

"Right for you. I don't know why you married me."

As soon as the words were out of her mouth she stared at him appalled, or so it seemed to him; as if there were words between which their minds could formulate, but which it would be fatal to speak aloud. He picked up one of the roses. The blossom drooped over his palm. He said, hearing the coldness in his voice:

"I married you because I was fond of you and because I thought we could be happy together. If you aren't happy you must try to tell me what's worrying you."

It was paradoxical that the truth could sound so false, could be so much less than the truth. If he had loved her enough he could have made himself lie and say, "Because I loved you." But if he had loved her enough the lie wouldn't have been necessary. She muttered:

"You needn't talk to me as if I'm one of your students. I know you think I'm stupid, but you don't have to patronize me."

He didn't reply, but stood watching her as she forced the last rose stem through the crumpled wire, grazing its stem. But the

194

arrangement was top-heavy and the entangled wire keeled over on to the table spilling rose petals, pollen and dollops of water. She gave a little moan and began dabbing at the water with her hand-kerchief. She said:

"Philippa leaving, you blamed me for that. I know what you thought. I couldn't give you a child of your own and I couldn't even make the adopted one stay with me."

"That's ridiculous, and you must know that it is. I could have stopped Philippa leaving, but I wasn't prepared to pay the price. Philippa must find her own way back to reality."

She said, so quietly that he could only just catch the words:

"It would have been different if I'd been able to have a baby."

He felt a tremor of pity, transitory, but strong enough to make him unwise. He heard himself speaking:

"That reminds me, there's something I meant to tell you. I went to see Dr Patterson last week. There's nothing wrong, it was only a check-up. But he got out my records and confirmed what I half guessed when we saw the specialist together twelve years ago. I'm the one who's infertile. It's nothing to do with you."

She stared at him, rose in hand. She said:

"But you had Orlando!"

He said sharply:

"It's nothing to do with Orlando. It happened after he was born. The doctor puts it down to an attack of mumps I had when he was six weeks old. These things aren't uncommon. There's nothing to be done about it."

She stared at him; her full unwinking gaze was unnerving. He wanted to turn away, dismissing the inconsequent detail of his infertility with a nonchalant shrug, a wry smile at the perversity of fate. But his eyes were held by that dumb unwinking stare. He cursed himself for his folly. Because of a bowl of ruined roses, because of a moment of futile compassion, he had blurted it out. Not the whole truth, he had never imagined himself telling that, but a part of the truth, the essential truth. A secret he had kept for twelve years, a part of him which he had become fond of, as one might a slightly disreputable friend, was his no longer. He had reacted to his particular guilty secret as he supposed the majority of his fellow men did to theirs. Most of the time he had been able to forget it, not by any conscious effort of will, but because it was as much a part of him as his digestion, unintrusive unless it gave trouble. Occasionally it would come into his mind and he would cogitate upon it as an interesting and intriguing complication of his personality which repaid study, much as he might cogitate about the complexities of a student's style. Sometimes he had even enjoyed

it. A guilty secret is, nevertheless, a secret and can be relished with
at least some of the innocence of childhood conspiracies. Sometimes,
but increasingly rarely, it had intruded into his waking thoughts and
provoked disagreeable sensations of distress and worry, even slight
physical manifestations of quickened breath which he would have
diagnosed as guilt and shame if those were words which he had ever
cared to use. And now it was no longer his secret. He had borne its
weight for twelve years and now he would have to shoulder the
burden of her reproach, her renewed disappointment. Self-pity took
hold of him. Why should she stare at him like that with those amazed
unbelieving eyes? He was the one who was entitled to understanding.
It was he, not she, who was maimed. She said:

"You've known all the time, haven't you? It isn't true that you've
been to Dr Patterson. You knew when we first had those tests, when
you said that you didn't want to go on with them any longer, that
you'd had enough. And you let me think it was my fault that we
couldn't have a child. All those years, you let me think it was me."

"It's no one's fault. It's not a question of fault."

He must have been mad to think for one moment that all that was
lacking between them was truth. The tragedy of his marriage
—except that tragedy was too grand a word for such a commonplace misfortune—was not that she always made the wrong response
to his needs; it was that there was no right response which it was
within her power to make. She said accusingly:

"I could have had a child if I hadn't married you."

"You might have had. That supposes that you would have
married someone else, that he wanted a child, that both of you were
capable of parenthood."

She had dropped her eyes at last. Clumsily gathering up the roses,
she whispered sulkily:

"There were other men that liked me. George Bocock liked me."

Who in God's name was George Bocock, he wondered. The name
struck a chord. Of course, that pimply youth who had been a clerk
in the university admissions office. So he had been competing with
George Bocock. If that didn't puncture his self-esteem, nothing
would.

At dinner she was more withdrawn than usual—less, he thought,
from her customary shyness, than because she was preoccupied
with her private thoughts. It wasn't until they were alone together
in the bedroom that they had an opportunity to talk. Then she
said, forcing out the words belligerently as if half expecting him to
remonstrate:

"I want to give up the juvenile Bench."

"Resign your commission. Why?"

"I'm not any good at it. I don't help anyone. And I don't like it. I'll finish this three-month stint, but I won't do any more."

"If you feel like that, then there's no point in going on. You'd better write to the Lord Chancellor's office. But I suggest you try to think of some less childish reason."

"Not doing any good, not being able to help anyone isn't a childish reason."

"What will you do with the extra time? Do you want me to talk to Gwen Marshall about the possibility of school-care work? They're always looking for suitable people."

"Why should I be any better at that? I can fill up my time."

She paused, and then said:

"I want a dog."

"In London? Is that fair? It won't be easy to exercise him."

"There are places, the Embankment Gardens, St James's Park."

"I should have thought there were enough dogs fouling the public parks. But if you're sure, you'd better decide what breed you want and we'll find some reputable kennels. We could do it this weekend."

His magnanimity surprised him. And perhaps it wasn't such a bad idea. She and Philippa hadn't exactly been companions, but the house probably seemed empty without her. A dog needn't inconvenience him if the animal were properly trained. They could drive to the kennels that weekend, make an excursion of it.

She said:

"I don't care about the breed. I want a stray from the Battersea Dogs' Home. I want to pick one out for myself."

He said irritably:

"Really Hilda, if you're determined on a dog, at least get a good-looking animal."

"I don't care about good looks. You and Philippa do, but I don't. I want a stray, a dog no one has claimed, one who'll have to be destroyed if they can't find it a home."

She turned from the dressing-table and spoke for the first time with animation, almost pleadingly:

"He won't make a mess in the garden. I know how you feel about the roses. I'll see he doesn't get on the flower beds. I could train him. He can live in a basket in the kitchen. And he won't be expensive. We waste a lot of food he could eat, and Mr Pantley would be obliging with bones for him. I'm a good customer."

He said:

"It's all right I suppose, as long as you take responsibility for him."

It was like humouring an importunate child. She said sadly:

"Oh yes, I'll do that. I'll look after him. That's one thing I can do."

"If in making your choice, you could contrive to be attracted to one of the smaller and less yapping varieties, you would oblige me."

She knew then that it was going to be all right. She remembered that Philippa had once said that when Maurice spoke like a character in a Jane Austen novel it meant that he was in a good mood. The literary allusion meant nothing to her, but she had learnt to recognize the tone. She would be able to have her dog. She pictured him, bright eyed, head cocked up at her, tail quivering. It was no good naming him before she'd chosen him. She would have to see what he looked like. But she rather liked the name Scamp. Maurice and Philippa would say that it was too ordinary, too common; but that was the kind of dog she wanted. Lying down in the single bed in which Maurice now so seldom joined her, she felt a surge of confidence, almost of power. She wasn't barren after all. It was his fault, not hers. She needn't spend her life making up to him for a deprivation which was nothing to do with her. And after this three-month stint she need never sit on the Bench again.

Book Three

ACT OF VIOLENCE

1

And now he moved with a mounting sense of excitement away from his settled routine at Pimlico and into a new world, their world. And the act itself was no longer hidden in an unknown future; the time had come to prepare himself physically and mentally for the deed. But he perceived a difference in himself. Shadowing Mrs Palfrey, he, the follower, had nevertheless felt himself to be in control. She led and he shadowed, but the invisible cord between them had reined her to his controlling hands. It seemed to him that he had followed her in a state of gentle euphoria, unstressed by anxiety, certain that in the end she would lead him to his prey. Her loneliness, the sad futility of her life, the inevitability of her betrayal, had even bred in him a sense of pity and comradeship.

It was different now; he was on enemy ground. He was shadowing two women, not one, and the girl had seen him and would recognize him again. He still remembered that moment in the rose garden with a mixture of shame and horror. And she was younger, keener-eyed, swifter, almost certainly more intelligent. His task had become infinitely more difficult and the risk of discovery greater. He would have to take his time, move with more cunning. The first task must be to watch from his hiding-place on the waste ground and try to get some idea of their daily routine.

It took him a week to discover where they went when they set out every evening at five o'clock. For three days he followed them at a distance up Mell Street, then watched from the shelter of a chemist's doorway until they mounted a number 16 bus going north up the Edgware Road. The next day he secreted himself closer to the bus stop until they arrived, then mounted the bus after them. They took seats on the lower deck, so he went quickly up the stairs. He took a ticket to the terminus to avoid giving a destination, then watched from the window at every stop to see where they got off. When at last, after a twenty-minute ride, he saw them alight at Cricklewood Broadway, he made his way down the stairs, jumped off at the first red traffic light, and hurried back. But he was too late, they were nowhere in sight.

The next evening he again took the bus, hurrying out of his hiding-place to join it once they were safely aboard, and again taking a seat on the top deck. But this time he was ready to alight, and he didn't lose them. He was thirty yards behind them as they entered a fish-and-chip restaurant, Sid's Plaice. He strolled past and joined a queue at the next bus stop, waiting to see if they emerged. After about ten minutes he strolled past the shop and looked through the glass window at the rows of formica-topped tables. They were nowhere to be seen. It didn't surprise him; he had hardly supposed they would travel so far for an evening meal. So this was where they worked. The choice surprised him; but then he understood. They needed to take a job where the daughter would be in no danger of meeting people she knew, could be sure that no one would ask questions.

After that he knew that he could relax his watch every evening between five o'clock and eleven. He couldn't kill her during their bus journeys, nor while she was at work. But what about that late lonely walk down Mell Street? He pictured himself waiting for them one night, straining himself against the door to avoid being seen, knife ready. Then the lunge at her throat, the one word "Julie" spoken so low that only she would hear, the vicious double twist, the tearing flesh as the knife was wrenched free, and then his feet pounding down Delaney Street to the shelter of—where? It wouldn't work; nothing about it rang true. That quick withdrawing knife, suppose it stuck, twisted in her muscles, was caught behind a bone? He would need time to force it out. He couldn't leave the knife in the wound. Surely the blood must flow freely if she were to die. And the girl would be there, younger, stronger, swifter than he. How could he hope to get away?

Never once during the first week of his surveillance did he see them apart. They were together all day and, more important, they stayed together all night. Since he had rejected the idea of an attack on the murderess in the street, his plan depended on knowing when the girl had left her alone in the flat. He would have to find an excuse for calling, particularly after dark, but that shouldn't be difficult. He would say that he had an urgent message from Caldecote Terrace for Philippa Palfrey. The fact that he knew the girl's name and previous address would ensure that the murderess would at least let him in. And that was all he needed. It would be better if he could kill her while she slept; cleaner, more certain, less horrible, more seemly. But all he needed was to come face to face with her in that flat, and alone.

He followed them on their daily excursions; not because he expected an opportunity to kill, but because he was restless when they weren't in sight. It was simple enough to trail them on the Underground. They usually went from Marylebone, the nearest station. He supposed that, on that first journey from King's Cross, the girl had chosen Baker Street or Edgware Road on the Circle line to save them the time and trouble of a change of line. He would walk behind them at a safe distance, linger in the entrance tunnel while they stood on the platform, then enter a different compartment and stand at the door throughout the journey so that he could watch when they got off. After that it became more difficult. Sometimes prudence made him hang back and lose them. Occasionally they walked along the lonelier reaches of the river, through remote Georgian squares in Islington or the City, where any follower would have been conspicuous. Then he would stand and watch them through his binoculars over the parapet of a bridge, or from the shelter of a church porch or shop doorway, motionless until the two golden heads were out of sight.

It had become less important to trail them, to keep them in sight, than to share their lives, to experience vicariously their interests and pleasures. He had become obsessed with them, itchy with restlessness when he was parted from them, terrified, despite the evidence of their settled way of life, that he might arrive one morning at Delaney Street to find them gone. He noted with obsessive concern the small details of their shared life: that it was the girl who seemed to be in control, who organized their lunching arrangements, taking the oblong plastic picnic box from her shoulder bag and handing it, opened, to her mother; that it was the girl who bought the tickets, who carried the map. He no longer thought of them apart and this, when it occurred to him, was worrying. One night he even had a confused nightmare in which it was the girl whom he killed. She was lying on his bed at the Casablanca, naked, and the wound in her throat was bloodless but gaping, like moistly parted lips. He turned round, the dripping knife in his hand, appalled at his mistake, to find his mother and the murderess standing together in the doorway and clutching at each other, screaming with laughter. The terror stayed with him next day and, for the first time since he had found them, it took an effort of will to leave the shelter of his room.

He was bound to them by hate; he was bound to them, too, by envy. He never saw them touch, they didn't often talk together; when they smiled it was the spontaneous smile of two people who laugh at the same things. They were like friends, undemonstrative, companionable, uneffusive, sharing their days because there was, at present, no other person with whom they preferred to be. So might he have walked and smiled and been companionable with his daughter.

He might have gone on like that for weeks, following them during the daytime, returning to the hotel for his dinner, then waiting behind the iron fence at night, until at last he heard their returning footsteps, the door of number 12 close behind them, and saw the twin oblongs of light shine out from their windows. He hardly knew what he was hoping for, crouching there in the darkness. The girl was hardly likely to leave her mother alone in the flat so late at night. But until the light was finally extinguished he could not bear to leave. And then, on the morning of Saturday 9 September, everything changed.

They were shopping in Mell Street market, as they had on the previous Saturday, and he was shadowing them, anonymous in the milling crowd, watching from the shelter of the antique supermarket, from behind the bric-à-brac stalls, stepping back if their heads turned his way to conceal himself among the swinging hangers of cotton shirts, summer dresses and long printed Indian skirts. It was a bright, warm morning after an early mist and Mell Street was crowded. He was standing at the stall which sold mangoes and huge bunches of unripe bananas to the West Indian women, listening to their high staccato jabber and looking across the road to where the murderess and her daughter were rummaging in a cardboard carton of old linen. They seemed to be searching for pieces of lace. On the edge of the stall was an Australian bushranger's hat, broad brimmed, turned up at the side. Suddenly the girl took it and perched it on her head. Her unbraided golden hair was flowing loose, a swinging curtain of gold. The strap of the hat hung under her chin. She turned on her heel towards her mother and tipped back the brim of the hat in a gesture defiant and debonair. Then she began searching in her shoulder bag for the money. She had bought it, that gallant, ridiculous hat. And the murderess laughed! Across the width of the road, above the rich West Indian voices, above the shouts of the hawkers, the hysterical barking of the dogs, he could hear the laughter, a peal of joyous, spontaneous mirth.

She was laughing. Julie was dead, Mavis was dead, and she was laughing. He was shaken not by anger, which he could have borne, but by a terrible grief. Julie was rotting in her grave. Her life had been choked out of her almost before it had begun. This woman was laughing, opening her throat to the sun. He had no child. She had her daughter alive, healthy, exulting in her candescent beauty as if nourished vampire-like by Julie's blood. They walked in freedom. He slunk behind them like a scavenging animal. They sat companionably together in their shared home and smiled, talked, listened to music. He crouched alone in the cold, night after night, peering like a sexual voyeur through that slit in the wall. He heard again the voice of his Auntie Gladys, dead now like his mother, like Mavis, like Julie. She, being dead, yet speaketh: "That boy gives me the willies. He creeps round the place like a sodding animal." Is thy servant a dog that he should do this thing? He might as well cock his leg against the door of the derelict car that sheltered him and void his inadequacy, his self-disgust. The voice of his mother, as

204

clear as if the words had once actually been spoken: "Murder! You! Don't make me laugh."

He found that he was crying, soundless, wordless, unassuageable tears. They poured over his face, seeped like salty rain into his quavering mouth, splashed over his unavailing hands. He walked on through the crowds, seeing nothing. There was nowhere he could go, nowhere he could hide. There was no place in London where a man could cry in peace. He thought of Julie, anxious eyes behind the steel National Health spectacles, the brace on her teeth, a thin face armoured with metal. He so seldom admitted that shadowy face into his mind. The greatest horror of murder was that it degraded the memory of the dead. If Julie had died in illness, been killed in a road accident, he could have thought of her now with sadness, but with a measure of acceptance and in peace. Now all memories of his child were corrupted by anger, by a half-salacious horror, by hate. All pictures of her childhood had superimposed on them like a faulty print the horror and humiliation of her dreadful end. The murderers had robbed him even of the common tribute which humanity pays to its dead. He seldom remembered, because it was too uncomfortable to remember. If both of them had hanged, would that have cleansed his thoughts or added a new dimension of horror to her death?

He found that he had walked the length of Mell Street and now trembled on the very edge of the pavement where the stream of traffic flowed down the Edgware Road. He found himself longing for what he now thought as home, that small high room at the Casablanca. But he had made a decision. This was the end of trailing after them like an animal twitching at the end of its string. If nothing could separate them, then he would have to get access to their flat. He would have to creep in at night when the murderess would be sleeping alone. And that meant that the time had come to steal the keys.

2

Since they had tacitly agreed that it was not yet time to talk about the lost years of their separation, they talked a great deal about books. With the past outlawed and the future uncertain, English literature was at least a shared experience which they could discuss without embarrassment or constraint, the safest of subjects. It was the more ironic that it should be a minute of commonplace literary chat over breakfast on Friday 15 September that led them directly to Gabriel Lomas.

Philippa asked:

"What did you read inside as well as Shakespeare?"

"The Victorian novelists mostly. The library was better than you'd think. There are two main requirements for cell literature: inordinate length and the writer's ability to create a distinctive and alternative world. I'm the prison-service authority on three-volume novels about intelligent, masochistic women who perversely marry the wrong man or no man at all; you know, *Portrait of a Lady*, *Middlemarch*, *The Small House at Allington*."

Philippa asked:

"Weren't the books spoilt for you, reading them in prison?"

"No, because, while I was reading them, I wasn't in prison. *Middlemarch* kept me sane for six weeks. There are eighty-six chapters and I rationed myself to two a day."

Middlemarch was first published in 1871. They would have hanged her mother then, but not in public. Surely public executions were stopped three years earlier. Maurice would know. She said:

"I don't think I'd have had that amount of self-control. *Middlemarch* is a marvellous novel."

"Yes, but it would be more marvellous if the sexual conventions had let George Eliot be more honest. A novel must be flawed if one of its main themes is the story of a marriage and we can't even be told whether the marriage is consummated. Do you think Casaubon was impotent?"

"Yes, don't you? All the evidence is there."

"But I don't want to have to deduce facts from evidence in a realistic novel. I want to be told. I know that the Victorians couldn't be explicit, but surely they needn't have been quite so timid."

Philippa said:

"Timidity is about the last adjective I'd associate with George Eliot. But if you're feeling critical about Victorian writing, why not indulge yourself with Victorian art? It might be fun to go to the exhibition of great Victorian paintings at the Royal Academy this morning. I think it closes on the seventeenth. Afterwards we could go on as planned to the Courtauld Institute, if that won't be a surfeit of painting."

"I don't think I could have a surfeit of anything now, not even of pleasure."

And so, at last, they met someone from Philippa's past. That didn't, in itself, matter. She had always known that it was inevitable. What did matter was that it should be Gabriel Lomas.

He came up behind them quietly while they were in the inner gallery, standing in front of Alma-Tadema's *The Baths of Caracalla* and studying the catalogue note. He was alone, which was surprising; but it was surprising that he should be there at all. There was no way in which Philippa could have avoided the introduction and she had no intention of trying. She touched her mother's arm and said:

"This is a friend of mine, Gabriel Lomas. Gabriel, my mother. She's in London and we're spending the day together."

He hid his surprise admirably. For a second—no more—his arrogant mobile face froze and his hands tightened on the catalogue. Then he said easily:

"How pleasant for you both. But why not tear yourselves away from these glittering eyeballs and recover with lunch at Fortnum and Mason? Afterwards I thought of going on to the Tate. The Henry Moore exhibition is finished, but one doesn't need an excuse for visiting the Tate."

His mouth smiled, his voice held exactly the right mixture of interest and pleasure, but his eyes, carefully avoiding too keen a scrutiny of her mother, were the eyes of an inquisitor. Gazing steadily at his face, Philippa said:

"No thank you, Gabriel. We're going on to the Courtauld Galleries and lunching later. We've planned rather a full day."

He would, she knew, be both too well bred and too proud to insist or to force his company on them. He said:

"I telephoned your adoptive mother a couple of weeks ago. She told me that you'd gone to earth. She was intriguingly mysterious."

"She needn't have been. Didn't she explain that I'm spending two months in London on my own? I'm trying to find out if I can support myself in anything approaching the manner Maurice has accustomed me to. And I'm gaining experience for a book."

That second explanation sounded pretentious and it was one she would have preferred not to make. But unlike the first, it rang true. Half the upper sixth were probably even now picking up experience for a first novel, as if experience lay like litter on the comfortable surface of their lives.

He said:

"What about Paris, Rome, Ravenna? I thought you said you'd been saving to embark on the Grand Tour before Cambridge."

"Not so grand. The mosaics at Ravenna will wait. I have a lifetime to see them. But this experiment is now or never."

"Why not take an evening off from it and come to the ballet—both of you?"

207

The flick of his eyes towards her mother was amused, inquisitive. She said:

"No thank you, Gabriel. I'm seeing no one. The whole thing will lose its point if I see friends whenever I'm lonely or go home as soon as I'm uncomfortable."

"You don't look at all comfortable now. On the other hand you're obviously not lonely."

Her mother had moved a little apart, ostensibly studying her catalogue, dissociating herself from them. He glanced at her, this time with overt curiosity and something like contempt. He said:

"Until Cambridge, then."

"Until Cambridge."

"Can I drive you up?"

"Oh Gabriel, I don't know! It all seems so far ahead. Perhaps. I'll be in touch."

"Ah well, *abiit*, *excessit*, *evasit*, *erupit*. Give my love to the Sisley."

"What Sisley?"

"*Snow at Lucienne*. That is, if you're really on your way to the Courtauld. And good luck with the experiment."

He raised his eyebrow and made a small rueful grimace which might have been intended to express regret, but in which she thought she detected a hint of complicity. Then he turned and bowed to her mother and was gone. Philippa went up to her and said:

"I'm sorry about that. I thought he was out of London. Actually he's the last person I should have expected to find here and alone. He affects to despise Victorian art. But we were bound to run across someone I knew sooner or later. I don't mind if you don't."

"I mind your not being able to invite them home."

Invite them home. The words conjured up suburban tea-time in the front room, home-made scones on doilies, fish-paste sandwiches, the best tea service brought out so that she wouldn't be disgraced by the family in front of this unknown, eligible young man. Since she had never sat in such a room, it was odd that she knew precisely how it would be. She said:

"But I don't want to. We're perfectly cosy on our own. I shall have three years of Gabriel at Cambridge. You're not bored are you?"

"No. Not bored. Never that."

"What did you think of him?"

"He's very good-looking, isn't he? Good-looking and confident."

"He can afford to be. Nothing has ever happened to him to dislodge him from the centre of his universe."

But one small thing had happened. She felt a twinge of anxiety.

Had he really accepted that sexual failure philosophically? Wasn't he a man who would need his small revenge? As if echoing her thoughts, her mother said:

"I think he could be dangerous."

"He'd be flattered to hear you say so; but he's no more dangerous than any other young male animal, and he's not dangerous to us. No one can be."

Donne's words came into her mind, but she did not speak them aloud: "Who is so safe as we where none can do Treason to us, except one of we two."

She wondered whether her mother had read Donne. She said:

"Forget him. He hasn't spoilt the day for you, has he?"

"No, he couldn't do that. No one could." She paused as if wondering whether to speak, and then added:

"Do you like him?"

"We don't seem able to stay apart from each other for long. But I don't think that what we have in common has anything to do with liking. Forget Gabriel. Let's fight our way into the coffee bar before it gets too crowded, and then go on to the Courtauld. I want to show you some real pictures."

3

That evening, just after half-past six, the strident ring of the telephone set Hilda's heart jumping. She had never liked answering it and during the day it seldom rang. Most of Maurice's colleagues telephoned him at the university and he or Philippa would answer it when they were at home, taking it for granted, she supposed, that the call wouldn't be for her. But since Philippa had left she had grown to dread that insistent, broken summons. She was tempted to take off the receiver, but then there might be a call from the court about one of her sittings, or Maurice might ring to say that he would be late home or was bringing a colleague back for dinner. She could think of no possible excuse why he should find the number continually engaged.

It was difficult to forget that the telephone was there. The house seemed infected with instruments. There was one on the table in the hall and another by their bed. Maurice had even had an extension fitted to the wall in the kitchen. Occasionally she would let it ring unanswered, standing stock-still, hardly daring to breathe, as if the instrument held its own secret, sinister life and could detect her presence. But the accusing silence after the final ring, the niggling guilt at her own inadequacy and weakness, were harder to bear than the fear of what she might hear. She hardly knew what it was she dreaded. She only knew that some catastrophe lay waiting in the future and that it would be heralded by this imperious ring.

Now she wiped her hands on her apron and took off the receiver and heard, at the other end, the coin being shot home. Her palms were moist and she felt the receiver slipping through her fingers. She steadied it with her other hand and spoke the number. To her relief it was a voice she knew.

"Mrs Palfrey? It's I, Gabriel Lomas."

As if she knew a dozen Gabriels; and anyone less pedantic would have said "It's me". She had always been a little in awe of him. He had taken too much trouble with her, confusing her with his easy charm. Sometimes his eyes had met hers in a mocking conspiracy, as if to say: "You know that you're not worth bothering about, I know it, so what are we both up to, my dear, delightful, dull Mrs Palfrey?" But at least this was a familiar voice, a lively voice, not the voice of a stranger, mysterious, heavy with imagined malice. She said:

"How are you, Gabriel?"

"Fine. Look, I've seen Philippa and her mother. I met them at the Arts Council exhibition of great Victorian pictures at the Royal Academy. They were looking at those two Abraham Solomon oils *Waiting for the Verdict* and *The Acquittal*. I oughtn't to have been surprised to meet her there. Philippa has always been fascinated by the Victorians. I must say I adore the peculiar awfulness of high Victorian art. Every picture tells a story. And what a story! A positively decadent feast of colour, my dear. Imperial confidence, pathos, Victorian eroticism and dreadful warnings about the horrid fate which awaited unfaithful wives. Have you seen the exhibition?"

"No, not yet."

He must have known that she didn't go to exhibitions. Maurice fitted in those that he wished to see during his lunch break and on the way home. Philippa went on her own or with her friends. Sometimes she had gone with Gabriel. Only once, in an effort to interest Hilda in art, she had taken her to an exhibition of paintings from the Prado. It hadn't been a success. There had been an uncomfortable crush of people. The pictures had seemed to Hilda very dark. She remembered only the long, gloomy Spanish faces, the dark heavy robes. It had been difficult to simulate interest.

None of the pictures had, she felt, any relation to her or to her life. She strained to hear Gabriel's voice which seemed suddenly to have got fainter. Then she heard it:

"It was unnerving. The pictures, I mean, not the encounter. Although that was unnerving too, in its way."

"How did she seem, Gabriel? Was she happy?"

"Philippa? Who can tell? No one is better at disguising emotion. She wanted to talk, but we only had about five seconds. Her mother moved tactfully away; at least I thought she was being tactful, giving us the chance for a private word, but now I'm not so sure. It may have been embarrassment. Anyway, she moved to the other wall and began rather ostentatiously studying Ford Madox Brown's *The Last of England*. Well, if one had to look at any picture that was the one most worth attention. It's an extraordinary situation, isn't it? Philippa and her mother, I mean."

Puzzled and confused, Hilda asked:

"Did Philippa tell you?"

"Oh yes, just the essentials. We only had a second. She wants me to visit her on Thursday at their place. Apparently the mother is going out. She said that there were things she wanted to talk over."

Hilda was aware of a transitory pain that Philippa should have confided her secret so casually, after all her careful and insistent instructions that no one was to be told under any circumstances. No one. But perhaps Gabriel was special. She had sometimes felt that he might be. But how much had she told? And what was that he had said earlier about a verdict and acquittal? She said:

"What things? Is she all right?"

"She isn't ill, if that's what you mean. A bit strained, perhaps, but that might have been a touch of the Alma-Tademas. They were on their way out when we met. As I said, there really wasn't time for confidences other than the main one, where her mother had been all these years."

So she had told him; he did know. Confused, she said:

"She told you that?"

"Well, I more or less guessed. There is a certain wariness about the eyes. I took one look and thought: either hospital or prison. I'm not sure that taking her to view high Victorian art is exactly calculated to adjust her to contemporary London. I did try to lure them to the Tate, but I got the impression from her mother that my company wasn't exactly welcome."

"How did they seem to you? Are you sure that Philippa's all right?"

"I'm not altogether sure that the experiment is working, if that's what you mean. I take it that that's what she wants to see me about."

"Gabriel, try to persuade her to come home. I don't mean permanently if she doesn't want to. Just to come and talk to us."

"That's what I had in mind. It's silly cutting herself off. It's this thing she has about the biological tie. It's completely irrational. You're her mother in any real sense of the word."

He didn't believe that. She didn't believe it. And it wasn't important anyway. Why should he need to tell her lies? Why did they all lie to her; obvious, commonplace, childish lies which they didn't even take the trouble to make convincing. But at least he had seen Philippa. At least she would be getting some news. Then she heard his voice again.

"I'm supposed to be there next Thursday at six. The trouble is that I've lost the address. I scribbled it down on the back of my catalogue and now I can't lay my hands on it. The name too."

"Ducton. The name's Ducton. And they're at 12 Delaney Street, north west one. It's off Mell Street."

"I remembered Mell Street and the number of the house. And, of course, she introduced her mother as Ducton. It was Delaney Street I couldn't remember. Have you any message for her?"

"Just my love. Give her my love. Perhaps you'd better not say that we've spoken, but Gabriel, try to persuade her to come home."

"Don't worry," he said. "She'll come home all right."

When she had put down the receiver Hilda's heart was lightened. She felt something very like happiness. After all, if they were visiting exhibitions, things couldn't be too bad. They would hardly be looking at pictures together if life were intolerable for them. And at least Philippa had got in touch with a friend, one of her own age-group. Gabriel would ring her back and give her the news. She wouldn't tell Maurice that he had rung. She knew that he was anxious about Philippa, but she knew, too, that it wasn't an anxiety he was willing to discuss. But, after next Thursday, she would get some news. Perhaps Philippa was ready to come home. Perhaps everything was going to be all right after all.

As she rinsed and dried her hands and went back to chopping the onions, she wondered briefly and totally without anxiety why Gabriel had troubled to telephone from a public box.

4

His plan was basically simple, although he knew that carrying it out would be trickier. He would lift the key ring from Monty's jacket pocket while, at the same time, dropping from his hand a bunch of keys roughly equal in size. Monty would be aware, even if only subconsciously, of the weight and jangle of the keys against his thigh. Simply to steal them would mean almost immediate discovery. Once the keys were in his possession he would have to get the two Yales copied as quickly as possible, preferably somewhere close but where there were plenty of customers so that one face might not be particularly remembered. Then the genuine keys would have to be returned and the substitutes recovered. It would mean two appearances at the shop within a comparatively short time. And there would be other customers; he would have to choose his moment carefully. But first he must get a close look at the key ring and the number and weight of the keys.

On the first day, Monday 11 September, he stationed himself at his watching post on the wasteland at eight-forty-five, binoculars at the ready. The greengrocer arrived on his bicycle at three minutes past nine, felt in the pocket of his close-fitting denim jacket and unlocked the door. But his back was firmly towards the street and it was impossible for Scase to get a glance at the keys. Two minutes later the shop front was cranked open and Monty began the business of dragging forward the crates of fruit and vegetables from the back of the shop, and arranging his display. He had exchanged his blue jacket for the shabby fawn working coat which he wore open. It had two large side-pockets, the left-hand one slightly ripped at the seam. The door between the shop and the ground-floor passage of the house was open.

Shortly after ten past nine a small van stopped outside the shop and the driver and a lad clambered down from the cabin and began lugging crates of fruit and vegetables on to the pavement. The street door was closed. Monty's hand went into his left pocket and he pressed something into the boy's palm. Then he began helping the driver to unload while the lad unlocked the door, wedged it open with a net of Spanish onions and began to hump in the crates of fresh produce. For a few seconds the key was left in the door, the bright ring of metal and the pendant keys hanging against the wood. But the driver, carrying a box of apples, moved across obscuring the view. Then the boy's hand fastened on the keys and he tossed them back to Monty. Scase glimpsed nothing but the flash of metal and Monty's hand snatching at the air.

For the next three days the routine was the same. Scase stayed all day at his post, fortified at mid-morning with sandwiches, but was still unable to get a close look at the keys. Monty worked alone. At midday he went over the road to the Blind Beggar and brought back a brimming pint-mug of beer, then dragged an upturned crate from the back of the shop and sat beside the stall drinking the beer and eating an immense roll of what looked like cheese and tomato. Occasionally during the morning he would go over to the pub. When this happened the wizened little man from the junk shop temporarily took over the stall. Scase guessed that they had this arrangement; that Monty would keep an eye on the junk from time to time while his neighbour covered his visits to the Blind Beggar. During the whole of the three days the connecting door between the shop and the rest of the house was left ajar, except when Monty was about to leave when he would firmly close it. Focusing his binoculars with some difficulty through the slit in the fence, Scase was able to confirm that this door, too, had a Yale lock and he guessed that Monty would be equally punctilious about closing this connecting door before leaving at night.

By Friday morning, frustrated, he knew that he must get closer, must be there early in the morning to watch while the door was unlocked. There was no reason why he shouldn't; someone had to be the first customer. It would mean that he was noticed; it added to the risk that he would be remembered. But that couldn't be helped. He would worry about that later when the time came to fabricate an alibi. Now all his thoughts were fixed on getting possession of that bunch of keys.

The timing was tricky. Monty invariably arrived between nine o'clock and nine-five in the morning. The murderess and her daughter left their apartment between nine-fifteen and nine-thirty. Provided Monty were on time and the other two didn't decide to leave early, he should be all right. But he couldn't safely loiter in Delaney Street before nine o'clock. Neither the junk shop nor the second-hand bookshop opened much before half-past nine, and his presence, unoccupied and aimlessly sauntering in the deserted street, might well be noticed from the window of number 12.

That afternoon he bought a canvas shopping basket from Woolworth's in Edgware Road and next morning began walking slowly down Mell Street towards the junction of Delaney Street just before nine o'clock. At two minutes past nine Monty appeared, cycling from the direction of Lisson Grove, and turned into Delaney Street.

214

Scase quickened his steps and caught him up just before he dismounted. He said:

"Good morning. Are you opening up now?"

"That's right. Take me about three minutes. You in a hurry?"

"Not really. I'll just pop round the corner to the station bookstall for a newspaper and come back later."

As he spoke, Monty, still with one hand on the bar of his cycle, inserted a Yale key into the lock. Scase kept his eyes fixed on the key ring, memorizing its size, its probable heaviness, the shape and number of the keys. It was a large ring and there hung on it two Yales, a small flat key about the size of a car key, and one heavier, solid Chubb about two inches long.

He bought his paper at Marylebone Station and sat reading it in the waiting-room, concealing his face behind it until ten o'clock. Then, when he could be sure that the murderess and her daughter would have left Delaney Street, he returned to Monty's stall and bought four oranges, a pound of apples and a bunch of grapes. He could lighten his load by eating them during the day. Then he walked quickly to Woolworth's and bought a large key ring. It had a tag attached bearing an ornamental initial, but this, without much difficulty, he was able to prise away.

He spent the rest of the morning searching for substitute keys in the junk shops and antique markets of Mell Street and Church Street. His first find was a substitute for the smallest key; this he took from the lock of a battered tea caddy. A Yale was discovered in a tobacco jar containing screws and pipe cleaners. The heavy Chubb proved more elusive and, in the end, he was forced to steal a key similar in weight and size from the top drawer of an old chest which was standing inside one of the shops. It pleased him that his fingers could act with speed and cunning. He found the second Yale in an old tin box of nails, screws, spectacles and broken pieces of electrical equipment stuck under the table outside the junk shop in Delaney Street. By the end of the morning he had succeeded in putting together a key ring which in appearance and weight was as close to Monty's as he could hope to find.

For the rest of the day he walked again the very streets of his childhood, euphoric, borne on a tide of excitement and terror, half pleasurable, wholly familiar. The concrete underpass at Edgware Road echoed with the distant thunder of the sea. He had only to close his eyes against the sun to feel again the gritty sand creeping between his toes, and to see once more the brightly patterned shore. The raucous voices of children calling to each other down the side streets jolted his heart with half-forgotten playground menace and the smell of the pavement after a squall of summer rain was the

215

smell of the sea. Now, as then, he knew exactly what he had to do, knew the necessity, the inevitability of the act. Now, as then, he was torn between the longing to get it over and the half-shameful hope that he still might have a choice, that it was within his power to stop now, to decide that the risk was too great. With part of his mind he wished that he had returned to the stall as soon as his key ring was complete, and had tried his luck then, carried forward on a tide of optimism and success. But he knew that it could have been fatal. He had yet to prove that the old skills remained to him.

He spent the whole of Sunday and Monday practising. He locked his room and hung his jacket over the corner of a chair. He hooked the new key ring over the little finger of his left hand and insinuated his hand under the flap of the pocket. With his thumb he gently lifted his own key ring at the same time as he slid the substitute ring from his finger. He performed the procedure over and over again, sometimes using his thumb, sometimes his middle finger, watching for the slightest movement of the jacket pocket, counting out the seconds to time himself. Speed meant safety. When he felt that he was proficient he started again, only this time using the fingers of his right hand. He had to be ambidextrous in skill. He couldn't be sure until the moment came, until he was close enough to Monty to press his hand against the jacket, which of the pockets would hold the keys. For two days he hardly left his hotel room except to buy sandwiches—hurrying through the hallway, almost oblivious to Violet's greeting as she recognized his footsteps and her dead eyes searched for him—grudging every moment away from his task. And by Monday evening 18 September he felt that he was ready.

5

The next day he collected together two pairs of underclothes and a couple of shirts and stuffed them into a plastic shopping bag. He went first to the Delaney Street launderette, arriving soon after nine o'clock. Once his washing was swirling in the machine he moved to a chair next to the open door from where he could watch number 12. One possibility worried him, that the murderess and her daughter might choose this morning to visit the launderette themselves. But he told himself that the risk of an encounter was small. If they came

216

out with a bag which might contain clothes, he would simply walk out before they arrived and return later to empty his machine.

But all was well. He saw them emerge as usual by nine-thirty, carrying nothing but their shoulder bags. He moved away from the window, but they passed on the other side of the street and without glancing his way. One or two pensioners, always the earliest out in the mornings, had made their way to Monty's door but business was slack, the street had not yet come alive. When the third customer, an elderly woman, had shuffled away with her load of potatoes, he judged that the moment had come. He picked up the empty bag and moved across the road to the stall. His right hand deep in his jacket pocket fingered the dummy set of keys. The metal grew warm and moist under his touch. It irritated him that his hands were sweating with fear until he remembered that the moistness would help, the keys would slip the more easily from his fingers. And at least his hands weren't trembling. Even at the height of childhood delinquency his hands had never trembled.

Monty, temporarily without a customer, was burnishing Cox's Orange Pippins on his sleeve and arranging them in a line across the front of the stall. Pretending to be interested in a carton of avocado pears, Scase brushed past him, his left hand briefly pressing against Monty's right-hand pocket. It felt padded; something was there, a handkerchief perhaps, or a rag. But he could detect nothing hard or metallic. So the keys, if they were on him at all, must be in the other pocket. He retreated from the back of the stall, and asked for four oranges, holding open his bag. Monty picked them out and dropped them in. Then Scase demanded and received four of the Cox's Orange Pippins. Lastly he asked for two bananas, not too ripe, and pointed to a couple which formed part of a bunch slung from a rail at the back of the stall. It was the most inaccessible bunch, and Monty had to stretch over to reach them, steadying himself by grasping the rail with his left hand. Scase moved close to him, his eyes fixed on the bananas. He hooked his little finger into the bunch of dummy keys, closed his fist round them, then insinuated his hand into Monty's coat pocket and felt with a surge of triumph the hard tangled coldness of the keys. He strengthened his middle finger and lifted the bunch, at the same time gently relinquishing the dummy ring. After the practice of the last few days, and with no occluding pocket-flap to hinder him, the ploy was surprisingly easy. He judged that it took less than three seconds. By the time Monty had straightened himself to tear the two selected bananas from the bunch and had tossed them into the pan of his scales, Scase was standing meekly by his side, stretching wide his shopping bag to receive them.

He made himself walk unhurriedly down Delaney Street, but as

217

soon as he turned the corner into Mell Street, his steps quickened. He was lucky, there were two taxis waiting outside Marylebone Station. He took the first to Selfridges and went to the key-cutting counter in the basement. Even at this early hour there were two people before him, but it was only minutes before he was prising the two Yale keys from Monty's bunch and handing them over. He asked for two copies of each, knowing that sometimes a newly-cut Yale would be defective. He left the store by the front entrance and, as he had hoped, had no difficulty in getting a taxi. They were arriving in a steady stream, dropping tourists for their morning shopping. He asked for Marylebone Station and, after paying off the cab, actually walked on to the concourse in case the driver should be watching. Within two minutes he was back in Delaney Street. His plan was to transfer his washing to the drying machine, then to watch the greengrocer's shop from the window until it seemed a propitious moment to change back the keys. But as he approached the stall his heart sank. Monty was no longer wearing the fawn working coat. The day had become hotter, the stall busier and he was serving now wearing nothing but his blue jeans and a singlet. The coat was nowhere to be seen.

He left Delaney Street and sat on a bench in Marylebone Station waiting for the clock to show five minutes to twelve. Monty invariably went across to the Blind Beggar for his beer just after the hour. The thirty-minute wait seemed interminable. He sat in a fever of anxiety and impatience which drove him every few minutes to pace up and down the concourse. It was unlikely that Monty would want the keys until it was time for him to shut up the shop at night. Even then he wouldn't need them; the locks were both Yales and all that was necessary was for him to close both the shop and street doors after him. He might not discover that he had a substitute set of keys until he tried to open the street door next morning. But there would be no possible chance of making the substitution after nightfall. It had to be done now.

He walked back to Delaney Street at eight minutes to twelve and pretended to browse in the bookshop. At twelve o'clock Monty called to his neighbour and, a second or two later, appeared from the back of the shop wearing his denim jacket and went across to the Blind Beggar. The old man from the junk shop settled himself on the upturned crate, lifted his face for a moment to the sun, then opened his newspaper. It had to be now. It might be only a couple of minutes, perhaps less, before Monty reappeared with his beer. And the only hope of success lay in boldness. He walked briskly across the road and into the recesses of the shop, so quickly that the old man hardly had time to raise his eyes as he brushed past. All was well. The fawn working coat hung on the nail above two sacks of potatoes piled against the wall. As his fingers met the smooth metal of the keys his heart leaped in triumph.

Ths old man was standing in the space between the wall and the counter. Before he could speak Scase said:

"I've left a Marks and Spencer bag somewhere where I've been shopping. I've only been here, over the road at the bookshop and to the dairy in Mell Street and it isn't there. I thought Monty might have found it and put it on one side for me."

The sharp little eyes were suspicious. But Scase hadn't been anywhere near the cash register. He wasn't helping himself to anything, hadn't been in the shop long enough to steal. What, anyway, was there worth stealing at the back of the counter? He said grumpily:

"Monty? He's not Monty. Been dead twenty year, Monty has. That's George. And he never said nothing to me."

"It's not at the back, and there's nowhere else he would have put it. It looks as if I must have left it in the launderette and someone's taken it. Thank you."

He walked briskly away, crossing the road and stepping on to the kerb outside the Blind Beggar just as Monty—it was difficult to think of him as George—emerged, carefully carrying a brimming pint in each hand.

The relief, the excitement, the exultation were greater than any he had experienced in childhood after the lesser, more innocent delinquencies. His heart sang a paean of undirected praise. If the keys had been strung on a ring he would have needed to spin them in a flashing arc, to have tossed and caught them like a toy. But none of this triumph showed in his face. As George passed he smiled at him. There must have been something strange about the smile. As he turned into Mell Street his last memory was of George's astonished face.

6

He had carefully matched the two sets of keys and had strung them on different lengths of string. One set would open the front door, the second the door leading from the hall into the shop. Until he tried them in the lock he couldn't know which was which. He hoped luck would be with him and that he would get it right first time. The longer he lingered or fumbled at the door, the greater the chance that he would be seen. He watched from his usual vantage point on the wasteland until the murderess and her daughter had left for work, then waited another forty minutes in case they should have forgotten something and return unexpectedly. From the narrow slit in the corrugated iron he had a very restricted view of Delaney Street, but he put his ear against it and listened until he could hear no footfalls. Then he edged his way quickly across the wasteland and slid through the gap in the fence as he had so many times. Delaney Street was deserted. Above the closed shops he could see a row of lit upstairs windows where he could imagine people eating an early supper or settling down to an evening's television. To his left the launderette shone brightly with light, but he could see only one customer, an elderly woman with a basket on wheels dragging her tangled linen from one of the machines.

He took one set of the keys from his pocket and concealed them in his clenched palm, then he walked quickly but deliberately across the street and inserted the key in the lock. It didn't turn. His lips moved. Silently he said to himself: gently, gently, gently. He felt for the second string of keys and this time the key turned without difficulty and he stepped into the hall, closing the door behind him.

And then there came a moment of atavistic horror. The house had shuddered at his entrance. He stood transfixed, holding his breath. Then he relaxed. The vibration was only the rumble of a passing tube train, presumably in the tunnel between Marylebone and Edgware Road. The noise receded, and the house settled into calmness. He closed the door and stood motionless, listening to the silence. The hall held the earthy, heavy smell of potatoes, with a trace of a lighter, sharper scent, perhaps of apples. At the end of the passage he could see a faint haze where a door with two panels of opaque glass led to a garden or back yard. He switched on his torch and followed the pool of light down the passage. The door was bolted, both at the top and at the bottom. That meant that the yard offered no sanctuary, no place to hide. The murderess and her daughter would almost certainly check those locks before they finally went to bed.

He shone his torch on the stairs and made his way up, testing each stair with his foot before he put his full weight on it. There was a small half landing. He paused, then made his way up the second short flight. Their door was on the left. He shone the torch full on it, and the pool of bright light illumined a security lock.

Disappointment rose in his throat like a hard core of bile which he had to resist the temptation to vomit away. He didn't beat his

220

hands against the door in frustration, but he rested his head against it for a moment, fighting down nausea. Then came anger and a sense of self-betrayal. How stupid of him not to have known that the door would be locked. But he had thought of the premises as the single house which once it had been, with one front door, one lock. And this was no Yale lock. Unless he could again steal a set of keys—and how could he?—he could only force his way through this barrier by breaking down the door.

He had intended to explore the flat in detail, to discover where the murderess slept, so that he could go unhesitatingly to her room and make his escape afterwards without blundering through the wrong door. This was now impossible. He had to change his plan. But there were things that he could do, preparations that he could make. He could begin by familiarizing himself with the house. He knew that the women weren't due back until midnight, but he walked on tip-toe, the torch beam sheltered by his left palm, his ears keen for the slightest sound. Gently and very quietly he pushed open the door to the bathroom, standing to one side as if expecting to find it occupied. The window was wide open at the top, and the air rushed at him, cool and strong as a wind, billowing the curtains. They were drawn back and he dared not switch on his torch, but the garish London sky, streaked with purple and crimson, showed him the outline of the gas boiler, the delicately-linked hanging chain with its bulbous handle, the great white bath. There was no cupboard, no curtained recess, nowhere here where he could conceal himself.

He spent the next five minutes mounting and descending the stairs, testing them for creaks. The fifth and ninth were particularly noisy; he would have to remember not to tread on them. Most of the others creaked under his tread, but it was possible, by keeping close to the wall, to reduce all but the slightest sound.

Lastly, he took the second set of keys from his pocket and unlocked the door leading into the shop. As he pushed it open, the rich smell of earth, the zest of lemons and oranges, met him so strongly that it caught at his breath. The darkness was absolute. No chink of light from the street lamps shone through the metal shutters, and if there were a window at the rear of the shop it must have been boarded up. No drawn curtains could so effectively exclude the sky. He leaned back against the door, staring into the blackness, breathing freely for the first time since he had entered the house. Even if the women returned early, they would have no key to this room. Here he could be sure of safety. Emboldened, he switched on his torch and swept it slowly over the shop, over the stall of potatoes and fruit, the folded trestle table, the rolled mat of synthetic grass, the piled boxes of tomatoes, apples and lettuces

221

waiting for the morning, the sacks of potatoes and the meshed bags of onions humped against the wall. At the rear and under the shuttered window was an old porcelain sink; one of the taps was missing, from the other a continuous bead of water formed, then fell. He had to resist the urge to turn it off, to stop the regular soft dripping. To one side his torch shone on a wooden table with a formica top on which was a gas ring, a kettle, and a brown stained teapot. Underneath the table was an orange box turned on its side, containing two blue-rimmed mugs, a tin marked "sugar" and a tea caddy with a coronation picture of King George V and Queen Mary.

He propped his torch against one of the boxes. Then, illumined by the single beam of light, he put on the long macintosh and the gloves, drawing them up over the tucked-in cuffs of the sleeves. Lastly he took the knife from the bottom of the rucksack. He squatted against the strong wooden upright at the back of the stall, knees bent under his chin, his thin buttocks hard against the unyielding floor, the sheathed knife between his palms. It wouldn't happen tonight. He knew that with complete certainty, although he was unable to say why. But he felt obscurely that the macintosh and the gloves were some protection against leaving a trace of himself for Monty to find, and it was right that he should thus formally garb himself for his task, should be prepared in case, by some miracle, the murderess returned alone. He sat on in the darkness, waiting, counting the regular dripping of the tap, smelling the warmth of the plastic macintosh superimposed on the loamy scent of the shop, holding his white-gloved hands before him, palm to palm, like the hands of a priest.

It was just before midnight when, at last, they returned and he heard the firm closing of the front door. He thought he could detect a low murmur of voices and the creaking of the stairs, but he wasn't sure. But then they were overhead. The house had not been built as two flats and there were only the joists and the wooden floor between them. The timbers creaked loudly as their feet struck them, and occasionally the wood cracked like a shot. Then his heart would leap and he would stare, petrified, at the ceiling, as if afraid that a foot would descend through the boards. He could hear every move. It seemed impossible that his presence, the very smell of him, the warmth of his spent breath, should not penetrate through to them. He could identify the two sets of footsteps, one lighter than the other. That would be the murderess; the girl was taller and walked with more confidence. Then the footsteps separated; they were moving about in different rooms. The quieter footfalls were in the front of the house; so the murderess must sleep in the bedroom overlooking the street. After about five minutes he heard her footsteps across the ceiling and, a few minutes later, there was the flush of the lavatory cistern and the muffled roar of the gas boiler. So the murderess was in the bathroom. This, if all else failed, could give him his chance. But he needed to know whether, with no one in the house at night except another woman, she would bother to lock the door, whether the door to the flat itself was propped open or closed when either of them went to the bathroom. Perhaps it would be instinctive to close both doors. If, in the end, he had to kill her in the bathroom, these were the facts it would be important to know.

By half-past twelve the last sounds had died away, but still he sat on, the wood of the upright hard against his backbone. The loamy smell of freshly turned earth from the sacks of potatoes was stronger than ever. He found himself trying to hold his breath against memory. But it was no use. Suddenly he was standing again with Mavis by the covered heap of red earth at the edge of Julie's grave in that vast east London cemetery, watching the small white coffin jerking slowly downwards into darkness. They had been the only two mourners; Mavis had insisted on a private funeral. They had always kept themselves to themselves; why should they be generous in grief? Why now should they expose themselves to the avid, salacious eyes of their neighbours? Their own minister had been ill and the young substitute had worn unpolished shoes. Mavis had kept her eyes on them throughout the words of committal. Listening to her complaints afterwards he had said:

"But he took the service very nicely dear, I thought he spoke very well."

And she had replied in the grudging, obstinate voice with which he was to grow so familiar:

"He should have cleaned his shoes."

He fixed his mind on the murderess sleeping overhead. Within a few days she would be dead. Perhaps he and the girl would be dead too. In that moment it seemed to him not to be important if they also died. There might be a necessity which he couldn't yet foresee or understand, but which, when the time came, he would be powerless to prevent. That the three of them should die together even had a certain rightness, a completion, an avoidance of future complications which he could almost welcome. For himself, he feared death less than he feared imprisonment. Perhaps it was the possibility of his own imminent death, which he faced now for the first time, more than the certainty of hers, which drove his thoughts back to the past. In his mind there clicked a series of bright, disjointed images, like pictures flashed on a screen. The tinsel Christmas tree on the bar of the Goat and Compasses, glimpsed through the open door; the seaweed hanging in swathes from the girders of the pier, moving in

223

slimy tentacles beneath the green onrushing tide, the grating dampness of the sand as he scuffed it over a stolen purse; Mr Micklewright, holding a knight between his first and second fingers and sliding it towards him across the board; Eli Watkin spooning out the cat meat and hissing endearments at his yowling brood; Julie in her new Girl Guide uniform; Julie sleeping in her pram under the apple tree on the lawn of Magenta Gardens; Mavis glancing at him across the scarred desk of the local secondary school where they had first met at evening classes in French. Why, he wondered, had they chosen French? Neither had ever been to France, neither had ever had any particular wish to go. But that had been the beginning. Nothing that had happened between them afterwards had ever persuaded him that he was lovable; only that, by some miracle of chance, Mavis had found him so.

From time to time he dozed, then woke and stretched his cramped legs. At last, before dawn, he got slowly to his feet, took off his gloves and macintosh and repacked them with the torch and the sheathed knife in his rucksack. His vigil was over; this was a new day. He wouldn't return that evening; it was important to stay at the Casablanca on alternate nights, to ensure that he kept his senses fresh and alert, that he didn't go too short of sleep. But he would come back on Thursday and on alternate nights after that until his chance came. Optimism had been reborn. He knew that the wait wouldn't be long.

He closed the shop door with infinite care, then crept down the few yards of the passage. There was still the front door to shut, but he didn't fear that that quiet click would wake the sleepers overhead. Even if the murderess still lay awake or stirred in her sleep, so small a sound would hardly disturb her. This was an old house; old houses were full of mysterious nocturnal noises. And by the time she switched on the light and got to the window he would be out of sight. The door closed behind him and he set off for Baker Street Station to wait for the first Circle line train.

7

It was mid-afternoon on Thursday 21 September, and Philippa was sitting in the basket chair at the open window of her room. She and her mother had just returned from a visit to Brompton Oratory to see the Mazzuoli Marbles and there was an hour before they needed to set out for work. Her mother had said that she would make the tea. From the kitchen Philippa could hear small noises like the scrapings of a secretive domestic animal, delicate tinklings, an occasional soft footfall. The sounds were extraordinarily pleasurable. The door of her mother's room was open, but Thursday was early-closing day and no sounds came up from the street. The voices which drifted in through her own window seemed far-away shouts of joy from another world. It had been a hot oppressive day with the threat of thunder, but in the last half-hour the sky had lightened and now the room was filled with the strong mellow light which comes before the dusk.

Philippa sat absolutely still in the silence, and there began to flow through her a sense of tingling delight, entrancing in its strangeness. Even the inanimate objects in the room, the air itself, were suffused with this iridescent joy. She fixed her eyes on the geranium on the window sill. Why had she never before realized how beautiful it was? She had seen geraniums as the gaudy expedient of municipal gardeners to be planted in park beds, massed on political platforms, a useful pot plant for the house, since it throve with so little atten-tion. But this plant was a miracle of beauty. Each flowerlet was curled like a miniature rosebud on the end of its furred, tender stem. Imperceptibly but inevitably as her own breathing they were opening to the light. The petals were a clear, transparent pink, faintly striped with yellow, and the fan-like leaves, how intricately veined they were, how varied in their greenness, each with its darker penumbra. Some words of William Blake fell into her mind, familiar but new. "Every-thing that lives is holy. Life delights in life." Even her body's flux, which she could feel as a gentle, almost controlled, flow, wasn't the in-convenient and disagreeable monthly discharge of the body's waste. There was no waste. Everything living was part of one great whole-ness. To breathe was to take in delight. She wished that she knew how to pray, that there was someone to whom she could say: "Thank you for this moment of happiness. Help me to make her happy." And then she thought of other words, familiar but untraceable to their source: "In whom we live and move and have our being."

She heard her mother calling her from the front room. There was a smell of cut lemons and freshly brewed China tea, and the pot, with their two special cups, the Worcester and the Staffordshire, was on a papier mâché tray on the bedside table. Her mother was smiling and holding out to her a tissue-wrapped package. She said:

"I made it for you."

Philippa took it and shook out from its folds a polo-necked jumper in a variety of soft browns and fawns, and with two oblongs of apple green, carefully placed above the right breast and at the back. The jumper had been constructed from every kind of knitting stitch, and the variety of textures between the panels, the subtle blending of colours, gave its basic simplicity such distinction that Philippa, tugging it over her head, exclaimed aloud with pleasure:

"It's lovely! Lovely! You are clever, but when did you knit it?"

"In my room, late at night. I didn't want you to see it until it was finished. It's quite simple really. The sleeves are just oblongs grafted on to the dropped shoulders. Of course, it's too warm to be worn now, but come the autumn in Cambridge you will be glad of it."

"I'm glad of it now. I'll always be glad of it. It's beautiful. Everyone will wonder where I bought it. I shall like saying that my mother knitted it for me."

They looked at each other, two faces transformed with pleasure. "I shall like saying that my mother knitted it for me." She had spoken the words spontaneously, without embarrassment. She couldn't remember in her private, self-conscious, fabricated life, when she had been able to speak so simply what was in her heart. She tugged her mane of hair free from the rolled collar and shook it free. Stretching both arms widely, she spun round in pleasure. In the oval glass which she had set between the two windows, she watched her spinning image, gold and fawn and brown and flashing green, and behind her the still flushed face of her mother, bright-eyed and alive.

The peal of the front doorbell, strident and peremptory, broke their mood. Philippa stopped spinning and they gazed at each other with surprised and anxious eyes. No one had rung that bell since the probation officer's last visit. Her mother said:

"Perhaps George has come back for something and has forgotten his key."

Philippa went to the door. She said:

"You stay here. I'll go."

The bell had rung again before she reached the bottom of the stairs. And with that second ring she knew that this was trouble. She opened the door.

"Miss Palfrey? I'm Terry Brewer."

The voice was cautious, almost apologetic. He was proffering a card. He must have had it ready in his hands as he heard her coming down the stairs. She didn't look at it. The police had cards too. There was a card for every purpose: warrants, authorizations, identity cards, licences, passes. They said: "Let me in. I exist. I am authorized, safe, respectable." She didn't need a card to know what business he was in. She kept her eyes on his face.

"What do you want?"

He was very young, not much older than she was, with strong, tightly curled hair low on his forehead, a heart-shaped face with a neatly cleft chin, jutting cheek-bones and a delicate, moistly pouting mouth. His eyes were large and luminous, pale brown speckled with green. She made herself look into them.

"Just a chat. I'm a feature writer, a freelance. I've been asked to do an article for the *Clarion*. About lifers and their readjustment to the world outside prison. Nothing sensational. You know the *Clarion*. They're not interested in morbid sensationalism. What I'm after is the human interest, how you discovered who your mother was, what it's like living together after all these years, how she survived her time in prison. I'd like to interview you both. Of course, the name will be changed. I shan't mention Ducton."

It was hopeless to try to close the door in his face. Already his foot was jammed against the wood. She said:

"I don't know what you're talking about and I don't want to see you."

"Oh, but I don't think you've got much choice, have you? Better me than a dozen others. One interview, exclusive, and I leave you strictly alone. No address printed. No names. The others might not be so accommodating. You don't need me to tell you that."

It was a lie about being a feature writer or a freelance. She doubted whether he were even a reporter. More likely he was a trainee journalist or had some minor job on the *Clarion* and he saw this as his first big chance. But someone must have tipped him off and there could be only one person. She asked:

"How did you find us?"

"I've got friends."

"One friend particularly. Gabriel Lomas?"

He didn't answer, but she knew at once that the guess had been correct. His muscles were too undisciplined, the face too mobile for dissembling. So Gabriel must have telephoned Caldecote Terrace, choosing his time so that Hilda would be likely to be there alone.

227

Maurice would have sniffed danger and deceit over the line, but Hilda, silly, innocent Hilda, was a predestined victim. She wondered by what guile Gabriel had extracted the truth from her and how much of it he had learned. He would have lied about their meeting, of course; even if it weren't strictly necessary he couldn't have resisted at least one lie. And then he would have done his research. He was to read history at Cambridge. He would have been meticulous about ascertaining the facts. And it wouldn't have been so very difficult. There weren't many crimes for which a woman would be imprisoned for ten years. He would only have had to study the press cuttings for 1968 and '69. She was surprised that it had taken him as long as a week to discover who her mother was. But, then, he might have had more important matters on his mind. Perhaps this small betrayal hadn't been given top priority.

Watching Brewer's predatory, ingratiating smile, she could understand why Gabriel had been attracted. Singularity and strangeness in a face had always drawn him. Why else, at first, had he bothered with her? He picked people over like bric-à-brac on a street stall. She had seen him at parties momentarily entranced by the fall of light on a turning cheek, a flash of unsuspected wit, the confident turn of a head. And, like bric-à-brac, people could be discarded if he made a bad buy. This face would have intrigued him. The farouche good looks, the hint of corruption and danger, the spurious vulnerability. He was trying to look deprecatory, harmless, but she could almost smell his excitement. He was rather too carefully dressed and not altogether at ease in his clothes. This must be his best suit, kept for job interviews, weddings, seductions, blackmail. It was a little too well-cut, the lapels too wide, the cloth, more synthetic than wool, already creasing. It was odd that Gabriel hadn't done something about his clothes. But he held himself well, he fancied himself, this common little pouf with his false, ingratiating smile.

"Look you'd better let me in. Get it over with. I'll only be back. And I don't want to discuss it here. I don't want to start shouting. After all, someone from the street might hear us. They think your mother is called Palfrey, I suppose? Better keep it that way."

Her mother had appeared at the top of the stairs. She whispered: "Let him in."

Philippa stepped aside and he slid through the door. Her mother was standing at the open door of the flat and he pushed past her and moved into the front room as confidently as if he had been there before. They followed, side by side, and stood in the doorway regarding him. How eagerly he had pranced up those narrow shabby stairs, despising their poverty, their vulnerability! Now he was frankly surveying the room, keen-eyed as a creditor pricing their few possessions, his glance resting at last on the Henry Walton. The picture, which even to Philippa's eyes looked suddenly out of place, seemed momentarily to confuse him.

It was an abomination that he should be there. Anger flowed through her. She was lifted exhilaratingly on a tide of passionate rage in which inspiration and action flowed together.

"Wait," she said. "Wait."

She ran into the kitchen and dragged the toolbox from the cupboard under the sink. Grasping the largest and strongest chisel, she walked past the front room with only a glance at Brewer's face, stupid and vacant with astonishment, then went out shutting the door of the flat behind her. Then she inserted the blade of the chisel in the narrow gap between the lock and the door-jamb and worked away at the lock. She had no energy to waste on wondering what was happening inside the flat; all her strength, all her mind were concentrated on the task in hand. The lock didn't break. It had been made to resist any such crude assaults. But the door itself was more fragile. It had never been intended as a front door and it had been there for over eighty years. She worked away, grunting with effort, and soon she heard the first creaks, saw the first splintering of the wood. After about two minutes it finally cracked and broke away. She gave a little moan and the door burst open under her hands. And now she was in the front room facing him, breathless, the chisel in her hand. When she could speak her voice was perfectly controlled.

"Right. Now get out. If you write a word, I'll complain to your paper and to the Press Council that you forced your way in here, broke down the door and threatened to betray us to everyone in the neighbourhood unless we gave you an exclusive story."

He backed against the wall, his eyes fixed on the chisel. His voice shook. He said in a hoarse whisper:

"You crazy bitch! Who's going to believe you?"

"More people than will believe you. Can you afford to take the risk? I'm eminently respectable, remember. Are you? And do you think a reputable newspaper will welcome that kind of publicity? My mother may be beyond compassion, but I'm not. I'm the dutiful daughter, risking my future to help her. Cambridge scholar in backstreet hideout. 'She's my mother,' says Mary Ducton's daughter. That's the kind of emotional muck you had in mind, isn't it? I qualify for pity. Do you seriously believe that anyone will believe that I broke down that door myself?"

"It isn't my chisel! Why should I come here with a chisel?"

"Why indeed, except perhaps to force open a door. It's a perfectly ordinary chisel. New, as you see. No distinguishing marks. Prove it isn't yours if you can. And remember, it's two against one. You seem to know who my mother is, what she did. Do you suppose a lie would stick in her throat? Not if it's going to destroy your career it won't."

He said, with a kind of wonder:

"Christ, I believe you'd do it!"

"I'm her daughter. If this didn't succeed and you got away with it, how long do you think I'd let you last?"

There could be no doubt now of his terror. She could smell it, rancid as vomit. He backed towards the door as she advanced, chisel in hand, the point at his throat. Then he was gone and they heard the clatter of his frantic feet on the stairs.

Her mother moved along from the wall, feeling it with outstretched hands like a blind woman. Philippa went to her and led her to the bed. They sat side by side, their shoulders touching. Her mother whispered:

"You frightened him."

"I did, didn't I? They won't print anything, and he won't write anything. Not yet anyway. Even if he tells, they'll check with their lawyers first."

"Couldn't we go away. Not for long, just for a few days so that he'll think he's scared us off. We could go to Ventnor, on the Isle of Wight. I went there once for a Sunday school treat when I was nine. There are cliffs and sand and little Victorian coloured houses. Once he finds we've gone he won't keep coming back."

"He won't come back at all. He won't dare. He knows that I wasn't bluffing. The *Clarion* is the last paper to print the kind of sentimental muck he had in mind. Even if they did print a story, they wouldn't identify either of us or print the address. They have their liberal conscience to preserve. They won't see it as their business to hunt you down. After all, as a lifer out on licence, in their eyes you're practically a protected species."

She was surprised that her mother was so shaken. She had seemed so strong when she first came out of prison. But perhaps nothing had mattered very much to her then. Perhaps it was only when she had stood on the canal bank in the green watery twilight, watching that shabby case finally topple out of sight that she had laid herself open to the pain of living. She moved closer to her mother and put her arm round the shaking shoulders. She laid her cheek against her mother's cheek, flesh against colder flesh. Then she kissed her. It was all so easy, so beautifully easy. Why had it taken her so long to learn that there was nothing to be afraid of in loving? She said:

"It's going to be all right. Nothing dreadful is going to happen. We're together and no one can touch us."

"But suppose he goes to another paper?"

"He won't, not while he's working for the *Clarion*. And if he does, we'll destroy his career. All you have to do is to confirm what I tell them. If you seem frightened—well that would be natural. All it needs is the capacity to lie."

"I don't think I'd be very good at lying."

"I don't see why you should worry about lying. Telling the truth didn't do you much good. But you won't have to lie. I tell you, he's not coming back."

"The door. How can we lock it?"

"I'll buy a bolt tomorrow and we can use that at night until I can get a new lock fixed. That isn't important, it's the least of our worries. He won't come back, and there's nothing worth stealing except the picture. A professional thief wouldn't bother with this kind of place. He certainly wouldn't take the Henry Walton. We were burgled once at Caldecote Terrace. What they like to pick up are the small, easily disposable valuables. There's nothing here that anyone could want."

She watched her mother's hands restlessly moving together. Her own fingers, long, bony, the nails strong and narrow, but on her mother's hands. Wringing her hands. It wasn't an expression one would ever write, too trite, too imprecise; but apparently it did happen, except that "wringing" wasn't the right word for this rhythmic pressing together of the palms. The hands seemed to be comforting each other. She was staring fixedly ahead, apparently oblivious of those kneading palms. Perhaps she was recalling the heavy smoothness of a sea-washed stone rolled between her hands, seeing in memory the layered sea, stretching to infinity, the mottled wave curving to crash in shingled foam against her naked feet. Then her eyes blinked again into the present. She said:

"How did he know?"

"Gabriel Lomas told him. Gabriel can smell out scandal, secrets, fear; it's a talent he has. He couldn't resist telling him. I can understand that. It was too important to him. Like me and the pregnant wife. In the end we think of no one but ourselves."

"What pregnant wife?"

"No one you know. Someone I did down. Someone who needed this flat."

"He seems a strange friend for Gabriel Lomas, a different class."

"Oh Gabriel has a personality like a hexagon. People need touch only one side for an illusion of closeness. Forget about him. Perhaps it would be a good idea to get out of London for a time. Ventnor is as good a place as any, but you mustn't expect to find it the same. No place ever is. And we'll need some money. I've some-

231

thing left in the bank but we must keep a small reserve for when this lease runs out. It won't be easy to find work in the Isle of Wight, not immediately, not at the end of the season."

Her mother turned to her with the eyes of a pleading child.

"I'm sure you'll like it there. And we needn't be away long."

Philippa said:

"And you could change your name you know. It would make things easier."

Her mother shook her head.

"No, I couldn't do that. That would be defeat. I have to know who I am."

Philippa got up from the bed.

"We'll go tomorrow, just as soon as I've got the door mended and a new lock fixed. But first I have to go to Caldecote Terrace. I won't be away long, not more than an hour. Will you be all right?"

Her mother nodded. She said, trying to smile:

"I'm sorry I'm being so stupid. Don't worry. I'll be all right."

Philippa slung her bag over her shoulder and made for the door. Suddenly her mother called her back. She said:

"Rose! You won't take anything that isn't yours?"

"Don't worry," she answered. "I shan't take anything that they don't owe us."

8

The things to take were the silver caddy spoons. They were small, portable, easily disposed of; silver was fetching a high price. Maurice had over a hundred in his collection. About half were kept in the wall safe in his dressing-room and the others on display in an eighteenth-century rosewood cabinet in the drawing-room. The cabinet was always kept locked, but she knew that the key was in the safe, and she knew, too, the combination. From time to time he would change the ones on display although, once they were arranged on the purple velvet, he seldom looked at them again. As a child she had enjoyed helping him to set them out, had liked the feel of their smooth bowls, their delicate balance in her fingers. He had taught her to recognize the hallmarks, handing the spoons to her as he took them from the box and asking her to guess their date and the name of the silversmith. Yes, it was right that she should take the caddy spoons. And it wouldn't be difficult. If Maurice hadn't changed the combination of his wall safe, and she thought this unlikely, there wouldn't even be a need to break the cabinet lock. It was a pretty object. It would have been a hurtful necessity to have had to damage it. It never once occurred to her to make the theft look like a burglary. She would take as many spoons as she needed to sell to keep herself and her mother without working for about a month. Maurice would know that it was she who had taken them, and one day she would tell him why. She knew which were the rarest and which, therefore, the most valuable. Even quite ordinary ones in Church Street market were fetching thirty pounds. She need only take twenty of the best and their immediate problems would be over. There wouldn't be any difficulty in getting rid of them provided she offered them singly and in the right shops. She wouldn't get what they were worth, but she would get enough.

Because she was in a hurry to get the job done and return to her mother, she decided on the extravagance of a cab from Marylebone Station. She paid it off at the corner of Caldecote Road, an instinctive precaution which, as soon as the taxi moved away, struck her as silly and unnecessary. The basement kitchen was in darkness, as she knew it would be. This was Thursday, Hilda would be in court. But she turned the key in the lock and shut the door behind her with extreme care, holding her breath, as if afraid to wake an echo in the white, clean-smelling hall. She was a stranger here, and it seemed to her that the house knew it. Then she ran lightly upstairs to the front bedroom. As she put her hand on the door, the second before she turned the knob, she knew instinctively and with absolute certainty that she wasn't alone. She stopped dead in the doorway, then slowly pushed the door open.

They were both on the bed, Maurice and the girl, half reclining, transfixed by that first sound of her footsteps on the landing. They had finished making love. The rumpled bed, the spread towel, told their own story, and she thought she could sniff in the air the unmistakable, doughy smell of sex. Maurice was wearing only his pants, but the girl was naked. She shoved herself clumsily from the bed and with a little cry began gathering up her clothes from the chair. Philippa stood at the door, half aware of Maurice's unembarrassed, ironic gaze, while the girl, scarlet-faced, diminished by shame, tried to cover herself with her skirt, and bent in an ungainly display of buttocks to scrabble under the bed for her shoes. Philippa knew that she had met her before, but for a moment she couldn't recall when or where. Absolute nakedness was intrusive, confusing to the senses. Paradoxically it both revealed and diminished identity.

233

She made herself stare at the girl's face, and then remembered. She was one of Maurice's students. The name came to her a second later. Sheila. Sheila Manning. Eighteen months ago she had come to dinner; it was an evening when Gabriel had also been invited. She had been an uncomfortable guest, voluble in her nervousness, alternately aggressive and aggrieved, treating them to a rehashed version of Maurice's latest seminar on the cycle of deprivation. Gabriel had taken trouble with her, resisting the frequent temptation to wit or sarcasm, steering the conversation from Marxist dogma to such innocuously boring subjects as food and holidays. It hadn't, Philippa thought, been done through kindness. Like most men, he reserved kindness for women who, beautiful or successful, had the least need of it. She had decided that he was acting either to disoblige her, or in obedience to some nursery dictate that it was the responsibility of a guest to attempt to rescue from social disaster even the most unpropitious dinner party. The girl, as had been painfully apparent, was in love with Maurice even then. Had it really taken her eighteen months to get into his bed?

Now they were face to face, and she stood silently to one side to let the girl pass. She was clutching a bundle of clothes to her chest. Encountering Philippa's disparaging stare she dropped her shoes; scarlet-faced she scrabbled for them, letting slip the rest of the bundle. Philippa noticed the strong body, curiously disproportionate to the etiolated neck and the thin face. Her breasts were as heavy as a nursing mother's, the nipples jutting like miniature udders from their brown concave aureoles. How could he have chosen to take them into his mouth? She thought complacently of her own high, tight breasts, the delicately furled nipples, only slightly raised. She was glad she approved of her body, even if, as yet, she hadn't taught it how to give her pleasure.

She came into the room and closed the door. She said:

"I would have thought you'd have had more pride than to bring her here, to fuck her on your own bed."

"Whose bed are you suggesting I should more properly use? Don't be predictable, Philippa. Do you have to react like a character in a second-rate TV soap opera?"

"But it's that kind of situation, isn't it? Commonplace. Farcical." And so, she thought, is this conversation. Like everything we say to each other, it's contrived.

He sat on the bed, pulling on his shirt. She was surprised that he hadn't first reached for his trousers. To be trouserless was surely to be vulnerable, ridiculous, the stock butt of bedroom farce. His pants were very short, white and narrowly striped with blue. She had seen Hilda pulling them out of the washing machine often enough. A tangle of male clothes. He was fastidious. Everything was clean every day. He said:

"It may seem farcical and commonplace—but doesn't it occur to you that I might be fond of her, might love her?"

"No. You're like me. We don't know how."

Once she had been afraid that she would never learn, but not now, not any more. She watched him dress. How long had it been going on, she wondered. Weeks, months, years? Had it perhaps started as soon as Hilda was appointed to the Bench? It must have seemed an ideal opportunity; the house free on the same day every week for three months. How many girls? A new one for each academic year? They would have had to avoid arriving together, but that wouldn't be difficult. He could come home through the mews service road leading to the garden door, then open the front door to her ring. The street was very quiet in the afternoon; but it wouldn't greatly matter if she were seen. After all, he was a lecturer, he had students to supervise. She asked:

"Where is she now?"

"I haven't the least idea. In the bathroom, I imagine."

"As long as she isn't drowning herself. That would take some explaining away."

"Oh, I don't think she's suicidal. Insecure and emotionally a bit intense, but not suicidal. But you'd better go and find out if you're worried."

"She's your responsibility, not mine. She's rather wet isn't she? I shouldn't have thought that she was your type. Is she really the best you can find?"

"Don't underrate her."

"That would be difficult, judging by her dinner conversation. She was so stupid with her talk about property and theft. Second-hand jargon and third-hand ideas. I got tired of waiting for her to make an original or amusing remark. No wonder you're reduced to fucking her. Anything would be less boring than listening to her conversation."

He had finished dressing now and was putting on his jacket, carefully transferring odd items from the dressing-table into his pockets. He said:

"Oddly enough, it was after that evening that we became lovers. I felt sorry for her. With me that's always dangerous."

"Is that why you married Hilda?"

As soon as the words were out she regretted them. But all he said was:

"No, that was because she was sorry for me."

She waited for him to explain, but he said no more. And suddenly, she thought of Orlando. She had never spoken his name to Maurice, but now she was filled with a sympathy which had to find expression. She said:

"I forgot about Orlando. I always do forget. I suppose it's because you've never talked about him, never even shown me a photograph. And I've never told you that I'm sorry he died. Until now I don't think I was particularly sorry. If he hadn't died I wouldn't be here. And I never knew him: if one can ever know a child. But you've lost him more completely than my mother was ever in danger of losing me. At least she'd have known that I was alive somewhere."

He didn't reply, but his hands ceased their careful busyness with his jacket. She looked at his face. In one second it had become as vacant as the face of a spent actor's in repose, all emotion, even the lines, smoothed away. Then there passed over it a look so momentary that she almost missed it, of pain, regret, of the rueful acceptance of defeat. She had seen that look once before. The picture came vividly to her mind, limed with the colour of blood. The screech of tyres followed immediately by a crash like an explosion. The young motor-cyclist, helmetless, lying on the kerb at the junction of Oxford Street and Charing Cross Road. The wheels of his motor cycle spinning in the air. A second of eerie silence, absolute, the air holding its breath. Then the babble of voices, cries. A woman with a face like lard, a cardigan stretched across her bolster of a chest, yelling in anger and remembered pain.

"He was coming too fast! He was too bloody fast! Oh Christ, those fucking machines!"

He was lying there, dying so publicly, and her railing voice was the last sound he heard on earth. Involuntarily she had stepped towards him and his eyes had met hers. She had seen in them that same look, the rueful acceptance of a terrible knowledge. Afterwards she had hurried home to write it down, an exercise in the creative recollection of trauma. She had torn up the passage. She always did tear up such exercises. Her life was encumbered enough, the wasteland between imagination and reality already too nebulous. But she wished that she hadn't recalled it now. This was a moment of small triumph, a time for planning and action. She hadn't wanted to think about death.

They were simultaneously aware that Sheila Manning had come into the room. She was dressed and was carrying a jacket and a heavy, old-fashioned handbag. Ignoring Philippa, she spoke directly to Maurice:

"You promised that it would be safe. You said no one would be here."

She was making a brave attempt at dignity, but she couldn't keep from her voice the note of querulous reproach. She sounded, thought Philippa, like Hilda when Maurice was late home for dinner. He wouldn't welcome that peevish reminder of small delinquencies. There was only one way for her to carry off this débâcle successfully, with humour and panache, but these weren't in her armoury. And whatever she said, this would be the end of the affair. The girl was as humiliated and inept as a child caught out in her first sexual experimenting. This room, this moment, most of all this man would be remembered only with self-disgust. She knew that she herself was part of the humiliation, sitting there calmly on the bed by Maurice's side in possession of more than herself.

She said:

"I'm sorry. It was unintentional."

She sounded insincere to her own ears. She would have despised anyone who believed her, and the girl didn't.

"It doesn't matter. You've done what you wanted to do."

She turned away. Watching the drooped head, Philippa wondered whether she had started to cry. Maurice at once got up from the bed and went to her. He put an arm round her shoulders and said gently:

"It was horrible for you. I'm so sorry. Please don't worry. These things aren't important, you know. In a few weeks you'll be able to laugh about it."

"It has never been important, not to you anyway. I shan't come back."

Perhaps she hoped, pathetically, that the threat would provoke some response from him; pain, anger, reproach. Instead he said, punctilious as a host:

"I'll see you out. Are you sure you've got everything?"

She nodded. They went out together, his arm still round her shoulder, and a minute later Philippa heard the closing thud of the front door. She waited for him in the bedroom, still sitting on the edge of the dishevelled bed. He stood at the door silently regarding her for a moment, then began to pace up and down the room. He said:

"You are enjoying yourself? You look happy and you look well."

"Yes. Yes I am. I suppose it's the first time in my life that I've been able to feel important to another human being."

"Indispensable, you mean. There's nothing so intoxicating to the ego as the knowledge that happiness is in one's gift. It's the foundation of every successful marriage. The other person has to be capable of being made happy, of course, and that capacity is rarer than one might imagine. I take it that your mother is?"

"For most of the time, yes."

237

"I suppose there are moments when she wonders whether she has the right to live."

She said:

"Why should she? The world is full of people who've killed a child: a wartime bomb released, a bullet in Belfast which hits the wrong target, a stamp on the car accelerator in a fit of impatience. And what about the drunken drivers, the incompetent doctors? They don't spend their days wondering whether they've a right to live. And she has survived ten years in prison. If anyone has the right to live, she has."

"And how do you spend your days? I take it you're enjoying the pleasure of patronage, giving her the benefit of your education."

She thought: "You should know about that. You enjoyed teaching me." She said:

"We look at pictures. And I'm showing her London."

"Didn't she know London already? She and Ducton lived close enough."

"I don't know. We never talk about the past. She doesn't want to."

"That's very wise of her. What, incidentally, have you come home for? It wasn't a particularly propitious moment to choose, but I take it that this *démarche* wasn't planned."

"I came to get some money. The Press have found out where we are. We've got to get away, at least for a time. I don't think they'll be back, but my mother's too upset to stay in Delaney Street. We're going to the Isle of Wight."

"So the running has started and she's dragging you with her."

"Not dragging. Never dragging. I'm going because I want to be with her."

"For God's sake why the Isle of Wight?"

"We think we'd like it there. She went there once as a girl, some kind of Sunday school treat."

"There are cheaper bolt holes. I suppose you intended to help yourself from the safe. What I keep in there will just about get you across the Solent."

"There are other things here I could take and sell. I thought of the caddy spoons. We only want enough cash for the first week or two. Then we can both get a job. That shouldn't be difficult even at the end of the season. We're not fussy what we do."

"How did the Press discover where you were?"

"We met Gabriel Lomas at the Royal Academy exhibition. I think he put his boyfriend on to us. But first he must have phoned Hilda and got the address out of her. That wouldn't be difficult, not for Gabriel."

"You might have expected it from that decadent Tory with his

238

high talking and squalid morality. Well, at least you've learned that betrayal isn't the prerogative of the extreme left."

"I never thought it was."

"So now you've got a choice between blackmail and theft. Why don't you sell the Henry Walton, by the way? You've got it. It's yours."

"We like it. We're taking it with us. Besides, you owe us something."

"Not any longer. You're eighteen, you're of age. When I adopted you I owed you a home, food, education, a reasonable standard of care. I owed you conscientious affection. Anything more isn't within my gift. I don't think there's anything on the slate."

"I'm not thinking about me. I'm thinking about my mother. You owe her my purchase price. You didn't have to adopt me. You could have fostered me, become my legal guardian. You could have given me a home and education without taking me away from her for ever. The experiment would have been the same—nearly the same anyway. You would still have been able to say: 'Look what I've done. Look what I've made of this odd, difficult, uncommunicative child, the daughter of a rapist and a murderer. It's not as if you ever cared about abstractions like justice or retribution. It's not as if you really worried about what she'd done. And you've never had a high regard for criminal justice, have you? Magistrates' courts, the Crown court; a formal system for ensuring that the poor and incompetent know their place, that the dispossessed don't get their grubby hands on the spoils. The petty thief ends in prison, the financier who makes his fortune dealing in currency ends up in the Lords. I've heard you often enough. Slice through society—you even know the precise socio-economic point at which the cut should be made—and the top half sits in judgement under the royal arms, the bottom half stands in the dock. The rich man in his castle, the poor man at his gate, law makes them high and lowly and orders their estate. So why didn't she qualify for your kind of mercy? She was poor enough, disadvantaged, under-educated, all the things you preach excuse crime. So why not excuse her?"

He said calmly:

"I'm not in the habit of confusing petty recidivism with murder and rape."

"But you know nothing about her! You don't know what pressures drove her to kill that child. You never bothered to find out. You only knew that she had something you wanted—experimental material—me. Scarce experimental material, no—unique. A child who might have been specially bred for your purpose, to demonstrate that man is the creature of his environment. And there were

239

incidental advantages, a child to keep your wife occupied while you fucked your students. No wonder you had to get your hands on me. But what about my mother? If she'd been hanged, if it had all happened before the death penalty was abolished, the hangman would have been more just. At least he'd have left her something. You were going to take me away for ever. She would have come out of prison and we'd never have known each other, never even have met. By what right did you do that to us? And then you say that you don't owe her anything!"

"Is this what she's told you?"

"No. It's what I've worked out for myself."

He came over to her, but he didn't sit beside her on the bed. Instead he stood over her, looking down. When he spoke his voice was harder. He said:

"Is that what you've really felt all these last ten years, that you were experimental material? No, don't answer hastily. Think about it. Be honest. Your generation make such a fetish of honesty. The more hurtful it is to others, the more necessary you appear to find it. When Hilda's excellent food slipped down your gullet, did you really see yourself as an experimental animal being fed its nicely calculated ration of protein, vitamins and minerals?"

"Hilda is different. I wish I could love Hilda."

He said:

"I daresay we both wish that we could love Hilda." He added: "She misses you."

She wanted to cry out: "But what about you? Do you miss me?" Instead she said:

"I'm sorry, but I'm not coming back."

"And what about Cambridge?"

"I'm beginning to think that Cambridge isn't as important as I thought it was."

"Do you mean you'll delay going up, wait a year?"

"Or not go up at all. After all, I'm going to be a novelist. A university education isn't essential for a writer. It could even be a disadvantage. There are better ways of spending the next three years."

"You mean with her?"

"Yes," she said simply. "With her."

He went across to the window and stood for a minute, parting the net curtains, looking down into the street. What, she wondered, was he expecting to see? What inspiration did he hope for from those brightly painted doors, the elegant fanlights, the brass-bound tubs and window boxes of the opposite terrace? After a moment he turned and began pacing between the two tall windows, eyes on the ground. Neither of them spoke. Then he said:

240

"There's something I've got to tell you. No, that's not strictly true, I don't have to tell you. Until this afternoon I didn't intend to tell you. But it's time you stopped living in a fantasy world and faced reality."

She thought: "He's trying to sound reluctant, concerned, but what he's really feeling is excitement, triumph." Something of the excitement communicated itself to her, and she felt, too, a spasm of fear. But it passed quickly. There was nothing he could say now which could harm her or her mother. Her eyes followed his careful pacing. Never before had she been so aware of his physical presence, of every breath he drew, of every bone of his head and hands, of every contraction of muscle; the air between them drummed with his heartbeat. And because of this intensity of awareness there was something else she knew, something that she couldn't explain. If now he wanted to hurt her, it had nothing to do with Sheila Manning. How lightly he had taken that humiliation! What had wounded him had been that blurted-out sympathy for the loss of Orlando. This moment was to do with her and him; but it was to do with Orlando too. She waited without speaking for him to begin. If he wanted to make a pretence of embarrassment, of reluctance, she wasn't going to help him. He said:

"You've assumed that Hilda and I adopted you after the murder, that your mother let you go because she was serving a life sentence, had no real choice. I thought when you started living together that she might have told you the truth. Obviously she hasn't. Your adoption order went through exactly two weeks before Julia Scase was killed, and we'd had you as a foster child for six months before then. The truth is quite simple: your mother let you go, because she didn't want you."

She wished that he'd stop his slow regular pacing, that he'd come over to her, sit beside her, look into her face, do anything except touch her. Instead he glanced at her, an artful, almost conspiratorial glance, so swift that she wondered whether she had imagined that slit-eyed momentary regard. Something, perhaps a speck of dust, was irritating his left eye. He took his handkerchief from his jacket pocket and rubbed it, then stood blinking. Satisfied, he started again on his slow perambulation. He said:

"I don't know what went wrong originally. She was pregnant when she married and it might have been that. I was told that she had a long and painful labour after a difficult pregnancy. That's one of the diagnostic pointers to child abuse. Anyway, there was no bonding of mother and child. I gather that you weren't easy. You were difficult to feed, an unresponsive, perpetually crying baby. She hardly slept at night for your first two years."

Q

He paused, but she didn't speak. His voice was as cool and controlled as if this were a dissertation before his students, an exposition that he had given so many times before that he knew it by heart. He went on:

"Things didn't improve. The screaming baby became an unloving child. Both of you had violent tempers, but you, of course, were too young to injure her except psychologically. She, unfortunately, could do more damage. One day she struck out at you and gave you a black eye. After that she became frightened. She decided she wasn't cut out for motherhood, so she went back to work and placed you with foster parents. I understand that it was a weekly arrangement; you came home for the weekends. She could stand you for two days a week."

Philippa said quietly:

"I remember. I remember Auntie May."

"There were, no doubt, a succession of spurious aunties of various degrees of suitability and of responsibility. In June 1968 one of them brought you down to Pennington; it was supposed to be a treat for you, a day in the country. It was just before the house was sold and the woman was visiting her sister who was the pastry cook there. She's retired now, of course. All the old servants have gone. I had to go down to Pennington to arrange about some of Helena's things before the sale, and Hilda and I met you and your foster parent in the garden. Hilda talked to her. She was a relief, I suppose, from the people in the house. And that's how we heard about you. Beddows was her name, Mrs Gladys Beddows. She wanted to stop fostering you—you weren't the easiest of children—but she was worried about letting you go back full time to your parents. She wasn't very bright and she didn't even like you but she had some sense of responsibility.

"After that meeting I couldn't get you out of my mind. The thought of you was like an irritation, something I would rather not have known but wasn't able to forget. I didn't want to get involved. I told myself that you were no concern of mine. I wasn't even thinking then about adopting a child. Hilda had mentioned the possibility, but it wasn't an idea that appealed to me. Certainly I wasn't looking for a child. I told myself that it would do no harm to find out what had happened to you. It was easy enough to trace Mrs Beddows through her sister. She told me that you were back full time with your mother. I nearly left it at that. But I was in the neighbourhood; it would do no harm to call. I didn't even bother to concoct an excuse for the visit, which was unlike me. I don't usually go into new situations unprepared. It was early evening by then and your mother had just come home from work. You weren't there. You

242

had been admitted two days earlier to King George V Hospital, Ilford, with a suspected fracture of the skull. And that was the most dangerous and the last time that your mother lost her temper with you."

She said through bloated lips, not realizing what tense she was using:

"Is that why the child could never remember anything that happened before she was eight?"

"The amnesia was partly the result of the injury, partly, I imagine, hysterical, the mind's natural reluctance to recall the unbearable. Neither Hilda nor I have ever attempted to cure it. Why should we?"

"And then what happened to her?"

"Your parents agreed that we should foster you when you came out of hospital, with a view to adoption if it worked out all right. There wasn't a prosecution. The hospital apparently accepted your mother's explanation that you'd fallen downstairs and cracked your head on the bottom banister. Those were the days before the Maria Colwell case and the authorities were less ready than now to suspect deliberate ill-treatment. But she told me the truth, she told me everything that June evening. I think she was glad to have someone, a stranger, to whom she could talk. You came to us straight from hospital and six months later we adopted you. Your parents both gave their consent without, I may say, any apparent reluctance. And that is the mother for whom you now propose to give up Cambridge, become a thief, and spend God knows how many years dragging after her from one watering place to another. The Scase murder, of course, is hardly relevant. She didn't murder you after all, although I gather it was a pretty close thing."

She didn't cry out in vehement protest that he was lying, that it wasn't true. Maurice only lied about important things, and then only when he could be certain that he wouldn't be found out. This wasn't important to him, and the truth could easily be proved. But she didn't need to check. She knew that it was the truth. She wished that she didn't feel so cold. Her face, her limbs, her fingers, were icy. He ought to have seen that she was shaking. Why didn't he tug a blanket from Hilda's bed and fold it round her? Even her lips were swollen with cold, stiff and numbed as if she had been given a dental injection. It was difficult to form words and her voice, when it came, sounded slurred.

"Why didn't you tell me?"

"I should like to believe that it was because I didn't want to hurt you. Perhaps it was. There are some cruelties which take courage. Mine are on a meaner scale. I did try to warn you. I told you to find out the facts, to read the Press accounts of the trial. Those would
243

have told you the date of the murder. You already knew your date of adoption. It might also have struck you as odd that the Press reports made no mention of a child. But then, you didn't want to know the facts, didn't want to talk to us about it; it seemed you were wilfully determined to be blind. It's odd that over something so important you never once used your intelligence, you who have always relied on intelligence, have had such a respect for your own mind."

She wanted to cry out: "What else have I had to rely on? What else had I on offer?" Instead she said:

"Thank you for telling me now."

"It needn't make any difference. It's an irrelevance. After all, you're not concerned with conduct or responsibility or nurture. If the blood tie is all that matters to you, well that at least is intact. But I did have you for ten years. I may not be entitled to make any claims on you, but at least I've a right to express a view about your future. And I'm not letting you give up Cambridge without a struggle. The chance of those three years won't come again, not now, not when you're young which is when they matter."

He added drily:

"I've also the right to my own Georgian silver. If you need money for her, sell the Henry Walton."

She said as humbly as a servant at the end of an interview:

"Is there anything else you want to tell me before I go?"

"Only that this is your home if you want it. This is where you belong. I've got an adoption order to prove it. And if that legalistic conveyance of possession lacks the emotional charge of the blood tie; hasn't your family had enough of blood?"

At the door she turned and looked back at him. She said:

"But why did you do it? Why me?"

"I told you. I couldn't put you out of my mind. And I was afraid of what might happen to you. I hate waste."

"But you must have hoped for something: gratitude, diversion, interest, the gratification of patronage, companionship for your old age, the ordinary things?"

"It didn't seem so at the time, but I suppose I did. My demands have always been presumptuous. Perhaps what I hoped for was love."

Three minutes later he stood at the window watching her leave. There was something different about her, a sense of brightness dulled, of limbs uncoordinated. Perhaps it was the hunch of the shoulders, diminishing height, foreshowing how she might look as an old woman, or the way in which she scurried from the front door, furtive as an interloper surprised. At the end of the terrace she broke into a run, swerving from the pavement into the path of a taxi. He gasped; his heart skidded. When he could bear to open his eyes he saw that she was safe. Even from this distance he could hear the screech of brakes, the shouted abuse. Then, without a backward glance, she had half run, half shambled out of sight.

He wasn't sorry that he had told her, nor was he seriously concerned about her. She had survived those first seven years; she would survive this. And, after all, she wanted to be a writer. Someone had said—he couldn't remember who—that an artist should suffer in childhood as much trauma as could be borne without breaking. And she wouldn't break. Others would break, but not she. There would be tatters and torn flesh enough on the barbed wire guarding that untender heart. But he was aware of a nag of anxiety, irritating because he guessed that it might be difficult to rationalize away, and because, like all his anxieties, it was allied to guilt. He wondered what she would say to her mother. Whatever the nature of the tie between them, he didn't suppose that she loved her mother in any sense in which he understood that ubiquitous word. After all, they had only been together for five weeks. She had lived with him and Hilda for ten years, undisturbed, apparently, by any need to love. He wondered what she would have said, how she would have looked, if sitting there on the bed in his post-coital depletion, he had spoken at least a part of the truth about Sheila Manning.

"I took her from egotism, boredom, curiosity, sexual conceit, pity, perhaps even from affection. But she's only a substitute. They're all of them substitutes. When she was in my arms I was imagining that she was you."

He saw that the bedcover was crooked and he smoothed it. That was the kind of detail that Hilda, obsessive housewife that she was, would notice. Then he went into the bathroom to check that Sheila had left no trace of herself there. He needn't worry that there would be an echo of her scent lingering in the bedroom. Before he had brought her to Caldecote Terrace for the first time he had warned her not to wear scent. She had replied:

"I never do."

He remembered her face, blotched with embarrassment and hurt, that he shouldn't have noticed that. The warning—revealing, as it had a calculation of risk, born perhaps of previous embarrassments and discoveries—had denigrated their love in her eyes, reduced their first time together to a commonplace, sordid intrigue. It hadn't been that; but for him it hadn't been much more. Why, he wondered, was he driven into these petty expedients of lust? Boredom? The ennui of the male menopause? A compensation for his sterility? The need to reassure himself that he was still virile, still attractive to younger women? A search, which he knew in advance to be hopeless, for the lost enchantments of love?

He felt physically and emotionally drained. He needed to cosset himself. He fetched a glass, a bottle of Niersteiner and the ice bucket and went to sit in the garden. The air was as heavy and oppressive as a sweaty blanket and he thought he could sniff the far-off metallic smell of thunder. He wished that the blanket would burst and the rain would fall, that he could lift up his face and feel the great cool sheets of it drenching his skin. He wondered why Hilda was so late, then remembered that she had said something at breakfast about late shopping in Oxford Street. He supposed that meant that they were to make do with a cold supper.

He wasn't distressed about Sheila Manning. Hilda was due to give up the juvenile Bench in two weeks' time, and he had planned to use that as an excuse for ending the affair. This evening's fiasco had saved him the protracted and emotionally wearing strategies, the appeals and reproaches, which usually accompanied the death of desire. The problem about wanting women who evoked his pity was that these were precisely the women who were the most difficult to get rid of. He wished he could be like some of his colleagues and take a succession of the guilt-free, experienced and cheerfully randy young who would ask nothing more of him than the occasional good dinner and the brief exchange of pleasure.

He supposed he would have to let Hilda know about Philippa's visit. He would tell the truth, merely editing out Sheila Manning. He could be confident that Philippa would never tell her, and it seemed to him not of immense importance if she did. Philippa would be coming home now and that should please Hilda. Life would go on as it had before. He supposed that that was what he wanted. He let his mind slip free of worry and guilt and closed his eyes. And in that moment of almost disembodied peace, the smell of wine and roses fused and he was back again, walking between the high hedges into the great circular rose garden at Pennington on a June day ten years ago. He was seeing Philippa for the first time.

9

He had never seen a child like her. She stood very still, a little apart from her keeper, a shapeless ungainly woman, querulous in the heat, and regarded him gravely with those extraordinary luminous green eyes under the curving brows. Her skin absorbed the mellow afternoon light, the shadowed green of the high hedge, so that it was like seeing her through water. Her hair was plaited corn drawn across her forehead in a mature, old-fashioned style which added to the contrast between the sixteenth-century Renaissance head held so proudly, and the childish body. He guessed that she was about seven. She was wearing a kilt too heavy for summer and reaching almost to her calves, with an immense safety-pin bunching it on one side. Her pale arms, downy and glinting in the sun, stuck out from a shirt so thin that it clung to her bony chest, brittle as a bird's. He could see her nipples, two pink delicate tags of flesh.

Hilda began talking to the woman, learning that her name was Gladys Beddows, that she was at Pennington to visit her sister. He spoke to the child:

"Isn't it dull for you here? What would you like to do?"

"Have you any books?"

"Lots, in the library. Would you like to see them?"

She nodded and they began walking across the lawn together, the two women following. She walked at his side, but distanced, her hands held in front of her, the palms folded together in a curiously formal, unchildish gesture. A few yards behind them Mrs Beddows seemed to be confiding her difficulties to Hilda. That type of woman usually did. Hilda, herself uncommunicative, gauche, somehow invited confidences, or lacked the assurance and ruthlessness to reject them. Whenever he entered the kitchen on the two days a week when the daily help was there he would find the two women drinking coffee together, Hilda's head docilely bowed under a spate of domestic disgruntlement. Now the whine of resentment came clearly to them, carried on the warm, rose-scented air.

"Not as if they pay much. And I have her all day, some nights as well. She's a difficult child. Never get a thank you out of her. And talk about temper! Screaming tantrums some of the time. Nightmares too. Not surprised her mother can't cope. Not what you'd call pretty, is she? Odd-looking child. Clever, mind you. Always got her head in a book. Oh, she's sharp, that one! So sharp she'll cut herself one of these days."

He glanced at the child. She must have heard. How could she help hearing? But she gave no sign. She walked on in her unchildish, hieratic dignity, but carefully, as if holding something precious between the clasped hands.

The woman was right. She wasn't a pretty child. But the fine bone structure of the face, the green eyes, gave promise of a spectacular if eccentric beauty. And she was intelligent, courageous and proud. These were the qualities he respected. Something could be made of such a child. He wanted to say to her: "I don't think you're plain. And I like clever children. Never be ashamed of being clever." But glancing again at her set face he said nothing. Pity would be an impertinence to this proud, self-absorbed child.

The southern aspect of Pennington stretched out before them, golden and serene, the great orangery shooting shafts of light so that his eyes dazzled. This was the view of the house he had seen when he had first visited Pennington with Helena. That, too, had been in high summer; but then he had been in love, intoxicated with the smell of roses and gillyflowers, with the wine they had drunk with their picnic on the drive down, with happiness, with the immensity of his prize. They had been coming to Pennington together to tell her father that they were to be married. Now walking that same lawn, the child's shadow moving with his like a ghost, he could look back almost dispassionately, with pity as well as with contempt, to that poor deluded fool frolicking in a dead summer which now seemed to have held the concentrated sweetness of all summers, invincibly arrogant in the high renaissance of the heart. And so they walked across the lawn together, the child with her pain, he with his.

The library was dark and cool after the glare of the sun. The books had been sold separately from the house, and already the archivists and workmen were there checking and packing the volumes. It should have pleased him that yet another aristocrat was reneging on his responsibilities, that this great house would no longer be the seat of a family, passing from father to son in the primogeniture of privilege, but would become institutionalized, debased. Instead, looking up at the fine stuccoed ceiling, and at the gorgeous Grinling Gibbons carvings on the bookcases, he was aware of a gentle nostalgic melancholy. If this room had belonged to him, he would never have let it go.

The child stood at his side, both of them looking in silence. Then he led her across the room to the chart table where a miscellany of Helena's books had been collected for him.

He said:

"How old are you? Can you read?"

248

Her voice rebuked him:

"I'm eight. I could read before I was four."

"Then let's see how you do with this."

He picked up the Shakespeare, opened it and handed it to her. He was behaving like a pedant with no particular intention. The afternoon was hot, he was bored, the child intrigued him. She took the book into her hands with difficulty and began to read. He had opened it at *King John*.

> "Grief fills the room up of my absent child,
> Lies in his bed, walks up and down with me,
> Puts on his pretty looks, repeats his words,
> Remembers me of all his gracious parts,
> Stuffs out his vacant garments with his form."

She read to the end of the speech, faultlessly. She didn't, of course, speak it in the cadence of blank verse. But she knew that it was poetry and she spoke it carefully in her childish, unemphatic voice, wary of unfamiliar words. It was the more poignant. He felt the tears stinging his eyes for the first time since he had learned that Orlando wasn't his son.

And that was how it had begun. It seemed to him that those two moments, so curiously linked by the memory of Orlando, the first in which he had watched the tears start from Hilda's eyes, the second in which the child's clear voice had brought tears to his, had been the only times in his life which had been free from self-regard. The one had resulted in his second marriage; the other in the adoption of Philippa. He wasn't asking himself now if they had led to disappointment. He wasn't sure what his expectations had been. The absence of expectation had been part of the purity of the moments, had brought them close to what he supposed some people might call goodness. He had almost forgotten the anguish of grief. Now it returned to him, less keen but more diffuse, embracing in one nostalgic melancholy the loss of Orlando, the unborn children he could never father, the stripped library at Pennington, and the child in her ridiculous skirt walking with him across the lawn in the mellow sunlight of a dead June day ten years ago.

10

For Philippa the journey from Caldecote Terrace to Delaney Street was a blank. Time was blotted out completely as if her mind were anaesthetized and her body was obeying some programmed instructions. She was aware of only one incident; running for the bus at Victoria and grasping the slippery rail, a moment of panic, and then the jerk of her armpit as a passenger on the platform caught her and hauled her aboard. Delaney Street was very quiet. The rain had begun to fall steadily in slivers of silver against the street lamps, and behind the patterned glass of the Blind Beggar the lights of the bar shone red and green. She turned her key in the Yale lock, closed the front door quietly behind her and walked up the stairs calmly without switching on the light. In the darkness she pushed the flat door, feeling under her palm the sharpness of the splintered wood. Her mother heard her and called out from the kitchen. She must be preparing supper, mixing the salad dressing; there hung on the air the sharp tang of vinegar. It was the same smell that had greeted her on her return to Caldecote Terrace after her visit to Seven Kings and the two moments fused together, the old pain reinforcing the new. Her mother's voice sounded happy, welcoming. Perhaps she had decided that they needn't move after all. She walked into the kitchen. Her mother turned, smiling, to greet her. Then the smile died, and Philippa watched as the face, so different yet so like her own, drained of blood. Her mother whispered:

"What is it? What's happened? What's happened, Philippa?"

She said:

"Why don't you call me Rose? You called me Rose earlier this evening. You had me christened Rose. I was Rose when you nearly killed me. I was Rose when you decided you didn't want me. I was Rose when you gave me away."

There was a moment of silence. Her mother felt for a chair and sat down. She said:

"I thought you knew. When you first came to Melcombe Grange I asked if you knew about your adoption. You said you did."

"I thought you meant did I know about the murder. I thought you were reminding me why it was that you had to give me up. You must have known that's what I thought."

"And I gave you my account of the murder, when she died, the date of my conviction. Even then, you didn't ask any questions."

"When I read it I wasn't thinking of dates and times. I was thinking of you."

Her mother went on as if she hadn't spoken:

"And afterwards, because I was so happy here, I said nothing. I told myself that the past wasn't our past. They were two different people in a different story. I thought I might let myself have just these two months. Whatever happened afterwards, I should have something worth remembering. But I meant to tell you. I would have told you in the end."

"When you could be sure that I'd got used to having a mother. When I didn't want to let you go. My God, you're clever! Maurice warned me that you were clever. At least I've learned one thing about myself, where I get my scheming intelligence. And what about my father? Did he hate me too? Or was he too ineffective to stop you, too timid to do anything except rape a child? What did you do to him that he needed that act to prove his manhood?"

Her mother looked up at her as if there was something which had to be explained, which could be explained.

"You mustn't blame your father. He wanted to keep you. I persuaded him to let you go. I was the one who thought it was better for you. And it *was* better for you. What had I to give you?"

"Was I such a nuisance, so much trouble? Couldn't you have tried with me a little longer? Oh God, why did I ever find you!"

"I did try. I wanted to love you. I wanted you to love me. But you didn't respond, ever. You cried endlessly. Nothing I could do comforted you. You wouldn't even let me feed you."

"Are you telling me that it was I who rejected you?"

"No, only that it seemed like it to me."

"How could I, a new-born child? I had no choice. I had to love you in order to survive."

Her mother asked with a humility which Philippa found almost unbearable:

"Do you want me to leave at once?"

"No, I'll go. I'll find somewhere. It's easier for me. I don't have to go back to Caldecote Terrace. I've got friends in London. You can stay here until the lease runs out. That'll give you time to find another place. I'll send for the picture. You can have the rest."

She heard her mother's voice. She spoke so softly that Philippa hardly caught the words:

"Is what I did to you so much more difficult to forgive than what I did to that child?"

She didn't reply. She snatched up her shoulder bag and made for the door. Then she turned and spoke to her mother for the last time:

"I don't want to see you ever again. I wish they'd hanged you nine years ago. I wish you were dead."

11

She controlled her crying until she was out of Delaney Street. Then it burst out in a scream of agony. Hair flying loose, she ran wildly through the rain, her shoulder bag bumping against her side. Instinctively, she turned up Lisson Grove seeking the dark solitude of the canal towpath. But the gate had long since been closed for the night. She pounded against it, but she knew that it wouldn't yield. On she ran, her face streaming with mingled tears and rain, seeing no one, careless now which way she ran, almost howling with pain. Suddenly a spasm of cramp twisted like a knife in her side. Doubled up, she gasped, gulping in the streaming air like a drowning woman. She clutched at some nearby railings, waiting for the pain to pass. Beyond the railings were tall trees and, even through the rain, she could smell the canal. She checked her crying and listened. The night was full of small secretive noises. And then there came a howl, alien and eerie, louder and wilder even than her own misery, answering pain with pain. It was the cry of an animal; she must be close to Regent's Park zoo.

She was calmer now. Her tears were still flowing but in a gentle, unbroken stream. She walked on through the night. The city was streaked with light, bleeding with light. The headlamps of the cars dazzled on the road and the crimson pools of the traffic lights lay on the surface like blood. The rain was falling in a solid wall of water, drenching her clothes, plastering her hair against her face and eyes; she could taste it on her lips as salty as the sea.

It seemed to her that her mind was a black and seething dungeon, too many thoughts fighting for air, pressing each other down, tortuous elongated thoughts writhing in rank darkness. And from that dense confusion rose the thin misery of a child's cry. It wasn't the peevish complaint one heard in supermarkets; this was a desolation of terror and anguish not to be comforted with a packet of sweets at the check-out. She told herself that she mustn't panic; to panic would be to go mad. She must sort out her thoughts, arrange them, impose order on chaos. But first she had to stop that dreadful crying. She put her hands up to her throat and squeezed, strangling the child into silence, and when she released her hands the crying had stopped.

They hadn't, in all their weeks together. once spoken of the dead child. They hadn't talked about the child's parents. How much had they cared? How long had they grieved? Perhaps they now had other children and this long-dead, violated child was only a painful, half-rejected memory. Grief fills the room up of my absent child. The child was dead. That fact had been less important to her than whether her mother had kept the kitchen clean. Her mother had killed a child, had clamped her small hand to a pram and dragged her faster and faster, until she fell under the spinning wheels. But that was a different child, another place. She had killed the child's father, too. He had come across the lawn in the summer sunshine, beautiful as a god, to where they used to meet in the rose garden at Pennington. And now he, too, was dead. She had buried him in the moist drifts of the forest. To lie in cold obstruction and to rot. He was rotting there under the trees. But that was someone else's father. Hers was under quicklime in an anonymous grave in a prison yard. Or was that only how they buried executed murderers? What did they do with the bodies of felons who died in prison? Did they carry them out secretly at night, cheaply coffined, to be disposed of at the nearest crematorium, without any comfortable words, the furnace flaring like the flames of hell? And what did they do with the ashes? That neatly packaged residue of ground bone must have been buried somewhere. She had never thought to ask, and her mother had never told her. Parthenophil is lost, and I would see him for he is like to something I remember a great while since, a long long time ago.

Suddenly there shone before her the glowing sign of Warwick Avenue Underground Station. The wide road, lined with its Italian-ate houses and stuccoed villas, ran with liquid light. As she half ran, half walked down the deserted pavement, the overhanging bushes in the front gardens rained a shower of white sodden petals and torn leaves over her hair. And here, at last, was the canal and she was standing on the elegant wrought-iron bridge which spanned the dividing waterway. At the corners of the bridge the high nineteenth-century lamps, each on its pedestal, cast a trembling light over the canal basin, the leafy island, the painted narrowboats moored at the canal wall, the long dark length of tree-shadowed water. Where the lamps shone brightest the plane trees seemed to burn with flickering green flames and below her, where the rain spurted from the roof of a narrowboat, there gleamed a brightly painted enamel jug filled with storm-tossed Michaelmas daisies.

Behind her the unceasing wheels of the cars swished past, slicing through the running gutters and hurling fountains of spray against the bridge. There were no pedestrians in sight and the avenues on each side of the canal were deserted. From the houses the lights shone out from balconied windows, illuminating the plane trees and laying a shivering path of light over the sluggish water.

She was still wearing the jumper her mother had knitted for her.

It was sodden and weighted with rain, the high collar cold against her neck. She pulled it over her head then, reaching up, she held it out and let it gently drop over the parapet and into the canal. For a minute it lay on the surface of the water illumined by the lamp-light, looking as frail and transparent as gossamer. The two sleeves were stretched out; it could have been a drowning child. Then, almost imperceptibly, it floated out of the path of light, sinking slowly as it moved, until her swollen watching eyes could only imagine its pattern on the dark water.

With the jumper gone she felt a physical sense of release. She was wearing nothing now but her trousers and a thin cotton shirt. The rain drenched it so that it clung to her like a second skin. And so, unencumbered, she walked on, under the great concrete arches of the Westway and south towards Kensington. She had no awareness of time, no sense of direction; all that mattered was that she should keep walking. She hardly noticed when the rain changed to slow, ponderous drops, then finally stopped, when the noisy bus routes gave way to quiet squares.

But at last she walked herself into exhaustion. It hit her suddenly, as unexpected and violent as a body blow. Her legs sagged and she tottered to the side of the pavement and grasped at a row of iron railings which surrounded the garden of a wide square. But the weariness which cramped her body had released her mind; thought was once again coherent, disciplined, rational. She leaned her head against the railings and felt the iron, parallel red-hot rods, branding her forehead. There was a privet hedge behind the railings, its pungent greenness filled her nostrils and spiked her cheeks. The wave of exhaustion flowed through her, leaving in its wake a gentle tiredness which was almost pleasurable.

Consciousness slipped away. She was jerked back to awareness by a high-pitched yell. The night was suddenly loud with running feet and raucous voices. From the far corner a gang of youths erupted into the square and reeled in a disorderly stream across the road to the garden. They were obviously drunk. Two of them, clutched together, were bawling a plaintive, discordant song. The others shouted meaningless staccato chants, slogans and tribal battle cries in a hoarse, broken cacophony of menace. Terrified that they would see her, that her shoulder bag, she herself, would present too easy a spoil, Philippa strained back against the railings. The gang had no clear purpose or direction. It was possible that they would stagger again into the road and miss seeing her.

But the voices grew louder. They were coming her way. One of them flung a toilet roll. It spun over the railings and into the garden, just missing her head. Its pale, undulating tail, transparent as a stream of light, floated and turned on the night breeze then came to rest on the surface of the hedge, light as a cobweb. And still they came, heads bobbing above the privet. She began to walk quickly away from them, still keeping close to the railings, but as soon as she moved they saw her. They gave a great shout, the jarring, unrelated voices raised in the united bellow of triumph.

She broke into a run, but they pounded after her, more purposeful and less drunk than she had expected. She forgot her tiredness in her fear, but she knew that she couldn't sustain the pace for long. She sped across the wide street and down a road of tall, decaying houses. She could hear her feet slapping the pavement, could see from the corner of her eyes the flashing railings, could feel the wild rhythmic drumming of her heart. They were still behind her, shouting less now, reserving energy for the chase. Suddenly she came to another road turning off to the left. She swerved down it and saw with a gasp of relief that a gate in the railings was open. She almost threw herself down the steps and into the dark, evil-smelling area, almost colliding with three battered dustbins. She squeezed herself behind them and crouched in the narrow space under the flight of steps leading to the front door. Bent almost double she folded her arms over her chest, trying to stifle the pounding of her heart. How could they fail to be drawn to that insistent drumming? But the running feet hesitated, then clattered past, then died. From down the street she heard their bay of frustrated anger. Then they broke again into the dis-organized shouts and singing. There was to be no search. They probably thought that she lived in the street and had gained the safety of her own home. More probably they were too drunk to think clearly. Once the quarry had gone to earth their interest died.

She stayed there long after their voices had faded away, crouched under the curve of the brick roof. She felt herself confined in a dark stinking cell, breathing dust and the spent breath of long-dead captives, bereft of the sky; the three malodorous dustbins, their shape imagined rather than seen, blocking her escape as effectively as a bolted door. There came to her in the darkness no blinding revelation, no healing of the spirit, only a measure of painful self-knowledge. From the moment of her counselling she had thought of no one but herself. Not of Hilda, who had so little to give but asked so little in return and needed that little so much. Hilda, who might reasonably have expected a greater return for those difficult years of caring than occasional help with the dining-room flowers. Not of Maurice, as arrogant and self-deceiving as herself, but who had done his best for her, had given with generosity even if he couldn't give with love, had somehow found the kindness to shield her from the worst knowledge. Not of her mother. What

255

had she been but a purveyor of information, the living pattern of her own physical life, the victim of her patronage and self-love? She told herself that she had to learn humility. She was not sure that the lesson lay within her competence, but this stinking corner of the sleeping city into which she had crept like a derelict was as good a place as any in which to begin. She knew, too, that what bound her to her mother was stronger than hate, or disappointment or the pain of rejection. Surely this need to see her again, to be comforted by her, was the beginning of love; and how could she have expected that there could be love without pain?

After a time she eased herself out of the area and again breathed the cool night air and saw the stars. She walked on, almost light-headed with tiredness, searching for the names of streets. They told her nothing except that she was in the W 10 district. She found herself in another square lying quiet and secret under the surging sky. In her mind the city seemed to stretch for ever, a silent half-derelict immensity, palely illumined by the recurrent moon. It was a dead city, plague-ridden and abandoned, from which all life had fled except for that band of scavenging louts. Now they too would have staggered into some filthy area, huddled together in death. She was completely alone. Behind the peeling stucco, the tall balus-trades, lay the rotting dead. The stench of the city's decay rose like a miasma from the basement areas.

And then she saw the woman walking quickly but lightly across the square towards her on high-arched elegant feet. She wore a long pale dress and a stole. Her yellow hair was piled high. Everything about her was pale, the floating dress, her hair, her night-bleached skin. As they came abreast, Philippa asked:

"Could you please tell me where I am? I'm trying to get to Marylebone Station."

The voice that answered her was pleasant, cheerful, cultured.

"You're in Moxford Square. Walk down this street for about a hundred yards. Take the first turning on the left and you'll find yourself at Ladbroke Grove Underground. I think you'll have missed the last train but you might pick up a late-night bus or a taxi."

Philippa said:

"Thank you. If I can get to Ladbroke Grove I know my way."

The woman smiled and walked on across the square. The en-counter had been so unexpected and yet so ordinary that Philippa found herself wondering whether her tired brain had conjured up an apparition. Who was she and where was she going, this confident walker of the night? What friend or lover had deposited her here, unescorted, in the early hours? From what party had she come or was she escaping? But the woman's directions proved correct. Five minutes later Philippa found herself at Ladbroke Grove and began walking southwards towards home.

Delaney Street was silent and empty, sleeping as quietly as a village street beneath the unthreatening sky. The rain-washed air smelled of the sea. The windows of all the houses were dark except where number 12 showed a faint haze of light behind the drawn curtains. It wasn't bright enough for the ceiling light. Her mother must be still awake, or if she had fallen asleep, must have done so before she remembered to switch off the bedside lamp. She hoped that she would still be awake. She wondered what they would say to each other. She knew that she wouldn't be able to say that she was sorry, not yet; she had never said that in all her life. But perhaps it was a beginning that she could feel it. Perhaps, too, her mother would understand without the need of words. She would hold out the key of the front door to her and say:

"I must have meant all the time to come back. I didn't remember to leave you the key."

She would stand there in her mother's doorway, and the fact that she was there would be enough. It would say:

"I love you. I need you. I have come home."

12

The bedside lamp was on and in its pool of softened light her mother lay on her back asleep. But there was someone else in the room. Sitting slumped forward at the foot of the bed, hands between his knees, was a man, white-robed, shimmering with light. He didn't move or look up as she walked over to the bed. Her mother's face was perfectly calm. But something strange had happened to her neck. An animal had her by the throat, a small white, slug-like beast with its pink snout buried in her flesh. Something was eating her alive, burrowing away, tearing out the sinews, voiding its leavings on her white skin. But still she didn't stir. Philippa turned to the man; and this time she saw in his dangling hands the blood-stained knife. And then she both saw and understood.

He looked so grotesque that her first thought was that he was the creature of delirium born of her exhaustion and the phantasmagoria of the night. But she knew that he was real. His being there by her mother's side was as inevitable as was her death. He was wearing a long raincoat of white transparent plastic, so thin that it clung to him like a film. On his hands were plastic gloves, surgeons' gloves, clinging to the pale flesh. They were too large for his tiny hands. At the end of each finger the plastic had gummed together and hung in pale flaps as if the skin itself were peeling away. Hiroshima hands. She said:

"Take off your gloves, they disgust me. You disgust me."

Obediently he peeled them off.

He looked up at her. He said, simply as a child craving reassurance: "She won't bleed. She won't bleed."

She moved closer to the bed. Her mother's eyes were closed. It was considerate of her to die with her eyes closed, but was that something one could choose to do? She tried to recall the pictured dead. It wasn't difficult; there were so many of them. The minds of her generation were patterned like nursery wallpaper with images of death; violence lay around their cradles. The corpses of Belsen piled like skinned rabbits in ungainly heaps, spike-bellied children of Ethiopia and India carrying their hunger like a monstrous foetus, the denuded bodies of soldiers sprawled in the clumsy dishevelment of death, all open-eyed. 'Tis a fine deceit to pass away in a dream. Indeed I've slept with mine eyes open a great while. But her mother's eyes were closed. Had she gone so gentle into her good night? She turned to the man and said fiercely:

"Have you touched her?"

He didn't reply. He made a movement of his bent head. It could have meant yes or no. There was an envelope propped against a small tablet bottle on the bedside table. The flap hadn't been stuck down. She read:

"If God can forgive her death then he will forgive mine. These five weeks have been worth every day of the last ten years. Nothing is your fault. Nothing. This is the better way for me, not just for you. I can die happy because you are alive and I love you. Never be afraid."

She put the note down on the table and looked again at the man. He was sitting on the edge of the bed, head bowed, the knife drooping from his hands. She took it from him and put it on the table. His hands were small, like a child's hands, a hamster's claws. He was beginning to shake and the bed shook with him. Her mother's body might have been shaking with laughter. She was afraid that the barely closed eyes would jolt open and that she would have to look on death. What was so terrible about grief was not grief itself, but that one got over it. It was strange to learn this truth even before the grieving had begun. She said, more gently:

258

"Come away from her. She won't bleed. The dead don't bleed. I got to her before you."

She took hold of his shoulder and, half lifting him from the bed, led him over to the basket chair. The two-bar electric fire was off, as if her mother had remembered that they needed to save electricity. She switched on a single bar and turned it towards him. She said:

"I know who you are. I saw you in Regent's Park and somewhere else too, somewhere before that. Did you always plan to kill her?"

"My wife did, from the moment our daughter died." Then he added: "We planned it together."

He seemed to need to explain.

"I came late tonight, but you hadn't left. The light in the front room was still on. I sat in the shop and listened and waited. But you didn't leave. There were no footsteps overhead, no sounds. At midnight I crept upstairs. The door was smashed and open. I thought she was asleep. She looked as if she was asleep. I didn't notice until I drove in the knife that her eyes were open. Her eyes were wide open and she was looking at me."

She said:

"You'd better go. You did what you came for. It wasn't your fault that she escaped you in the end." Death of one person can be paid but once and that she hath discharged. What thou wouldst do is done unto thy hand.

She said more loudly, shaking him gently by the shoulder:

"I shall have to call the police. If you don't want to be here when they come you'd better go now. There's no need for you to get involved."

He didn't move. He was staring at the bar of the fire. He muttered something. She had to bend her head to hear him:

"I didn't know it would be like this. I want to be sick."

She supported him into the kitchen and held his head while he retched over the sink, surprised that she could touch him without revulsion, could be so aware of the curiously silken texture of his hair, sliding over the hard skull. It seemed to her that her hand experienced simultaneously every single hair and the soft moving mass. She wanted to say: "She didn't mean to kill. It was a burst of anger which she couldn't control. She never wanted your child dead in the way that you and I wanted her dead, willed her death." But what was the use? What did it matter? His child was dead. Her mother was dead. Words, explanations, excuses, were an irrelevance. About that final negation there was nothing new to be thought, nothing new to be said, nothing that could be put right.

Everything in the kitchen was the same. As his head shuddered between her hands and the stink of vomit rose to her nostrils, she gazed round at the familiar objects, marvelling that they were unchanged. The teapot and two cups on the round papier mâché tray; the glistening pellets of coffee beans in their glass jar, how erotically beautiful they were—freshly-ground coffee had been one of their extravagances; the row of herbs in their pots on the window ledge. The north-facing window wasn't the best light for them, but still they had thrived. Tomorrow they had planned to snip the first chives for a herb omelette. The dressing her mother had made was still there in a jug on the table, the tang of vinegar still in the air. She wondered if she would be able to smell it in the future without thinking of this moment. She looked at the carefully folded tea towels, the two mugs on their hooks, the saucepans with their handles carefully aligned. How excessively neat they had been, imposing order and permanence on their insubstantial and precarious lives.

He was still retching but now it was only bile. The worst of the sickness was over. She handed him a towel and said:

"The bathroom's on the half landing if you want it."

"Yes, I know." He wiped his face and his mild eyes met hers. "Won't you get into trouble? With the police, I mean."

"No. She killed herself. The knife wound was made after death. Doctors can prove that. You saw yourself that she didn't bleed. I don't think there is a criminal offence of mutilating the dead. Even if there is, I don't suppose they'll charge me. All anyone will want is to get the whole unsavoury affair neatly tidied up. You see, no one cares about her. No one will mind that she's dead. She doesn't count as a human being. They think that she should have been killed nine years ago. She should have been hanged, that's what they'll all say."

"But the police might think you killed her."

"There's a suicide note to prove I didn't."

"But suppose they think that you forged it."

How extraordinary that he should get that idea. What a sophistical mind he must have. She looked into the meek, anxious eyes. Behind them a clever little brain must be scheming away. He ought to be writing thrillers. He had the mind of a thriller writer, obsessive, guilt-ridden, preoccupied with trivia. He had lived too long with thoughts of death. She said:

I can prove that she wrote it. I've got a long specimen of her handwriting, a story she wrote in prison, a story about a rapist and his wife. Look, you'd better go. There's no point in letting the police find you unless you like the idea of seeing your face in all the newspapers. Some people do; is that what you want?"

He shook his head. He said:

"I want to go home."

"Home?" she asked. She hadn't thought of him as having a home, this nocturnal predator with his finicky hands that could do so much damage, his stink of vomit. She thought he whispered something about Casablanca being home, but that was surely absurd.

He asked:

"Shall we see each other again?"

"I don't suppose so. Why should we? All we have in common is that we both wanted her dead. I don't see that as a basis for social acquaintance."

"Are you sure you'll be all right?"

"Oh yes," she said. "I'll be all right. There'll be plenty of people to make sure that I'm all right."

There was a rucksack on the floor beside the door. She hadn't noticed it before. He took off his macintosh, rolled it, and stuffed it inside. It was, she thought, something he had done many times before. But when he reached for the knife, she said:

"Leave it. Leave it where it is. I'll see that it has my finger-prints on it."

They went down the stairs together as if he were a dilatory visitor whom she was managing to see off at last. He walked quickly up Delaney Street without a backward glance, and she watched him out of sight. She returned to the bedroom. She couldn't look at her mother, but she made herself take up the knife and hold it for a moment in her hand. Then she ran out of the flat to Marylebone Station to telephone Maurice.

The entrance to the concourse was deserted, the row of telephone booths empty, except for one figure. A young man was huddled in the furthest booth. She couldn't tell whether he was drunk or asleep. Perhaps he might even be dead. But she recognized him. She had seen him before, patiently trying to hand out texts in Mell Street market.

She found a tenpenny piece in her purse, dialled the seven familiar digits, then pushed the coin home as Maurice's voice repeated the number. He had answered at once. But then, the telephone was by his bed. She said:

"It's Philippa. Please come. My mother's dead. I wanted her to kill herself and she has."

He said:

"Are you sure she's dead?"

"I'm sure."

"Where are you ringing from?"

"Marylebone Station."

"I'll come straight away. Wait where you are. Don't talk to anyone. Do nothing until I come."

The streets were almost empty in the calm of the early hours, but, even so, he must have driven very fast. It seemed only a matter of minutes before she heard the Rover.

She walked towards him and into his arms. Suddenly they were round her, fierce and stiff, a clasp of possession not a gesture of comfort. Then, as suddenly, he let her go and she tottered and nearly fell. She felt his fingers gripping her shoulder, propelling her towards the car. He said:

"Show me."

The Rover slid to a stop outside the door of number 12. He took his time over locking it, looking up and down the street, calm and unhurried as if this were a late social visit and he would prefer on the whole not to be observed. She turned the key in the Yale lock and he followed her upstairs. Their climbing feet echoed in the hall. If he noticed the smashed lock on the flat door, he said nothing. She led the way to her mother's room and stood aside, waiting and watching while he walked over to the bed and looked down. He read the suicide note, his face expressionless. He picked up the empty bottle and studied the label, then tipped out on to his palm the one white bullet-shaped pellet. He said:

"Distalgesic. Considerate of her to have left this. It'll save the analyst time and trouble. I wonder how she got hold of it. Distalgesic is on prescription; you can't just buy it across the counter. Someone must have smuggled it into prison for her, if she didn't steal it from the hospital wing or have it prescribed for her. That's probably something we'll never know. She's not the first person to have mistaken the strength of this stuff. It's got paracetamol in it; but that isn't the danger. It contains an opium-type compound. An overdose kills very quickly. She was planning the usual histrionic gesture and misjudged the strength."

Philippa wanted to reply: "She didn't misjudge anything or any-one. She killed herself because she meant to kill herself, because she knew that's what I wanted her to do. You might at least give her the credit of knowing what she did." But she said nothing. He bent his head slightly and looked at the savaged throat intently, like a doctor. Then he frowned. It was a frown of worried distaste, as if he were faced with a technical problem and had encountered an unexpected snag. He said:

"Who did this?"

"I did. At least I suppose I did."

"You suppose you did?"

"I can remember wanting to kill her. I can remember going into the kitchen and getting the knife. That's all."

"When you talk to the police, forget the first sentence. You didn't kill her, so what you intended or wanted isn't relevant. Did you break down the door, too?"

So he had noticed. But of course he had. She said:

"After I got back from Caldecote Terrace we quarrelled. I ran out of the flat. I didn't intend to come back. But then I did come back. We've only one pair of keys and I'd forgotten to take them. I banged on the door but she wouldn't let me in, so I broke it down. I had a chisel with me from the tool chest. I'm not sure why. I think I might have been threatening her with it before I ran out, but I can't remember now."

He said:

"If you didn't take the keys with you, how did you get in at the street door? Aren't they on the same ring?"

She had forgotten that. She said quickly:

"There's only a Yale there. I slipped the latch up. I got used to doing that if I went out briefly at night."

"Where is the chisel, the one you used on the door?"

"I put it back in the tool box."

The inquisition had ended. He moved from the bed and said:

"Come away from here. Is there another room or somewhere comfortable?"

"No, not very comfortable. There's only my room and the kitchen."

He placed his arm round her shoulders and pushed her gently into the passage. They went into the kitchen. He said:

"I'm going to ring the police now from Marylebone Station. Do you want to come with me, or are you all right here?"

"I'll come with you."

"Yes, that would be best. Get your coat. It's cold."

He made her wait in the car while he telephoned. It didn't take long. When he came back to the car he said:

"They'll be here very quickly. When they come just tell them what you told me. You can't remember anything between going to the kitchen drawer for the knife and running out to telephone me."

The police came quickly too. There seemed a lot of them for so unimportant a death. She was put to wait in her own room. They lit the gas fire. They brought her tea. She wanted to explain that it was the wrong cup, her mother's cup. There was a policewoman with her, blonde, pretty, almost as young as herself. She looked attractive in her dark blue, well-cut uniform. Her face, disciplined of pity, watchful, was carefully neutral. Philippa thought:

"She isn't sure whether she's guarding a victim or a villain. Normally she would have put a consoling hand round my shoulders. But then, there is that slit in my mother's throat." When the detective came in to question her Maurice was with him, and another man whom she recognized as Maurice's solicitor. He introduced him formally.

"Philippa, I don't know whether you remember Charles Cullingford, my solicitor. This is my daughter."

She stood up and shook hands. It was as punctilious and ordinary as if they were meeting in the drawing-room at Caldecote Terrace. He kept his eyes rather too carefully from looking round the bleak little bedroom. The police brought in two chairs from her mother's room. They introduced the inspector to her but she didn't take in his name. He was dark and fitted rather too well into his clothes and his eyes had no kindness in them. But he questioned her gently and Maurice was at her side.

"Has anyone else been here this evening?"

"No. Only us."

"Who broke in the door?"

"I did it. I did it with the chisel in the kitchen drawer."

"Why did you take the chisel with you when you left the flat?"

"In case she tried to lock me out."

"Had your mother ever done that before?"

"No."

"Why did you think she might lock you out tonight?"

"We had a quarrel after my father had told me that she'd given me away."

"Your father says that you ran out of the flat and walked for about three hours. What happened when you came back?"

"I found that the door was locked and she didn't answer, so I broke in with the chisel."

"Did you know when you found her that she was dead?"

"I think so. I can't remember what I felt. I can't remember what happened after I broke down the door. I think I wanted to kill her."

"Where did you get the knife?"

"From the kitchen drawer."

"But before that? It's new isn't it?"

"My mother bought it. We wanted a sharp knife. I don't know where she got it."

They went away again. There was a knock at the door, loud voices, confident feet. Her door was ajar. The policewoman got up and closed it. The feet were moving more slowly now, half-shuffling down the passage. They were taking her mother away. When she realized this she sprang up with a cry, but the policewoman was quicker. She felt her shoulder seized in a surprisingly strong grip and, gently but firmly, she was forced back into her chair.

The blur of voices came through the door, disconnected words,

". . . clearly dead when she stuck the knife in. You didn't need to pull me out of bed to tell you that. I suppose you've got a charge somewhere which fits the case if you want to find one, but it can't be homicide."

Maurice's voice:

"This place is pathetic. God knows what these six weeks have been like for her. I couldn't stop her . . . she's of age . . . my fault. I should never have told her that her mother battered and then abandoned her."

She thought she heard someone say:

"It's all for the best." But perhaps that was imagination. Perhaps that was only what they were all thinking. Then Maurice was standing over her.

"We're going home now, Philippa. It's going to be all right."

But of course it would be all right. Maurice would arrange it all. He would dispose of the flat, selling the last few weeks of the lease, get rid of all that was left of their life together. She would never see any of their belongings again. The Henry Walton would be replaced on her wall at Caldecote Terrace. That was too expensive to be discarded. But it was spoilt for her. She would look at it now with different eyes, seeing behind the elegance and order the prison hulks lying off Gravesend, the flogging-block, the public hangman. But there had to be some limit to the indulgence of sensitivity. She would be expected to go on living with the Walton. But everything else would go. The rest would be treated as the rubbish it was. His lawyers would handle the police, would gentle her through the further questioning, the inquest, the publicity. Only there wasn't likely to be much publicity. Maurice would see to that too. Everyone—police, coroner, Press—would be sympathetic. When they remembered that ravaged throat they would fight down repulsion or dislike, remembering whose daughter she was. They would be sorry for her; but they would be a little frightened too. Had she only imagined the inspector's final words, bluff, almost humorous:

"You can take her home now, sir. And for God's sake keep her away from knives."

Afterwards, he would take her away, perhaps to Italy since an Italian visit had always been his personal therapy. They would see together the cities she had planned one day to see with her mother. How long would it be before he could look into her eyes without wondering whether she was, after all, her mother's daughter, without asking himself whether she would have plunged that knife into a living throat. Perhaps the thought would excite him; people were excited by violence. What, after all, was the sexual act but a voluntarily endured assault, a momentary death?

265

And now they were alone. Before they left together, she went to her room and came back with her mother's manuscript. She held it out to him.

"I want you to read this, please. It's her account of the murder. She wrote it in prison long before she met me."

"Is that what she told you? Look at the colour and newness of the paper. Feel it. This hasn't lain about in a cell for years. This was written recently. Didn't that strike you?"

He took it over to the fireplace, then paused. He didn't smoke and carried no matches. While she watched he went into the kitchen and came back with a box. He held up the manuscript and the flame bit, crept in a widening circle across the writing, then burst into flame. He held the paper almost until his fingers were burnt, then dropped it into the grate.

Suddenly she was aware of her tiredness, the stains and filth on her shirt, her trousers grimed with coal dust where she had crouched behind the bins in that distant area. She felt a gout of blood discharge and roll down her leg. He looked at her and said gently:

"Go to the bathroom. Take your time. I'll be waiting for you."

When she came back five minutes later he had taken down the oil painting and had in his arms one of the blankets from her bed. He put it round her shoulders. Without speaking they went together down the stairs and out of the flat.

The drive home seemed very short through the deserted streets. No one had seen them go. Tomorrow George would open his shop and wonder why they were so silent, where they had gone. No one would miss them for long.

At Caldecote Terrace there was a light on in the hall and in the drawing-room but the kitchen was in darkness. The door opened to them before Maurice had time to fit his key in the lock. Hilda stood there, anxious-eyed, wearing her blue quilted dressing-gown. Maurice said to her quietly:

"She's all right. Don't worry. Everything's all right. Her mother's dead. Suicide."

She was smothered in Hilda's padded arms. She heard her say:

"Your room's still waiting for you, darling," as if it might have taken off and vanished during her absence. And then she heard a dog barking and Hilda's face was suddenly tender with concern.

"You've woken Scamp. I'd better go down to him."

At the bottom of the stairs he took the blanket from her shoulders and tossed it aside. When she came down next morning it would be gone. Even an old blanket from Delaney Street wouldn't be allowed to contaminate memory. He followed her upstairs; his footsteps firm behind her faltering ones. She felt like a prisoner under escort.

But the room to which her feet weakly but unhesitatingly led her was white and peaceful and the single bed looked comfortable. It had nothing to do with her; she didn't belong here. But she thought that the girl who did wouldn't mind if she used it. She peeled off her dirt-stained shirt and filthy trousers, let herself drop face downwards on the bed grasping the pillows with her hands and felt Maurice drawing the blankets over her shoulders. She hadn't bathed; but that didn't matter, she didn't think the girl would mind. Just before she fell asleep she remembered that there was someone for whom she needed to weep. But she had no tears left, and she had never found it easy to cry. And that didn't matter either. She had a lifetime ahead of her in which to learn how.

Book Four

EPILOGUE AT EVENSONG

1

Sunday afternoon evensong was over. The packed congregation, released from their role of silent participants in the music, joined with cheerful abandon in the concluding hymn. The boy choristers, their calm candle-lit faces rising translucent as flowers from their ruffs, had closed their books and were filing from their stalls. Philippa rose from her knees, shook free her hair, twitched the pleated cotton more comfortably on her shoulders and joined the small band of similarly white-gowned members of college who were following the procession out through the carved screen and into the cool, light-filled immensity of the ante-chapel.

She saw him almost immediately, but then she would have recognized this insignificant little man anywhere in the world. He was standing in his neat over-pressed suit at the end of the first row, diminished under the marvel of Wastell's surging vault, but with his own small human dignity. His hands, those well-remembered hands, were resting on the back of the chair in front of him. As she came within touching distance, the knuckles tightened into shining pebbles. Their eyes met and he looked steadily at her with what she thought was a mute appeal that she shouldn't escape him. It never occurred to her to try; nor did she believe for one moment that this encounter was by chance. After she left the chapel she lingered at the south porch until he came up quietly beside her. They didn't greet each other but turned, as if by mutual consent, and began pacing the sunlit path beside the Gibbs Building. She said:

"How did you find me? But I'd forgotten; you're an expert at tracking people down."

"It was your book. I read the reviews and two of them said that you were a student at King's. You published it under your name, Philippa Ducton."

"Ducton's my name. I dropped the Rose. It didn't suit me. I thought I was entitled to one small personal preference of identity. But you didn't come here, surely, to congratulate me on the novel. Did you read it?"

"I asked for it at the library."

She laughed, and looking at her he flushed and said:

"Is that the wrong thing to say to a writer? I suppose I ought to have bought it."

"Why should you? And you couldn't have welcomed it—the name Ducton on your shelves. Did you enjoy it?"

She could see from his face that he wasn't sure whether she was teasing him. At last he said, surprisingly:

"It was clever, of course. Some of the critics said that it was brilliant. But I thought that it was harsh, unfeeling."

"Yes it was. That's just what it was, unfeeling. But you didn't take all this trouble to track me down just so that we could have a literary discussion."

Looking at his face, she said quickly:

"I'm not sorry to see you. You had to leave suddenly when we last met. I've had that feeling, too, that there's unfinished business between us. I've wondered from time to time about you, what you were doing, where you were."

She wanted to add: "And whether you were happier knowing that my mother was dead." But looking at his calm, untroubled face, that was a question which she didn't need to ask. Perhaps that was why revenge was so satisfying; it worked.

He answered her eagerly, as if he were glad to be telling her.

"I left London after the inquest on your mother and travelled about England and Wales for about two years. I stayed at cheap boarding-houses in the summer and moved into better-class ones in the autumn and winter. You get special rates out of season. I spent my time looking at places, buildings, thinking about myself. I wasn't unhappy. Six months ago I returned to London and went back to the Casablanca. That's the hotel where I took a room when I was tracking you down. I'm not sure why I went back, except that I felt at home there. It was just the same; the blind telephonist, the one you saw me with in Regent's Park, was still there. Her name's Violet Tetley. We started going out together on her free afternoons. We're going to get married."

So this was why he had come. She said:

"And you don't know how much you ought to tell her?"

"She knows about Julie, of course. And I told her that both the Ductons were dead. But I'm not sure whether I ought to tell her what I tried to do. There's no one in the world but you I can talk to about it, no one else to consult. I had to find you."

She said:

"If you're marrying a blind woman, I shouldn't advise you to tell her that you once twisted a knife in another woman's throat. It could be unsettling."

The shock and the hurt on his face were as palpable as if she had struck him. Even the physical manifestation was the same. He flushed, and then became very pale, except for one scarlet lash on his cheek. She said more gently:

"I'm sorry. I'm not a kind person. I try to be sometimes, but I'm

272

not very good at it yet." She nearly added: "And the person who could have taught me how is dead." She went on:

"It's your bad luck that you're stuck with me as a confidante. But the advice is still sound. We none of us know another human being so well that we can be absolutely sure about him. I can't see what you gain by telling. Why distress her?"

"But I love her. We love each other. Doesn't that mean that I ought to be honest with her?"

She said:

"This conversation between us is honest as far as I can make it so. That doesn't mean that either of us likes it the better. You have the whole of your past life to be honest about. One incident in it isn't important."

"It was an important incident to me. And it brought us together. I wouldn't have been at the Casablanca, wouldn't have met Violet, if I hadn't tried to kill your mother."

She could have replied that his child and her mother would both have been alive if he had kept his daughter at home on a foggy January night twelve and a half years ago. But what point was there in tracing back the long concatenation of chance. She said, interested:

"How are you going to manage? Have you a job?"

"I've lived simply during the last three years. I've got about twelve thousand pounds left from the sale of the house. That will be enough to put down on a cottage somewhere. And my local authority pension starts in a few months' time. We should be all right. We don't want a large place, just somewhere with a garden. Violet loves the smell of roses. She became blind when she was eight; before that she could see, so she has some memories, and if I describe things to her carefully, buildings, the sky, flowers, it helps. I have to look at things differently now, more carefully, so that I can remember them. We're so happy together, I can't believe it."

She wondered if the happiness included going to bed together. Probably it did. He wasn't sexually repulsive, this poor little murderer manqué. And even Crippen had had his Ethel Le Neve. The unlikeliest couples found their way to that irrational joy. She remembered the feel of his hair under her hand, silkier than her own. And his skin was soft, unblemished. Besides, his Violet wouldn't have to see him. It must be strange to be blind, making love always with one's eyes shut. She caught a glance at his smile, secret, reminiscent, almost lubricious. He had come to her with his anxieties, but that wasn't one of them. Remembering the girl she had seen in the park, she wondered whether his Violet was young enough to have a child. As if his mind had flowed with hers, he said:

273

"She's much younger than I am. If she has a baby I could help look after him. There's nothing we can't manage together."

He turned to her.

"Do you ever feel that you don't deserve happiness? The time I first went out with her, the day you saw us in the rose garden, I was exploiting her, making use of her blindness. I was lonely and she was the only person I could feel safe with, because she couldn't see."

How early he must have learned that primeval lesson, the distrust of joy. Touch wood, cross fingers, light a candle, please God don't notice that I'm happy. She wanted to say:

"I used my mother to avenge myself on my adoptive father. We all use each other. Why should you expect to be less corrupt than the rest of us." Instead she said:

"Why not learn to be gentle with yourself, to accept the possibility of happiness? Forget about my mother and me. That's over."

"But suppose Violet found out? She'd find it hard to forgive, the deception or what I did."

"There's nothing for her to forgive. It wasn't her throat. Besides, we can forgive anything as long as it isn't done to us. Haven't you learned that? And how could she find out? You needn't worry about me. I shan't ever tell."

"But you're a writer; you might want to use it one day."

She nearly laughed aloud. So that was what was worrying him. He must have borrowed her novel from the library in trepidation. What, she wondered, had he been expecting? Some lurid Gothic romance with himself as a pathetic Eumenides? But he would hardly be expecting a dissertation on the nature of the creative imagination. She said:

"Some writers can only write about their own direct experience. That's not the kind of writer I am or want to be. I said that we all use each other, but I hope to use people with rather more subtlety than that."

He said, tentatively, as if venturing on dangerous ground:

"Do they know about your mother here? After all, you do call yourself Ducton."

"Some of them know and some of them guess. It's hardly a subject that comes up naturally in conversation."

"And does it make any difference, to you I mean?"

"Only, perhaps, to make them a little afraid of me. For someone who values privacy that's no bad thing."

They had reached the bridge over the Cam. Philippa paused and gazed down at the shimmering water. He stood beside her, his tiny hands grasping the parapet. And then he asked:

"Do you miss her?"

She thought: "I shall miss her every day of my life." But she said: "Yes. I'm not sure that I really knew her. We only lived together for five weeks. She didn't say very much. But when she was there she was more there than anyone I've ever known. And I was there too."

He seemed to understand what she meant. They walked on, again in silence, and then he said:

"I've wondered about you. I'm grateful to you for what you did for me. I'm frightened of authority, frightened of being locked up. If you'd called the police that night I know I would never have been able to cope. And I would never have met Violet again. I've wondered many times how things were with you, what happened after I left you, whether your mother—I mean Mrs Palfrey—is well."

He could have been asking after any casual acquaintance. She said: "She's very well. She has a dog now. His name is Scamp. And nothing very much happened to me. My adoptive father arranged everything; he's a great fixer. Afterwards he took me on a long holiday to Italy. We went to see the mosaics at Ravenna."

She didn't add: "And in Ravenna I went to bed with him." She wondered how he would have looked, what he would have said, if she had responded to his confidence with that gratuitous news. And it wasn't, after all, important. What, she wondered, had it meant exactly, that gentle, tender, surprisingly uncomplicated coupling; an affirmation, a curiosity satisfied, a test successfully passed, an obstacle ceremoniously moved out of the way so that they could again take up their roles of father and daughter, the excitement of incest without its legal prohibition, without any more guilt than they carried already? That single night together, the windows open to the smell of cypresses, to the warm Italian night, had been necessary, inevitable, but it was no longer important. She said:

"My mother insured her life for five hundred pounds so that she could pay her share of the flat. There wasn't a suicide prohibition in the policy—I don't suppose they bothered with so small a sum—so I got the money. She must have arranged it secretly soon after we started living together, perhaps when she went to see her probation officer. No one knows for certain how she got hold of the distalgesic but she must have been secreting those tablets away for months. I tell myself that it shows that she was thinking of killing herself even before she came out of prison, that her death had nothing to do with me. There are so many expedients for getting rid of guilt. You'll find one for yourself in time."

He said nothing more. He seemed satisfied. Suddenly he stopped and held out his hand. She shook it. The gesture seemed to be important to him. Then he walked on alone down the avenue in the

275